Marcus Sulliva
but very little abou
inherited—and di
Fortunately the beautiful blond screenwriter Marcus was working with had a way with kids as well as words. But it was Annie de Witt's plan to replot his love life that had the perennial single guy stymied...

A gruff bachelor—and instant father!—finds his assistant helpful in matters professional and of the heart, in Marie Ferrarella's enchanting novel.

"Marie Ferrarella is a charming storyteller who will steal your heart away."
—*Romantic Times*

❧ ❧ ❧

When single—and clueless-about-babies!—TV producer Elaine Lewis learned she was pregnant, she knew she needed help, fast. And she got it, from her handsome employee Brent Clark. He knew all about babies and was happy to play stand-in father-to-be. But to Elaine, was the game becoming all too real?

A scared single mom-to-be and her baby-savvy employee play at being a happy family—and find the roles suit them, in Carolyn Zane's lighthearted novel!

"Readers will enjoy Ms. Zane's zippy writing style… (and) touches of humor."
—*Romantic Times*

MARIE FERRARELLA

sold her first contemporary romance novel to Silhouette Books over seventeen years ago. She is part of Silhouette's exclusive five-star club, having sold more than five million copies of her books. Recently she had a ten-part serial launched on Harlequin's newly remodeled Web page, www.eHarlequin.com. Her romances are beloved by fans worldwide and have been translated into seven languages. In March 2001 she celebrated the publication of her 100th title for Silhouette.

She earned a master's degree in Shakespearean comedy and, perhaps as a result, her writing is distinguished by humor and realistic dialogue. Marie Ferrarella describes herself as the proud mother of two and the lucky wife of a man who still knows how to make the room fade away for her. This multi-nominated, RITA Award-winning author is thrilled to be following her dream of writing full-time, and loves nothing more than to entertain her readers.

CAROLYN ZANE

lives with her husband, Matt, their preschool daughter, Madeline, and their latest addition, baby daughter Olivia, in the rolling countryside near Portland, Oregon's Willamette River. Like Chevy Chase's character in the movie *Funny Farm,* Carolyn finally decided to trade in a decade of city dwelling and producing local television commercials for the quaint country life of a novelist. And even though they have bitten off decidedly more than they can chew in the remodeling of their hundred-year-plus-old farmhouse, life is somewhat saner for her than for poor Chevy. The neighbors are friendly, the mail carrier actually stops at the box and the dog, Bob Barker, sticks close to home.

THE FAMILY FACTOR

MARIE FERRARELLA
CAROLYN ZANE

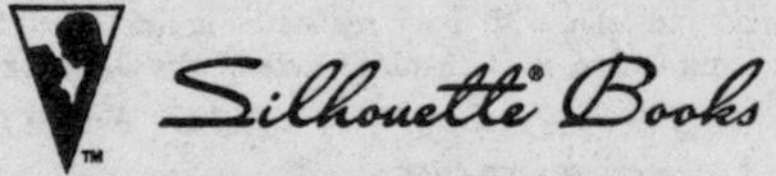

Published by Silhouette Books
America's Publisher of Contemporary Romance

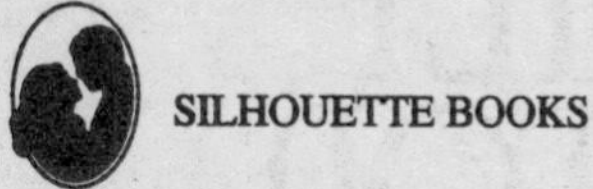

ISBN 0-373-21727-7

by Request

THE FAMILY FACTOR

This edition published by arrangement with Harlequin Books S.A.

Visit Silhouette at www.eHarlequin.com

Printed In U.S.A.

CONTENTS

Dear Reader,

I feel as if I'm revisiting an old friend. I have honestly never written a book I didn't like, but as with everything, there are favorite stories you look back on more fondly than the rest. *Blessing in Disguise* is such a story. I loved Annie's character right from the beginning, and also right from the beginning the characters would suddenly talk to me. There would be dialogue I just had to save popping into my head at the most inopportune times. I specifically remember one instance when I had to put Tigger's adventures on hold (those were the days when I used to read to my son Nik until he fell asleep each night) while I grabbed my ever-present pad and scribbled for dear life (I have the world's worst handwriting) while my son complained that he had to hear the end of the story (Tigger's, not mine) NOW. I also remember smiling a lot while I wrote this book. I hope you smile a lot when you read this book.

As always, I thank you for reading and for taking this journey down memory lane with me. From the bottom of my heart, I wish you love.

Marie Ferrarella

BLESSING IN DISGUISE

Marie Ferrarella

To my brother Mark,
who is finally learning
that being optimistic
is the only way
to survive

Chapter One

"But why can't I write it alone? It's based on my book."

The question echoed through Marcus Sullivan's mind as he moved restlessly around his living room. He paused briefly at the window and noted subconsciously that the early morning drizzle had evolved into a torrential downpour. The question had been posed during lunch with his agent more than a month ago. They had been discussing the production of a screenplay based on *The Treasured Few*, a book, he had pointed out with alacrity, that had been on the *New York Times* bestseller list for more than half a year.

But Richard had remained adamant. He had steepled his freckle-laced fingers together, his orange-marmalade brows rising innocently as he regarded his number one client.

"But my dear Marcus," he had intoned soothingly in his crisp British accent, "you are a novelist, and this project requires the hand of a screenwriter. A very good, talented screenwriter."

What Richard had said made sense, of course, Marcus thought grudgingly. But it was his baby, and he didn't want to just hand it over to someone else, no matter how good that person was supposed to be. And he had said as much. Very firmly. Besides, he had no use for movies. Movies pandered to the public. Marcus Sullivan was not a panderer by any stretch of the imagination.

Richard had turned a shade of light, unbecoming pink when Marcus proceeded to threaten to turn down the lucrative fee that Addison Taylor was dangling before them. Of all the offers that had come pouring in from the various producers, Addison's had been the most substantial. But neither Addison nor Richard had reckoned with the possessive ardor of a writer.

Richard, after considerable effort, had devised a compromise that was just barely acceptable to Marcus. He had convinced a doubtful Marcus to acquiesce, arguing that he should at least give the project a chance. He could work with the screenwriter.

After having more time to think things over, Marcus wondered why in heaven's name he had initially agreed to any of this. It wasn't really a compromise. He had surrendered. Lock, stock and barrel. In a moment of temporary insanity, he had given up. It was all Richard's fault. Richard had reminded him that he was, after all, the one who had originally seen the hidden promise of his talent in his scattered writings when all the other agents had roundly rejected him.

Marcus owed him a little faith and trust, he went on. Richard had a wonderful screenwriter in mind who just happened to be under contract to him as well. Finally Marcus had agreed. And now he had a cross to bear.

The wind howled as rain pounded angry fists against the window. The cross, he thought as he glanced at his watch, was over forty-five minutes late. He didn't like to be kept waiting.

From where he stood in the living room, he could see the tip of a book peering out from beneath the white marble coffee table. Muttering, he stooped down to pick it up. He hated disorder. And that was just what his life had fallen into, disorder.

He glanced at the colorful book in his hand. It was a children's book worn down by the constant turning of pages. His godson's book. No, not his godson anymore. His ward. It was an antiseptic term to gloss over the fact that suddenly, terrifyingly, within the last three weeks, he had become responsible for another human being's life. A life he had absolutely no idea what to do with.

That, he supposed, thinking of Nathan, made two of them.

He set the book aside on the coffee table, its binding parallel to the edge. He made a mental note to take it into Nathan's room later.

Where *was* that screenwriter?

Collaboration. The whole thing was a damn stupid notion. It would have only taken him a little time to learn the basic fundamentals of scriptwriting, and a little longer to apply them to his own book. Instead, he was expected to greet an interloper with open arms, to allow her to put her name next to his on his work.

That was the way he viewed it. *His* work. Writing was a labor of love for Marcus, but it was first and foremost *labor*. When he was into a book, nothing else mattered, not time, not space, nor unanswered phone calls. Nothing. He gave himself totally to his work. It made up for the loneliness within his life. There were times he went for entire stretches of days in his den, writing furiously. He worked, *slaved*, until it was finished. How could he be expected to admit someone else into this most private of worlds? To share such an intimate process as that?

The simple answer was that he couldn't.

He let out a sigh and dragged his hand restlessly through

the thick mane of straight black hair. Five more minutes, that was all he gave her. Just five more minutes. After that, he felt justified in calling the whole thing off. If Miss Hollywood Screenwriter couldn't even arrive on time for their first meeting, she certainly couldn't be expected to work to a schedule. They had exactly six weeks before production started. Six weeks to turn four-hundred-and-eighty-nine pages into a two-and-a-half hour movie. He doubted it could be done, and he was certain it couldn't be done if *she* was late.

Why wait five minutes? he decided. He'd call Richard now.

Marcus was halfway across the room to his telephone when the doorbell pealed.

He glanced at the door in mute disappointment, regretting that Holly, his housekeeper, wasn't here to tell the woman that he wasn't in. He thought of just not answering. The door chimes rang, and rang again. There was nothing to do but get this over with as quickly as possible.

Marcus crossed the floor and threw open the door. It was not a hospitable gesture and he knew it, but he wasn't feeling gracious at the moment.

The figure in the doorway was wrapped from head to foot in a huge electric-blue cape. "Hi, I'm Anne de Witt." The sunny, cheerful voice was a direct contrast to the weather.

"You're late," he announced. "Do all screenwriters show up late?"

Annie looked up at him, only mildly surprised at the curt, sarcastic tone he used. Richard had warned her. "They do if a truck jackknifes on their freeway."

He wasn't sure just what he had expected her to look like. But it wasn't what he saw standing in front of him now. She was about five foot two—maybe. The blond hair that was peering out from beneath the hood of her cape was plastered across her forehead, hanging into her eyes. She looked like something that the cat had dragged in, and she was standing, dripping, on his front step.

He was blocking the doorway and didn't appear ready to move. Annie stood on her toes and made an exaggerated attempt to look over his shoulder.

"You've got a very nice living room. Do I get to see any more of it?"

He saw the tiniest of dimples form on her right cheek as she grinned at him. Her fragile appearance diluted the edge of his antagonism. She looked like a child, he thought. How did Richard expect him to work with someone who probably popped gum as she talked? Nevertheless, he stepped back and allowed her to enter.

He was better-looking than the photograph on the back cover of his book, Annie thought as she walked in. And much, much bigger. For a moment, she felt a little overwhelmed. He had to be at least a foot taller than she was. She wondered if his aristocratic features appeared any softer when he was smiling. The photo on the book had captured a pensive expression, the same one he was wearing now. Well, Richard had told her it wasn't going to be easy. But that had made her all the more interested.

Annie pushed back her hood, revealing a wealth of swirling blond hair. The tips brushed against her shoulder, absorbing the moisture on her cape and turning darker. In a fluid movement, she removed her cape. She was dressed in a crisp gray skirt that fell an inch short of her knees and a soft pink blouse that struck Marcus as devastatingly feminine.

A feminine child, he mused. She wasn't getting her hands on his book, he decided firmly. She didn't look like she knew the first thing about life.

She turned her green eyes on him. They sparkled and momentarily held him in place, and he felt just the slightest bit disoriented. He realized that she was holding out her cape.

"Richard warned me that you were going to be difficult." She said it so matter-of-factly, she might have just said that Richard had told her his hat size. She raised the cape higher. "Where can I—?"

He took it from her grudgingly. "I am *not* difficult," he informed her tersely as he thrust the dripping cape onto the hook of an antique coatrack that stood sentry in the corner next to the front door.

"Terrific. Then we'll get along great."

I seriously doubt that, Marcus thought.

He turned from the coatrack, about to tell her why this temporary partnership Richard had planned didn't have a prayer of working, only to find that she had moved on to his living room.

Certainly makes herself at home.

He walked in after her. She was walking about the room, looking. And touching. It seemed almost a natural gesture, as if she were a spring breeze, passing through the room. But that was a ridiculous analogy, he thought.

Quickly his eyes washed over the petite figure. She looked as if she were there to baby-sit Nathan rather than to get acquainted and discuss the project. She was definitely too young to be any good, he thought again. Richard had mentioned that she was twenty-nine, but Marcus strongly doubted it. If she was twenty-nine, it was a damned young twenty-nine.

He felt far older at thirty-one.

For a moment, he studied her in silence. She seemed totally comfortable with her surroundings. Like a chameleon that could easily blend into its environment. In a way, he admitted, the ability was to be admired. He had never managed to blend in, or even attempt it. Instead, he had always stood off to the side, watching. Even in the midst of the parties that he was, from time to time, obligated to attend, he always felt alone. It had been that way ever since he was a child.

He watched now as she moved about the room, running her slender fingers along nearly everything that came her way. What was she doing? he wondered.

"Into heavy reading?" She indicated the book on the coffee table, an amused smile lifting the corners of her mouth.

"That belongs to my godson," he answered stiffly, wishing he had put it away when he'd picked it up.

"Good book." She grinned. "I've read it myself."

"I'm sure it's just your speed."

His tongue was every bit as rapier sharp as Richard had told her it was. Rather than take offense, she enjoyed his retort. She'd always found pacific to be synonymous with dull.

Annie came to a halt in front of his fireplace. She looked briefly at the dying embers on the hearth. Then she turned her attention to the mantel. In one corner stood a small cluster of trophies, very precisely arranged. There was an inscription on the one closest to her heralding Marcus's prowess as a long-distance runner.

A godson who left books in his wake and a host of trophies. So, he does more than lock himself away and write, she mused.

She placed a tentative finger along the base of one cup. A smudge of dust marked her finger.

"Don't dust very often, do you?"

He looked at her in disbelief, half annoyed and half amused despite himself. Holly hated dusting. "Thank you for sharing that with me."

She shouldn't have said that, she thought, biting the tip of her tongue. Sometimes words just seemed to pop out before she thought them through. But it had showed her his mettle. He was going to be a challenge all right. So much the better. She worked best when challenged. Able to make herself comfortable in any given situation, she enjoyed collaboration as much as she enjoyed working on her own.

Each project was an adventure, something to be savored, the same way life was. She had gotten that enthusiasm from her father, who had gotten it from his. Anne Kathleen de Witt was a third-generation screenwriter with an impressive list of credits to call her own.

She wondered if it was wariness she saw in his eyes, or something else. It was hard to decipher the message. The color of his eyes was so distracting. They were a deep, cobalt blue. And, she thought, they seemed to veil some sort of pain. He wasn't quite handsome, she decided, but there was definitely something there, something disturbing that went deep. She was going to like this assignment, she told herself. She could feel it. It was going to be difficult, but with tenacity, she knew she could turn out a movie that was even better than the book. And get to know a fascinating man in the process.

Silently Marcus removed her hand from the trophy.

She seemed unperturbed as she continued moving about. She stopped by the window. The storm was still raging. Running the drapes through her thumb and forefinger as if to get the feel, she looked over her shoulder at him and smiled innocently.

What the hell was she doing, he thought impatiently, taking inventory?

"I've never worked with anyone before," he began by way of an opening. He was going to tell her to go home. Having seen her, he knew that his initial feelings were correct. This was going to be *all wrong.*

"So Richard told me." She dropped the drapes and turned around. "It's a little like a marriage. You have to work at it a lot."

Her hand was hovering over an expensive vase that was the only tangible article he had taken from home when he finally left the East coast and the chilling aura of his family's house. It had always been the family house to him. He had never thought of it as home.

Protectively he placed himself before the vase. "Do you *have* to touch everything?"

She was a little surprised at his rebuke. She dropped her hands, and a slight flush came to her cheeks. She was doing it again, she thought. And she hadn't even been aware of it, really. It was second nature to her. "Sorry. I guess it just helps."

"Helps what?" How could he work with a woman who didn't speak English?

"Helps me to get a feeling for you."

The dimple appeared again. Even with her hair slightly disheveled by the wind and rain, she was lovely to look at. But lovely or not, she wasn't getting her hands on his book. He upbraided himself for having given in. If he had remained firm, he would have gotten his way. If not—well, he could certainly live without having his novel turned into a movie. There were far worse tragedies in life.

He was going through one now, he thought, then abruptly shut away the haunting sadness.

"And you're trying to accomplish that by touching?" His tone was nothing short of sarcastic.

It didn't faze her. "Best way I know how." Her green eyes crinkled a little as she smiled easily. "Vibrations." She was enjoying putting him on.

Marcus nearly looked up to heaven for help. "Oh, God, a renegade flower child."

"No, a people toucher."

Until she said it, he hadn't realized that she was now touching him. Her hand was on his shoulder. Not only was she moving in on his book, she was infringing on his space.

He took a step back. By nature, Marcus was a solitary creature, preferring to observe life at a distance and not get involved. This screenwriter from hell looked like the type who jumped in with both feet before she checked if the pool had any water. She might bear watching, but not when she was touching his novel.

His eye caught the gleam of a gold band on her hand as it dropped to her side. "Are you married?" He found himself voicing the question before he even clearly formed it in his mind.

"It's my mother's ring. I wear it for sentimental reasons. I've never been married." She congratulated herself for not giving in to the lump that rose in her throat. Briefly she shut her eyes, as if that would shut away the memory.

Yes, Marcus could definitely understand why she wasn't married. Who would want to say "I do" to a moving violation? "Never found anyone who could last, I presume?"

The slight edge of sarcasm tickled her. *I bet your bark is a hell of a lot worse than your bite, Marc Sullivan,* she thought. The sarcasm roused her and helped her shut away the pain.

"No, never met that Mr. Wonderful all those 1940s movies were written about," she said flippantly, mentally apologizing to Charlie's memory. It would have been two years this fall, she thought.

Purposely she turned her attention to the painting on the wall. It was a lonely seascape. So lonely it made her feel desolate for a moment. "And Jimmy Stewart is just a wee bit too old for me," she added as a postscript.

Lucky for Jimmy Stewart, he thought. He watched as she began to browse through his books that lined the wall on one side of the room. Enough was enough.

"Do you sit?" he asked in exasperation.

She turned and gave him a beguiling look. "Periodically."

His patience, never an abundant commodity, was at a low ebb. "Would it be too much to ask if one of these periods was coming soon?"

She pushed the book back on the shelf. They hardly looked touched. She wondered if he read them, or kept them for show.

"I make you nervous, don't I?" she asked. The wide

grin was back. Her mouth was too large, he decided, even though it was strangely attractive. He wondered if she ever closed it completely. He'd wager that she didn't know how.

"Frankly?"

She shrugged. "Sure."

"Yes."

"I'll sit."

Annie sat down on his white couch. It was so pristine. Did he ever have company? Was he as lonely as the seascape indicated?

She discovered that the seat was too wide to accommodate her frame. If she sat flush against the back of the sofa, she couldn't bend her knees. It was a couch made for a big man, a man like Marcus Sullivan. She wondered where he let his godson sit in this room. It wasn't a room that really invited people in, especially not little boys.

She kicked off her shoes and curled her legs under her. "I hope you don't have anything against feet," she quipped impishly.

"Only if they're walking all over me."

The features of her slender face grew grave. As they did so, Marcus saw that she looked a bit older than the teenager he had first perceived her to be.

"Marc," she began.

"Marcus," he corrected her as he sat down himself, keeping a good distance between them.

"No," she countered with a firm shake of her head, "that makes you even more stuffy."

He didn't like being labeled. "And I suppose you want me to call you 'Annie'?"

She laughed. "Unless you prefer Witty."

"What?"

"Some of my friends call me Witty."

"Some of your friends obviously have a low threshold of amusement."

"It's a derivative of my last name," she pointed out, nonplussed.

And she was a derivative of he-didn't-know-what.

Marcus took a deep breath and tried again before she had a chance to say anything more. "I think there's been a mistake made."

She tilted her head slightly, the beguiling, childlike enthusiasm back. "Why?"

"I've decided not to do the screenplay."

That didn't sound like the man Richard told her about. "You're giving the whole project to me?"

He rose to his feet. "I'm giving none of the project to you. I'm withdrawing it."

Now that sounded like the man Richard had described. She pursed her lips, remaining quiet for the longest period of time since she got there. Exactly one second.

"Afraid?"

He saw something akin to mischief cross her face. "Of what?" he demanded.

"Of the fact that someone else might have some insight into your characters besides you." She saw a frown forming on his face. "I liked your book," she added easily.

"Thank you." There was ice in his response. Pure ice.

"And," she went on, undaunted, "I'd like to try my hand at bringing your people to the screen. I've got a lot of ideas."

"I bet you do." He loomed over her. "But the fact remains that—"

She propped herself up, tucking her arm around one of the embroidered cushions, totally unintimidated. "I'm really very good, you know."

"No, I don't know."

He was going to be a tough nut to crack, she thought, but challenges were what life was all about and she bit into this one with relish. "I wrote *The Wayward Children.*" She set down the pillow.

"Never saw it."

"Did you see *Allison in the Morning?*"

"No."

"Tears of a Nation?"

"No."

Annie put her shoes back on and noticed that the action caught his eye. "How about *Casablanca?*"

The almost sensuous ritual made him lose his train of thought for a moment. He looked at her accusingly. "You didn't write that."

"No," she admitted cheerfully, "but I was beginning to wonder if you watched any movies."

"Not very often." He shoved his hands into his pockets, damning Richard for putting him in this spot. Unconsciously he moved away from her. His keen instinct of self-preservation had kicked in. "I'm too busy watching people."

"Good." She nodded as she rose and followed him. "I'll let you watch me work."

Why couldn't the woman stay put? She offended his sense of orderliness just by being. How could they possibly think of working together?

"That wasn't—" he began and got no further.

"No, probably not," she said, second-guessing him. "But it might be good for openers."

He began to wonder if he stood a chance against her rapid-fire delivery. "What's good for closers?"

She grinned impishly. "The screen credits rolling by."

He felt himself being reeled in. "You're determined, aren't you?"

"Yup."

"Why?"

"I like you, Marc Sullivan."

His eyes narrowed. "You don't even know me."

Again, she tilted her head, looking, he thought, rather

vulnerable and confident at the same time. He hadn't thought that was humanly possible.

"You'd be surprised." She winked mysteriously. "I've read your book. As a matter of fact, I've read all of them."

"Now I can die a happy man." He paused. "And?" The writer within him always sought reaction to his work, even from people whose opinion didn't matter.

He expected her to spout glowing reviews just to get on his good side. He dared her.

"And," she responded thoughtfully, "I think you need to practice some of that sensitivity and emotion you pack into your books."

"What?" The word burst out before he could stop it, carrying with it the full weight of his annoyance.

"Anger's a start, of course," she said, neatly sidestepping the fact that he was being annoyed with her. "With luck, it might even lead to other emotions."

She was good with word games, he could see that, but it would take more than being clever to change his mind.

"All this collaboration will lead to," he informed her, "is trouble."

She smiled, contemplating his words. "That might be interesting, too."

He could feel himself wavering. She was intriguing in an offbeat sort of way. What did he really have to lose except a little time? Maybe, just maybe—

No, getting a screenplay accomplished with her was impossible. Still—

"All right," he heard himself saying. Shock began to set in. "I'll give it a week."

"To start." Annie took his large hand in hers, sealing the bargain.

"Or finish," he countered.

"We'll see." Her eyes laughed as she said it, but for some reason, he wasn't offended this time. Mesmerized would have been a better word.

He felt a warm sensation seeping into him despite his prophecy. A part of him warned that he was getting in over his head. Another part whispered that he'd be missing a chance to experience something unique if he turned his back on this. Curiosity was an important quality for a writer.

Curiosity won.

But even as he gave in, he got the very distinct impression that he had just allowed the storm to move into his house.

Chapter Two

"Oh, there is just one other thing about your books, Marc."

He knew it. Marcus let go of her hand and gave her a piercing look. He didn't mind constructive, intelligent criticism from people he respected. But that comprised a very small circle of people. She didn't fall into that category.

"Yes?"

Despite his defensive stance, Annie sensed that this was a man who didn't care for empty compliments. That was fortunate because she wasn't any good at them. "They could stand a dose of humor."

He had heard the horror stories that other novelists had to recount about what happened to their works in the process of being brought to the screen. He was not about to join their legion.

"Let's get one thing straight here, Miss de Witt—" He looked down at her from a vantage point of twelve-and-a-half inches.

If his height was supposed to intimidate her into silence, it didn't work. Instead, Annie just shook her head. "We're not going to get anywhere, Marc, if you keep insisting on addressing me as if I were an aging librarian out of some Victorian novel."

He was rapidly losing his patience. Using her nickname implied a degree of familiarity, and above all, he didn't want to foster that. She was already giving too freely of her thoughts. He wanted to maintain a professional distance between them. But to avoid any further discussion and digression, he decided to acquiesce, at least for the time being. Anything to get things cleared up and set straight. "All right. Annie—"

"There, that's better," she interrupted with a nod.

Marcus doubted it. If anything, it was worse. She was the kind, he was sure, who if given an inch, took a mile—and probably built a condo on it.

"Better," he informed her, summoning all the cool, aloof dignity he could, hoping to put her in her place, "would be if I were sitting in my den, working on another book." He saw no reason to tell her that right now, his creative process was running on empty.

His manner left her totally undaunted. "You will be," she assured him, once more meandering toward his neatly arranged book shelves, "as soon as you get this screenplay out of the way."

In her rambling, she had stumbled upon exactly the right words. That was the way he thought of the project. If he couldn't terminate his agreement, then he wanted to get this thing out of the way. Fast. Besides, there were other things, greater things, to occupy his mind. But they weren't going to get anywhere if she constantly kept intruding on his thoughts and flitting about. Like now.

He followed her over to the shelves, watching slender fingers slide along gilt-edged bindings. "You're changing the subject."

Pulling out a volume, Annie looked through it, then carefully placed it back. From her cursory glance, she saw that all the books were of a literary nature. Nothing frivolous or light. She wondered if he had a man's adventure story or a science fiction paperback tucked away somewhere. No, she thought, looking at him, probably not. His mind didn't seem to move in those directions. He needed to loosen up.

"I wasn't aware that there was a subject under discussion," she murmured, reading another title.

Marcus closed his eyes and sighed heavily. "Why do I get the feeling that I'm trapped inside a Burns and Allen routine?"

With a wide grin, she turned from the shelves. "Aha! Then you did watch television."

"Radio," he corrected evenly. Actually they had been tapes that were made of old radio shows. He had listened to them in college at Jason's behest. But Marcus didn't feel like explaining that to her. He didn't feel like explaining *anything* to her. The less said, the less ammunition she had to go off on another tangent. "And you're—"

"Not trapped at all, you know," she put in, crossing back to the sofa behind him.

Marcus turned around. Couldn't the woman stay put? His head was beginning to hurt. "What?"

"That's your problem, you know." Annie picked up the children's book again. The vivid cover was the brightest spot in the room. Flipping through the oversize pages, she wondered about Marcus's relationship with the boy.

He knew damn well what his problem was. Having an agent who was an idiot. How could Richard have ever dreamed this was going to work out between the two of them?

Firmly he lifted the book out of her hands and replaced it on the table. His unconscious drive for symmetry and order made him place it perfectly straight. "I don't need you to—"

"Tell you what your problem is?" Annie guessed, knowing she was right. "Of course you don't. But if you don't mind my saying so—"

"I do." He knew the protest fell on deaf ears, but he felt he had to make it, anyway.

"I think it's your attitude about this whole thing that's at the core of your discomfort." She turned her bright green eyes up to look at his face. "You're not trapped, Marc."

Yes he was. In quicksand. Up to his knees, and he felt as if he were sinking deep. For some odd reason, when he looked into her eyes he had the sensation that time had stood still, even as he was sinking. With great effort, he roused himself. Could an intelligent man be hypnotized by being assaulted with endless rhetoric? It was a definite possibility. He felt that way, dazed, hypnotized. Disoriented.

"Think of working on this screenplay as tapping unknown resources within you," she was saying. Her eyes on him, she moved the book slightly with the tip of her finger until it was askew. "This is a whole new field you're going into." Her grin challenged him. "It's different. You might even find it fun."

"Fun." Deliberately he moved Nathan's book to its original position. He wasn't about to let her gain any ground whatsoever, even with something so minor. "Like going over Niagara Falls in a barrel." He eyed her, waiting.

Hand raised to move the book again, she shrugged carelessly, letting it stay. It wasn't her wish to irritate him, just to test him. She had her answer. He resisted change. "If that's your idea of fun."

Marcus held up a hand, calling time out. He had wanted to say something at the beginning of all this. What was it? She had talked so much, everything had started swirling around in his head.

Then he remembered. "I don't want you tampering with my dialogue, or any part of the book."

"I'm not going to be tampering, Marc." Seating herself

again, she raised her eyes upward, looking for all the world as if she were innocent of creating this turmoil that had suddenly appeared between them. "I'm going to be tempering." Carefully she enunciated the last word.

The hell she would. This was ridiculous. He had always been in control before, why should this be any different just because she talked faster than he could think? Firmly, he took a seat next to her and tried to take up the reins of leadership. "We need ground rules."

That got no argument from her. "Every partnership should have them."

Her choice of words sent a prophetic chill down his spine. That would be his idea of everlasting hell. "This is not a partnership, it's a temporary—" He threw up his hands as he rose. "Abomination." There was no other word to cover the situation.

Annie got up as well, her straight skirt clinging to her thighs. She had great legs, he thought unexpectedly, surprising himself. But he was not about to let her drop-kick him over her goalpost just because of that.

"Marc," she said calmly, "we're not going to get anywhere if you're going to throw tantrums."

"I'm *not* throwing a tantrum." Yes, he thought, he was doing just that. What was she *doing* to him? He was a calm, reasonable man who never even raised his voice.

"Good. Then what were the ground rules you wanted to set up?"

"I just—" Oh, what was the use? She'd debate over every word out of his mouth, and he suddenly felt very tired. He sighed, thinking that he needed some time and space before he could successfully tackle this. "We'll work it out as we go along."

"Good plan," she approved.

He felt like wringing her long, slender neck.

"Want to get started?" She turned and unzipped the large portfolio she had brought with her.

What he wanted was a stiff drink and a long cruise. Or maybe just a good lawyer to get him out of the contract he had so blindly signed in Richard's office, bonding him to this woman for the next six weeks.

But he had always managed to make the best of a bad situation before. He just needed time to reconnoiter, that was all. She had caught him completely off guard. Anticipating a problem with working with another writer, he had still naturally assumed that the other person would be a normal human being. He hadn't been prepared for a woman who made auctioneers sound as if they were speaking in slow motion.

He glanced at her. There was amusement gleaming in her eyes. He wondered if there was enough time in the world to get prepared for her.

Unfortunately time was at a premium and he knew it. "No, we'll get started tomorrow." It wasn't very much, but at least it was something.

Annie frowned and looked down at the notes she had taken out. She had read Marcus's book three times and was dying to get started. Jumping right into a project was one of the most exhilarating things in life for her. And, at one point, it had been all that had seen her through. "That doesn't make the deadline any easier."

"No," he agreed, wondering if he held the door open, would she take the hint. "But it might help my blood pressure."

Annie shoved her notes away again, then stopped as she zipped her case. "High?"

He disregarded the trace of concern in her eyes. They were strangers; why should she be concerned? That didn't make any sense. "Not until this moment."

"Oh." She laughed knowingly then closed the portfolio the rest of the way. "You're being dramatic again. You had me worried for a second."

Marcus was about to turn toward the coatrack. Her comment stopped him. "What do you mean, 'again'?"

Annie dropped her case to the sofa carelessly. Rocking forward on the balls of her feet, she placed her hands on either side of his shoulders. It was an intimate, friendly gesture that Marcus deemed should be reserved for old friends.

There was a smile in her eyes as she regarded him. "Marc, you do tend to get a little worked up, you know."

With a very deliberate movement, he removed her hands from his person. Contact between them was not quite as antiseptic as it had initially been. It was almost as if the light pressure of her hands cut through his apparel and *really* touched him. She was like some sort of an alien creature that was slowly, relentlessly infiltrating his system.

No, it was something much more down-to-earth than that. She was like a germ, he thought, liking the simile better. A cold germ to be warded off at all costs or be laid low.

"I think in this case I have just cause," he told her. "Normally I'm a very easygoing man."

Artfully, when he had removed her hands, she had turned them so that now she was holding his. "I'd say that you were a very uptight man."

He glanced down at their linked hands. How had she managed to accomplish that? Was this a sign of things to come? Her turning everything inside out? To his disadvantage? "And I'd say—"

They stopped as they heard a key in the door and the murmur of a voice. Annie couldn't quite discern if it belonged to a woman or a man.

She cocked her head at him questioningly. "Does someone else live here?"

Why was she always changing the subject before he could have his say? "No," he said in exasperation, pulling his hands free of hers. Then he realized what she was asking. "Yes."

It couldn't be both. "They live here part-time?" she prompted helpfully.

She was exhausting. More exhausting than sweating out a chapter in a book or making a character come to life. He began to think that for some unknown reason, Richard had it in for him.

He was momentarily spared the effort of answering her as the door opened. Her attention, he noticed almost gratefully, had shifted toward the two people entering.

"Hi!" she said brightly when Holly Hudson, a comfortable-looking, heavyset woman in her late fifties entered, bringing in the rain and ushering in a wide-eyed, thin little boy before her. The boy stared at Annie and didn't return her grin.

"Hello." Holly nodded at Annie. "The movie," Holly said to Marcus without any preamble, her small, sharp eyes looking Annie over quickly, "let out early, and he didn't want to stop for pizza." With a twist of her ample posterior, she shut the door behind them. Closing the umbrella, Holly tucked it into the stand.

"Not stop for pizza?" Annie crossed the room to the boy. "Don't you like pizza?"

Marcus thought it was only fair to warn his godson. After all, the boy was only seven, and that wasn't nearly old enough to be able to hold his own with someone like Anne de Witt. Thinking it over, neither was thirty-one.

"Brace yourself, Nathan. You're in for the Spanish Inquisition."

Nathan raised his brown eyes uncertainly, shifting them from Annie to Marcus and then back again. Behind him, Holly was busy removing his rain slicker. He stood as still as a mannequin until the older woman was finished. He clearly didn't understand what Marcus was telling him, though it was evident that he tried. "The what?"

Annie tossed a look over her shoulder at Marcus. There was a touch of exaggerated disappointment in her expression. "If that's your attempt at humor, it's lucky I'm here to help."

"I don't think the word 'lucky' can be stretched that far," Marcus muttered.

But she had already turned back to Nathan and was now squatting down to be on his level. "Hi, I'm Annie." She extended her hand to him.

Nathan took it solemnly and shook it, the epitome of good manners. It occurred to Annie that she had never seen a boy look so old before.

"And you're—?" Though she had heard Marcus say his name, she thought that the boy might want to introduce himself.

"Nathan Danridge."

Maybe he was shy. Taking a closer look, Annie decided that it went deeper than that. She glanced up at Marcus. Maybe the boy just took after his godfather. Marcus was probably like this as a child, she judged. "Well, I'm pleased to meet you, Nathan Danridge."

"Why?"

He *did* take after his godfather. "Because I'm hoping that someone in this household knows how to smile." There was no visible response to her words. Nathan continued to look at her with sad, serious eyes. "Do you?" Annie prodded.

The corners of the boy's thin face lifted slightly for politeness' sake, but his eyes did not follow suit. The expression drooped once more. Annie felt a pang, and if she hadn't been involved before, she knew that she was certainly involved now.

"We're going to have to work on that." It was a promise. She patted the boy's shoulder and then rose to her feet.

"Is there anything you don't plan to work on and rearrange?" Marcus's words fairly crackled in the air.

Marcus found himself thoroughly annoyed. Though he had no way of communicating with Nathan himself, never having mastered the art of conversing with children even when he was one, he still didn't want to see this capricious female hurt the boy by her mindless chatter. He knew that Nathan had more than enough reason for being the way he was.

Annie turned, her eyes on Marcus's face. This time, she gleaned, the reason for his curt remark didn't have anything to do with inflated ego or the right of possession. What had she stumbled onto?

"I'll draw up a schedule," she quipped, though there was no smile to go with it this time.

"Did you like the movie, Nathan?" Marcus asked. He had instructed Holly to take Nathan out in hopes that it would provide the boy with some badly needed diversion.

Nathan shrugged. "It was okay, I guess."

It was too soon yet, Marcus thought. He saw the housekeeper watching him, taking all this in. Privacy was at a high premium. "Holly, get Nathan into some dry clothes and see if you can't get him to eat something."

Holly nodded, taking Nathan's small hand into her own wide one. She looked like the perfect grandmother, Annie thought, but it seemed to have no effect on Nathan. He followed along obediently but with no life to his step whatsoever.

"Why is he so terribly solemn?" she asked quietly as she watched Nathan leave.

Marcus was surprised at her tone of voice. So, it could go down a few decibels and lose its wild exuberance. Maybe there was some sort of hope of being able to work with this woman after all, he thought. That still didn't give her a reason to ask personal questions. "I don't think that's any of your business, de Witt."

Annie turned to face him. Well, at least he had dropped

the formal "Miss" part. Maybe she could ease him into this working relationship yet.

"Maybe not," she agreed, "but I'd still like to know."

The absolute audacity of the woman overwhelmed him. She didn't even entertain the notion that there were things out there that were out of her so-called jurisdiction, things that she had no business poking around in. He found her presumption incredible. And fascinating in an odd sort of way, just like her eyes.

"His parents were killed in a car accident on a day much like today." Marcus's voice was flat as he said the simple sentence.

He turned to watch the rain beat relentlessly against the windowpane, trying not to remember the horrible desolation he had felt when he had heard the news. Jason Danridge had been his best friend all through college, the only person Marcus had ever been able to open up to. They had studied together, shared their dreams and forged careers in two totally unrelated fields. Jason had been a football player in college. A star quarterback. He had turned pro shortly after graduation. The athlete and the scholar, that had been them. Yet there had been common ground. A lot of it. And laughter.

Sometimes Marcus missed him so much, he didn't think he could stand it, though no one ever guessed at the depth of his sorrow. As always, he kept that locked away.

Annie watched Marcus's back and saw the tension in his shoulders. Instinctively she sensed that she wasn't the cause of it right now. The death of Nathan's parents was. Another woman would have left the subject where it was, content to wait until the time was right to ask. But Annie had to have at least one answer with which to build her conception of the total man. He wasn't just a waspish-tongued egotist. There was more here. Much more. And she wanted to know.

"How long ago was that?"

Her voice was low, intruding into his private thoughts so subtly that he wasn't aware, at first, of her even asking the question. He didn't turn around. "Three weeks ago."

"And you took Nathan in?" She couldn't see the man who had snapped at her as she had first come in doing that. Obviously there was more to the man than met the eye. More than he wanted others to see. She thought of some of the almost poetic passages in his books. Perhaps they weren't accidental.

"Jason and Linda made me Nathan's guardian," he said quietly, as if that explained it all.

He remembered the day it happened. They had been drinking more than a few toasts to his first bestseller, and Jason had lifted a glass of champagne high, laughingly saying that now he could breathe easier. If anything ever happened to him and Linda, he knew that Nathan would never lack for anything, living with Marcus.

Even in the slightly hazy state that the alcohol had led him to, Marcus had hesitated. He knew that neither Linda nor Jason had any family to speak of. And Jason was like the brother he hadn't had, a friend to cherish forever. Still, he didn't feel qualified to be his son's guardian, entrusted with raising a living being. He didn't know the first thing about that.

And he had said so, but his fears were waved away by Jason. Both he and Linda had been adamant.

"There isn't anyone else I'd trust with Nathan except you," Jason had said solemnly, all deluding traces of alcohol instantly vanishing from the large, rugged face.

Deeply touched by the gesture of faith, Marcus had agreed and legal papers were drawn up the next day. Numbed by their death, Marcus had forgotten about his promise until Jason's lawyer had called him the day before the funeral to discuss Nathan's situation.

He had accepted his responsibility, but protested that he wasn't equipped for the job. Now that the boy was here, quiet and withdrawn, it didn't get any easier. Marcus hadn't the faintest idea on how to proceed.

"They must have thought a lot of you," Annie said softly, lightly placing her hand on his arm.

Marcus turned, surprised at the kindness he heard in her voice. "I suppose they did," he murmured.

But you don't, she guessed. Because she could see it made him feel awkward, she withdrew her hand. "That means they thought you were up to it."

He raised his head. He didn't need her advice. "Who says I'm not?"

She had read the troubled doubt in his eyes a second before he had shut it away. "No one," she said cheerfully.

How had they even gotten onto this subject? He didn't want to talk about Jason and Linda or Nathan. He really didn't want to talk to this woman at all.

Casually Annie crossed to the coatrack and retrieved her cape. "Did you come from a large family, Marc?"

There she was, probing again. "No, did you?" The question was purely a reflex action. He certainly didn't care.

"No." With a flourish Dracula would have envied, Marcus thought, she slipped the cape around her shoulders. "There were just two of us, my brother and me. But I had a lot of cousins," she added. A thoughtful look came into her eyes as she glanced in the direction Nathan had taken. "They're all married with kids of their own now. My brother had two children."

He was about to take her elbow and usher her toward the door when she swung around to look at him again, catching him off guard. It was getting to be a habit. "Maybe I can bring them over to play with Nathan."

God, she really did want to take over. "We'll discuss it." It was one of those throwaway lines meant to shut her up. He might have known better.

"Okay. Tomorrow. When I come back."

It was like making plans for the next attack of locusts. "About tomorrow—"

Once again, she didn't let him finish. "I thought that we'd work here, instead of my place, at least for the first week or so." She walked back into the room to pick up the portfolio she had left on the sofa. "It might make you relax a little."

He had the feeling that a handful of Valium wouldn't be enough to make him relax around her and nearly said so before he stopped himself.

"What time?" he asked wearily.

"Nine's good for me."

He usually got up at six. That would give him three hours to pull himself together before having to face her again. "Nine'll be fine."

Never, he thought as he started to close the door behind her, would be even better.

"I'll see you then," she promised.

Marcus closed the door and frowned. Maybe the world would end before tomorrow morning.

At least, he mused, he could hope.

Chapter Three

She was late again.

With an impatient oath, Marcus let the curtain at the front window drop. A feeling of déjà vu danced through him. It was yesterday all over again, except that this time, it wasn't raining.

Well, what did he expect? Of course she was late. It wasn't as if she had exactly struck Marcus as being the conscientious type. He had had her pegged right from the start.

How on earth had he managed to convince himself yesterday that this collaboration had a ghost of a chance of working? Obviously the rain must have seeped through his brain, Marcus speculated in mounting irritation.

If he were being honest with himself, he was in a worse frame of mind about this project than he had been to begin with. When he had initially agreed to give in to Richard and go along with this, Jason had been alive. There would have been someone to talk to, to unwind with. If working with a writing "partner" would have gotten to be too much, Marcus knew that he could always kick back at Jason and Linda's house, nursing a cold beer while Jason burned steaks on the grill and called them barbecued.

Marcus sighed as he dragged his hand through his hair. All that was gone now.

He moved about the living room restlessly. One quick moment in time and everything changed drastically. He didn't have that safety valve any longer. More than that, everything felt as if it didn't fit right, not his world, not his work, not his skin. Try as he might, he couldn't find his place anymore. He supposed it served him right for letting down his guard. Living with his parents had taught him how cold, how austere, life really was. How not to expect anything more. If he had remembered that, if he hadn't gotten involved with Jason, with his family, he wouldn't be going through this now.

He hadn't been able to write a single word in three weeks. Not since the accident. It just wouldn't come. He'd sit down at his desk and then just stare at the blank computer screen, feeling hollow. What was the use? his mind would taunt him, encroaching on the emptiness that was eating him alive. What the hell was the use? What was it all about, anyway?

He had no answers. Maybe there weren't any.

But there had to be. There was Nathan.

Nathan.

Marcus loosened his tie slightly and took off his jacket, draping it over the back of the sofa as he tried to rid himself of the sense of confinement that hounded him. He glanced toward the window. There was no car approaching the house. It figured.

His thoughts returned to Nathan. Lately, the orderliness in his life that had always given him peace of mind was deserting him. Even his thoughts were becoming scattered. What in God's name was he going to do with a seven-year-old boy who didn't laugh, didn't play and only spoke when spoken to? Perhaps Nathan would have been considered a parent's dream come true, except that Marcus remembered that Nathan *had* laughed, *had* played. And it wasn't just a simple matter of sending him outside to play, either. With whom? There were no children in the neighborhood, at least, not any near Nathan's age. Besides, that wouldn't have been the answer even if there were children around.

Absently he picked up a gold lighter from the coffee table. A gift from Jason and Linda on his birthday, his twenty-ninth, he remembered with a smile. The year he had decided to give up smoking. He fingered it as he went on pacing, went on thinking. He thought too damn much, he knew, but there was nothing else.

Except for a seven-year-old boy.

The look in Nathan's eyes, a look that he knew mirrored his own, tortured Marcus, yet he had absolutely no clue how to even broach the subject of his parents' death, how to go about easing the boy's pain. Marcus knew exactly what Nathan was going through. The ache in his own heart was almost unbearable. He felt as if he had lost his brother, his kindred soul. Before Jason, there had been no one Marcus could relate to, talk to. Withdrawn, with books as his companions, he never seemed to have much in common with other young men.

As for the women, they were just names and faces and little more. Warmth for the evening. Physical warmth, not emotional. Emotionally he was withdrawn, starved, driven into himself by an uncaring, cold mother and a self-absorbed father. There was never a raised voice in his house. Never a hand raised in anger. But neither had there been a hand ready to stroke, to comfort, to hug. After a while, the boy had gotten used to it and grown into a man who thought he didn't need emotional nourishment. It had been Jason and Linda who had showed him a brief look at a world that might have been. But the curtain had dropped on that scene much too soon.

A noise had Marcus glancing over his shoulder. He thought he caught a glimpse of Nathan peeking into the room. But when he looked, there was no one there.

Marcus shrugged. Probably just his imagination. Maybe he was just remembering himself as a boy, feeling as lost as Nathan. There had been no kind words to free him of his cold cell then. Consequently Marcus had none to pass on to Nathan.

Maybe a military school, Marcus thought in desperation. He could enroll Nathan in a military school in the fall. They knew what to do with little boys there. At least it would give Nathan a sense of order, of structure. It would be the best thing that he could do for Nathan. That had been all that had seen Marcus through his own childhood. Structure was all he had to cling to. That and books. And his writing.

But writing wasn't there for him now. His ability to cocoon himself within the worlds he created had deserted him now when he needed it most. Marcus couldn't even express his anguish on paper. He needed something, a catalyst, to set him free, to make him write. It was that need, he realized now, that had made him act so out of character and continue to agree to this screenwriting project. Subconsciously he had understood that he needed something to stir him, to get him going again. Much as he hated to admit it, he needed some outside force to push him out of this dark and lonely place he found himself in.

He glanced at his watch impatiently. Abruptly he turned and, this time, saw Nathan before the boy had a chance to pull out of sight.

''Nathan.'' Marcus made it across the room in five quick strides.

But the boy was nowhere to be seen.

Marcus blew out an exasperated, frustrated breath. Nathan had been here at the house for almost two full weeks, and his suitcase still stood in the corner of his room, packed, ready to go at a moment's notice. It was as if he thought of this as just a transition period in his life, as if he hoped that his parents would return to take him home again.

Except that they weren't coming back.

"Not to either of us, Nathan," Marcus murmured under his breath. In his heart, Marcus wanted to be able to reach out to Nathan, to make things a little easier for him. But the words refused to come. He wasn't very good with words unless he could write them down.

And he couldn't even seem to do that right now, he thought, struggling against the clammy grasp of despair. God, he felt so helpless.

Damn it, where *was* she?

The doorbell rang in answer.

"Finally!" His annoyance flamed, red-hot. He considered being chronically late the ultimate, unprofessional insult. In the background, he heard the clatter of a pot being set down. "Don't bother, Holly," he called, reaching the foyer, "I've got it."

He threw open the door, his expression dark. This time, he planned to put the woman in her place. "Another jack-knifed truck, Miss de Witt?"

She wasn't alone. Some of his thunder faded, to be replaced by bewilderment. Flanking her on either side was a child, one boy, one girl. The boy was slightly taller than the girl, and he was clutching a brown paper sack. Both were blond and delicate-looking, although already the boy had a determined tilt to his chin. Just like Annie.

Hers?

Annie opened her mouth and then shut it, the rush of explanatory words dying on her lips in the face of Marcus's piercing, black look. She had been about to explain that her sister-in-law, Kathy, had called just as she was leaving the house and begged her to take Stevie and Erin for a few hours.

"You know I wouldn't ask if I had anywhere else to turn," Kathy had pleaded breathlessly. The woman was always breathless, always doing twelve things at once and eleven of them well.

Annie never said no to family, but she had hesitated, thinking of the flippant remark Marcus would have if she called and canceled their first work session. Then she remembered Nathan, and things just seemed to fall into place for her. There was no need to cancel. She'd take the children with her. Annie firmly believed in making lemonade out of every lemon sent her way.

"Sure," she had said to the harried voice on the telephone. "I'll swing by and pick them up on my way to my appointment."

The relief came flooding over the phone. "Annie, you're a saint."

"That's not an opinion shared by everyone," she had laughed, thinking of Marcus.

Now, facing him, she had trouble summoning some of that laughter. He looked as if he were contemplating having her drawn and quartered for being late. The man was definitely going to have to lighten up if they were going to work together.

"No, no jackknifed truck." Her hand tightened around the small hands lodged in hers. "There was a song on the radio I liked, so I stopped to listen."

He stared at her. "You can't be serious."

The little girl, frightened by his voice, hid behind Annie's legs, Marcus noticed, and he felt a tinge of guilt for scaring her. He also noticed something else. Annie wasn't wearing a skirt. Or slacks. The woman had come dressed for a picnic, wearing a pair of blue shorts with a blue-and-white button-down blouse knotted at her waist. Her legs were long and firm and tanned. She had the best calves he had ever seen.

No, this wasn't going to work.

"No, I'm not serious." She regretted her previous retort, but his attitude had annoyed her and she had answered before she thought. It was one of her failings.

Marcus shook his head. She wasn't making any sense. His best defense, he decided in mounting desperation, was a strong offense. It worked in war and he was beginning to think that there was more than a passing analogy here. He tried again.

"If we're going to—" *heaven help me,* he thought "—work together, I want you to understand that I won't put up with such laxness and unprofessionalism. You were supposed to be here thirty minutes ago."

She didn't particularly like being late, even when it couldn't be helped. She also didn't like being lectured to. Her chin rose rebelliously as she swept into the room, pulling the children along with her. "Why, did I miss something?"

Marcus pushed the door closed behind him without looking. She walked past him, her hips swaying slightly, reminding him of the woman he had envisioned as the heroine of his last novel. He tried not to concentrate on the effect it was having on him. He wasn't successful. "No, but I must be."

Annie turned to look at him. "What?"

"My sanity." There was an edge to his voice. This just wasn't working. She no sooner walked through the door than he lost his patience. He nodded towards her bookends. "Who are these children?"

"Lower your voice, you're scaring them." She raised their hands slightly as if to remind him of their presence. "And me."

Marcus arched a dubious brow. "I doubt if a raging bull would scare you."

She grinned, tickled at the comment. "Depends on how loud you bellow." She looked at the two children who were taking this in with wide-eyed interest. The boy was holding a large paper sack that was filled with his precious dinosaurs. "As for the children, they're my niece and nephew. Remember, I mentioned them yesterday."

"Yes, I remember." He remembered everything about yesterday's visit. It lived in his mind with the clarity of an overwhelming nightmare. He glanced at the children. They didn't look the least bit frightened of him anymore. Even the girl was merely staring at him curiously. "However, I didn't expect you to bring them here for show-and-tell." She was bringing out the very worst in him, he thought. Two minutes in her company and he was behaving like an ill-mannered boor. And he couldn't seem to help himself.

She bit her lower lip, wondering where Nathan was. She glanced toward the hallway, but didn't see him. "They're the reason I'm late."

He looked down at them. They were now studying him and the pristine, white room with unabashed interest. To their credit, they weren't wandering around and touching things. Unlike their aunt, he thought, remembering yesterday. Her flippant remark came back to him. "They wanted to hear the song on the radio?"

Rather than take offense, she laughed. It was a smoky, silky laugh that went straight down to the bone. He tried not to notice that, too. He was batting zero so far. "Very witty, Sullivan. There's hope for you yet."

"Not until this project is over."

Marcus looked at the boy and girl and consciously softened his expression. More children in his house. Just what he needed. He could see that the girl was staring at him with wide, slightly uncertain eyes. She was about six, he'd guess. Or perhaps a very petite seven. She reminded him of a doll. The boy was sturdier, almost a head taller. With his arms wrapped around his sack, he stood protectively next to his sister. Marcus liked that. He didn't care for people who were easily intimidated, and the child, he had often maintained, was the father of the man.

He was living proof of that.

"Why did you—?" His voice trailed off as he remembered what she had said yesterday. She had talked about bringing children over to see Nathan. He had thought he had cut her off by saying they'd discuss it later. Obviously he had thought wrong. "I don't think Nathan is really ready for this, Miss—"

Still formal, she thought. Well, she'd have to break him of that, too. She certainly had her work cut out for her, she mused. "Annie," she corrected him.

Erin looked up at her aunt, bewildered. "He calls you Miss Annie?"

Annie ruffled Erin's short blond hair, but her eyes were on Marcus. "No, I think he has another name for me, but he's not going to use it, are you?" she ended, putting the question to him.

He liked symmetry. Her grin, he realized, was lopsided. There was no reason on earth why that should be appealing. "Only when pressed," Marcus muttered. "Look—" he tried again, "I don't think that Nathan is ready for two children to descend upon him—"

A flash of a dark head in the doorway caught her eye. So, he was listening. "I think we'll let Nathan decide that." Annie put her hand out toward the empty space the slight boy had vacated. "Right, Nathan?"

Shyly Nathan reappeared in the doorway. Marcus turned in time to see him take a step inside the room.

Annie pretended not to notice how heart-wrenchingly shy Nathan was. "Nathan, I'd like you to meet Erin and Stevie." With a hand on each shoulder, she ushered the two toward the boy. She smiled at him encouragingly. "I think the three of you might have a lot in common."

The awkward look on Nathan's face had Marcus remembering another time, another place. "And what makes you think that?" Marcus wanted to know, a protective feeling for Nathan springing up within him. Just who the hell did this woman think she was, rearranging lives like this? She should have asked if she could bring these children along with her. Asked so that he could have turned her down.

"Nathan, if you'd rather not—" Marcus was about to give the boy a way out. But, again, he didn't get a chance to finish.

Annie turned slowly to face Marcus, her head tilted a little. He noticed that she swallowed before speaking. The flicker of pain caught his attention, cutting short his words. "Well, for one thing," Annie told him, "they lost their dad, too."

She saw that she had startled Marcus with her words. "It was a couple of years ago, but I thought that perhaps they could talk to one another. Sometimes, talking is all we have." She turned her attention back to the children. "Nathan, is there somewhere you could take Erin and Stevie so you could play together while Mr. Sullivan and I try to get a little work done? You'd really be doing me a tremendous favor."

Hesitantly Nathan looked over his shoulder toward the stairs, and then nodded. "Sure," he answered quietly. "I'm staying upstairs if you want to come up."

Hefting up the sack with one hand, Stevie put his arm around Nathan's shoulders, having sized him up favorably. "Got any video games?" He motioned for his sister to fall into step.

"No."

Stevie mulled the information over for a minute. "That's okay. I've got my dinosaurs. We can play with them." Because she wasn't following fast enough, Stevie let his hand drop from Nathan's shoulder, took hold of Erin's hand and pulled her along in his wake.

Annie watched the three make their way up the stairs

before she turned toward Marcus. "You're going to have to get video games for him."

She would have made a hell of a drill sergeant if he were in the market for one. Which he wasn't. "Anything else?"

"Yes, a better attitude wouldn't hurt." She saw the frown and decided to take another approach. He wasn't used to her yet. "Look, Sullivan, I know I have a tendency to come on a little strong—"

Obviously the woman was given to understatements. "Nothing that can't be measured on the Richter scale."

She laughed, enjoying the joke at her expense. "Touché. But I think we'll get along much better if you don't try to thrust and parry every time I open my mouth."

"What should I do when you open your mouth?" Suddenly, precisely, he knew what he would like to do. He would like to kiss her. No, like was too tame a word. *Wanted* fitted much better.

My God, what was he thinking of? The realization startled him. He would have thought that gagging her would have been foremost in his mind. He wondered if she dabbled in witchcraft on the side. Why else would he want to kiss someone who annoyed him so completely?

She turned her face up to his, her eyes innocent. "You could try listening."

He forced air into his lungs slowly. Her green eyes had him forgetting to breathe. "You mean I have a choice in this matter?"

"No," she answered cheerfully.

"Somehow, I didn't think so." He relented, looking away for his own safety. "You really should have called about the children."

Yes, she should have, she thought. But she had been in a hurry, and besides, it was too late for that. She shrugged. "They were a last-minute surprise."

He looked at her, confused. "You didn't know you had a niece and nephew?"

"I didn't know I had a niece and nephew who were going to be coming along. Kathy, my sister-in-law," she interjected quickly, "had an emergency crop up. She didn't have any place to leave the children. I knew if she called me, she was desperate."

"People only call you when they're desperate?"

She looked up at him. What had caused all that awful, wary sadness she saw in his eyes? Was it in some way connected to the fact that he kept trying to make her keep her distance? People didn't normally react to her that way. She usually got as close to them as she chose. Not him, she thought.

"Sometimes," she told him. "Other times they call me because they enjoy it."

He had a hard time picturing someone voluntarily calling her just to talk. To listen, maybe, but not just to talk. Therein lay only frustration.

She wandered off into the hallway. "I like your house, Marc. Do I get a tour later?"

He looked at her, still debating the wisdom of all this. He kept telling himself that it wasn't too late to back out. "If there *is* a later."

She looked at him over her shoulder, amused. "Oh, there will be."

There was an inverse relationship here, he thought. The more negative he was, the more positive she became. What made her like that? Was she merely a grinning idiot, an infuriating female who meddled with everything that came in contact with her, or—

Or what? And why did knowing what she was even matter to him?

The answer was, he told himself firmly, that it didn't. They had work to do, and he had to get started if there was ever going to be a way to get this woman out of his hair and get his life—his and Nathan's—back in order.

Was there ever going to be order again? he wondered, the overbearing sadness gnawing at him again.

He thought of the children she had brought with her. "Umm, the children's father—"

"My brother?"

"Yes. How did he—?"

"Die?"

He was beginning to feel as if he was an unwilling contestant in a game show, one where he was required to speak in tandem with someone else. "Yes."

"You have trouble saying that word, don't you?" she asked sympathetically.

"I have trouble," he told her in a moment of unguarded honesty, "accepting that word."

She could appreciate that. She knew how she had felt when it had struck in her life, leaving gaps that burned into her soul.

"My brother died of leukemia. It was fast. Very fast. We didn't even know there was anything wrong until the end. He was lucky."

"Lucky?!" he cried incredulously. How could death be lucky?

"Yes," she said simply. "Usually the patient lingers and suffers a lot. Daniel had just enough time to say the things that counted—I love you and goodbye." With effort, she shut away the pain. It was never easy. Part of it, she knew, would always be there.

She skimmed her hand through her hair, looking up the stairs where the children had disappeared. "I explained about Nathan's situation to the children on the way over here. I think that talking to children his own age who've gone through the experience of losing someone close to them might help Nathan cope with this a little better."

It was something he would have liked to have done for Nathan, he thought. But he hadn't known how.

"Perhaps."

She merely grinned. ''I'll take that as a thank-you.''

''It wasn't meant to be.''

''I know, but I'll take what I can get.''

He bet she did. He just bet she did. Marcus had a very uneasy feeling that the next six weeks were going to be quite an endurance test. One he wasn't completely certain that he could pass.

Chapter Four

She was here; Nathan was occupied. There were no excuses left. He had to begin this project. Marcus realized with growing discomfort that he had no idea how to proceed. How exactly did one collaborate?

She knew. She had said as much. But it was his book and he wanted to maintain control. He didn't want to surrender the lead to her right from the outset. Permitting her to have control was tantamount to Custer asking the Indians how to shoot a gun. Hands in his pockets, staring at the multiple panes on the front window, Marcus cast about for a way to start, for something to say.

"You did read the book." It was a stupid thing for him to ask. He knew she had. Annoyed with himself, he shoved his hands deeper into his pockets. Once again, he wished he had never agreed to this.

He looked uncomfortable, restless, and it bothered her. Annie wished she could put Marcus at ease. But she was uncertain how to approach him. Being friendly, the way she always was, didn't seem to work with him. She really didn't have another approach. He looked as if he took offense at everything she said. It was as if he was intentionally fostering discord between them. She wanted to know why.

"Every golden word," she answered.

He interpreted her response as sarcasm. Adrenaline shot through his veins. "Then you have no objections to talking over the plot."

Marcus looked at Annie, daring her to voice an objection. Traces of a smile were just visible at the corners of her mouth. What was so amusing? he wondered.

It was a place to start, she thought. She had her notes and her PC in the car. She could always get them later. "None."

Stiffly he gestured toward the sofa. "All right, let's sit down and get started."

"Okay." She sat down, kicked off her sandals and tucked her feet under her the way she had done the day before. The woman looked as if she felt right at home.

Too bad he didn't, he thought.

She distracted him. Unsettled him. Suddenly he couldn't remember the details of his book. He had written it, sweated over it, made slow, deliberate love to it in a way he never had to a woman. Why then couldn't he remember the plot? This was embarrassing, frustrating. What the hell was wrong with him? Disoriented panic threaded through him as he lowered himself onto the sofa.

He came in contact with something soft, yet firm. Instinctively he jerked to the side. Without looking, he had managed to pick the exact same spot on the sofa as she had.

She was too damn soft, he thought, annoyed with himself and with her. Too soft and, if he wasn't misreading his reactions, too attractive for his own good.

He cleared his throat as he looked down into her amused eyes. She could sense his discomfort. She was enjoying it.

"Sorry," he muttered.

"Nothing to be sorry for. A simple law of physics states that two objects can't occupy the same space at the same time." She paused. "But they can try." Her dimple was prominent in the corner of her mouth as she laughed. The sound washed over him like a warm, caressing hand. "This better?" She slid over to the corner of the sofa and looked up at him, one arm carelessly hooked over the side, her toes curled beneath her.

He could have strangled her for the totally innocent look she gave him and for the fact that it had his blood warming. If this so-called collaboration was going to work in any shape, manner or form, he had to think of her in the neuter gender. Better yet, he would think of her as some sort of a challenge from God and his agent. Under no circumstances could he think of her as a flesh-and-blood woman who was at this moment packaged in such a way as to wreak havoc on his every coherent thought.

He sat on the edge of the sofa and gave her a long, penetrating look. "Why are you wearing shorts?"

Annie glanced down at her attire. She hadn't given it a second thought when she left her house. This was the way she usually looked when she worked. She had, though, taken a little extra care with her hair.

"Because they make me feel comfortable." She looked at what he was wearing. He was dressed as if he were on his way to a formal meeting. His suit jacket was slung over the arm of the sofa. He'd probably just taken it off. "The same way I guess a shirt and tie make you comfortable." Although for the life of her, she couldn't see how.

He didn't care for the laughter he detected in her voice. "Comfort isn't the point here. We're professionals."

No one was disputing that. But what did clothes have to do with it? Just what was he driving at? "Yes?"

She was goading him on. How could he work if everything was reduced to a debate? "And I thought that we should dress the part.'' There was a certain way to do things, and he had always found a certain amount of solace in rituals and routines, just as he did in order. It was a poor substitute for warmth, but he had learned to live with it.

She still didn't understand what he was trying to say. ''Of mannequins?''

''Are you deliberately trying to annoy me?'' His formidable manner didn't intimidate her. He would have found it admirable if it didn't have a direct effect on his position.

''No, not deliberately. Look, Marc.'' She reached over and touched his arm. He didn't care to be touched. But he left his arm where it was. ''I really think that we'll get along better if we loosen up.'' She used the word ''we'' to be polite. They both knew she meant him. If *she* were any looser, he thought, she'd come in liquid form. ''Do you mind?''

''Do I mind what?'' Suspicion brushed over him.

Annie leaned forward, her fingers reaching for his tie. ''My father always said this was more of a noose than a fashion statement.'' She undid the already loosened knot, her eyes on his. ''Cuts off the circulation to your brain.''

Marcus put his hands over hers, intent on stopping her. Her hands felt so small under his. Small and delicate and fragile.

So much for his having an astute sense of touch, he thought.

''The circulation to my brain is just fine.'' *Except, perhaps, where thoughts of you are concerned,* he added silently. *There I seem to be somewhat addled.* ''Can we dispense with the word play and the disruptions and just get down to work?''

She raised her hands high, fingers spread wide. The tie hung loosely about his neck. ''That's why I'm here.''

''Nice to know,'' he muttered, straightening his tie. She was right, it did suddenly feel too tight. But he wasn't about to admit it.

Annie cocked her head. "Now who's bantering?"

He wanted to wipe the grin off her face. He wanted—

He stopped himself from completing the thought. It wasn't going to end the way he would have liked.

Filling his lungs with air, he let the breath out slowly. There, that was better.

He looked straight ahead and moved back on the sofa. "The story starts—" He looked at her, about to make a point. Her eyes were wide as she prepared herself to listen. Her lips were slightly parted as if she were about to savor what he was about to say. Except that he wasn't saying anything. "The story starts," he began again.

To his horror, his mind went blank again, utterly, completely blank.

Annie leaned forward. She seemed to fill the small space around him, crowding him, her hands on her knees, her body arched forward, as if every fiber was alert, poised. Ready. How had the distance between them evaporated? He didn't remember moving closer. When had she?

"Yes?" Annie encouraged, waiting. He seemed to have gone into a holding pattern, and she wondered if this was some sort of a test on his part. He was bent on making her withdraw from the collaboration, that much she would have been sure of even if Richard hadn't warned her that this might happen.

But what Marcus didn't know was that she needed to work, that she thrived on it, for all his theories about her laxness. She had her own style, her own way of working. There were no hard-and-fast rules to slavishly adhere to, except to finish what she started and to produce the best possible product she could. When she worked, she was dedicated, but she never lost sight of the fact that for her, work was fun and she felt very, very fortunate to dearly love the thing that paid for her food and provided the luxuries in her life.

He had never had this much trouble gathering his

thoughts together, had never felt this sort of an inability to concentrate on something that was basically second nature to him. It had to be her. He didn't quite understand how, but it had to be her. "Answer me a question."

"Okay. What is it you want to know?"

He was at the end of his patience. "Are you a plague from God?" He wouldn't have been the least surprised if she said yes. He had never, ever, met anyone so infuriating, so inflammatory.

"No." There was mischief in her eyes as she lifted her chin. "Were you expecting one?" If ever a man had a right to expect to be set straight by the powers that be for being so perverse, it was him.

His anger intensified. He would have had difficulty deciding who he was angrier at, her or himself for responding to her. "I was expecting another writer."

She spread her hands wide. "That's what you've got."

"No, that's not what I've got. What I've got—" What I've got is an all-consuming headache for the next six weeks.

Marcus cleared his throat again. What was the use of debating this? He glanced at her tanned legs. "Can you wear slacks tomorrow?"

She grinned, pleased. It was nice to know. "Am I distracting you?"

"No," he retorted, knowing it was useless. She saw through him. "Yes."

Annie weighed his words. "Half distracting, then. I'm glad. It makes you human."

All too human right now, he thought, and it wasn't going to do.

Lightly she placed her hand on his forearm. She felt it tense, then watched as he made a conscious effort to relax at least this much of his body. She was glad that she was having an effect on him. God knew something was humming through her own body, not giving her any peace. It had been like this, she realized, since she had met him yesterday. Something had just snapped into place for her, although what that was she wouldn't have been able to explain. Yet. "Maybe we can take that tour of your house now. Showing me around might make you feel more in control."

Marcus managed to hold on to his temper, but just barely. "I wish you'd stop analyzing me."

"I'm not analyzing," she corrected him. "I'm trying to help."

"If you really wanted to help—" He was very close to saying that she shouldn't bother coming by anymore, but knew that was impossible. He settled for second best. "You'd dress more appropriately." At least then he wouldn't keep getting distracted.

"Tomorrow—" she raised her hand "—sackcloth and ashes. I promise."

Some wars, he knew, were won by retreating and fighting another day. He needed a few minutes to regroup. "C'mon, I'll take you on that tour now."

When she raised her hand to him, he took it instinctively. Feelings and thoughts came rushing up at him when her fingers entwined around his. As she rose to stand next to him, his body tensed, a low vibration beginning in his very core. It was because of her nearness. He could smell a very light, feminine fragrance that wafted along her skin. It seemed to him as if every pore of his body opened up in the face of this unabashed radiance that was emanating from Annie. Disjointed, lax, with a mind that he knew was probably as scattered as the four winds, she still radiated sexuality. More than that, she radiated sensuality, which in his book was the far more deadly of the two.

Even brooding, he was handsome. Maybe more so, Annie thought. "You know, you look kind of cute with your nostrils flaring like that."

Consciously he disengaged himself from her and dropped her hand. "I wasn't aware that they were."

"They were. They are." She placed a gentling hand on his shoulder. She wasn't used to this sort of resistance. People always liked her. She really just wanted to be friends.

No, her mind whispered, she wanted to be more. Much more. But first came friendship. And trust. Nothing was worth anything without trust. "I don't bite, Marc."

His brows drew together. Words were all he had. "It'd probably be toxic if you did."

This, she thought, was going to be very, very interesting. He was going to keep her on her toes, and she liked that, liked being stimulated. But there was more here, she thought, more than just the clash of wits. He *did* interest her, as a writer. As a man.

A slow smile curved her lips as a bittersweet feeling begged to be allowed out. She pushed it away with both hands. Now wasn't the time to think of that. Or to feel that, either.

"C'mon, show me Nathan's room," she urged, grabbing his hand again and tugging.

The look on her face told him that she was enjoying herself immensely. She was as at ease with all this as he was not. He realized suddenly that his malaise and sense of apathy were gone. At least she had done that much for him. "This way."

Holly appeared just as he walked into the foyer. She looked at Annie, and there was neither approval nor disapproval on her face. Holly was the type to reserve judgment. But she saw everything. Like their linked hands. "How many for lunch, Mr. Sullivan?"

Aware of Holly's gaze, Marcus pulled to free his hand. "Are you planning on staying, Annie?"

Lunch was only a little more than two hours away. "I thought we could work it in, yes," Annie responded, amused. "Maybe we can eat with the children." She cocked her head, waiting for his comment, a hopeful expression on her face.

The meals he had shared with Nathan in the past two weeks had been painfully quiet and formal. Perhaps eating with this woman and the children she had brought would break the ice for them. If nothing else, he and Nathan could join forces against this hurricane that had blown into their lives. He wondered how the boy was faring with the children. Better than he was with her, Marcus hoped. "There'll be five for lunch, Holly."

Holly nodded briskly and marched off to see what could be done about that.

"You know, Marc—" Annie easily slipped her arm through his "—you have definite possibilities."

She was attached to him again. The woman had more sticking power than industrial-strength glue. "Thank you for noticing."

She ignored the cool put-down. "You're welcome."

The woman was impossible. And Marcus had absolutely no idea why he found himself smiling. But it did feel good, as did the touch of her hand on his arm.

When they came to the landing, the sound of childish laughter greeted them. Marcus looked questioningly at Annie, then down the hall at the source of the sound.

"Nathan?" she asked. It was a rhetorical question. She already knew it was. Stevie laughed like a young blue jay, and Erin giggled almost silently.

"I'm not sure." Afraid to find out it wasn't, he moved slowly down the subtly wallpapered hall.

"Must be." Annie kept abreast of him. "Stevie has a very distinct, high-pitched laugh." With a nod of her head, she urged him to push open Nathan's door.

When they peered into the room, they saw the three children on the floor, playing with the dinosaurs that Stevie was never without.

"He's a meat-eater," Stevie declared, pointing to the figure Nathan held for the benefit of the two adults in the doorway, "but I can fly away."

To prove it, he moved his pterodactyl up and down, gliding it on the air.

Not to be left out, Erin quickly announced, "I'm a princess."

Stevie frowned. "There were no princesses back then," he told her authoritatively.

"She can be a princess if she wants," Nathan said softly. "Maybe a cave princess."

Annie smiled. He was a kind-hearted boy, just as she had surmised. "Destined to be some girl's knight in shining armor," she told Marcus quietly. *Are you?* she wondered.

There was a question in Annie's eyes that Marcus chose to ignore.

Nathan's solution pleased Erin greatly, and Stevie grudgingly accepted it, his interests immediately turning to staging another battle with the flying attacker.

"See you at lunch," Annie told the children. She tugged on Marcus's arm and indicated the hall with a slight incline of her head.

He followed her out, mystified and relieved at what he had witnessed. "You knew that was going to happen, didn't you?"

She nodded. "I was hoping. It's not so much that misery likes company as sadness needs a shoulder to cry on—a shoulder it can reach." She patted his for emphasis, indicating that she wasn't trying to criticize him. "I asked Stevie to tell Nathan about his dad and see if he could make Nathan feel a little better." She fell into step as Marcus led her away from Nathan's room. "It made Stevie feel important, and in turn, I was hoping that he could help Nathan. See," she said, looking up at him. "Simple."

"Right, simple." There was nothing simple about her mind, he thought, or the way it worked. "Well, this is my bedroom." Feeling uncommonly awkward, Marcus opened the double doors and watched her face as she looked inside.

Annie didn't just look; she walked in and somehow, Marcus noted, took possession just by entering. Hands on hips, she surveyed the room carefully.

She could have picked it out of a lineup, she thought. It reminded her of him. Everything was very neat, very clean, very precise. The black curtains with their bold floral pattern hung just so, each fold in place. The king-size bed with its matching bedspread was made, four pillows scattered at exactly the same distance from one another along the carved headboard. There wasn't a slipper showing, a tie left out, or any change left uncollected on the bureau. It wasn't a bedroom; it was a room out of a museum. Cheerless and dignified.

Annie thought of the jumble her own bedroom was in. "You sure you sleep here?"

He kept his post by the doorway, his arms folded across his chest. "Yes, why?"

She had an urge to open the closets and see if everything was hung in descending order. Probably. "I didn't think a human being could be this neat."

Leave it to her to make a virtue sound like a failing. "It's in the genes."

"Must be." She turned around to face him. "Me, I live in subtle chaos."

Live in it and create it around you, he thought. "Subtle?"

For the first time, Annie saw amusement highlighting his eyes. It was a change for the better. He might look sexy with smoldering moodiness, but this was devastatingly appealing.

"All right," she conceded, "not so subtle." She let him lead her out into the hall again. "But I find order within it. Not worrying about keeping things neat gives me time for other things."

"I don't have any trouble coordinating both."

He pointed out a guest room, but she hardly noticed it. She was too busy watching him. "No, I don't doubt you would." At least, not on the surface, she wanted to add.

No one could be so precise, so controlled and not be on the verge of erupting, she thought. She wondered if she'd be around when that finally happened. A shiver swept through her as she walked along beside him. She hoped she'd be there. She had a feeling that there would be a great deal of passion involved, passion and emotion when he finally let go. He was capable of passion. His works had showed her that. No one could write the way he did and not feel it somewhere, in the privacy of his own mind, his own heart.

Because she urged him on, he went through the entire house, room by room. He watched her take it all in, commenting, approving, sometimes silently nodding her head as if she were agreeing with something in her own mind. The silence proved as unsettling as the banter. He wanted to know what was going on in her mind. Forewarned, he told himself, was forearmed. And he was going to need all the forearming he could manage.

He noted that she absorbed everything like a sponge. What went on in that chaotic space she called a mind? Why did all this matter to her, how the rooms were decorated, if he had chosen the furnishings himself or if he had handed it over, carte blanche, to a decorator? He hadn't, and she had guessed that, too.

"What makes you say that?" he asked, returning to the living room.

"Easy. Because you're not the type to let anyone make decisions for you. You like being in control."

At least she understood that much, he thought. "Try to remember that." He had little hope, though, that she would.

"I'll try." The emphasis was on the last word.

He had no doubts that "try" was as far as it was going

to go. "All right, we've done the tour. Now I think we should finally get down to work." He said it as if it hadn't been he who had procrastinated in the first place.

"Whatever you say." She began walking to the front door.

"Where are you going?" he called after her.

"Just to get some things."

He had scarcely assimilated her words when she was back at his side, a portfolio under one arm, her PC held in the other.

Marcus took the PC from her and led the way into the den. "You're being very agreeable," he said. Suspicion tinged his words. He knew better than to believe that she would just docilely go along with what he suggested.

The den, she noticed, was just like the rest of the house. Neat, slightly austere. The smell of leather, wood and polish blended and lent a pleasantness to the room. But it was as pristine as the rest. If there hadn't been a computer on his desk, she would have never guessed that he worked here. There were no signs of the agony of creation. Yet she had read his books and knew that he was capable of it.

Carefully placing her portfolio on the corner of the desk, she unzipped it.

"I'm always agreeable."

"News to me," he muttered. He placed her PC next to his. Hers was small, portable, almost a toy. His was a permanent fixture, massive, sturdy. They didn't blend. Yet both, he noticed, were made by the same company and had been created to complement each other. Maybe there was a message to be picked up here.

He was being unfair to her, but he was also fighting for life as he knew it. Something in the corners of his mind whispered, like an elusive melody, that things were never going to be the same again.

Marcus glanced again at the papers she had taken out

and was now placing on the desk in a haphazard pile. He stifled the urge to stack them neatly.

"What are those?"

"My notes," she answered cheerfully, twisting a chair around to face his.

He no longer thought he was in danger of bidding good-bye to life as he knew it. He *knew* he was.

Chapter Five

Well, she certainly had gotten his adrenaline flowing yesterday, he'd give her that. There had been little time to become really anxious over whether he was suffering from writer's block or to mourn the fact that he might never give birth to another creative thought again.

Before the day was out, he had devised a dozen ways to do away with her. If that wasn't creativity, then he didn't know the meaning of the word.

They had sparred all afternoon. It seemed as if they just couldn't agree on anything. Strangely enough, although she made him terribly annoyed to begin with, by the end of the day he felt invigorated. It was almost as if he was beginning to enjoy the tension between them.

No, that didn't quite describe it. He wondered how he would have labeled the scene if he were writing about it. It wasn't just tension. It was *sexual* tension.

Marcus froze mentally. No, it couldn't be that. And yet, if he were being honest...

If he were being honest, he told himself, shifting in the passenger seat in Richard's car, he was just a man who had gone through a terrible emotional ordeal and was consequently not responsible for what he *thought* he was feeling.

He tried to concentrate on the way the session had gone yesterday and not on the participant. All things considered, it hadn't been as bad as he had expected. Of course, it hadn't gone as smoothly as it would have if he'd been working on this alone, he thought, giving his agent an intense, sidelong glance that seemed to bounce off the man as they drove toward Shalimar Studios. In her own chaotic way, Annie had raised credible points.

Given a choice, though, he still preferred working alone. It grated on Marcus that he probably wouldn't have accomplished anything if it hadn't been for her. She had been the catalyst he had unfortunately needed, the fire that had set him off.

He didn't like being in debt to anyone, especially when he had no idea how to repay the debt.

He also didn't like having to put in a command appearance before anyone. And he definitely didn't feel like having to protect his work from the "creative input" of a producer who envisioned the movie as his own. That was the problem here, he thought—too many cooks wanting to spoil *his* broth, however unintentionally.

Richard brought his Bentley to a stop at the studio gate. "I still don't see why I have to come, Richard. That's why you're getting ten percent."

Richard showed his identification and was waved onto the grounds by the guard. He slipped his wallet back into his jacket. "Dear boy, I do think you should meet the man who's putting money into your pocket. Now, make nice for my sake."

It wasn't enough of a reason. Again, Marcus shifted restlessly in his seat, wishing he was back in his den and working. "My readers put money in my pocket. I don't have a burning desire to meet every one of them."

The redheaded man parted his lips. Something that passed for a smile slipped into place for a moment, then was gone. "You would if they slipped an *obscene* amount of money into your pocket."

Marcus reflected on all his years of struggling, of making do with one meal a day. "There's nothing obscene about money, Richard."

Richard rolled his eyes heavenward. There at least they were in agreement. "Amen to that."

A blonde in a harem outfit came into Marcus's line of vision, her head inclined toward a tall, muscular man as they shared a joke. Involuntarily Marcus thought of Annie, then wondered why. It was bad enough to have to put up with her during working hours. To allow her to materialize in his thoughts was like having his mind rebel against him.

His body, it seemed, had already gone that route, but that, he felt, could be restrained with a simple act of control.

Richard carefully brought his pride and joy to a stop before an imposing one-story Spanish hacienda in the center of the studio lot. Richard angled the car across two parking spaces.

"All right." He turned to the younger man. "You haven't said a word about her since I picked you up. Don't play stoic with me. I know you far too well. How did yesterday work out?"

Marcus thought of the way their words and thoughts had kept overlapping throughout the entire day. "Does the phrase 'unorganized chaos' give you a clue?"

Richard lifted a red eyebrow. "Then I take it that things did not go well." With a shake of his head, he got out.

Marcus slammed his door and crossed to the hacienda's entrance. "That all depends."

Richard rang the bell. The first few bars of the theme song from *The Alamo* floated through the air. "On what?"

"On just how little you're expecting by the word 'well.'"

"You're exaggerating again."

Marcus gave a short laugh. "That's not possible this time."

One of Addison's assistants, a slight, scholarly-looking youth dressed in shades of brown, opened the door, mumbled a greeting and motioned them inside.

Allowing Richard in first, Marcus had just enough time to cross the threshold before someone raced up breathlessly behind him. He knew who it was before he turned around. He recognized the "whoosh."

"Hi." Annie beamed at Richard as she placed herself between the two men. "Have I missed something?" The question was for Marcus's benefit, a reminder of yesterday's lecture about punctuality.

Marcus looked accusingly over her head at Richard. "You didn't say she was going to be here."

Bony shoulders rose and fell beneath the expensive designer jacket. "You didn't ask."

Addison's assistant silently turned on his heel and began leading them down a wide hallway, the walls lined with framed photographs of all the celebrities who had ever worked on an Addison Taylor movie. Every one bore an intimate inscription.

Annie looked up at Marcus. "I'm your other half, remember?"

Marcus sighed. "Unfortunately my memory is alive and well."

"And so are you." Hurrying to keep in step, Annie looked Marcus over. He was dressed in a pearl-gray suit with a light blue shirt and tie that brought out the color of his eyes. "Nice suit," she noted. The assistant led them all past a brightly lit, windowless reception area that held a large, round desk and three secretaries. "You're looking well, too, Richard."

"As well as can be expected when my two prize clients are at each other's throats."

"Singular, Richard. I am not going for the jugular. Marc, I'm afraid, is still having trouble working out his differences."

"Wait here, please," the assistant instructed, ducking into another office. Annie noticed that he looked relieved to leave.

"My differences?" Marcus echoed incredulously. At the moment, his only difficulty seemed to be a rather short, headstrong woman.

"Well, they're not mine," she answered innocently. "I have no problems with working together. How's Nathan?" The question came quickly, forestalling the response she knew would follow.

She was good at ducking and weaving, he thought with something distantly akin to admiration. "He's fine."

"Good. Stevie and Erin would like him to come over and visit."

"All right." He looked at Addison's closed door and wondered just how long he was expected to wait before he had an excuse to leave.

"When?" Annie pressed.

Her question was unexpected. "When what?"

"When can Nathan come over?"

Marcus shrugged, pulling his thoughts together. He had surmised that she was just making aimless conversation while they waited. He should have known better. She wasn't the aimless sort. Instead, she seemed to aim straight for any available vital organ. "You need an answer now?"

"It would be nice."

Marcus threw up his hands. "I don't know." Her expression told him she wanted something more definite. "Saturday."

"Good. I'll pick him up."

"I'm sure you will. What are you grinning at?" he snapped at Richard.

Hands that were unusually wide-palmed for such a thin man went up to ward off Marcus's ire. "Nothing. I've just never seen a Hepburn and Tracy movie in action before, that's all."

"And what's that supposed to mean?" Marcus wanted to know. Had everyone gone crazy on him? Or was it him?

"Catch one and you'll understand, dear boy."

He needed another agent, Marcus thought. And if he went along with this farce any longer, he needed his head examined.

The unobtrusive assistant reappeared, leaving the door open this time. "Mr. Taylor will see you now." He motioned them into the inner sanctum.

"My prayers have been answered," Marcus muttered sarcastically, passing the young man.

Annie threaded her arm through Marcus's and entered with him. "Have you had your rabies shots, Marc?" she asked sweetly.

"Why, are you planning to bite?"

She laughed, undaunted. "Touché."

Why did the sound of her laughter have to affect him? Wasn't he dealing with enough problems as it was? Jason and Linda's deaths. Nathan. Writer's block. What in the world was he doing, collaborating with a woman who looked as if she were more suited to reclining on the beach in a bikini? A small, scarlet bikini…

He banished the image before he made a total idiot of himself.

"You're breathing harder," she murmured.

He looked straight ahead. "It's suddenly gotten very stuffy in here."

She gave Marcus a knowing look. "It's bound to get stuffier." Releasing his arm, she moved toward the thin, angular man seated behind the gleaming black desk. "Hello, Addison."

The man in the round, black-rimmed glasses rose slightly in his seat and took her hand in both of his. "Annie, you're getting more gorgeous every day." The affection in his voice sounded genuine.

Marcus stared at Annie's back. She wore an attractive white suit with a straight skirt and a vivid red silk blouse. As if she needed color to enliven her. "You know each other?"

Annie looked over her shoulder as Addison released her hands. "Sure."

"Of course." Why had he thought differently? Marcus told himself to be patient, that this too shall pass. The sooner they got this over with, the sooner he'd be back at work. He thrust his hand at Addison. For a diminutive man, he thought, Taylor had a strong grip. "I'm Marcus Sullivan."

"I know." When he smiled, Addison Taylor looked like a boy play-acting in an adult world. He didn't look anywhere near thirty-seven. "I'm paying you a lot of money to be."

Marcus raised an eyebrow in Richard's direction. In return, Richard gave him his patented, all-enduring half smile. Nothing seemed to ruffle Richard. Marcus's theory was that someday, Richard was going to explode. No one could remain continually calm. Especially, he thought glancing at Annie, with her as his client.

Addison gestured toward the blue brocade chairs before his desk. Annie took the one closest to the producer, Marcus noticed. The center of the storm. "This meeting is predominantly being held because of you, Marcus."

"And why is that?"

Marcus looked tense, on guard. Why? Annie wondered. Did he think they were going to attack him? What an awful way to face life, always being on your guard, always anticipating the worst, she thought. Had he always been like this? Or had something happened to make him this way? For a moment, she didn't hear what Addison was saying to them. She was far more interested in the man who had seated himself to her right.

"I like to meet the people I work with," Addison told Marcus. "Get to know them. Share my thoughts."

Marcus wasn't so annoyed that he didn't take note of the fact that Addison had said "people I work with," not "people working for me." He revised his opinion of the man. Slightly.

Still, Addison wanted to "share" his thoughts. "About the novel," Marcus began.

"Hell, no, about the screenplay," Addison interjected enthusiastically, unconsciously rubbing his hands together. "The novel is yours. The movie, however—" he leaned back in his well-padded chair and looked at the trio as he rocked "—is ours."

Annie could see that communal possession of his story didn't sit well with Marcus. There was a slight furrow over his brow even though his expression hadn't actually changed. It had, however, hardened. She didn't want things to rise to a head here. Although Addison had a congenial approach toward business, it only went so far. He was strong-willed. An iron hand in a velvet glove. He liked to hear the right words come his way.

"My name," Addison was saying, "appears above the title of the movie." With a sweep of his long, delicate hands, he stretched out an imaginary banner. "Therefore, you understand, I have a great deal besides money invested in this—"

"I understand," Marcus began. He understood very well. He was being led deeper and deeper into Oz by Dorothy and a misguided Scarecrow. He had no intentions of playing the part of the Cowardly Lion. Certain things had to be made clear, no matter what the consequences. "I understand quite well—"

Marcus looked down at the armrest. Annie's hand was covering his, as if that single, small gesture could keep him in his seat and the words in his mouth. It couldn't. But the surprise it generated within him could and did.

"I do have all your notes, Addison, and naturally, we will be taking them into account," Annie said quickly before horns were locked. The glance she gave Marcus warned him to keep still. "But don't you think that we should have something concrete in the way of a script before we discuss this any further?"

"Further?" Marcus echoed. "We haven't—"

"We have," Annie cut in.

"You have," he corrected her. If he disliked having his work dissected in front of him, he disliked the fact of having it dissected behind his back even more.

The pressure on his hand increased. She was pushing it into the delicately carved wood. "Right now," she reminded him calmly, wondering if she should be hitting this man between the eyes with a two-by-four to get through, "I am part of 'we.'"

But not for long, God help me, Marcus thought. "And that's another thing—"

"That he'd like to thank you for," Richard put in, taking Annie's cue. He knew the danger signs far better than she did. "Marcus had no idea what working with a partner would be like and feels—"

"That you made a splendid choice, Addison," Annie ended. "As always."

The thin lips parted into a full-bloomed smile that seemed to fill out the man's face. It emphasized his boyishness further. The product of his mind, Marcus thought, was in the hands of a teenager.

"Well, if things are going well and you have my notes, I suppose there's no reason to repeat myself. If none of you has any objections, we can conclude this meeting. I've got a comedy on Lot Six that is anything but funny.'' Addison rose and moved around his desk. He was hardly taller than Annie. It surprised Marcus. The producer thrust his hand toward him again. "Nice meeting you after all this time, Marcus. I've been a fan for a long while.''

Marcus encircled the bony fingers in his large palm. "Thank you.'' He meant the words sincerely. If people stopped buying his books tomorrow, Marcus knew that he would still go on writing. He had to in order to survive. For him it was as necessary as breathing. Maybe more. But it was still gratifying to hear that people enjoyed reading his books. He never took it for granted. He had learned that nothing could be taken that way.

Addison preceded them out the door, followed by his assistant.

"What was that all about?'' Marcus asked, taking Annie's arm and hustling her out of the office, toward the front door.

"All what about?'' Annie nodded toward Addison's secretary as they sailed past her desk. The woman looked curiously at Marcus's hold on her arm. "It's all right. He likes to get physical,'' Annie told her. There was only envy shining in the older woman's eyes as she looked on.

It was a nightmare, Marcus thought as he strode out into the hallway, and it was his. "Do you really have to do that?''

"Do what?'' She wondered how long he could keep up this pace.

He pushed the front door open with the flat of his hand, still holding on to her arm. "Call attention to yourself, to us?''

"Who's hustling who out the door?'' Abruptly he let go of her arm and sighed. Momentarily he looked befuddled. She felt sorry for him. "You had a question earlier?'' Annie prompted. Richard came out and joined them in the parking lot, standing off to the side and enjoying the fireworks.

She had gotten him so muddled, he forgot he had a question. Marcus jerked a thumb back at the building. "What was all that tap dancing you were doing in there?"

She had a strong suspicion that if she said black, he would say white. Why was he so pigheaded? Couldn't he see that she had done him a favor? "Did you want to discuss Addison's changes?"

"No." He bit off the word.

"Did you want to tell him that you'd work them in?" The dark look he gave her answered that. "Well, in case you haven't noticed, Sullivan, I just saved you the trouble. Addison softens up when he hears that people are working in harmony with him."

As far as he could see, it was only a stalling tactic, putting off the inevitable. "What happens when the script comes on his desk and his changes aren't in it?"

"He won't make a fuss as long as the story works." She smiled brilliantly. "Trust me."

That was just the trouble; he couldn't. Something told him it would be very dangerous if he began to trust her. Trust only led to disappointment. "You've been through this before, I take it?" Marcus asked, suddenly fascinated by how the sun was tangled in her hair.

Annie was aware of the way he was looking at her. She felt a momentary scramble of her pulse before she answered. "About six or seven times."

Marcus looked at his watch. It was only ten o'clock. Too early for lunch. "I guess I owe you a cup of coffee."

She grinned. "At the very least."

It was better not to answer that. Suddenly remembering Richard's presence, Marcus turned toward the agent. "Join us?"

Richard held up his hands. "Unlike the curious observers at the Battle of Bull Run, I have no desire to get a front-row seat for the beginning of the war. Besides—'' he glanced at his watch ''—I have an appointment at eleven. You'll take him home for me?'' he asked, dropping a kiss on Annie's temple.

''If he lets me.''

He was stuck. It occurred to Marcus that he had precious little control over his life lately. None where she was concerned. ''Coward,'' Marcus called after Richard's retreating back.

''Down to the long yellow streak between my skinny shoulder blades,'' Richard agreed cheerfully. ''Have fun, you two.''

For a second, they just stood there, a moment of awkwardness shimmering between them. She pointed vaguely to the left. ''There's a little restaurant just off the lot on the next block, if you were serious about the coffee. Felicity's.''

He had no idea what had made him extend that invitation. Temporary insanity was becoming a way of life with him. ''All right,'' he muttered stoically. He approached her car. ''Mind if I drive?''

''I figured you'd want to.'' Tossing him the keys, she slid in on the passenger side.

Marcus closed the door behind her a little too firmly. ''One-upmanship your specialty?'' He came around the hood.

''How did you guess?''

Allowing him a few moments' grace, she watched him start the car. His were large, capable hands, hands that would always know what to do, instinctively know how to touch a woman and make her want more. She settled back, taking a deep breath, pushing aside thoughts that were coming too soon.

And then she turned toward him, her smile wider, if that was possible. ''Is this a date?''

If he had been driving a standard transmission, he knew

he would have stalled out. As it was, he swerved. A car honked behind him. "What?"

"The restaurant. Coffee. Is this a date?"

"No." The answer came tersely. "It's a cup of coffee." The implications of an actual social outing with this woman were far too jarring.

"Oh."

Her expression told him that she didn't believe him. Well, what did he care what she believed or didn't believe? He knew what he was thinking.

What was he doing, anyway, driving off to a restaurant to have a sociable cup of coffee with a woman who—who— He was being polite, that's what he was doing. Nothing wrong with manners. It made up the backbone of this country. He almost believed the excuse.

The restaurant was bright and noisy, with a prominent counter that ran along the length of one wall. Almost every seat was occupied by someone in costume. He and Annie were the only ones in street clothes. He should have known.

"Felicity's is open almost all the time. It's a favorite with the extras." Annie nodded over toward the corner. There were two people whose gender he couldn't begin to guess at dressed as fruit. He looked quizzically at Annie. "They're probably shooting a commercial. Or a science fiction movie."

All of this felt like a science fiction movie, Marcus thought.

"Want to sit at the counter?" She pointed toward two vacant seats between a gunslinger and a Viking. "Or a table?"

"Table."

She was already weaving her way through the crowd toward an empty one. "I had a hunch."

A tall woman with a pink-feathered boa dripping off her shoulders deliberately brushed against Marcus as she walked by. She gave him an appreciative, come-hither look.

The boa tickled his nose. He tried not to sneeze. "I wish you'd stop second-guessing me," he said to the back of Annie's head.

"I will if you do something against type."

"And just what is my type?"

She seated herself neatly, then looked up at him, innocence in her eyes. "Reticent."

She was doing it to him again, making his blood rise to its boiling point. If there hadn't been people all around them, he would have taken that moving target she called a mouth and kissed her to show her just how reticent he was.

No, it wasn't the people stopping him. It was his common sense. He knew the danger of that sort of action. He had no intentions of working without a net. He wasn't a complete fool.

Oh no? Then what was he doing here with her? Holly had plenty of coffee at home.

He had no answer for that, only an odd, sinking sense of foreboding.

Chapter Six

Marcus sat nursing his coffee and mulling over the situation he was in now. At least the coffee was good, surprisingly so. He liked his coffee strong and eye-opening. Most restaurants didn't.

He tried not to be aware of the fact that sitting so close to Annie was a problem. It shouldn't have been. But it was. She made him conscious of things that had absolutely nothing to do with writing.

"Come here often?" Coming from a bestselling novelist, Marcus thought in contempt, that was pitiful.

If it was, she didn't seem to notice. "Only when I'm in the neighborhood to see Addison."

"So, have you known him long?" He didn't like the idea much. He liked the fact that it bothered him even less. There was no reason for it, he told himself.

An actual personal question. Finally, Annie thought. The stone wall around him was beginning to wear down. It was about time. It would make working together easier. It would make a lot of things easier.

"Forever. He used to come over to the house a lot when he was first starting out. My parents' house," she clarified. The dark look in his eyes made the clarification seem necessary. "Addison was simply rabid to learn everything he could about every facet of filmmaking. He said the only thing he wanted to do was make movies, quality movies. My father liked his dedication and sort of took him under his wing, introducing him to a lot of people on the lot."

She leaned over the small, chipped table that separated them. He couldn't explain why it seemed like such an intimate movement. It just did. He was beginning to have the feeling that if she so chose, she could make reading the phone book an intimate experience.

"If Addison chose your novel to put his name to, it's going to make a great movie. He has faith in it."

Now that he had gotten over that huge blank wall in his head and had begun writing again, he felt he could take it from there. "Enough faith to leave it to me?"

"He doesn't have that much faith in God, let alone a human." She laughed, remembering. "The first film he ever made under his own name was based on one of my father's scripts. Addison was everywhere. Directing, checking cameras, props, sites, doing everything himself before the people responsible had a chance to get to it. By the time the movie was finished, he had made everyone crazy, including himself. But it was a wonderful movie."

The glow in her eyes as she spoke prompted Marcus's next question. "Are you involved with him?" Subtle, damn subtle, Marcus thought, irritated with himself.

"With Addison?" The idea tickled her. The producer was like a brother to her. "No, not in the way you mean." She couldn't resist. "What makes you ask?"

He shrugged, unusually preoccupied with his coffee. "No reason. It just came up in the conversation."

"Oh." Annie hid her smile behind the coffee cup, which she then placed back on the saucer. It took her a moment to compose herself. If she laughed now, she knew he'd get up and walk right out of her life. "But he does have very good judgment, Marc. And I'd take his suggestions—as well as mine—into consideration."

Yes, he was sure she would. But she wasn't him. "He bought my book, therefore he bought my conception of the characters."

"True," she agreed, "but you can't stuff almost five hundred pages onto the screen. At least, not without subjecting the audience to kidney problems." He was about to suggest a solution to that, but only got as far as opening his mouth. "Besides," she went on quickly, "some things just can't be translated onto the screen no matter how well they read." She knew he wasn't going to like this. "I'm afraid we're going to have to cut out whole sections of the book."

She was talking rapidly, even for her. It made him uneasy. He found it difficult to assimilate so much so fast. He should be alert, ready to defend his turf, yet he was just listening to her, practically hypnotized by the sound of her voice. He shook his head in an unconscious effort to regain control over his thoughts. "It's not going to work, you know."

"What?" For a moment, she thought she detected an inviting look in his eyes. She began to fantasize just a little. Something, possibly something very good, was going to happen between them. She wanted it to. She wasn't going to vacate his life until it did. "The screenplay, or us?"

"Us?" She read him too well. He was right in wanting to terminate this association. He had no desire to see this—whatever "this" was—through.

"Yes, us." She felt a very strong attraction to him, but knew that there was an equally strong probability that it could go nowhere, due to his resistance, his barriers. Because they both needed the safety of the lie to save face, she gave it. "Working together."

He drained his cup, then placed it down with a clatter. "Both."

"You're wrong."

He wondered if there was anything she didn't challenge. "About which part?"

"Both." She grinned. It camouflaged the shakiness she felt coursing through her body. "Everything'll work out. If you let it."

His chest felt tight. His breath struggled to escape from his lungs. Her very presence seemed to have a way of cutting off his air supply.

"And if I chose to maintain control instead of 'going with the flow'?" It would be simpler, far simpler, not to see this woman again. He didn't need this. The money and the glory were irrelevant. He had more than enough of both. Neither made him particularly happy. Instinct told him to cut bait and run. Why didn't he just go with it?

Everyone, he mused, had a self-destructive edge. This was his.

"Then you're probably in for a big legal hassle. You signed papers, my friend, and Addison may be a pussycat in some respects, but he takes his business—and his contracts—very, very seriously." She pushed aside her cup. The coffee was cold. "Why are you so against working with someone? Is it me?"

It would have been easy to say yes, but it was no longer as simple as it had been two days ago. He decided to play it safe, safe according to his definition. "I don't like sharing my thoughts with someone." He hadn't meant to be quite that honest. "I've never worked with a partner before." The creative process was far too intimate an act. To share it with someone, to let her be part of it, would leave him wide open, make him feel exposed, vulnerable. He didn't want that.

But I want you to share your thoughts with me, she mused silently. *I want to know what you're thinking and why. I want you to tell me everything.* The smile on her face hid what she was feeling. "Perhaps it's time for a new experience."

That's what she was all right. An experience. He thought of the constant arguing over interpretation yesterday. The nonstop battle of wits. The scent of her cologne that had kept wafting up to him and had preyed on his senses long after she had left with her brood.

"I'm not sure I can work with someone on a day-to-day basis." That much was honest. There was no need to add that she made his palms feel sweaty even while he contemplated strangling her.

A roar of laughter rose from the back of the restaurant, and five spacemen strode out together, their antennae bobbing as they walked. Annie gave them a cursory glance and smiled unconsciously. "We've already gone over ground rules and plot line. The rest should be easy."

Was she serious? Hadn't she been there for yesterday's session? Wasn't this the same woman who had absolutely refused to let him use the prostitute in the bar scene because she insisted that it would hurt the main character's heroic appeal? They had spent the better part of three hours on that. "Are you always this optimistic?"

His tone was sarcastic, but she was learning to ignore that. "Almost always. I cringe a little when I go to the dentist, but even then, why anticipate the worst? Most of the time, there aren't any cavities."

That's because the main cavity was in her head, he was tempted to say.

Annie rested her chin on the bridge formed by her clasped hands, her elbows leaning on the table. She barely noticed the waitress who came by with the check. Marcus made her think of a homeless puppy in need of a lot of understanding. He took a great deal of pleasure in biting off her head, but she didn't think it was just because he was being perverse. True, he was possessive of his work, but there was more to it than that.

She had to admit that she had been intrigued by the man behind the words when she had finished his first book. By the sixth, she was hooked. And if she had any doubts as to the basic nobility of his character, well, there had been a late football player who shared her belief that there was much more to this man than a frown and flashes of wit aimed at keeping people at bay.

She wasn't much for football, but she had heard of Jason Danridge. He had made all-American in college. The world had been at his feet, and he had a lot to give in return. It was a crime that his life had been cut so short. But while he lived, he could have had his pick of friends, his pick of associates. He had chosen Marcus to be his friend and to take care of his son. There had to be a reason.

She wanted to know what it was. Maybe it would tell her why she was so attracted to him. She had to know why the deeply sensitive human being who wrote stirring prose, who had such insight about people on paper, was so distant in person.

She had given up hope of ever being attracted to anyone again, not in that special, mind-spinning way that made her blood hum. Exceedingly gregarious and friendly with the world at large, Annie still held a little of herself in reserve. It had been the part she had given Charlie. The part, she had been so sure, that had died when he did. To know it didn't please her. And frightened her just a little.

"Well—" Annie began to rise. Marcus mechanically moved to her side and pulled out her chair. "Now that we're stimulated—"

It was getting to the point that every time she opened her mouth, it was to say something that befuddled him. "What?"

"The coffee." The expression on her face was nothing short of mischievous.

Once again, he hadn't understood her. He wondered if there was anyone who could accomplish that magic feat. "Oh, that." He left a few bills on the table and let her lead the way out.

"Are you game to go back and work, or are you going to have to think this through, too?" Annie stood on the curb, waiting for him to catch up.

He was never one to shrug off responsibility. "I suppose the sooner we get this over with, the sooner my life will be back in order."

Taking his arm, Annie walked over to the lot where they had left her car. "You do have a way of making a girl feel that she's the center of your world, Marc."

The sun was high overhead and the smog seemed to hang around them like a leftover witch's curse. The lot, with its gravelly terrain, seemed dustier than it should be. "Marcus," he corrected. "I'd really rather have you call me Marcus."

Annie put her key into the car door, then looked at him questioningly. "Only when I'm issuing a formal request for a duel, Marc. Do you want to drive again?"

He was surprised that she would relinquish her car to him twice in one day. He got in behind the wheel. "Don't you ever get serious?"

"Yes." The seatbelt clinked as she buckled it.

"When?"

"When I work. My work is very, very important to me." She saw several people she knew entering the restaurant and waved out of the window.

"And mine is to me." Marcus saw his chance and pulled the car out onto the street.

"Fine, we're in agreement about something. The rest'll follow."

Traffic looked annoyingly heavy, he thought as he inched along. "Like an avalanche."

The temperature was rising. Annie rolled up her window and turned on the air conditioner. She spared him a disapproving look. "We're going to have to do something about your pessimistic attitude, Marc."

"You could tell me that this is all a bad dream. Maybe then I'd wake up full of optimism."

"No," she said, shaking her head. "That was done on TV once. No one bought it."

"Then we're stuck."

"Afraid so."

He managed to angle the car out from behind a truck. Visibility improved. Traffic did not. "Not nearly as much as I am. Not nearly as much as I am."

"Are you any good with cars?"

He looked up, startled at the sound of her voice. They had just put in over six hours of solid work, most of which had been spent quarreling. Exhausted, he had let her win more than half the points. The operative word, he had told himself, was "let." He wanted to believe that if he had insisted enough, the matter would have gone his way. Deep in his heart, though, he had his doubts that even God could have won an argument with her.

Five minutes ago she had bidden him goodbye and walked out of the den. He had let out a sigh of relief and begun looking forward to an evening listening to quiet music. Maybe he would ask Nathan if there was something he wanted to listen to. He didn't think he had enough energy left to face her again so soon.

But then, the woman was full of surprises, as well as questions he wasn't expecting.

Rubbing the bridge of his nose, he tried to focus on her. She didn't look half as tired as he felt. "Am I what?"

"Any good with cars," she repeated. She gestured abstractly to her left, not having the vaguest sense of direction of where the driveway actually was. "My car seems to be sitting, dead, in your driveway."

He was tempted to make a remark about her joining it, but restrained himself. There was no point in being nasty, even though she deserved it.

Marcus stood up and ran his hand through his hair. "What's wrong with it?"

"If I knew that, I wouldn't be asking you if you were any good with cars." There was a touch of irritation in her voice.

Well, well, well, he thought, suddenly amused. So, something did get to her once in a while. That was encouraging. "I'm not. I'm good with phones." He picked up the receiver. "I can call someone to tow your car to my mechanic if you like."

She nodded. She didn't need to ask if his mechanic was good. She knew that if Marcus used him, the man had already been thoroughly checked out. She glanced at the pile of papers neatly stacked next to the printer while he made his call. It was a nice amount of work that they had produced today. A good start for a first draft. They might even be finished ahead of schedule. Bet that made him happy, she thought.

"He'll send someone over in the morning," he told her, about to hang up.

Annie nodded, taking the receiver from him. He surrendered it, looking at her curiously. Annie glanced around, knowing that it wouldn't be in plain sight. He was too neat for that. "Do you have a Yellow Pages around somewhere?"

He took one out of the bottom drawer and handed the hefty tome to her. "Who are you calling?"

"A cab." She flipped through the pages quickly, then found what she was looking for. "I don't think you want me camping out here until the car's fixed. Besides, I have a pregnant dog to feed.''

Impulse was not something he allowed into his life very often. It had been something that he had only experienced when he was with Jason and Linda. Because he was so comfortable with them, they had brought it out. There was no reason for it flourishing now. But it did. Inexplicably he found himself putting his finger on the telephone button and cutting her off.

Annie looked at him, waiting for an explanation.

''I'll take you home.''

''If it's not too much trouble,'' she said cautiously, enough to be polite, not enough to force him to change his mind.

''It is,'' he said with undue harshness because his own actions confused him.

Chivalrous to the end. ''Then why—''

''Are you going to stand here, debating this with me, too?''

''Heaven forbid. I never look a gift horse in the mouth. Here.'' She handed him her keys. ''The mechanic might want these.''

He pocketed them absently, scribbled a quick note for Holly, then led the way outside. He refused to think about what he was doing or why. He was tired; he needed fresh air and a break. That's all there was to it.

He jammed the key into his car's ignition and turned it. ''Where do you live?''

It took him a moment to orient himself after she gave him the Malibu address. ''That's near the beach,'' Marcus said, heading the car in that direction.

''No, that's *on* the beach. I like listening to the waves beat against the shore at night. It's very soothing.'' She had contemplated moving out after Charlie had died because the memories there were so painful. But she loved the old house, and she knew that wherever she went, she'd be taking her memories with her. They would always be a part of her and would contribute to making her what she was.

"Real estate's expensive there."

She knew that. Enough realtors had knocked on her door telling her of the fantastic price she could get if she sold. "It's been in the family a long time. My grandfather bought it when he first moved out here. It was his until he died. He left it to me in his will."

He heard the fondness in her voice. "Were you close to him?"

He didn't know why he asked, except that a deep-seated hunger made him do it. He had never been close to anyone in his family. Affection was unheard of, unwelcome. Both of his parents reacted badly to such displays the few times that he had attempted them as a young child. It made them uncomfortable. Marcus eventually realized that *he* made them uncomfortable. He had left after high school graduation and he hadn't been back since. He didn't miss his parents. But he missed the idea of them sometimes, the idea of a family, of closeness. She, he thought, raising a brow, had probably been close to everyone when she was growing up, including the mailman.

When Annie thought of her grandfather, she thought of strong hands that had held her high and a robust laugh that told her to reach for the sky; not the stoop-shouldered old man he was before he died. "Very. I worshiped the ground Grandpa walked on. I thought he was next to God, or at the very least, Walt Disney. I lived a good deal of my life in Disneyland," she explained.

"I could have guessed that part."

"What about you?"

He took a turn down a long, winding road. "What about me?"

She watched as early evening shadows played hide-and-seek with the planes of his angular, aristocratic face. He had the brooding, sensitive face of a poet. Byron. No doubt about it, the man raised her pulse. "Whose ground did you worship?"

"No one's."

The answer was so pat, so curt, it hurt her to hear it. "What about Jason? Did you and he—"

"We went to school together." His answer dismissed the subject. But as he said it, a collage of memories spun through his mind, bits and pieces feeding into one another. His parents had robbed him of love and so the person he might have been withdrew. Jason had seen what there was hidden within him and had brought it out. Marcus had allowed himself to become part of Jason's family, to be part of Jason and Linda's lives. It had felt good. But it had ended.

"And you—"

Why didn't she leave it alone? Everyone else left him alone. Everyone else knew when to back off. Everyone, he remembered, but Jason. Jason had never allowed him to pull his cloak around himself and retreat. He was always there, cajoling, pushing, daring him to try things. Jason would have understood someone like Annie. He would have been equipped to deal with her. But Marcus didn't have the faintest clue how to handle this woman.

"I'd rather not talk about Jason."

She could appreciate the fact that the wound was still raw. To lose a friend, to lose someone who mattered, was very hard. She knew about that twice over. "Okay, what do you want to talk about?"

"I'm all talked out for tonight. Silence would be nice."

"If you say so."

"I say so."

She lasted a little over three minutes, then turned on the radio. Johnny Mathis was singing something warm and romantic. Marcus switched the station. The sound of drums and guitars vibrated through the car, melding with the cooling night air. They reached her house ten minutes later, and Marcus walked her to the front door.

"I don't suppose you want to come in?" She bit her lower lip and waited, hoping.

He almost did, just to prove her wrong, but he was tired and not up to tilting at her windmills.

"I think I'd feel a lot safer not entering your lair." The words were prompted by self-preservation. The less he knew about her, the better. It would keep the barriers up between them.

He made the fatal mistake of looking down into her eyes. There were worlds to get lost in in her eyes, teasing worlds, worlds that knew his secrets. They were the sexiest pair of eyes he had ever seen.

They matched the rest of her.

Without fully knowing or understanding, he reached for her. Another impulse had taken him over. Dangerous habit, giving in to impulses. It was totally out of character for him. He was beginning to be confused as to what was *in* character for him, or who and what he was. He had thought he knew. He had felt comfortable with that knowledge, with himself. Now he was no longer sure. He was acting strangely and he didn't know if he even liked it.

Impulse made him sample what he had been craving all day.

Framing her face, he filled his hands with waves of blond hair and brought his mouth down to hers. It was an action that he had done countless times. He couldn't remember one of them. He knew, instantly, that he would remember this no matter how long he lived.

He had thought of her as a hurricane, as mischievous. There hadn't been the slightest hint of the exotic about her. Yet she tasted exotic, electrifyingly so. She made him think of strange, mysterious foreign lands, with the scent of silks and heady perfumes.

A surprise. It was all a wondrous, unique surprise.

He had kissed her to get it out of the way and to satisfy his own curiosity, which had nagged him since the first time he had seen her standing on his doorstep, dripping wet.

But he wasn't satisfied. As the kiss deepened, as it revealed things to him that he had never known before, as he drew her body closer against his, Marcus grew only hungrier.

Hungrier for something that he knew would lead to his undoing. He grew hungrier for soothing, for passion, for the feeling of peace. Hungrier for a hundred conflicting things that swirled through his mind as his lips slanted over hers. None of that had anything to do with the woman in his arms.

It had everything to do with the woman in his arms.

Lips sought, tested, gained and retreated, leaving fiery imprints in their wake. Tongues touched hesitantly, then explored, first shyly, then boldly, sending sensations soaring, blood pumping. Neither one of them was left unchanged.

A kiss begun in curiosity rose quickly in intensity until there was no air left in his lungs and only whirling, disjointed thoughts in his head. He had the unmistakable feeling that he had just put a match to a very dangerous fuse, a fuse that was going to have lasting effects on his life somewhere down the line when it came to journey's end.

She hadn't expected this. She had hoped, but she hadn't even begun to dream that there was this waiting for her. It was every single happy experience rolled up into one. Her head filled with fireworks, and there was nothing and no one but him. The scent of the beach, the quiet night sounds, everything disappeared as if it didn't exist. The only thing that did was this man holding her, this man whose body was supporting hers, keeping her from falling. And yet she was falling, falling into a deep, dark tunnel with bright lights shining at the other end.

Shaken, Marcus let his hands drop and dragged himself

away, knowing if he didn't stop now, he'd pick her up in his arms and carry her into her house, to take her just beyond the door.

She didn't know what to say. The taste of his mouth had been dark, powerful and had robbed her totally of her control. He had left her stunned. And more than convinced that the attraction she thought was there was *definitely* there.

He could apologize, he thought. He could turn on his heel and just leave. He could have himself committed. Since she thought a cup of coffee was a date, she might see this as a proposal of marriage.

"This isn't to be misconstrued, either," he warned her. Damn, even his voice sounded shaken.

"Is it all right to construe it as a kiss?" Somehow, she summoned a smile. Her impish grin belied the turmoil going on inside her. She felt like a washing machine on spin dry with all the towels tangled up and pulling against the force.

He had no words to answer her. Retreat seemed best at the moment until he could gather his thoughts together. "Yes. I'll see you tomorrow."

"Count on it." Annie hugged herself as she watched him move quickly back to the safety of his car.

Chapter Seven

Marcus stood before the multipaned windows, staring at the rainbow of colors created by the sun breaking through the prismlike thick glass. He was staring, but he wasn't seeing. His mind was elsewhere.

Behind him were the muted sounds of some golden oldie he half remembered. Annie had won that concession from him their third morning together. She worked better, she had insisted, with music. He had expected Beethoven. He had gotten Beatles.

He had gotten a hell of a lot more than that, he thought, rubbing his hand along the back of his neck, and probably more than he could safely handle.

Above the music he could hear the continuous, rhythmic clatter of computer keys. She had an idea, he knew, and was working it through. Though she could talk and write at the same time, mercifully, right now she was busy communing exclusively with the machine. Even with his back to her, Marcus could visualize the scene clearly. Total chaos. She worked in the center of turmoil, oblivious to it, possibly even thriving on it. Around her were piles of papers arranged in no particular order, as scattered in their composition as she was. His side of the desk, as always, was organized.

Marcus was neat and meticulous when he worked. He needed to be. That was how he coped. Everything in his life had to be in order. Everything was done in measured steps. There was little or no spontaneity, but that was the price he paid. The only release Marcus had was through the actual act of writing.

His outlet, his verve, had abruptly dried up with Jason and Linda's deaths. A vast, overwhelming sense of loss, of loneliness, of being cast emotionally adrift, had sucked everything out of him. For days on end, words refused to come. Half thoughts fell together haphazardly in piecemeal fashion, only to fall apart. Nothing he wrote made sense and so he had stopped writing, stopped trying. It had panicked him. Without his writing, he was lost.

He couldn't think straight, couldn't pull his thoughts together.

He felt desolate, as alone as he had before Jason and Linda had happened into his life. More, because now he knew the difference. There was no need for speculation anymore. He knew what it meant to share, to talk, to sound off innermost thoughts without fear of ridicule, of censure or of misunderstanding. Jason and he, so different, yet so alike, were like the left and right sides of a brain. Different, yet harmonious.

With Jason's death, the harmony within life had ceased. Jason was the only human being with whom he had ever really connected.

But if that were true, Marcus thought as he fingered a plant on the shelf behind his desk, watching Annie's fingers fly over the PC keyboard, then where were all these thoughts coming from? All these feelings? God, he wished he had Jason and Linda here now to talk to, to tell them about this crazy woman who had been dropped into his life with the aplomb and fanfare of a wartime soldier parachuting onto his front lawn.

The light that broke through the panes of glass scattered and lit the room, bathing the den in its warm brightness. No brighter than the expression on her face, he noted, still watching her. Whatever she was doing, she was obviously happy with it.

He winced, knowing that another battle was probably in the works, erupting as soon as he read what she had written.

She was a lot better at dialogue than he was, he thought. He was good at thoughts, at constructing moods. Talking on paper seemed second nature to her. Now why didn't that surprise him?

In her own way, he had to admit, she was good. Different, but good. That didn't mean he had to let her into his private life.

The past week and a half had been like living in a battle zone, and he was most definitely suffering from combat fatigue. But what he wasn't suffering from any longer, he thought with no small amount of relief, was writer's block. She made things happen, explode, in his mind. Undoubtedly it was all due to a self-defense mechanism. If his mind hadn't reared into life, he knew she was capable of just rolling over him and continuing merrily on her way, unperturbed.

They might call the wind Maria, he mused, but hurricanes could really learn a lot from this woman.

She always came prepared, he'd give her that. Armed with her PC, piles of notes and ungodly cheer, she'd come, late, but she'd come, marching undoubtedly to some inner clock the world hadn't, mercifully, tapped into yet.

She'd come not only prepared to work, but prepared to nose her way into his life the way he had never allowed anyone, except for Jason and his wife, to come into his life before. She was impervious to frost, let sarcasm roll off her back and had absolutely no idea what the word privacy meant. She was even on a first-name, friendly basis with his housekeeper, who, for the first time since Marcus had employed her, had lost some of that dour expression he had assumed had been stamped on her face at birth.

More important, Annie had an amazing effect on Nathan. She had accomplished what Marcus had wanted to do. Too timid and withdrawn at first to venture into the den, Nathan soon took advantage of the path Annie forged for him into Marcus's life. He was evolving from a quiet guest into a normal seven-year-old boy.

Because of her.

She had no idea what the word "no" meant. And nothing seemed to stop her. He longed to know what could, yet put off finding out.

She took to rearranging his life. "What in God's name is that?" he had demanded just this morning when she had arrived overloaded and fairly staggering under the combined weight of her briefcase and the rather large box she was hefting. He took the latter from her. "Did it ever occur to you to take two trips to the car?"

"Wastes too much time."

She was slightly breathless and her voice was husky and warm. He couldn't help wondering if her voice would sound that way after she made love. Something he wouldn't find out, he warned himself. Not if he was smart. This was not a lady who would pass through his life leaving no impression, no mark. This one, if he let her, would hurt. It seemed almost ridiculous to believe that, but he saw the signs, had felt it when he had kissed her. He really didn't want to get close.

"Aren't you the one who's always trying to save time?" she asked, walking into the den.

Marcus deposited the box on his side of the desk. There

was no room on her side. "You don't save anything by getting a hernia."

"Why, Marc." She dropped her briefcase casually on the chair. It slid to the floor. She left it there. "You care." She fluttered her lashes at him coquettishly, then laughed.

As always, her laugh stirred him. "I care about finishing this damn screenplay on time."

The slim shoulders, gracefully bare thanks to an electric-blue halter top, moved up and down. "I'll take what I can get." Purse met briefcase on the floor. She glanced toward the hall. "Where's Nathan?"

He itched to pick up her things and put them in their proper place, but forced himself to leave them where they were. "Probably pacing up and down in the living room, waiting for you."

"Well, at least one member of the household looks forward to seeing me." She flashed Marcus a dazzling smile, then turned on her heel before he could respond to that. "Well, let's not keep him waiting."

He caught up to her at the doorway. "You didn't answer my question."

Her blond hair was pulled up in an outrageous ponytail that perched on the crown of her head and bobbed as she moved. She made him think of an ad for suntan lotion. "Oh, I thought I did. What question did I miss?"

"What did I just bring into the house?" Besides my undoing, he thought.

"A video game system."

He looked at her, his brain failing to register what she was saying. "And what am I going to do with it?"

Was he serious? What cave had he been hiding in? "You're going to hook it up for Nathan so that he can practice."

"Practice?"

"You're beginning to sound unoriginal, Marcus. We can't have that." Her eyes smiled as she patted his cheek.

Her touch made him remember the single kiss they had shared. He shifted his eyes to her mouth. It made things worse. There wasn't a part of her that he could look at safely, he thought.

"Stevie and Erin would love to see him again if it's all right with you." She had already brought Nathan to her sister-in-law's house on Saturday, as promised, and the three children were well on their way to becoming fast friends. She intended to nurture that. "And I thought they might play a few video games to keep out of your hair."

"Very thoughtful of you to try to preserve my hair." Why couldn't Richard have sent him a man to work with? Or at least someone who didn't smell so good, who didn't have creamy white shoulders that tempted him to reach out and touch. He wasn't used to not being able to concentrate, and she kept making him lose his train of thought. Just by being.

She insisted, when he proved to be all thumbs, on hooking up the video game system for the boy right then and there herself. And secretly, he had taken pleasure at the light that had risen in Nathan's eyes. She was, all in all, like a ray of sunshine in their lives.

At least, he amended, in Nathan's.

After Annie played one game with amazing dexterity, he had disengaged her from the game and led her off to the den where she attacked their screenplay with exactly the same amount of gusto.

Their screenplay.

When had it become "their" screenplay and not exclusively "his" in his mind? The line was blurred, as was most of his life in the past week and a half. A wild, exhilarating, breath-taking blur filled with arguments, regroupings and then wars over interpretations. The woman actually had the unmitigated gall to explain his characters to him.

"Women interpret things differently than men," she had told him.

He had been restrained enough to keep the reason for that to himself. He noted that no matter how heated the arguments got, they were only heated on his side. She was adamant without raising her voice, without so much as changing her expression.

It made him long to change her expression. The way he had last week. Eight days ago, precisely. When nothing less ordinary than skin touching skin, lips touching lips, had occurred.

And haunted him every night.

Finally, now, he decided to reply to her statement. "Women are more emotional than men."

Annie looked up from the screen. She had been frowning over a word. "You say that as if it's a bad thing."

"It is." He came away from the window. "Emotions are fine in books. But they get in the way of things in real life. They cloud our judgment, color our decisions."

"Color." Annie seized on the word, a poised finger raised in the air, the keyboard temporarily abandoned. "That's exactly it. Without emotion, there is no color, only shades of gray."

He was arguing with her because she seemed to constantly push that button within him, yet in his heart, he agreed with her. Where they really differed was that he thought, apart from his writing, that shades of gray were preferable to pain. And he told her so.

Annie stared at him, silent for a moment. He would have savored the silence, except that it made him uncomfortable. The look in her eyes made him uncomfortable. Inadvertently admitting to pain—he knew how her mind worked by now—had been a momentary slip on his part, and he regretted it immediately. She reached out and placed a hand on his shoulder. Because he thought he recognized pity when he saw it, he moved aside.

It was obvious that he had been hurt very badly once, she thought. They had that much in common, and the kindred ache within her reached out to him, making her want to soothe, to take away the unspeakable pain she knew he was dealing with. She had lived with it herself.

"Was it someone you loved?"

He didn't want to answer, but knew she'd only press until he did. He tried evasion. "What?"

"The pain in your eyes," she said quietly. "Did you lose someone you loved?" Whoever she was, Annie felt herself suddenly envying the woman he had loved enough to take into his life.

Maybe it would have done him good to talk about it. But reaching out to another human being had always been difficult for Marcus at best. As a child, it had been drummed into him not to let his feelings show until he found that he *couldn't* let them show even if he had wanted to.

"There's no pain in my eyes. That's a squint. The sun's too bright." As he tugged the chord, the opposite ends of the drapes flew toward each other, shutting out the daylight.

Though she was sure he thought she didn't know how, Annie retreated. If she pushed too hard, she'd only succeed in pushing him away. He'd talk about it when the time came. Everyone needed to talk, to let the hurt out. Talking heightened happiness and dissipated fears and pain. It was something she firmly believed.

"Have it your way."

A reprieve. She was something else again, he thought. "Thank you."

"You're welcome." Annie arched her back, linked her fingers and stretched her arms above her head slowly. It had been a long day and she felt it.

Marcus watched her, fascinated. If he had been in the midst of producing the great American novel, it would have evaporated from his brain.

Nothing he knew of could have competed with the utterly feminine, utterly feline, gracefulness of Annie's body. Each movement was captivating, lyrical, and brought his blood pounding through every vein in his body. The ache he felt in his loins was very real, very demanding and very difficult to shut away.

With a sigh, he put down the pages he was perusing. "I wish you wouldn't do that."

She stopped, puzzled. She was just sitting on a chair. "Do what?"

He gestured, helpless. Frustrated. "Stretch like that."

Annie relaxed, her body almost fluid in the chair now. "Does it disturb you?" Her eyes were wide with surprised amusement. And pleasure.

"Yes." What was the point in denying it? Even if he did, she could read the signs.

"Good." She rose and crossed to him. "Because I have to admit, you disturb me."

He had never met anyone like her before, which he took to be God's kindness to him. "Do you always say what you think?"

She smiled, and the smile spread across her face, moving up into her eyes. It was a smile that made him feel like smiling, although there was nothing to smile about.

"I'm not saying what I'm thinking now," she told him.

He had a thousand responses milling around in his head. Not a single one materialized on his lips. What did materialize, though it had not been far from the surface the past eight days, was his desire.

His hands slid down her back. He memorized each inch as his fingers skimmed along her spine. The sensation of her bare skin aroused him to such a point that it seriously worried him. It was as if he had no control over his own actions, his own thoughts. And he had always had control. Female companionship was pleasant, but he could take it or leave it, and he had always chosen women who didn't tax him on every level of his existence.

He seemed to have no choice whatsoever in this matter. He wanted her, and he resisted as long as he could. But it seemed hopeless to go on trying. He had only to touch her, ever so lightly, and the demands within him would begin, linking themselves to pleasures he had experienced the last time he had kissed her. He was always going to want her. It seemed hopeless.

He knew that they had absolutely no business being together, not professionally, not socially. She didn't fit into his world. She represented chaos, disorder, constant tension.

There were a thousand reasons to back away and only one not to.

Because he didn't want to.

He had always been one not to go with the odds.

Gathering her to him, he sought and found what his soul had been lacking these last few days. It was as if he were stepping into a warm haven after freezing in the darkness. He crushed his mouth against hers, cursing himself for his weakness, cursing her for making him weak.

Curses faded. All he wanted to do was go on kissing her, feeling this strange combination of being safe, yet being breathlessly swept away at the same time.

He had never known anything remotely like this sensation that held him in its grip. He knew he never would. But for now, he hung on to it with both hands, savoring it, savoring her.

Annie was surprised by the force of his kiss, by the force with which she reacted to it. He stirred up all the needs that she had swept so carefully away, under a rug somewhere in the corners of her soul.

They were back, brought to her in a misty cauldron by a man who professed not to care, not to feel. She knew better. And now she had proof. Though she had sampled the passion within his pages, to have it here, now, was beyond anything she had imagined. His kiss was hot and urgent, creating a complete meltdown within her. She had thought she could handle this, thought that whatever happened between them could be contained within ramifications that she drew up.

She was wrong.

And she was frightened. He resurrected things within the ashes in her heart that she would have sworn were forever gone. While she rejoiced that they weren't, their very existence brought new fears. She had lost someone she loved once; could she risk living with that hurt again? Should she? Especially with a man who kissed her as if he were angry with her for making him want her.

Annie drew back, her fingers still digging into his forearms, as much for strength as to push him away. She closed and then opened her eyes again, trying to refocus. "You're going to have to warn me the next time. My supply of oxygen is gone."

She pulled in a ragged breath and looked at him, her eyes saying things her banter couldn't. She knew they were filled with awe and wonder. She did her best to hide the fear.

There was anger in his eyes, anger amid the desire. When would it leave? *Would* it ever leave? she wondered. "Are we going to argue about this, too?" she asked.

"What are you talking about?" He forced himself to let her go, even though he wanted to go on holding her, go on touching her, perhaps until the end of time.

Her stomach was all tied up in knots. She wanted her relationship with him to be perfect, effortless. The last time she had loved, it had been so easy. It wasn't like that now. "You look angry."

"I am." Caution seemed to be eluding him. He couldn't lie to her, even though it would be easier. "I don't want to want you."

"But you do?"

He didn't want to see happiness in her eyes. Didn't she

know things like this were only temporary? That happiness, if it came at all, hadn't a prayer of lasting? He knew that. Why didn't she? "Yes."

"I see." Her heart was pounding, but she maintained her composure, forcing herself to keep it light. It was enough for now that she knew. She'd work out the rest as they went along. "I could come in wearing sackcloth and ashes tomorrow." She wanted to ask why he thought that wanting her was so bad, but she didn't want to hear his answer.

"You promised that once before." It wouldn't help. Underneath, she'd still be her, maddening, infuriating and incredibly desirable. But the image of her so attired brought a slight smile to his lips.

"I forgot." She wanted to touch him, to make him see that it was all right. For once, she was at a loss.

"So it would seem." He sighed. "Let's get back to work."

"Okay." She sat down again. The words she had written were still on the screen, green letters against black. She had to concentrate intently to remember what she was working on. He had completely stripped her mind. "I still think the love scene has to be moved up in the timetable in order to snare the audience's attention."

How many lovers had she had? he wondered. An annoying spark of jealousy zipped through him, but he wasn't going to ask her. It wasn't his business who she had taken to her bed, who she had touched and kissed and loved.

"Just what do you know of love scenes?" The question was not as innocently phrased as he had wanted it to be, but it was too late. Anything he said now to fix it would only make it worse.

Annie looked up at him, not seeing Marcus at all. "Enough."

Her voice had a quiet, melancholy note he had never heard before. He wanted to press and ask her questions, but asking would only open up channels that were best left closed.

Yet he couldn't shake the desire to hold her and ask who it was that she had loved. It wasn't jealousy exactly that prompted him now, although there was a shade of that, too. It was the slight flinch and flicker of pain he had seen in her eyes. She had loved someone. And lost him.

And he wanted to comfort her. Her, the woman who put his life into total chaos.

Marcus had the uncomfortable, panicky sensation that he was steadily, inevitably sinking into quicksand. And there wasn't a limb or anything that might save him in sight.

Chapter Eight

It took considerable effort, it always did, but she shut out the pain the memories generated. It would do no good to relive the past. Not when there was someone who needed her in the present. A man on the radio was singing about his girl being sweet sixteen. She hadn't been sixteen for quite a while. She hadn't felt like this about a man in quite a while.

A smile chased away any signs of sadness on her face. "You know, Sullivan, if you're trying to get me to quit, you're going to have to try harder."

Moving around him, Annie crossed to the window and tried to open it. The room needed fresh air and so did she. "I've worked with some incredibly maddening people in my life and never once walked out on a project. I've contemplated justifiable homicide a time or two, but never quitting." Try as she might, the window wouldn't budge.

Marcus stood back and watched her struggle, amused,

waiting to see how long it would take before she asked for help.

"Compared to them, you're just a pussycat." Annie looked around the window casement. How did this darn thing open?

A pussycat. Did she mean he was a pushover? "I'm not sure how to take that."

"In the best possible sense, trust me." Her forearms strained, a nail broke, but the window wouldn't move an inch. Annie swallowed an expletive.

"I'm also not sure how to take you." *And I damn well know I shouldn't even try,* he thought.

"Also in the best possible sense." She half turned toward him. "Okay, what's the secret? How do you open this darn thing?"

He came up behind her. With an arm around her on either side, he grasped the sash. It wasn't the most convenient way to do it, but he wasn't looking for convenience, just excuses. "You have to jiggle it, first on one side, then the other." He demonstrated. "It's temperamental."

She felt his body brush up against hers. His warm breath whispered along her back. It was as if her very skin was sensitized to him. Any second, there'd be goose bumps. Goose bumps, for heaven's sake.

The thought made her smile to herself. She relished the small, pulsating excitement that danced through her.

"Like a lot of things here," she murmured, carefully turning around so that she faced him.

There was no room between their bodies. There wasn't meant to be.

"You do have a way of getting under a person's skin." He played with a wisp of hair at her neck that moved in the breeze from the open window. He saw the desire that rose in her eyes. It matched the fire that burned within him.

This was counterproductive. But he didn't care.

"I've been working on it." Her words feathered along his lips.

He looked down. She was standing on her toes. It made him smile. Marcus let his hands drop to her small waist. It was as if his hands were meant to fit there, his fingers dipping down slightly and resting on the feminine curve of her hips.

God, he wanted her. He had never truly wanted a woman before. When he had taken one to his bed, it was unpremeditated, just a spontaneous reaction that lasted for the pleasure of the moment. He couldn't remember his pulse scrambling like this, couldn't remember his body throbbing and aching with demands.

Annie wound her arms around his neck. "Kiss me, Marc. I can't stay on my toes forever. My calves are cramping up."

He pulled her body to him, close enough to feel every soft contour against his, close enough to feel the tempting swell of her breasts rubbing against his chest. "Can't have that." Softly, gently, he nipped at her lower lip. Then his mouth covered hers.

He went with it because she had asked him to, he told himself.

He kissed her because he would have blown apart inside if he hadn't.

Surprised, worried about the speed with which his emotions surfaced, Marcus was swept out to sea again. He had only to touch his lips to hers, only to taste the flavors that were hers alone, to lose touch with reality. His mind filled with thoughts of only her as he lost himself to the passion that consumed him.

Her lips parted invitingly beneath his as he heard her moan. It vibrated against his mouth, filled his throat. His tongue teased hers, exciting him, pushing him closer and closer to the guardrail.

She tasted wonderful, *was* wonderful. He felt as if he

were drugged, spinning on the rim of the universe, having control spin away from him.

He didn't want to get involved. He didn't. It had been far better as a child. Then there had only been the pain of rejection. Before long, the barrier around his heart had hardened and he had told himself it didn't matter anymore. He didn't need love, didn't need to feel loved. It made life simpler.

It was infinitely preferable to the pain of losing someone. If he were to care about her, if it came to the point where it mattered if she left, then he would be opening himself up to devastation. He had been emotionally rejected by his parents, abandoned, in a manner of speaking, by Jason and Linda. He didn't want to risk facing the pain of opening up and then losing a third time.

He took a deep breath as his lips parted from hers. Her eyes were wide and slightly dazed, the outline of her mouth blurred from the force of his. "We can't keep doing this."

She found it difficult to think clearly. And even more difficult to deal with his barriers than she had thought. "Why?"

For a thousand reasons. Because I'm afraid. Because it won't work between us. Because I'll care too much. Better not to care at all. "Because we won't get any work done."

He would slip behind that excuse. She had no recourse but to go along with it. But she didn't have to make it easy for him. She smiled as she took a step back. "Man does not live by work alone."

He dragged his hand through his hair, wishing he could do the same through his life and have it fall into place as easily. "I do."

She studied him a moment. He was fighting too hard. "I don't think so."

His eyes narrowed. She was always presuming to know him better than he knew himself. If he could just hold onto his irritation, he'd be in the clear. "Then you think wrong."

Annie slowly shook her head. "Uh-uh."

He felt like taking her by the shoulders and shaking her. "Are you always this smug?"

"No. Only when I'm right."

He had heard of a succulent plant that shot off a poisonous substance when it was touched. Maybe he could make her a gift of it. She was always touching things....

Annie continued to look at him, trying to understand. It was a nice face, even, if allowed, a kind face. But he wasn't allowing it, wasn't allowing anything to touch him or to come in, perhaps not even the boy in the next room. A boy, if she was any judge of things, who desperately needed him.

Marcus's defenses had to be broken down for more than just a fragmentary moment. *She* needed to break them down. For Nathan. For herself. Annie curbed her impatience. For now, she knew she had to retreat. If you pushed too hard, you could break something that was frail.

She turned her attention to the screenplay. There were people counting on her and Marcus. Work would go a lot faster if he'd stop arguing with her. After working with her for over a week, he still didn't think of her as an equal.

"That's part of your problem."

Now what? He found it frustrating not being able to keep up with the workings of her mind, which seemed to shift around like a sidewinder on the hot desert sand, moving ever forward but in a complex, sideways pattern.

"Part of my problem—no, *most* of my problem—is trying to follow what it is you're talking about. It's like you're feeding me bits and pieces of conversations you start in your head."

She grinned. He had found her out. "The man is absolutely right." She made her decision. Abruptly she moved over to her computer and pushed the storing sequence. Green messages flashed at her. "What I am talking about, as you so deftly put it, is that part of the problem is that you don't respect my judgment."

He was relieved that they were talking about work. At least there he had a foothold. Respect, in his book, had to be earned. He watched as her fingers flew across the keyboard. "Forgive me, but why should I?"

She typed in the segment name and pushed the key marked "return." The computer began making low, grunting noises. "Good point."

"Good point?" He looked at her suspiciously. This was too easy. She was up to something.

Annie looked up. "Yes, good point. The reason you don't respect my judgment, the reason you don't treat me as a competent equal, is because you haven't seen any of my work. I've read all your books, but by your own admission, you haven't seen any of my movies."

He'd be damned if she was going to make him feel guilty about that. "I don't see—"

She glanced at the screen. It was blank again. Satisfied, she shut the computer off. "No, but you will once you watch."

"Watch what?" Any moment now, he was going to give in to another passion and wrap his hands around her slender, tempting throat. Maybe he could squeeze something out of her that made sense. But he doubted it.

Annie looked up at him, mystified that he still didn't follow her. It was obvious. "One of my movies. *Until Tomorrow* is currently out."

"And you want me to see it?"

She smiled. "Yes."

"When?"

"Now."

"No." She never ceased to astound him.

Annie put her hands on her hips, telling herself that losing her temper wasn't going to accomplish anything. She wasn't going to let him be obstinate this time. "Once you've seen one of my movies, maybe you'll stop treating me as if you were Moses bringing down the Ten Commandments and I was a lowly goatherd allowed to witness you do it."

She was babbling again. He went for the obvious. "Goatherds are men."

"We'll quibble about gender later, now c'mon." She moved around to his side of the desk and looked at his monitor. The screen was empty. "Anything there to save?" She knew there wasn't, but if she tried to shut off his computer without asking, he'd probably take her fingers off.

"No, but—" They hadn't gotten nearly as far in the script as he had intended. In any event, he had no desire to go off and see one of her movies. He was still trying to hold on to the idea that the less he knew about her, the better he could keep her at bay.

The perverse little voice that everyone carries within them laughed at the paper-thin hope.

"Good." She switched his computer off, and a single swirl appeared on the fading green screen before it went black.

He glared at her, not knowing whether to admire her guts or have her shot for the same reason. "You take too much on yourself."

"Yes, I know," she answered cheerfully. "It's self-defense." With one efficient movement of her hip, she pushed in her chair. "Let's go get Nathan."

She was already out of the room. He had to grab her arm to get her to slow down. "Why are we dragging him into this?" Somehow, he realized, in the last minute or so she had gotten him to go along with her impetuous suggestion.

"Because he needs to do things with you." She saw by the look that came into his eyes that she had overstepped her ground. Again. "Besides, it's a very entertaining movie," she added quickly. "Rated PG because of a couple of 'damns' and a 'hell.' I'm sure Nathan's heard as much or worse from you.''

''I don't swear around the boy.'' *Although around you it's getting to be a habit.*

''Very admirable. Do you talk around him—or to him?''

He decided that the woman couldn't help meddling. It was in her blood. ''I talk *to* him.'' And it was, he was relieved to note, getting steadily better all the time. He looked down at Annie. ''Just how long have you been a social worker?''

She could match him, flippant remark for flippant remark. ''I was born in 1962.''

Marcus was fighting a losing battle.

''Nathan,'' Annie called as she entered the foyer. There was no answer.

Going on instinct, she went to the family room. Nathan was still there, sitting cross-legged in front of the television set. She arrived in time to see a green goblin make off with the princess. Nathan maneuvered the control panel, his tongue caught between his teeth, trying to save her.

She knew he'd be hooked once he started playing. ''Nathan, we're going to see a movie. Would you like to come along?''

Nathan, his fingers curled around the hand control, his eyes glued to the set, didn't look up. He gave no indication that he'd even heard her. His body swayed as he tried to make a hit and failed. The princess disappeared into the goblin's dark castle.

''I think I've created a monster,'' Annie confided to Marcus.

He thought of the effect she kept having on him. ''In more ways than one,'' he muttered.

Annie gave him a curious look. She didn't know if he was being flippant, or not. For now, she let it pass. ''Nathan, honey.'' She tapped the boy on the shoulder and he jerked as he looked up, surprised to see anyone else in the room. "I think it's time we gave that thing a rest. You don't want to beat Stevie too badly, do you?"

Nathan grinned sheepishly. He was going to be a heartbreaker when he got older, Annie thought fondly.

"No." He shook his head.

She took the control panel out of his hand and placed it on top of the television set, then switched the power off. "Marc and I are going to see one of my movies. Would you like to join us?"

Nathan scrambled to his feet. "One of your movies?" he echoed. "Like a video you own?"

"No, like a screenplay I wrote. Do you know what a screenplay is, Nathan?"

He had heard Marcus talking about it to someone named Richard over the telephone. He hadn't sounded happy about it. "A story for a movie?" he guessed.

"You're very bright." Nathan beamed at her approval. "I'd like your opinion of the movie." She draped her arm around his shoulder casually. "Got anything better planned for this afternoon?"

"Heck, no." The video game was already forgotten.

"Then it's settled. We'll let Marcus take us to the movies." She moved toward the door, her arm still around Nathan, who she could see was enjoying being included.

"Let?" Marcus repeated, following. "I think the FBI would file this particular 'outing' under the heading of kidnapping."

Annie playfully lifted her chin, a challenge twinkling in her eyes. "You're much stronger than I am, Sullivan. Nobody'd believe it."

At this angle, her chin made a very tempting target. He wondered what she'd do if he clipped her one. "That doesn't make it untrue."

"Nope." Her eyes laughed at him.

He let Nathan and Annie precede him out the door to the driveway. Nathan seemed very excited over the prospect of going out with them. The change from the withdrawn, morose child he had been just a month ago to the well-adjusted boy he now appeared to be was astounding. The only time Nathan still acted somewhat subdued was when he was alone with Marcus. But Marcus wasn't vain enough to be jealous of the fact that Hurricane Annie could evoke responses in Nathan that he couldn't. He was just glad that Jason's son was back among the living.

He made no conscious acknowledgment of the fact that Annie was working the same miracle on him.

Annie turned as he slammed the front door. "Mind if we use my car?"

He descended the three steps that it took to join her. "And if I did?"

"We'd use yours." He was halfway to his car when she added, "but I know the way better."

He preferred driving. Just one more thing he liked having control over. But it was a petty matter. There were bigger things to fight over. And he had every confidence that they would.

Resigned, Marcus nodded for Nathan to climb into her car.

Annie hid a smile when the boy settled himself in the front seat next to her, leaving the back door open for Marcus. She turned slightly to get a better view as Marcus got in. "You don't mind being chauffeured around, do you, Marc?"

He closed the door after him. "As a matter of fact," he answered truthfully, "I hate it."

"Oh, I forgot. You like to be in control." She raised her hands from the steering wheel. "I have no problem with that."

"Ha!" Marcus stayed where he was, and Annie turned on the engine. He tugged at his seatbelt, which obstinately refused to budge. It was stubborn. Like her. It was with no small satisfaction that he finally wrestled it out of its inertia.

No sooner had he buckled up than she peeled out of the driveway. His stomach lurched. "Are we in a hurry?" he wanted to know.

Annie changed lanes to get in front of another car. "Not particularly."

The woman drove like she talked. "Then why are you trying to break the sound barrier?" he asked.

"Sorry." Annie eased her foot off the gas pedal. "Habit. I drive fast when I'm alone."

"Which is why you probably drive alone," he muttered under his breath. "Just what is it we're going to see?"

He forgot. It just proved her point. He didn't think what she had to say was important enough to pay attention to. "I told you. *Until Tomorrow*. It's a comedy."

Marcus looked out the side window, watching scenery and cars whiz by. "I'd never have guessed."

Annie glanced at the boy on her right before looking back at the road. "You know him better, Nathan. Is he always this grumpy or am I special?"

"I think you're special."

Nathan's words made her throat tighten the way it did every time she watched greeting card commercials that heralded the best that life had to offer. The precious moments. This was most definitely one of them. She reached over and squeezed his hand. "I think you're special, too, Nathan."

Marcus tried hard not to feel as if he were intruding.

They didn't have far to go. She made it a practice to know the exact locations of the theaters where her films were playing. It never ceased to give her a kick. This time the closest one was at a triplex nestled within a well-frequented minimall.

Annie parked as close as she could to the triplex. *Until Tomorrow* was playing in theater number three. "We're here," she announced as she turned off the ignition.

Marcus didn't move. He had thought this through on the ride over and had decided that while he had every intention of seeing one of her movies eventually, he didn't care for the fact that she had decided that it was going to be here and now. Until she had turned up, he had made all his own decisions. Now she swept in, arguing every point, making him want her when there was no sane reason to do so, and turning everything in his world upside down. He had to take a stand somewhere before she had him crowded against a wall.

Annie closed her door and then looked into the car. Marcus was still sitting in the back seat, making no effort to get out. She looked at Nathan. The boy shrugged and shook his head. She peered into the back seat. ''This isn't a drive in, Marc. You have to come inside to see the film.''

''You know, it seems to me as if you always get your way.''

She knew that look. There was an argument in the making. ''Not always.''

He knew she'd contradict him. ''Then what are we doing here?''

Why was he being so stubborn? ''We're here to see my movie.''

''When we should be working.''

Annie felt her patience draining. And she felt hurt because he didn't want to see the movie she had written.

''You wouldn't have come if you hadn't wanted to,'' she pointed out.

''What I really wanted to do was finish the scene we were working on. I wasn't particularly in the mood to see a movie.''

She opened her mouth, flabbergasted, then thought better of it. The phrase about leading a horse to water but not making him drink ran through her mind. She couldn't make him want to see her movie, or make him like it once he had. That was up to him. She quietly closed the car door.

If he wanted to be pigheaded, that was certainly his privilege.

"In that case, you really don't have to come in. But it's a shame to waste a trip. I'll go by myself."

He was fully annoyed at this point. He was through being led around by the nose. "Fine."

"Fine," she shot back

The man was insufferable. Nathan was looking at her eagerly. She wanted to take him with her, but that would mean coming between them or forcing the boy to make a choice. She had no desire to put Nathan through an ordeal. "You take care of him, okay?" She tried not to notice that his expression fell.

Stunned, Marcus watched Annie walk up to the booth, buy a ticket and walk inside without so much as a backward glance. What had started out as a bid for control had degenerated into a petulant act on his part. He didn't care to feel that he was behaving like an idiot. If he wasn't mistaken, there had been a hurt look in her eyes just as she turned away. He didn't want to hurt her. He just wanted to prove a point, a point that suddenly didn't mean that much anymore. Moreover, there was no denying one disconcerting fact. He *wanted* to be with her in the theater.

"Mr. Sullivan?"

The high voice had him looking up. He had forgotten about Nathan. "Yes?"

The boy climbed into the back seat next to him. "I think we should go in with her." He looked uncertainly at Marcus, obviously worried that he might have said the wrong thing.

So do I. "Why?" Curiosity had him asking for the boy's reasons.

Nathan struggled to put his feelings into words. "Well, she's a lady and she's all alone. Shouldn't we protect her or something?"

"It's more of a matter of protecting the world from her."

Marcus laughed, then ruffled Nathan's hair. The boy smiled up at him shyly. It was, Marcus realized, the first time they had actually had any physical contact with each other. The boy had been so withdrawn, so self-contained with his hurt tightly wrapped inside him, that Marcus hadn't been able to bridge the gap. Talking about Annie was helping. It figured. He couldn't seem to get away from her influence no matter how hard he tried. What was worse, he was beginning to be at odds with himself about the problem as well. "You really want to go in and see it?" Nathan nodded. "Why?"

"Well, I like movies."

What else didn't he know about this young life that had been thrust into his? Marcus wondered. "Do you?"

Again, the dark brown head nodded up and down. "My dad and I—" Nathan's voice broke as tears suddenly sprang up into his eyes.

"Yes?" Marcus urged kindly.

Nathan cleared his throat of the tears lodged there. "My dad and I, we used to go all the time, when he was playing in town, I mean. Sometimes we used to go out real late." Remembering made him smile. "He liked science fiction best."

"Yes, he did." Marcus looked down at the small, delicate face. Nathan had Linda's soft eyes and bone structure, but the grin belonged to Jason. "He used to drag me to awful old movies all the time when we were in college. *Flash Gordon and the Mole Woman* was one of his favorites. He made me sit through it three times."

Nathan tucked his legs under his body as he sat up. "Really?"

"Really." Marcus looked at the boy, the eager expression getting to him. "Maybe you and I could see it together. They must have it at some video store."

"Sure!"

There were no science fiction movies to see now. Just a

comedy by a woman whose intrusion into his life was no laughing matter. "Well," Marcus said slowly, looking toward the theater. "I guess we'd better go in there and find her, eh, Nathan?" Marcus got out and held the door open for the boy.

Nathan tumbled out. "Can we stay and watch, maybe?"

"Sure, why not?" Trying not to seem obvious, he guided the boy across the street.

"Can we have popcorn?" Nathan asked as Marcus handed the woman in the booth a ten-dollar bill.

Marcus grinned at the eager note in Nathan's voice. "What's a movie without popcorn?"

Nathan cocked his head, testing the waters a little further. "With butter?"

"Absolutely."

Nathan grinned happily as Marcus ushered him inside the theater.

Chapter Nine

Annie held the box of popcorn steady on her lap. She had bought the small container more to have something to do with her hands than because she was actually hungry. It was still full. She hadn't touched any of it. Though her eyes were on the screen, her mind was somewhere else. On the occupants of a blue car in the parking lot.

Maybe she had been a little overbearing, she thought. She did have a tendency to come on strong sometimes. A rueful smile curved her lips. More like ninety-eight percent of the time. She really didn't mean to. It just happened, especially when she cared about something. About *someone.*

Maybe she should have tried coaxing him into the theater instead of just giving him his choice. The trouble was, she didn't know how to coax gently. Her own eagerness and good intentions always got in the way. Marcus was probably hailing a cab right now, Nathan in tow, on his way home.

She was annoyed with him, with herself and with her failure to get him to open up. She was certain he liked her, and she could sense that he was coming around, but each time it looked as if there was a little headway being made between them, suddenly the antagonism was back along with that damned impregnable wall of his.

Annie plunged her hand into the container, grabbing a fistful of popcorn. She bit down on an unpopped kernel and flinched as the shaft of pain registered, radiating from her tooth through her jaw.

Pulling the kernel out, she moved the perfectly round shape back and forth, rolling it between her thumb and forefinger. It made her think of Marcus, stubbornly retaining its original shape even under considerable pressure.

She sighed. Maybe he was happy that way, but she doubted it. It was this doubt, this belief, that everyone preferred being happy to angry, integrated to isolated, that drove her on with people in general.

And Marcus in particular.

That, and the very persistent, very sensual pull she felt whenever she was around him, despite his standoffish demeanor.

"Some way, somehow," she murmured to herself, scarcely aware that she was talking out loud, "it's going to happen between us."

"What is?"

Marcus caught her container of popcorn before it hit the floor. Annie stared, surprised, as he took the seat next to her. An overwhelming sense of contentment washed over her.

"Only good things," Annie managed to answer finally. She nodded at the container Marcus handed her. "Nice catch."

"Jason used to like to throw passes. He needed a receiver."

Annie tried to imagine that—Marcus out on a field, running back as his friend threw a football toward him. It gave her a good feeling.

She leaned forward and looked past him to the boy who sat down to his right. "Did you have to twist his arm?" she asked Nathan.

"No. He thought it was a good idea."

Someone two rows in front turned and shooshed them. Annie bit her lower lip sheepishly and grinned. "I guess they want to hear this," she whispered to Marcus.

So, he had come into the theater voluntarily. Miracle number one hundred and seventy-three, Annie thought happily.

Marcus cocked a brow. He couldn't see her facial expression. The scene up on the screen was taking place on a moonless night and the theater was shrouded in darkness. She sounded smug, though, and he would have bet six months' royalties from his last book that she felt that way. She had read him right all along. Why was it he couldn't say no to her and stick to it?

"Pretty pleased with yourself, aren't you?" Marcus couldn't help whispering.

She continued to look at the screen, but he could make out the slight curve of the smile as she said, "No, I'm always this happy."

"Shh," the person directly behind them said sharply.

"He's right," Annie responded, inclining her head toward Marcus. "You don't want to miss a word of this." She indicated the screen with fingers that were filled with popcorn. Suddenly she had an appetite.

Marcus had his doubts whether he'd feel as if he were missing anything if a line or two of dialogue were lost to him, but he had ultimately come to see the movie because he believed in being fair. And because he was a firm believer that one way or another, a person was always reflected in his or her work.

For reasons that he didn't care to delve into, he decided

that he wanted to scratch more than just the surface with Annie de Witt. Never mind about the less he knew about someone, the less involved he'd be. He *was* involved; there was no use in denying that any longer. And since he was, he needed to know things about her. Knowledge, after all, was power. He couldn't let her have all of it.

Besides, she seemed determined to scratch him down to his inner core. A core that hadn't been touched or disturbed before, not this way.

That was the word for it, he thought, absently taking a handful of popcorn from the container Nathan offered. Disturbed. More than anything else, she disturbed him. Disturbed him emotionally, professionally. Physically. It had to stop. But in order for it to stop, he had to know what made it happen. He had to have a key as to what it was about her that made him react so strongly.

Marcus watched Annie as much as he watched the action on the screen. She seemed completely absorbed in the movie, as if she didn't know what was going to happen next. But of course she did, he thought, fascinated by this reaction. She wrote it. If he hadn't known it before, he would have guessed by the contented glow that radiated from her when the audience laughed in all the right places. Annie's rapt attention prompted him to start watching the movie in earnest.

Without knowing exactly when it happened, Marcus became involved.

The dialogue, crisp and quick, was riveting and funny, intelligently written so that it could appeal to an adult audience and yet draw in the younger crowd as well. He had to admire her for that feat. Marcus caught himself actually wondering how the story would resolve itself and what would happen to the characters on the screen. The story made him care about the people whose lives he was watching evolve—not a small accomplishment, he silently admitted. He wasn't easily roped in.

He glanced at Annie again. At least he hadn't been until now.

When the credits finally rolled by, he heard her draw a breath as her name scrolled upward. It was little more than a soft sigh, but he heard it. His eyes narrowed. She still got a thrill out of it, he marveled, the thrill of knowing that something she had created was there for all the world to see, to enjoy. He understood that. He had felt it once, the first time a work of his had been accepted for publishing. When it had finally hit the shelves, he had haunted all the bookstores to see it, to stand back and just admire the collection of books with his name on it. Somewhere along the line, the thrill had faded, replaced by work, responsibility, contracts and details. The excitement had gotten lost, he thought, envying her the fact that she could still feel it.

Annie didn't have a clue as to whether or not he liked the movie. He hadn't laughed. She was acutely aware that all through the showing she had been waiting for the sound of his laugh, listening for it above the sound of others. It hadn't come. He didn't like the movie. Her movie.

So what? Thousands of other people did. Why should it matter that one black-hearted man didn't?

Because it did.

Falling in step with the other people as they surged out of the theater, Marcus, Annie and Nathan made their way through the lobby and out of the building. Outside, the sun was a glaring white, baking everything in sight, as if atoning for the fact that it had rained outside the perimeters of the rainy season just the week before.

Annie blinked several times as her eyes slowly became accustomed to the brightness that surrounded them. She drew a breath and found it hurt her lungs. In the last two hours, it had gotten almost unbearably hot.

"I feel like my eyelashes are going to burn off any second." She knew she was making small talk, but if he thought she was going to beg a response out of him, he had a long wait coming. "How about an ice cream?" The question was directed toward Nathan more than to Marcus.

"Sure." Nathan knew he would have said yes to anything she suggested. She was the prettiest lady he had ever seen and she made him feel good. She made him feel as if he still mattered. After his parents had died and left him, Nathan didn't think that he did. Shyly he reached for her hand.

Annie squeezed it, touched by the loving look she saw in the boy's eyes. "Never met anyone who could say no to ice cream on a hot day. C'mon." She tossed the word over her shoulder, knowing that Marcus was lagging behind. "There's this great ice-cream parlor just on the other side of the theater complex. And it's air-conditioned." She said the last words reverently.

Marcus had to walk quickly to keep up with her. Even in this heat—the weather bureau had predicted a hundred degrees for today, and he could feel that they had passed this conservative estimate—the woman had the energy to move fast. Maybe she wasn't human, just a fast-talking, over-energized android in a pair of short shorts and a skimpy halter top.

Android, hell. No android could create the kind of reactions he was experiencing around her, he thought. One did not daydream about stripping androids of their clothing slowly.

The blast of cold air that hit them when they walked into the ice-cream parlor was a welcome relief from the heat, and for Marcus, a welcome relief from his own thoughts. He needed, he decided as he followed Annie and Nathan to a table, a cold shower.

The halter dipped slightly as she sat down, giving him a fleeting glimpse of firm, small breasts that had his gut tightening and his loins following suit.

A long, cold shower, Marcus amended, taking the seat

opposite her. Nathan slid in next to her with no hesitation, his allegiance clear.

After ordering something called a Kitchen Sink Sundae for herself and for Nathan, Annie settled back, her hands folded neatly on the table. She eyed Marcus expectantly. He gave no indication that he knew why. "Okay, I think I've shown restraint long enough."

"You?" Marcus nearly laughed out loud. Restraint and Annie was a contradiction in terms. "Restraint? I'm glad you told me. I would have never noticed on my own."

"There's a lot of things you don't notice on your own." She ignored the darkening look in his eyes. "Yes, I was showing restraint. I didn't ask you what you thought of the movie."

"No," he agreed, "you didn't."

She waited a beat. Nothing. She felt like hitting him. "Well?" she demanded. He was doing this on purpose, but she decided that she wasn't too proud to ask, to push. Pride was just a cumbersome, empty thing that could only get in the way of things for her. "You know, you are an infuriating man."

The water glass felt comfortingly cold against his hands as he held it. Marcus raised his eyes to her face. "Must be catching."

She wasn't about to be put off any longer. Bracing herself for his response, she forged ahead. "What did you think of the movie?"

He shrugged. "I'm not much for movies."

She gave a frustrated little huff. "We've already established that. You're not answering the question, Sullivan."

"It was better than most."

Annie clutched at her heart, rolled her eyes toward the ceiling and gasped, "A compliment. Quick, Nathan, check to see if the sky is falling."

Nathan was bright enough to laugh rather than to run

outside the little shop and do as she said. He didn't even look at her oddly.

The waitress, however, did. As quickly as she could, the woman set down their order. Giving Marcus an interested glance that spoke volumes if he had only bothered to look, the waitress hurried away.

Marcus's attention wasn't on the waitress but the over-animated woman sitting opposite him. What made her tick? "Haven't you ever written anything serious?"

"Everything I write—" Annie sank her spoon into a mound of hot fudge "—is serious." Sampling, she closed her eyes and sighed. Heaven, pure heaven. When she opened her eyes she saw that Marcus was watching her. "Comedy is a very serious subject."

Was that the way she looked when she made love? As if ecstasy had touched her? It didn't seem possible that a person could take such joy in everything. He gathered his thoughts. He was drifting again. "Are you really going to eat that?" The dish in front of her was filled to overflowing with different flavors of ice cream.

She grinned. "Every last bit, or die trying."

Marcus watched her as he took a tentative lick of the single scoop of vanilla he had ordered.

"Really dig right in, don't you?" Her voice was teasing. She took another spoonful, savoring the cool feeling that the ice cream created. When she looked to her right, she saw Nathan mimicking her every move. It made her smile.

Damn, how could a woman make eating ice cream look so erotic? What the hell was wrong with him lately? Just being around her generated desire within him, made him want her in crazy, unconventional ways.

Unconventional for him. She, he had no doubts, would probably think that being covered in ice cream and having it slowly licked off her body was equal to making love in the missionary position.

He sucked in his breath, struggling to clear his mind. It

was due to the heat, that was all. In an effort to put things in perspective, he tried to remember when he had been with a woman last. No woman's face came into his mind. Only hers.

Damn.

She thought he had said something. Their eyes met and held as time froze. She saw desire, hot and impatient, in his eyes. Cobalt blue and desire, an unbeatable combination, she thought.

"I like vanilla." The words were said defensively. He couldn't remember what it was he was responding to. If this kept up, he'd be declared totally senile by the end of the month.

Annie lowered her eyes, knowing enough to hide her pleasure. "I'm sure you do."

Grown-ups were strange, even nice ones, Nathan thought, watching the two with him. "Vanilla's a good flavor," he volunteered. "My dad liked it."

Annie tried not to be obvious when she looked at the boy. To her relief, there was no sign of the deadening, soul-wrenching sadness she had seen the first time she met Nathan. She put her arm around him. "Vanilla's a terrific flavor."

"He liked mint chip better," Marcus recalled.

Nathan's face lit up as he remembered, a vivid memory flashing by. "Yeah, he did."

They were sharing a moment, Annie thought. Whether they were aware of it or not, they were sharing a moment. Jason Danridge, she decided, had been one smart man. He had known who to leave his son with.

"Annie?" Nathan ventured in between mouthfuls of fudge-covered ice cream.

"Hmm?"

"Did you really write that movie?"

"Yes, I did." She watched Marcus's face as she said it. The condescending smile she expected didn't materialize.

Maybe we're making headway here, too, she thought. Hope spun out, casting slender threads of steel that caught and held.

"I thought it was really neat. Especially when that guy's boat sank when he was in it."

Yes, that would appeal to someone his age. "That was one of my favorite parts, too." So, she was a kid at heart; there was nothing wrong with that.

"Are you really writing a movie with Mr. Sullivan?" He had heard them talking loud, when they thought he wasn't around, but it was still hard to believe that big people actually wrote what he saw.

Annie gave Marcus a long, penetrating look that he couldn't quite read. "I'm doing my best."

"Was than an insult?" Marcus wanted to know. With her, he was sure of nothing except his own confusion.

She shook her head, another tendril coming loose. "That was a statement. You'll definitely know when I insult you," she promised, taking another spoonful.

He eyed the half-eaten concoction before her. His stomach hurt just to look at it. "If you don't explode first."

She merely laughed and went on eating.

"Do you *really* enjoy writing such frivolous stuff?" He didn't even know why he felt compelled to make it sound like a put-down. She was competent in her own offbeat way, and he had to admit, if only to himself, that the movie had been well written—for what it was. But something kept goading him on, as if he were fighting for his own survival, fighting to keep her at bay. Disparaging remarks about her work could accomplish that.

She knew what he was doing and reacted accordingly. "I enjoy writing *entertainment,* Marc. If I didn't, I wouldn't do it. I never do anything I don't like."

He was silent for a moment. "You can't possibly be as happy as you let on."

She raised her eyes. It was nothing if not seductive. He wondered if she knew just how seductive. "Try me."

"If you are," he said quite seriously, "I really envy you. You're very lucky."

Lucky. If she had been lucky, she thought, truly lucky, she would have sampled more than just a taste of what real love would have been like. She almost said that to him, experiencing a sudden need to say the words aloud.

But then she buried it. The pain she carried with her was something very, very personal. It was something she didn't share. Not with anyone. She hadn't let it out even when all her family had done their best to divest her of it. They had been there for her and she had wept a little, but then she had carried on the way she always had. It was only the look that sometimes came into her eyes that gave her away.

The sudden sadness in Annie's eyes made Marcus want to reach out, made him want to ask: What? Why?

Who?

But Nathan was there, and it wasn't a subject Marcus sensed that could be shared with a child present. Meticulously Marcus folded his napkin and placed it on the table without thinking.

The woman was really getting to him. And that wasn't good. But he wouldn't have stopped it if he could, and he suspected that he couldn't.

Probably had something to do with a death wish, he thought.

For the first time, the silence growing between them felt very painful. "Have you always written for the movies?" Marcus heard himself asking.

"Always." She nodded, reinforcing her words. "My grandfather started in this business when it was just getting on its feet, right after the talkies blossomed. My dad followed because there was nothing else he wanted to do. He had different plans for me, something more stable and dependable—"

"But you wouldn't listen," Marcus put in knowingly. He felt a twinge of pity for her father, for any man who had come up against her.

"Why start a precedent?" She pushed her bangs away from her face. "I went into the business because making up stories was my whole world. It still is. Between my dad and grandpa, they garnered five Academy Awards and twelve nominations. I've got one of my own," she said with a touch of awe and pride he found strangely irresistible. In some ways, she was almost an innocent.

Annie raised her spoon and used it to emphasize her point. "And this project of ours just might net us another one."

It wasn't until later that Marcus realized he had taken the word "us" in stride.

Chapter Ten

Nathan had finished his giant sundae, although it involved a major effort on his part toward the end. But he didn't want Annie to think that he was ungrateful. The attention she gave him meant everything.

Annie maintained a cheerful stream of conversation during the drive home, receiving occasional answers from Marcus. Nathan hardly murmured at all. She cast a side glance at him as she stopped at a light. This time, she suspected, the boy's silence didn't have anything to do with his emotional state. The problem went a little lower than that. Poor thing. His hands were clasped over his stomach, his expression slightly pained. She took care to drive a lot slower returning to Marcus's house than she had leaving it.

"What's the matter, Nathan?" she asked gently as they approached the house. "You look a little peaked. The sundae not agreeing with you?"

"That sundae couldn't have agreed with anyone who doesn't have a cast-iron stomach," Marcus commented.

Annie looked up into the rearview mirror and caught a glimpse of Marcus's eyes. "I ate it."

"I rest my case." Marcus moved to the edge of his seat in order to see Nathan's face. The boy pressed his lips together and raised his eyebrows helplessly as he nodded in response to Annie's question. "You didn't have to finish it," Marcus reminded him.

"Yes, I did." Nathan felt miserable now, but the sundae had tasted good to begin with. "It was there."

"Spoken like a trouper." Annie laughed fondly. She coasted into the driveway and stopped her car next to Marcus's navy Jaguar. "A little bicarbonate of soda should have you feeling a lot better." She yanked up the emergency brake and turned off the engine. "Or, barring that, try some club soda."

"I'll see if we have any," Marcus promised Nathan. He got out first and opened the boy's door. Nathan climbed out slowly. He looked green, Marcus thought. He placed a comforting hand on Nathan's shoulder. "C'mon, fella, we'll see if we can fix you up."

She wondered if he knew how natural he seemed with the boy. The stiffness, the hesitation she had witnessed just a few short days ago, was dissipating. This was the man she wanted to get to know. Not the man who insisted on matching wits with her, although she did enjoy that. But this man, this gentle person who resided within the stern, demanding, competent writer, was the one who awakened her dormant emotions, who stirred her vulnerability at the same time that he made her feel safe.

Marcus stopped and looked over his shoulder. "In view of the situation, I think we'll call it a day. I'll see you tomorrow."

"Right." It pleased her immensely that he put a small boy's comfort ahead of his work ethic. Annie turned on the ignition again. She hadn't been wrong about him. For some reason, he just wanted to keep his better traits hidden from view. Those days were numbered.

An impish grin spread across her face. "Oh, Marcus," she called after him.

He turned, ready, he thought, for anything. "Yes?"

"This *was* a date."

She drove away before he could say anything.

"I think she likes you," Nathan mumbled, holding his stomach as if he was afraid that if he didn't, it would explode.

Marcus opened the front door. "If she does, it'll probably mean sealing my doom."

Nathan shuffled in, trying manfully not to moan. "What's doom, Mr. Sullivan?"

Marcus glanced down the street. Annie was making a U-turn. One slender hand waved jauntily out of the driver's side as Annie stepped down on the gas pedal and sped off. With a sigh, he closed the door behind them.

"Something that seems to shiver up my spine every time that woman walks into my line of vision." He led the way into the kitchen.

Nathan screwed up his face, trying to understand as he hurried to keep up. "You mean Annie?"

He tried to remember if there was any club soda in the refrigerator. "That's the one."

Nathan sat down on the first available chair he came to. "I think she's neat."

Marcus rummaged through the refrigerator. No club soda. "You, Nathan, are very young and very naive." He found a half-filled bottle of ginger ale. Holly's. Maybe that would do. "Live grenades are never 'neat.'" He reached inside the overhead cabinet for a glass. "One cure coming up."

She hummed along with the song on the radio as she drove, feeling very, very content with herself, with life in general. The screenplay was coming along, albeit slowly. And so was her campaign to break down Marcus's defenses, albeit even slower. But the bottom line was that it *was* progressing, which was all that counted.

It was really wonderful just to be alive. Annie sang out loud the rest of the way home.

She opened the front door and was assaulted by hot, almost stagnant, air. With quick strides, she crossed the living room and flipped the switch on her air conditioner. It rattled into life. An off-white dust mop on four legs scurried up to greet her.

"Hiya, Beatrice, how's my girl?" Annie bent down to scratch the small animal behind the ears. Beatrice thumped her tail madly against the floor.

Annie eyed her pet's very rounded stomach. It was almost dragging on the floor. She patted the dog gently. "How's the family coming along?" Beatrice was very much in the family way due to a very brief but passionate encounter with the feisty Scottie on the next street. Chauncey, his owner had whimsically called him. "Couldn't resist you, could he? Someday you'll have to teach me that trick. C'mon." Annie rose to her feet. "It's time to feed all of you."

The dog waddled after her mistress to the kitchen. Annie refilled Beatrice's water dish, then hunted through the refrigerator for the last of the leftover roast beef. Since she had gotten pregnant, Beatrice had demonstrated a definite fondness for roast beef.

Annie cut up the remaining meat into small bite-size pieces. "Here, this should satisfy your cravings." She set the dish in front of the dog. Crossing her arms and leaning against the refrigerator, she watched as the animal ate hungrily. "Well, we have that much in common. We both love food. And we've both thrown our lots in with men who are poles apart from us in temperament."

As she listened, Annie could hear the faint sound of barking. The Scottish terrier had a bark that could have belonged to a dog three or four times larger than he was. It really carried in the daytime when everyone else in the area was at work or school.

Sighing, Annie shoved her hands in her pockets and wandered into the living room. Beneath her contentment a bittersweet feeling gnawed at her. She knew she was saying goodbye to something, finally letting go. Her eyes wandered to the piano that dominated the room, a beautiful white baby grand that had been a housewarming gift from her father. She hadn't touched it in over a year. Not since Charlie had died.

Annie sat down and slowly lifted the cover from the keyboard. He had loved to pick out tunes on the piano. Sometimes he had composed things for her, silly, nonsensical songs that had touched her heart and made them laugh. After the accident, she had found that she couldn't bear to play it any more.

Slowly, hesitantly, she placed her fingers on the keys and began to play. She closed her eyes, and the notes came back to her. *Moon River.* One of the first songs she had ever learned.

Music filled the air, surrounding her. When she opened her eyes, the room was still there. Nothing had changed. Except for her.

Annie slid the cover back down over the keys. Rising, she picked up the silver-framed photograph that she kept on the piano. A thin, dark-haired man with sensitive eyes looked back at her. Charlie. The photograph had been taken just a few months after they had gotten engaged. A week before he had died.

Slowly she ran her fingertips along the glass, remembering what it had been like to touch him, remembering how it felt to be near him. The sweetness was still there. The pain had faded.

"I've met someone, Charlie," she said softly to the image she held in her hands. "He's not a thing like you, but I think he needs me. As a matter of fact, I'm sure of it, although he probably thinks otherwise," she added with a laugh.

Turning the frame around, she removed the back. With shaky fingers, she took out the photograph. She set the frame aside and crossed to the coffee table where she kept her album.

"I'll always love you, Charlie. But it's time to get on with my life. I need sunshine." She sat down on the sofa, pulling the photo album onto her lap. "I need love, and most of all, I need to give it." Searching through the book, she found an empty page. "But you always knew that, didn't you?"

Charlie would have understood. Somehow it helped to know that.

Tenderly she placed the photograph on the empty page and smoothed down the clear plastic over it. Then slowly she closed the book.

No, she thought, Marc was nothing like Charlie. Nothing like her, either, but he was someone she could love, someone who could love her. There was something basic within him, something sensitive beneath the surface that spoke to her, moved her.

Sensitivity had been easy to see in Charlie. With Marcus, it wasn't that simple. But she knew it was there. It was in his words. His written words. She felt confident that Marcus Sullivan was every bit as sensitive, as passionate, as his writing. She had had a taste of it in his kisses. He just needed help to release the real man.

And if she couldn't do it, she thought as she rose, leaving the album behind her, no one could.

He didn't want to be stirred up like this. But that was exactly what she was doing. He was used to going along a nice, unemotional, straight path. She had him zigzagging, filling up with emotions, with wants, with needs suddenly exploding within him, with no more cause than the fact that the sun had highlighted her face or a corner of her mouth lifted higher than the other. It all seemed so ridiculous. And yet, Marcus couldn't reason himself out of it even though he knew what the dangers were of following the path he was on.

His childhood had been nothing if not a stark reminder of where emotions, if released, led. To disappointment. To pain. He could remember making a card for his mother. It had been her birthday, and his father was taking her to a party to celebrate. Marcus wasn't included. But he had worked feverishly to make her a card, oblivious to the mess he generated in its creation. When he had handed his mother the card, she had carelessly tossed it aside and then scolded him for the mess he had made. Most of his childhood had been marked with incidents like that, until he had been afraid to reach out.

With the Danridges, it had been different. It had been safer. He was allowed to experience all the warmth, all the love, of a family unit without being completely involved. All the good parts, none of the problems. But when Nathan came to live with him, it made Marcus realize how deficient he was, how unequipped he was to deal with another human being. He still couldn't open up all the way.

And no one made him see his problem more clearly than Annie. He realized how difficult it was to express his feelings, feelings other than anger and annoyance. The easy way she got Nathan to open up simply emphasized his own inability to do so. He was accustomed to repressing his emotions, yet with her there was a strong desire not to. But in order to survive, he knew he had to.

Restless, unable to sort out the jumbled thoughts in his head, Marcus paced around his den. He had seen to Nathan's needs, then left the boy in Holly's care and thrown himself into the script. He thought he'd feel better, calmer, if he worked by himself, without her distracting him.

Methodically he reviewed the work they had completed that morning, fully intending to rework everything they had done. He didn't need to. The pages were still in rough-draft form, certainly not polished enough, but they were good. And they reflected the combination of both their feelings, both their philosophies. The fact that they were good worried him. It meant that the collaboration was working. His world was being dismantled. He had been so certain that a collaboration with Annie wouldn't work. But it seemed to be. Maybe he was wrong about other things, too.

They were good together. The thought throbbed in his brain like the relentless tattoo of the rain beating against a windowpane.

He hadn't wanted to give an inch today, had hung on to every piece, every principle, tenaciously like a junkyard dog. But she had managed, somehow, to temper, to add, to augment. He refused to use the word "change" because she hadn't actually changed anything. She had, God help him, *enhanced* it.

Just as she had somehow managed to enhance his relationship with Nathan. The awkwardness he had felt, that both he and Nathan had felt, was peeling away, layer by layer. They were finding each other in their need to grieve over the same loss, the same emptiness. Annie was the catalyst. He'd like to think that somehow the relationship between Nathan and him would have evolved on its own, but he knew that before Annie had walked into the house, it was going nowhere. He had felt frozen inside. His grief had him sealing himself off from Nathan.

She, either consciously or not, had helped him open up to the boy. She had talked and coaxed and wheedled until a crack within his armor had been found.

And then she had slipped in.

Damn her. Damn her for making him feel. He didn't

want to feel, not again. Feelings had consequences. With feelings, there was always that awful risk of losing. He didn't think the risk was worth the pain.

Annie. The name made him think of a little girl with frizzy red hair and black dots for eyes. Anne de Witt wasn't quite "Annie" to him. He thought of her as that *woman*, the screenwriter, the hurricane.

A self-deprecating smile came to his lips. That seemed like a lot of titles for such a little woman. A little woman who took up an awful lot of space in his life, he thought, pacing the length of the room with the pages still in his hand. He really didn't want to get involved, not with anyone. He didn't want someone to matter. He didn't want to give her that kind of control over his life. He had worked too hard to become independent and self-sufficient.

And yet the hole, the aching emptiness in his life, demanded it.

It was too jumbled a mess to be straightened out now. Later.

Marcus looked at his watch. She had probably gotten home by now. Impulse overtook him again. Without thinking through his actions and their consequences, he dialed her number. He didn't even realize that he knew it until now.

He almost hung up when he heard her voice on the other end. Bright, soft, sensual, it filled his head like trapped sunshine. "Hello?"

Hang up the phone, you idiot, before you make a fool of yourself, Marcus thought angrily. His hold on the receiver tightened. It got no closer to the cradle than it had been a moment before.

"De Witt?" he fairly snapped out her surname.

The man was a born romantic, she thought. Now what was wrong? "Marcus."

It wasn't a question, he realized. It was a pleased identification. As if she knew all along that he was going to call. "Predictable" she had called him. He was tempted to hang up just to show her she was wrong.

He didn't.

If he was going to do this, it best be done quickly. Wasn't that a line out of *Macbeth*? he wondered. Macbeth died at the end of the play, he reminded himself. He was walking into a trap of his own making. What the hell was the matter with him?

He didn't know. Just as he didn't know what possessed him to ask, "Do you have any plans for tonight?"

Annie thought of the old MGM musical she had found listed in the *TV Guide*. The bowl of potato chips stood waiting by her chair. She felt a smile spread through her. "None."

He knew he had to talk quickly before she jumped in and invited him over. He wanted to be the one doing the asking. The balance of control between them was very delicate at this moment, and she had a penchant for pulling it over in her direction. "All right, dress. I'm taking you to dinner."

"I never eat dinner naked."

It was a teasing line, but it conjured up an image in his mind that was very hard to shake. He could picture her across from him at a table, nude, candlelight playing on her smooth, soft skin, tempting him, making him burn. Making him want.

There was silence at the other end. Had he changed his mind? "Marc, are you still there?"

All too much so, he thought as he glanced down, glad for the distance between them at this particular moment. He was letting his desires run away with him. God knew his mind had already fled. The phone call was evidence of that. "Yes, I'm still here."

She cupped the receiver in her hand, cradling it. Beatrice had waddled by for another scratch. Annie stooped down to oblige the dog. "We're making real progress, you and I."

He knew he was losing ground and that it was of his own making, but he didn't have to give in without some sort of a semblance of a fight. "We're making plans for dinner."

"Yes, we are."

Why did she always have to make everything sound as if it had another meaning behind it? Maybe, he thought, because it did this time. He just wasn't ready to admit it. "How soon can you be ready?"

It had never taken her long to get dressed. Like everything else, she did it quickly. "How soon can you be over?"

Marcus glanced at his watch, gauged his time and heard himself saying, "I'll be by to pick you up in an hour."

More than ample time. "Then I'll be ready in forty-five minutes."

"I'll see you then." He hung up, then caught a reflection of his face in the multipaned window. "You are an idiot, you know that, don't you?"

Yes, he knew that. Muttering, he went off to change.

Annie hung up and grinned broadly. She gave herself two thumbs-up, savoring the moment. "That was him, Beatrice. Think you can entertain yourself for the evening?"

The dog yipped.

"Atta girl." Annie dashed off to do a million things in forty-five minutes.

Marcus showed up exactly fifty-three minutes later. She didn't keep him waiting. The door flew open almost immediately in response to his knock.

She looked the same. Bright, glowing, the speed of light trapped under glass.

She looked entirely different.

It was her hair, swept up from her neck, piled high in a

haphazard way, secured by pins, he imagined. What he couldn't fathom was why it looked so terribly appealing.

She wore a hot pink dress that had a halter top and absolutely no back to speak of. If he placed his hand on the small of her back to guide her out the door, she would feel naked. It made his hand burn.

The dress's skirt came around like a sarong. A very short sarong. The woman might be small, but she was very long on leg. A physical impossibility, except that she managed.

"You're staring." She liked the look in his eyes. Dazed. She decided to hunt for a compliment. Just a little one. She needed to hear words. "Is that because I look very good, or very bad?"

Marcus looked away, nonplussed at being caught. "The former."

"Flatterer. You do carry on." Her laugh was low and sexy. His hand tightened on the flowers he was holding. He had made no move to enter her house. "I love flowers. Are those for me?"

Feeling none of the polish he had so painstakingly developed, he thrust the bouquet forward. "These were Nathan's idea."

"They're lovely." He could have brought her a string of pop tops from soda cans and she would have felt the same. Very, very pleased. Hooking an arm through his, she drew him inside. "You told Nathan you were taking me out?"

Nathan had come to his room just as he was leaving. It had seemed natural to tell the boy. He didn't know why the fact pleased her so much. But Nathan made a good topic of conversation. Marcus found himself in need of one. "Yes. He says he thinks you're 'neat.'"

"I think he's neat."

Releasing Marcus, she looked around for a vase. She found one on a shelf on the breakfront. A cut-glass vase that had been a gift from her mother on her last birthday.

Deftly she arranged the bouquet and placed the vase on the piano. Perfect.

Annie turned then and looked at Marcus. "What do you think?"

He wished he had a drink to toy with. "I think he's a nice kid."

"He is, but I was asking about me." She took a step forward, then turned slowly around. When she faced him, Marcus was eyeing her warily. "What do you think of me?"

"I try to think of you as little as is humanly possible." The operative word here, he added silently, was "try."

"Are you succeeding?"

He could have lied, but he didn't. She had a way of knowing when he lied. "No."

She tucked her arm through his again. "I'm glad. So, would you like a drink before we leave?"

Several, he thought, wondering again how he could have put himself in this situation of his own free will. *Had* he had a free will where she was concerned? He no longer knew the answer to that.

The drink tempted him, but if he had one here, his control might dissipate permanently. "No, our reservations are for seven-thirty, and I think we'd better be on our way."

"Whatever you say." She handed him a shawl that seemed to be spun out of silvery threads and little else.

"I wish I could believe that."

Since she stood waiting, he draped the shawl around her shoulders. Her skin felt soft, silky. He caught himself lingering there a little longer than he knew was safe. For either of them.

He remembered he was supposed to be the one in charge. It wasn't easy. "By the way—"

"Yes?"

When she looked up at him like that, he could almost

believe that she was innocent, sweet, without a contrary bone in her body. Almost. "*This* is a date."

With that, he ushered her out to the car. He didn't look at her, but he knew she was smiling to herself.

In charge? Marcus thought. Who was he kidding? If he was lucky, he'd come out of this alive.

Chapter Eleven

The restaurant was subdued and dimly lit. Conversation around them was discreet enough to be hardly audible. Marcus felt completely alone with her in the booth. Yet it wasn't the kind of isolation he was familiar with. This was different. It was an intimate solitude. Because of the inner reserve he had developed over the years, he had felt alone in the midst of people at parties and at meetings. He had always stood apart from everyone, observing. It was what he was used to.

It had been different, of course, with Jason and Linda, but that had been a very special case.

And this, it seemed, was another.

He knew he couldn't really let himself believe that, not even for a moment. If he did, if he let his guard slip, if he started to believe that he could reach out to someone and not be rebuffed at some point, then he would start believing that perhaps a relationship could actually evolve and last.

But it couldn't. Not for him.

If ever a man had laid the plans for his own self-destruction, Marcus thought, it was he. Why else grab a rubber raft and deliberately run straight for the point where the rapids plummeted?

That was exactly what he was doing, he mused, putting himself into this vulnerable position with a woman who thought taking charge was one of the inalienable rights guaranteed to her by Thomas Jefferson and the other founding fathers. With every passing moment, she continued drawing him to her, pulling him toward her.

Knowing this, knowing what was in store, why had he made this overt move? Why had he asked her out? And why did he find her harder and harder to resist? It was the quicksand principle again, he thought. The more he tugged, the more he strained, the deeper he was being sucked in.

So why was he so stimulated, so excited? What was it about those almond-shaped eyes that made him lose his thoughts? What was this anticipation that kept slicing through him at unexpected moments when she'd look up at him?

People probably faced approaching death the same way, he thought.

"You've been awfully quiet," she observed over dessert. She had hoped, when he had asked her out, to finally get to know him, *really* get to know him.

As always, she seemed to be enjoying her meal. If someone would have asked him at this moment what he was eating, he wouldn't have been able to answer. "So have you. I didn't think that was possible."

Finished, Annie set down her fork. "I have my quiet moments," she told him. "I just happen to like conversation, preferably with someone who's living."

She leaned forward, the single familiar movement signaling privacy, intimacy. Marcus felt himself being drawn to her, slowly, inevitably, like the needle of a compass was destined to be always magnetized to the north.

"Why did you ask me out?"

Because after working with you for over a week, I'm nine-tenths certifiably crazy. The response flashed through his mind, but he didn't give it. Why did she always have to be so direct? Didn't she understand subtlety? Didn't she know when not to probe with embarrassing questions he had no answer to?

Marcus shrugged. "I think there used to be a line in the late sixties that went, 'The devil made me do it.'"

She laughed as she took a sip of wine. He watched the slight movement of her throat as she swallowed and wanted to trace the path the wine took with the tip of his finger. He wanted to press his lips to that throat, lose himself in her scent and her touch and her taste.

More than anything else in the world, Marcus wanted to make love with Annie before speculation about it drove him insane with desire.

Yes, he thought, definitely nine-tenths certifiably crazy. The other tenth wasn't that far off.

"Sometimes," Annie murmured, watching the light shine within her wine glass, "the 'devil' can be a very nice guy." She raised her eyes to his. He had such beautiful eyes. "Talk to me tonight, Marc. Don't waltz around with words. You're so good at that, but—"

She reached for his hand. He turned his palm up, his fingers slipping around hers. It was an action as natural as breathing. "I feel disarmed around you," he said in a moment of honesty.

She shook her head. "Never that. You'd never be disarmed. But that's exactly what I mean. You've got too many words to hide behind."

She understood that, he thought. Understood that he had always used words to shield him, to separate him from others. A cloak, a barrier. Safe, he couldn't be hurt. How much else did she know?

She saw that look entering his eyes. He was distancing

himself from her. She didn't want to be shut out, not tonight. "Talk to me, Marc. Really talk to me," she pressed. "As if I'm a woman you want to get to know. A woman who wants to get to know you." A smile curved her generous mouth. "Pretend."

There would be no pretending necessary, he thought. But he wanted to know her reasons. "Why?"

"Because when you pretend, nice things happen and things can end happily ever after."

It wasn't exactly what he had wanted to know, but it would do. This wasn't the time or place for rewrites. She looked so earnest when she spoke. She believed in what she said. He knew better. "There is no happily ever after."

"There is for a while," she insisted.

He thought of his parents. Of the motherless boy waiting for him. He felt his own anger rising at the injustice of that. Didn't she understand? "Are you really that naive?"

"No." There was an unshakable firmness within the quiet tone. "I'm that hopeful. There's no point in cutting yourself off from life because it might end badly. You can't live expecting only the worst."

"Why not?" His words displayed the raw bitterness he felt. "Disappointments don't happen then."

Oh, God, how deeply did his wound run? There had to be more to it than just the loss of his friend. But how could she get him to open up, to trust her enough to tell her what he felt? She bit back an impatient retort.

"Neither does the joy." She saw his expression harden. She beat him to his response. "Are you going to disagree with everything I say?"

He took a long swallow of his own drink. An incurable optimist, that was instinctively what she was. Jason and Linda would have loved her. His need to back off from her warred with his need to grasp hold of the things she believed in, if only for a little while. "Probably."

Annie felt her annoyance dissipating. She never could

manage to maintain it for long. "So long as I know." Annie studied him for a moment over the rim of her glass. "I don't believe you, you know."

When she looked at him like that, he felt as if she could see right through him, see him better than he saw himself. "Believe what?"

A waiter at her elbow swept away their plates. Annie kept her attention focused on Marcus. "That you're the man you're trying to project."

His hand slid over the tray with the check the waiter had left in his wake. "It's not a projection." Marcus placed his credit card on top of the tab.

"I think it is. The real man lives in his books."

She hit too quick, too deep. The lady was as astute about real life as she was about the world of make-believe. And she was truly rattling his cage. But then, he knew she was capable of that. "Those books are just works of fiction."

He wasn't convincing. "The feeling in them isn't. Tell me about you," she asked again.

He couldn't share himself with her. It was too hard, too painful. He didn't know exactly what he had had in mind, coming here, being with her, but it wasn't to talk about himself. "There's a bio on the back cover of every book."

She knew, she had read it. It had said next to nothing. Nothing about his family, his past, except that he had gone to school in the Midwest. Who was he? Why were his eyes so eloquently sad?

"I want to know more."

He said nothing. Annie folded her hands before her. "If you died tomorrow, what would your obituary say?"

She certainly didn't give up easily. He couldn't help the grin. "That I knew there wasn't any happily-ever-after all along."

Annie laughed. She had met her match as far as words were considered. Perhaps as far as everything was concerned. "You're impossible."

He toasted her with his half-empty wine glass. "I try my best."

The waiter took the tray with Marcus's card. Annie looked on as a couple walked by their booth. They were crossing to the area in the back that had been cleared off for dancing. The song that came drifting from there was low and bluesy. Annie had a need to be held in a man's arms. His arms. "Dance with me?"

Marcus knew it would be a mistake. To hold her in his arms would be a mistake right now. He felt particularly vulnerable, particularly in need of her warmth. When the waiter reappeared, he took the diversion gratefully and signed his name to the receipt. "I don't dance."

His body, tall and graceful, was made for dancing, for smooth movements. She couldn't picture him being awkward. "You're kidding."

She never stopped, did she? A lot of people didn't know how to dance. "When have you known me to kid?"

"Well, then, it's high time you learned. To do both." Annie rose and took his hand. The retreating waiter grinned at them.

Marcus stayed where he was. "Even if I was so inclined to let you teach me—and I have absolutely no desire to learn—it wouldn't be in the middle of a crowded floor." Although, if he were to hold her, that probably would be the safest place to do it.

No, touching her was never safe. He knew that.

She prided herself on knowing when to back off. "Sorry." Lifting her hands up in surrender, she sat down again. "I forgot who I was dealing with. Maybe we can find room in your closet."

He was amused. "It's occupied."

She gave him a knowing look. "I bet it is." With skeletons from his past that he had yet to set free.

His had been a flippant retort. He wasn't about to ask

her what she meant by hers if his life depended on it. "Ready to leave?"

"No, but you are." She picked up her clutch purse and rose with a sigh. "I don't know any more about you than I did before. You shadowbox well."

"I've been getting a lot of practice lately," he said as he escorted her out.

Leaving the close, intimate atmosphere of the restaurant didn't help. Filling his lungs with fresh, cool air didn't help. It didn't stop him from wanting her, from knowing that if he had taken her in his arms on the dance floor, he wouldn't have wanted to let go. He would have wanted to take her home with him and make love with her until he had rid himself of his need for her. Or until the twelfth of never, whichever came first.

He was beginning to have a frightening feeling that if nothing else, he knew the answer to that part.

Asking her over to his home was still on the tip of his tongue even as he brought his car down the narrow street to her front door.

Overwhelming things, urges, he thought. But he wouldn't allow himself to be governed by physical wants or emotional cravings.

The light on her front porch was on. Marcus brought his car up to the curb, then cut off the engine. For a moment, he just sat there, silent, watching the pale moonlight filtering through the interior of his car. It bathed half her face in light and half in shadow. He didn't know which he found more alluring.

And which would spell his ultimate defeat.

"We're here," Marcus murmured, his hands still gripping the steering wheel tightly.

"I recognize the house." She wanted him to come in. Why didn't he ask her if he could?

Never say die, she told herself. He had overcome one

obstacle and met her part of the way. She could go the rest of the distance. ''Want to come in?''

Yes. A great deal. He didn't release the wheel. ''It's late.''

''I have a watch.'' She raised her right hand. ''I know what time it is. That wasn't what I asked.'' She saw his brow furrow. He probably thought she was being flippant again. ''Okay, I'll ask an easier question. Would you like to take a walk? It's a beautiful night, and I don't want the evening to end yet.''

When she looked at him like that, he couldn't say no. Besides, what harm would it do? And he did want to be with her for a little while longer. ''All right.''

''One point for the home team.''

But she smiled softly as she said it so he didn't bother to retort. Instead, he got out and opened her door, then took her hand. She curled her fingers around his and left it there. It seemed natural.

''It's really a very nice neighborhood,'' she told him. ''Grandpa picked it because he loved the ocean. Do you?''

He let her choose the direction, trying not to think how right her hand felt in his. She was only a temporary part of his life. It was senseless to form an attachment. Worse than senseless. It was stupid. ''When I get the time to get down.''

''Marc,'' she chided indulgently, ''you're in Southern California. There's always beach around somewhere within a few miles. You're shattering our surfboard, sun-bleached image.''

The lights in the beach community were muted, just as the restaurant's had been. The night was warm, but the breeze from the ocean kept it from being hot. It was a night made for loving, Marcus thought.

So would Nome, Alaska, have been. With her.

Get a grip, Sullivan, he ordered. ''I was never one for images.''

"No, I didn't think you would be."

As they walked past the next house, a weather-beaten two-story building, a dog began barking ferociously. Marcus started.

"That's Chauncey, Beatrice's lover," Annie explained. "He's a lot smaller than he sounds."

Marcus looked down at her face. She was being absolutely serious. "Who the hell is Beatrice?"

"My dog. She tempted Chauncey once too often." An affectionate grin spread on her face as she thought of her pet. "She's going to have puppies any day now."

Marcus pitied Chauncey. The dog probably never stood a chance if Beatrice was anything like her mistress. "Fascinating."

"Attraction always is."

He didn't answer. Because she knew he'd prefer it, they walked in silence for a bit.

He discovered another unnerving thing. He felt relaxed with the silence between them. Felt oddly comfortable with her despite the need to possess her, to finally discover the secrets that were waiting for him. But he wasn't ready for a relationship, knowing the pain and disappointment that was involved in caring about someone. He wasn't going to risk rejection.

He never wanted to care about anyone again. Only writing was a constant. It was the only thing he could depend on.

And yet, why couldn't he stop this powerful need rising within him, this need to matter to someone, to make a difference? To connect?

They came to a halt at the end of the long winding block next to a darkened art gallery on the corner. Across the street was a restaurant, brightly lit in contrast. The outdoor tables were filled with people, couples enjoying each other. He didn't want to walk past them. "I think I'd better take you home."

Annie looked across the street. Why did the sight of happiness make him retreat? "My place or yours?" Her eyes were twinkling.

"Your doorstep."

"You are precise." She raised herself up on her toes just before he turned to make his way up the block again and whispered, "Coward," teasingly into his ear.

Her warm breath sent a shiver down his spine, and he reacted before he could stop himself. Forgetting the people at the café, forgetting everything but the woman in front of him, he framed her face in his hands and kissed her.

He felt alive for the first time all day.

The kiss was rougher than she had come to expect from him and all the more thrilling because of it. Anticipation hummed through every pore of her body as she gave herself to the wonderful sensation that Marcus created within her. Without her realizing it, a little moan of pleasure escaped.

Marcus felt her soft gasp vibrate against his lips. The excitement it triggered couldn't be measured by any scale man had created. Sliding his hands along her back, he felt Annie arch her body into his. The feast she offered him was far more sumptuous than anything he had had tonight. Above the passion he detected a trusting innocence that overwhelmed him. She was vulnerable. Dear God, he had never thought of her in that light, not really. It was an awesome responsibility.

With the utmost effort, Marcus regained himself and slowly pulled free of the vortex. He didn't have to look to see the smile of satisfaction on her face. He knew it was there. He *felt* it. "Let's go," he muttered.

"To the ends of the earth if you want."

Her laughter had the same effect on him as her kiss did. How the hell was he going to get through the next few weeks with his soul intact? He walked faster.

She trotted to keep pace. "Why are we jogging, Marc?"

"We're not jogging. I suddenly remembered something I have to do at home." *Like get there.*

They reached her front door in a few minutes. "It was a lovely evening, Marc, even though you had trouble getting out of the phone booth."

He was all set to go. That stopped him. "*Now* what are you talking about?"

She turned her face up to him, amusement in her eyes. "Clark Kent, shedding his disguise and becoming Superman." She lightly placed a fingertip in the center of his chest and tapped it. "I know he's in there somewhere."

He took her hand and elaborately returned it to her side. "Now you're babbling."

"Speaking metaphorically," she corrected him.

"Babbling," he repeated.

She pretended to shiver and ran her hands up and down her arms. "I love it when you're forceful."

"You are an infuriating, exasperating, crazy woman." So why did she reduce the pit of his stomach to a semiliquid consistency every time he kissed her?

"Thank you."

He tried his best to look annoyed, but he knew he really wasn't. "I didn't mean it as a compliment."

She could read the look in his eyes. He was weakening. "Yes you did."

He shook his head. "There you go again, putting words into my mouth."

"If I were to put anything into your mouth—" she raised herself on her toes again "—or near your mouth—" her arms were on his for balance "—it would be this." She tilted her head back, her eyes half shut, her mouth inviting, inches away from his.

It wasn't an invitation he could refuse, especially with the impression of her last kiss still blazing hot on his lips. But he hoped he was in control enough to just kiss her this time and break free quickly.

He was wrong. He would never be able to break free.

The quick, gentle kiss blossomed in proportions until a tiny daisy had evolved into a giant sunflower, startling the planter beyond words. The power and intensity of his passion, of hers meeting his, rocked him. He heard his own blood rushing in his ears, exhilarating him, lifting him to plateaus he would have staunchly maintained did not exist.

Until he scaled them.

He couldn't deny their existence anymore. He was a believer. A shaken, reluctant believer.

Yes, she thought, yes! She arched against him, tangling her fingers in his thick, dark hair.

She hadn't imagined it, hadn't just wished it into being. It was there. She could taste it. The desire, the passion, the need, dark and exciting. All there in proportions that enveloped her and made her feel safe even as it spun her on the rim of a giant top going faster, ever faster.

She felt his hands go up her back as she gripped his arms again. Her hold tightened until the fabric beneath bunched and wrinkled as she clung. She didn't dare let go. If she did, she'd spin out to the edge of the universe and no one would ever find her again.

He felt every inch of her body against his. Hunger burned bright. The sensation in his soul could only be likened to the way he felt standing on the beach after a wave had washed over him and then tried to reclaim the sand beneath his feet. He was being pulled out to sea.

He was going to go under.

When he could finally think clearly enough to stop, he found that he was shaken and struggling for a semblance of balance. For a moment, there were no words, no sounds. His own emotions and hers had rendered him speechless.

Trouble. He was in deep trouble. He didn't want this, couldn't want this. And yet, he wanted nothing more. Yes, he thought, he was in deep trouble.

Marcus took a step back from her. "You'd better get some sleep if we're going to work tomorrow."

"Right." The word was hardly a whisper as she pressed her lips together, sealing in the taste of his.

This was something big, she thought. She was tottering on the brink of something very big. Maybe she should slow down before she burnt up like a meteor plummeting into the earth's atmosphere.

She stood on her doorstep, taking a slow, deep breath as he moved away from her and toward his car. She was still standing there when he pulled away.

He reached home. He wasn't exactly certain of the route, only of the thoughts that were crowding through his brain, falling into one another. Each thought was reinforced with the word *no*.

As Marcus walked into his house, the phone in his den began to ring. Perfect timing, he thought, wondering who would be calling at this time of night.

Holly, her square body wrapped in a sensible beige robe that whispered along the wooden stairs as she descended, was en route to the den to answer. It was his private line and there were no extensions in the house.

"Never mind," Marcus called up to her, slamming the front door behind him, "I'll get it."

Holly changed direction without a word and trudged up the stairs again.

He got to the phone on the seventh ring. Whoever it was, he thought, was persistent. "Hello?" When he heard her voice, he realized he should have known.

"I think it's time," she said, drawing out each word as if it was just occurring to her, "for you to work at my place. We can get started tomorrow."

"I think we already have," he answered, but he was giving his reply to a dial tone.

The sound of her voice vibrated through his brain long after she hung up.

Chapter Twelve

He couldn't sleep.

It wasn't the sudden, unexpected storm that had materialized with its repeated cracks of thunder, threatening the land like an angry fist of God. It was the sound of his blood pounding in his veins that created the restlessness that kept Marcus from finding a place for himself in his bed.

More simply put, it was Annie.

Every time he closed his eyes, he would see her before him: warm, inviting. Making his mouth go dry. A siren on the rocks of destruction, beckoning him on to eventual heartbreak. He had told her the truth. He didn't believe in things continuing "happily ever after." Happiness, if it came at all, came in short, minuscule amounts and then evaporated, leaving devastation and bereavement in its wake. The lesson had been taught to him by his parents' behavior and brought even closer home by Jason and Linda's deaths. That had been the final straw—to venture out, to hope, only to be beaten down and deprived at the end. He didn't want to experience that sense of loss again. He didn't want what she had to offer.

He didn't think he could live without it.

Marcus swore under his breath and sorely wished for once that he was a drinking man. He wanted to numb his senses, douse his brain so that his emotions were doused as well. It wouldn't solve a damn thing, but at least for a little while, it would let him forget. It would let him sleep.

Marcus threw off his sheet and got up. He was too keyed up, too wired, to stay in bed and wait for sleep that refused to come.

And then he heard it.

The sound was faint, almost muffled, but it stood out against the sharp crack of thunder. It was—

Marcus listened closer, turning his head to find the direction the sound was coming from.

It was whimpering. Someone was whimpering.

Nathan.

Forgetting his robe in his haste, Marcus opened the double doors of his bedroom and stepped out into the dark hallway. He inclined his head toward Nathan's room. He heard it again. He'd been right. First came the thunder, then the sound of a frightened whimper.

God, how many nights had he cowered as a child, listening to thunder and not having someone there to tell him that it was all right? Too many to count. Enough to make him always remember.

Marcus placed his hand on the doorknob, then stopped before he could open the door. Not from restraint, but for Nathan's sake.

Instead, he knocked, giving the boy a moment to pull himself together. "Nathan, the storm's got me up and I was wondering if you'd mind keeping me company."

Behind the door, Nathan rubbed away tear stains with the back of his hand, gulping in snatches of air. His father had never told him that it was wrong for a man to cry, but he didn't think that his father's friend shared that belief. He didn't want to displease Mr. Sullivan. Mr. Sullivan was all Nathan had left of his father. "Su-sure."

Marcus opened the door a little at a time, hoping that the boy wouldn't be embarrassed, yet wanting to let him know that he wasn't alone. Being alone at that age was the worst thing in the world.

He remembered how awful it felt.

"Thanks." Marcus walked in and shut the door behind him. "I—um—"

Now what? He was as unsure of how to proceed with the boy as he was with the woman. Except that the boy needed him, and need was something he couldn't turn his back on.

Marcus studied the small, flushed face. Nathan was trying so hard to look unconcerned, but the tension was evident everywhere, in the way he sat, in his eyes. Marcus's heart went out to him.

"Want to come into my room? It's bigger. And we can talk."

Nathan flashed a relieved smile that told Marcus he had made the right move.

"About what?" the boy wanted to know, climbing out to join him. He felt safer next to Mr. Sullivan. Protected. The thunder couldn't get him as long as there was light and someone to talk to.

Guided by instincts that Annie kept telling him she saw in his writing, a fact that she was more convinced of than he, Marcus ran his hand lightly over Nathan's fine, dark brown hair.

"Anything you want to talk about." *And I sincerely hope you've got a subject handy,* he added silently, momentarily wishing that Annie was here. She was better at this than he was. A lot better.

He saw the fear flicker in Nathan's face as they approached his darkened room. Nonchalantly Marcus switched on the light. Nathan relaxed.

Small round eyes looked up at the tall man, half hopefully, half fearfully. "Can we talk about Dad?"

Marcus let half a beat go by because the question had found him unprepared. "If you like."

"I think I would. It'll kinda help." He could put it in no better words than that. But it was enough.

Marcus pulled down the rest of the covers on his bed. "Want to climb in?" He sat down on one edge and pretended to test the mattress. "It's a pretty comfortable bed as far as those things go."

There was nothing Nathan wanted more than to spend the rest of the night beneath Marcus's protective wing. At home, when he had had a home, he'd climb in with his parents whenever a storm or a scary dream had frightened him. His father had always made the monsters go away. They were afraid of him. Monsters were always afraid of football players, his dad had told him. Nathan stared at Marcus, wondering about his powers over monsters.

Marcus saw the question in Nathan's eyes. "What?"

"Are monsters afraid of writers?"

Marcus went with it. "Terrified."

"Really?"

"Absolutely." Without waiting, Marcus got in on his side and left the choice up to Nathan. "Writers can make them disappear into thin air without a trace."

Nathan had pictured his father beating monsters up and knocking them out. This was something new. Carefully the boy climbed into the bed, trying not to pull the sheets out of place. "How can they do that?"

Marcus leaned over, elaborately looked around to make sure that "no one" was listening, and whispered, "We erase them."

Nathan covered his mouth and giggled. It immediately occurred to Marcus that he had never heard a more heartwarming sound. Except, perhaps, the sound of Annie's laughter, but then another part of him had been warmed besides his heart.

He couldn't help thinking of Annie, even now. She would have approved of this, he thought, approved of his letting a frightened boy share his room. Well, he hadn't done it because of her. He had done it because once, a long time ago, he had been terrified of thunder, of the sky suddenly lighting up at night for no reason and making angry sounds. He had wanted to be reassured that it wasn't seeking him out for some boyish wrongdoing. He would have given his soul to have crept into either one of his parents' separate bedrooms, into either one of their beds. But he had been rebuffed by both and told to be a little man. He had been a frightened little man for many long nights.

"That's pretty cool," Nathan commented, in awe of Marcus.

Marcus tucked the sheets around the boy. "I think so." It was getting easier to play along.

"My dad was never afraid of monsters." There was love and longing in each word.

"No," Marcus said, leaning back and remembering, "the only thing your dad was ever afraid of was low grades."

Pencil-thin crescent eyebrows drew together as Nathan tried to understand. "Why?"

"Because then he couldn't play football." Marcus looked at Nathan to see if he was following him. He wasn't. "Colleges have rules. If you have low grades, you can't play on the team."

"Oh."

Marcus thought back to the long, all-night sessions he had spent with Jason, staying up to try to cram enough information into Jason's head to help him through. Jason hadn't been bad in math and science, but English, English was a subject that his brain seemed to retain like a sieve.

Marcus would tutor him until Jason could parrot the right phrases, hit the right buzzwords and eventually even distinguish a sonnet from a limerick. It hadn't been easy. But it had been infinitely rewarding to know he had had a hand in giving the university its star quarterback.

And as Jason rose in prominence, he pulled a protesting Marcus along with him for the ride, letting him sample the limelight. Letting him find the people that eventually lived on in his books.

Marcus blinked, realizing that Nathan was asking him something. "What?"

"Was he stupid?" Nathan didn't think so, but then he wasn't as smart as Mr. Sullivan. Maybe he knew better. Adults always thought they did, anyway.

"Your dad?" Marcus shook his head. "No, he wasn't stupid. He was the smartest man I ever knew." As he said the words, he knew that he meant them, had always meant them. "He knew how to enjoy life, how to find that joy and make it work for him."

Nathan's eyes were getting heavy, but he could still see that there was something sad about the man sitting next to him. "Don't you know how to find joy, Mr. Sullivan?"

His laugh was small, self-deprecating. "Not even if you drew me a map."

Nathan looked at Marcus uncertainly. "I don't draw maps very well."

Marcus laughed and ruffled the boy's hair. "Your dad couldn't draw very well, either."

Another peal of thunder and the boy cringed slightly, glancing over his shoulder. Effortlessly, naturally, Marcus gathered him close. "Why, I could remember a time when he had to do this relief map of..."

Marcus continued to talk, his voice soft, soothing. Story after story came back to him, and he talked until the boy was asleep. Suddenly he knew the subject of his next book. The last of the writer's block broke apart as if it had never existed. His next book would be about Jason, about them. About the friendship that blossomed between two out-of-state boys on their own for the first time who found something within each other to help them face the world.

Gently Marcus slipped his arm away from Nathan's slight shoulders, taking care not to wake him. Tucking the sheet around the small body again, Marcus was surprised, and gratified, to discover what he was feeling at this moment. He loved Nathan. Really loved him like his own son.

"You don't ever have to be afraid of thunder again," he promised the sleeping boy.

Her house looked smaller in the daylight. Smaller and somehow cozier. The exterior was stark white. Marcus guessed that the house had been painted in the not too distant past. The salty sea air hadn't had a chance to eat away at it.

With conscious effort, he unclenched his hands that hung at his sides.

This was ridiculous. There was absolutely no reason to feel uncomfortable, standing on her front step, like a suitor about to embark on a first date. This wasn't a date, for God's sake. That was last night, and he had gotten through *that* without any bloodshed. Just barely.

This was just another work day.

So why did he feel as if he were about to face the firing squad without having had a chance to have his last wish granted?

He rang the bell. No one answered. He knocked sharply. Nothing. He pictured her in bed, still asleep. Impatiently he knocked again. And again. By the fourth time, he decided that she had forgotten about telling him to come over and had gone to his house. That would have been par for the course. It wasn't as if she was exactly stable.

No, he amended, that was unfair. She was stable. She was just—

Enthusiastic was the only word that he could think of that would even begin to describe what she was, the *way* she was.

He was all set to leave, then he remembered that she loved the sea. Hadn't she mentioned something about a terrace? Knowing her and her regard for punctuality, she was probably sitting there right now.

Picking his way around the white picket fence—it figured, he thought—with scads of colored flowers leaning against it, he circled to the rear of the house. The land sloped so that the back was half a story above him. He shaded his eyes and looked up.

She was there, sitting in a white rattan chair, nursing a steaming mug of something or other.

He felt like throttling her. Why couldn't the woman be more professional? She didn't look the least bit surprised or chagrined to find him glaring at her.

She had lost track of time, thinking about him. It didn't faze her. "Hi."

"Didn't you hear me?" he wanted to know. "I was banging on your door for the last five minutes." The woman was totally irresponsible.

"Sorry." She flashed an apologetic smile and his annoyance vanished immediately. "The ocean tends to drown things out. Why don't you come in?" She indicated a path that led right to the stairs to the terrace.

He looked down. The decorator stones ended abruptly. The "path" was nothing but sand. "I'll get sand in my shoes."

She smiled down at him. "It shakes out."

Right now, he had the urge to shake her out. Out of his life, out of his dreams. Out of his fantasies. He crossed the sand and took the stairs up to her, a disgruntled Romeo approaching his Juliet.

He didn't take the chair she indicated with her eyes. He

held the briefcase full of manuscript pages aloft. "Are we going to work out here?"

"No, we're going to drink coffee out here and enjoy the view." She was already pouring coffee into a mug. A scene from a popular cartoon movie danced around the sides of the mug. She'd been waiting for him to join her, he realized. "*Then* we're going to work."

He didn't want to be comfortable with her. It might become a habit. "I don't want to waste time—" There was no heart in his protest.

"Enjoying nature's handiwork is never a waste of time."

Seeing no way out, he sat down and took the mug she pressed on him.

"Sit back, enjoy," she coaxed, her voice as hypnotic as the repetitive rhythm of the sea. She picked up her mug and leaned back. "Isn't it breathtaking?"

Yes. But he was looking at her, not the view. Her lips were slightly parted as she stared out at the ocean endlessly caressing the shore with curled fingers of white foam. She seemed in awe of it, with her hair tied back away from her face, her face bare of makeup, dressed only in the glow of enthusiasm.

"Breathtaking," he agreed.

She looked toward him, aware that he wasn't looking at the ocean. The glint of desire in his eyes made her want, yet there was a part of her that was still fearful, a part that was still the tiniest bit raw.

"Well—" she took a breath "—since we've agreed on something, I think we should get to work. Might as well strike while the moment's promising." She rose and took his hand. "C'mon, I've cleared off a work area for us inside."

She opened the sliding glass door and led the way into the family room. Unaccustomed to the decreased light, Marcus almost tripped over something on the floor. There were several things scattered haphazardly on the floor, he noted. She wasn't exactly a fanatic about housekeeping. But this "something" was shaggy. And moving.

"Careful!" Annie cried, dropping to her knees. "Are you all right?"

"I'm fine." He felt self-conscious. Why was she on her knees? After all, he hadn't fallen. And he knew her well enough to know she wasn't about to start cleaning now. "I regained my bal—"

She looked up, confused, and then amused. "No, not you. I was talking to Beatrice."

The woman talked to mops. It fitted. He looked at her, then at it. "To whom?"

"My dog, remember?" She held the dog in her arms as she rose to her feet. With a light, gentle touch, she stroked the dog, murmuring endearments. "I told you last night. She's going to have pups any day now, and I don't want to upset her."

Maybe that was the answer. Maybe he should pretend to have pups and she'd try not to upset him.

He dragged both hands through his hair. He was beyond "upset" and on his way to a nervous breakdown, total and complete, he judged. If he weren't, he wouldn't have had that insane thought, even cynically.

"Oh yes, the tryst with Chauncey." Because the dog's face was adorable, Marcus petted the animal. Beatrice responded by licking him. He pulled his hand back, then saw Annie looking at him curiously.

"It felt rough," he explained.

"All dogs' tongues are rough." Annie scratched Beatrice behind the ears. "Haven't you ever been licked by a dog before?"

"No."

His dog probably graduated top in his class in obedience school and repressed the urge to lick. Annie looked at the expression on Marcus's face. A thought dawned on her. "Didn't you ever have one?"

"No."

No one should live their life without having a pet at some point. The solution was obvious. "Well, when she has pups—"

He saw the look entering her eyes. He knew how her mind worked. That fact that he did was a sobering thought. "No." He raised his hands as if to ward her off for emphasis. "Absolutely not. Don't even think it. Now can you please put Lassie down so we can get to work?"

Annie obliged, sending Beatrice on her way. "Lassie would be too large for me to hold."

He let the remark pass. And then he looked around, really looked. "How can you work here in all this chaos?" There was too much clutter. It made him feel claustrophobic. She had knickknacks on every conceivable surface.

He felt hemmed in here, trapped. Just as he had suspected he would. He wasn't meant to be with her in such a tiny space. He searched for his temper, because temper was all he had to protect him from her. From himself. It wouldn't come.

"I—" she looked up at him "—can work anywhere, anytime." She thought of his den. "Even under pristine conditions." She felt the electricity crackling between them. There was no escaping it. "You'd better kiss me and get that out of the way before we get down to work."

It was no longer a surprise to him how correctly she read him and even less of a surprise how much he wanted to kiss her.

"All right, anything to get this screenplay over with," he murmured against her mouth.

He didn't give her a chance to laugh the way she seemed ready to. He was too hungry for her. God, the more he had, the more he wanted. It was like being addicted, like having no say in his life anymore.

He had a say. He could say no. But he didn't want to. Not yet. Soon, but not yet. Slowly his lips moved on a languid, exhilarating journey of her mouth, her cheekbones, her eyes, his own breath catching fast as the beat of his heart increased.

His hands tugged out the final inch of her T-shirt from her jeans, then slipped beneath. He needed to hold her, to touch her, to feel her skin. She moaned and moved closer. He found himself going on instincts alone, instincts that fueled the fire raging within him. Almost reverently, he moved his hands up her body until he cupped the swell of her breasts. He fought to keep the spasm that traveled through his body from seizing him.

She had wanted to let herself drift, to flow with this feeling, to let him mold her. His hands were gentle, warm, possessive, and she wanted him desperately. She found she had to hang on with both hands. Needs slammed through her, making her heart thud against her rib cage. There had been only one other man she had allowed to come so far, both physically and emotionally, and she was hungry to go the distance, to love again.

His mouth was greedy and passionate, and excited so much more than it soothed. She felt his lips framing her face, touching her jawline, her throat. Pulses jumped everywhere he touched. And then his lips were covering hers again.

The kiss was hard and impatient, draining her as much as it drained him. Over and over, his lips slid over hers, challenging, daring, taking, losing and winning.

If he didn't stop now, he'd be beyond the point of no return. He would take her right here and now, in the midst of all this clutter. Something, fear, held him back.

Forcing himself back before he tumbled into the abyss she had cracked open for him, he buried his face in her hair.

It smelled of the sea. And flowers. "I think we've gotten that out of the way," he said into her hair, trying to steady the erratic beating of his heart. "Let's get to work."

Out of the way? she thought, still dazed. *No, my friend, we've gotten more into the way. Much, much more than we bargained for. But have it your way for now.*

"All right." Braced, she took a step back, then tucked her T-shirt back into the waistband of her jeans. "We'll work here, by the window. It's almost the same view as from the terrace."

The same view. The same world. But nothing, he knew, was ever going to be the same again. Not for him, not after her.

He looked at the woman who stimulated him beyond belief and wondered if the devil tended toward disguises of long blond hair and almond-shaped blue eyes. He decided that he must. For Marcus knew that he was surely losing his soul as well as his mind.

Chapter Thirteen

It was progressing.

They were four weeks into the screenplay, and it was going far better than he had initially anticipated. It was actually going according to schedule, no thanks to her, he thought irritably as he glanced at his watch and wondered where she was. Annie argued with him over every point, every scene, every bit of dialogue.

Of course she said *he* argued, but he knew better. If she would only go along with things, there would have been no arguments. After all, it took two to argue.

But she insisted on putting her stamp on things, telling him that *The Treasured Few* needed "the woman's point of view." He had pointed out that it hadn't needed "the woman's point of view" to explode on the bestseller list. She had only smiled that infuriating, inscrutable smile of hers and gone on defending her position like a dog hanging on to a bone until he threw up his hands and surrendered.

With a critical eye, he perused the pages that she had

printed on the computer yesterday and was forced to grudgingly admit that, despite his peppered words to the contrary, what was evolving was a piece of quality entertainment fit to captivate even the toughest audience. She brought out the best in him. At least on paper.

They were different, he thought. So different. She wrote with people in mind. He wrote only to please himself. That way, there was no danger of feeling the sting of someone's disapproval. He had told himself that he was above that, that he no longer felt hurt when someone rejected his effort, but deep within his soul, he still did.

He let the pages fall back on his desk and went over to the window.

Where *was* she? It was her idea to work here today. They kept shifting work areas like gypsies moving from camp to camp. He should have insisted that they continue working at her place. At least he'd know where she was.

He let the curtain drop. She was late—again—and he was watching for her like a schoolboy watching for the girl next door. He laughed at his own thought. The only way she could have qualified for that title was if he was living next door to some sort of an amusement park.

The screech of tires on his driveway told him she had finally arrived. The flying figure that passed his den on the way to the front door he identified as Nathan. A Nathan whose cheeks were no longer hollow, whose eyes were no longer haunted and sad. Marcus would have liked to have felt that he alone was responsible for the change, but knew it was only partly because of him. A small part. The main contributor to Nathan's transformation was Annie.

Annie, always Annie.

No, not always, he reminded himself. She'd be gone soon. As soon as the screenplay was wrapped up, she would flow mercurially out of their lives the same way she had flowed into them. It was her nature.

Marcus heard Nathan's voice as the boy greeted Annie and then squealed. "For me?"

Now what? It was obvious that she had brought something for the boy. Again. She had already presented Nathan with a video game system, not to mention a collection of children's videos, both games and movies. By the cry that Nathan uttered, Marcus judged that this was something more exciting than just a game. Nathan sounded completely animated. Like her. It made for a frightening thought.

Maybe she had brought along her niece and nephew. No, Nathan sounded as if whatever it was entitled him to possession. The boy hadn't learned Annie's trick about possessing souls yet.

Okay, so what was it? Consumed with curiosity, Marcus left the sanctuary of his den and walked into the foyer. Nathan and Annie, with Holly hovering close by, were still at the front door.

Holly was clucking and circling Annie and Nathan like a mother hen, her attention, as well as Nathan's, on the contents of the box Annie was carrying. A box that was making noise.

Annie looked his way just as Marcus crossed to them, her eyes wide, smiling. It disarmed him every time even when he thought he was braced for it. "Hi."

He hid the fact that he had been impatiently anticipating her arrival for reasons other than their work. "You're late."

She was used to that tone of voice by now. And immune to the censure. "You're predictable."

"That's one thing no one'll ever accuse you of being." Marcus saw that the pronouncement pleased her. "What did you bring this time?"

"It's a puppy!" Nathan exclaimed just as a wet, pink tongue got him on the cheek and branded him for life. Nathan was instantly and completely in love. The euphoric look abated only a little as the boy looked Marcus's way. "Is it all right, Mr. Sullivan? Can I keep him?"

Nathan still wasn't completely secure here, Marcus realized. He still acted like a guest who expected to be evicted for the smallest transgression.

Marcus reached out and scratched the taffy-colored fur. The puppy twirled about in his small space and eagerly licked his hand as well. "If I said no, I'd feel guilty to my dying day."

Annie laughed, satisfied. "Good. It worked." She pushed the box into Nathan's hands. "I now pronounce you boy and dog."

She had engineered this, just as she did everything else. Marcus knew he could say no, that he *had* said no when she had offered to bring him a puppy. But was control so important to him that he could disappoint Nathan? He knew the answer to that. Establishing and maintaining control around Annie wasn't nearly as important as the radiant smile of a seven-year-old boy.

"Yes," Marcus agreed. "It worked. I take it Beatrice is willing to part with this one?"

Beatrice had had her litter over five weeks ago. It was time to start finding them homes before she grew too attached to all of them. By she, Annie was thinking of herself, not her dog. Annie hated parting with anything that was a piece of her life.

"This one is the runt of the litter and keeps getting pushed out of the way by the others. I thought Nathan might want to lend a hand and help him get his proper nourishment." She ruffled Nathan's hair. He was so involved with the bundle of fluff that he hardly noticed. "How about it, Nathan? Are you up to helping?"

The puppy licked his face again and kept on licking. Nathan laughed with glee. "Yes!"

Annie raised her eyes to the housekeeper. "Holly?" The request went without saying.

Holly's mouth puckered as she pressed her lips together.

"It always comes down to that, doesn't it? Let Holly tend to it."

"Well, I—" Holly wasn't fooling her. She was as pleased about Nathan getting a pet as she was in giving him one.

Holly raised a hand to dismiss any further words from Annie. Nice trick, Marcus thought. Maybe he could ask her to teach it to him.

"C'mon," Holly said to Nathan as she put an arm around his shoulders and turned him in the direction of the kitchen. "I think I can rig up a bottle for him."

One down and one to go, Annie thought, turning to Marcus. "Thank you for letting him keep the puppy."

He shrugged away her words carelessly, turning toward the den. "I never had a choice, you know."

Another man might have. A harder man. "Yes, I know. You know, Marc, I've been thinking—"

Marcus stopped in the doorway. "Oh God, should I head for the hills?"

Annie grinned. "Yes."

Someday, if he lived to be that old, he was going to understand her without benefit of explanations. The fact that he was even remotely planning to wait around that long in her company amazed him. "Would you care to elaborate a little on that?"

"Absolutely." She crossed to him, winding her arm through his. He was trapped in every sense of the word and only a little uncomfortable about it. Had he been more alert, he would have been worried. "The second half of this movie takes place near Santa Barbara, right?"

He raised a brow, wondering what she was up to. "You *have* been paying attention."

"Cynic." She laughed. "I just thought that maybe we should go up there for the day, you know, soak up the atmosphere a little and bring the flavor back with us."

The only flavor he really wanted to soak up was the

flavor of her mouth. Especially when her lips were so close to his.

With effort, he disentangled his arm from her grasp. "I *was* up there," he informed her. It had been there that the idea for the story had germinated, in a quaint little town that hadn't quite hurried its way into the last quarter of the century.

She wasn't about to let him talk his way out of this. She wanted to go away with him for even just a day. They needed this time together, needed more than just an hour or two shared in a restaurant. She wanted him to herself. "When?"

"When I first started writing it. Three years ago. Maybe four." He switched on his computer and sat down, ready to work.

She said nothing in reply. Instead, when he looked at her, there was that look on her face, that look that said she knew she had made her point.

He leaned back in his chair, staring at the empty screen thoughtfully. It had been a long time since he had been up there last. Too long. He thought back. It had been a peaceful time. A good time. Suddenly he wanted to show it to her, share it with her, and though he knew he was probably making an error, he went with it as if, like with the puppy, he had no choice. Because as far as he was concerned, he hadn't.

"All right, we'll go."

"When?"

The woman was never satisfied. "I suppose you'd like to go today." He did know her. It was scary. And strangely exhilarating.

Unsuccessfully she attempted to appear submissive and patient. "If it's all right with you."

He gave a short laugh and switched off his computer. There was no use pretending that any work was going to get done today. "As if my opinion mattered."

Annie stood in the doorway. Suddenly there was nothing and no one. "But it does," she said quietly. And more than anything else, she wanted his opinion to meld with hers.

God, he could almost believe her. If he let himself. Shaking his head to clear it, he picked up the telephone receiver. "I need to make a few arrangements," he muttered, turning so that he couldn't look at her. If he didn't see her, he couldn't want her.

And the river only flowed when you watched it. He *was* a fool, and he was quickly getting past the point where he cared.

With determination, he jabbed at several numbers on the telephone. There was an appointment he had to cancel. And a redwood he had to see.

He had just ended his phone conversation and hung up when Annie walked back into the den, a large basket slung over her arm.

They really were on the road to Oz, he thought, and she was carrying Toto in her hamper.

"What's this?" He tapped the hamper as Annie set it down on his desk. "Did you bring another dog you wanted to get rid of?"

He didn't really understand her yet, did he? she thought. "I didn't really want to get rid of the first one."

But she had brought it to Nathan. "Then why—?"

"I thought that Nathan needed a friend—besides you," she added pointedly.

Her statement made him self-conscious. "I'm not—" He was about to say that he didn't think that Nathan saw him in that light.

She was quick to stop his denial. "Nathan thinks you are."

"Does he?"

He sounded almost eager when he asked, Annie thought.

No, she hadn't been wrong about the man. She had been very, very right. "Yes. He does."

Marcus cleared his throat, embarrassed by his own show of emotion. "Okay, now what's that?" He nodded at the basket.

She let him retreat. "That's lunch. Holly packed a picnic lunch for us."

Marcus could only stare at the hamper. "Holly? A short, squat woman in orthopedic shoes? The one who gives lectures about the importance of having hot meals? The woman who wants to outlaw fast-food places?"

"The very same." For his benefit, Annie lifted the lid. "You'll note the abundance of fruits and nuts." She moved aside the linen napkins. "No cold cuts. Only pieces of cold fried chicken."

Only Annie could have managed this, he thought. Holly believed in decorum, in meals served on time and at the table. His respect for Annie's powers of persuasion went up another notch. But then, look at the hoops she had him jumping through.

He ran his fingers over the woven hamper. "I didn't even know we had a picnic basket."

Annie let the lid fall again and picked up the basket. "You don't. I do."

"And you brought it." She was running true to form. She might act as if she were scattered, but he was beginning to believe that she left very little to chance.

Delicate shoulders lifted and fell in an innocent shrug. "Just in case."

Right. He'd just bet.

She was already ushering him to the door, one arm linked through his. Marcus looked around for Nathan. "What about Nathan?"

"He's opted to stay with the puppy." Annie opened the front door.

Marcus eyed her as he stepped over the threshold. "Is

this a planned seduction?'' Not that he had any objections to one. Another clear sign that he was losing his grip and his mind.

The innocent expression on her face made her look like an angel. ''We're only going to see trees and recapture a mood. Besides, you're the one who made the decision to go today.''

The front door closed behind him. Now that he noticed it, it was a perfect day for a picnic. His first picnic, he realized. There were a lot of firsts with her. ''As if I had a choice.''

''Why, Mr. Sullivan.'' Annie fluttered her lashes at him and her voice took on a slow, southern lilt. ''I thought that you above all people had a choice.'' She grinned at him, the lilt fading. ''You're not a man to be bullied into anything. You wouldn't be doing this if you didn't want to.'' She wanted him to know that. She stood next to the car, waiting for him to unlock the door.

She was right. He *did* want to. Which, he supposed, made it all the worse. It was something he was going to have to ponder.

Later.

It was a three-hour drive, much of it through sparsely populated country. In a subtle way, it renewed his faith in nature, in life, in the importance of using his senses to take in beauty. When they finally reached their destination, a hundred and fifty miles later, Marcus had lost some of his hard-edged cynicism. It seemed that it had been unraveling steadily as the miles registered on the odometer. The farther away they were from the hub of the city, from L.A. and his home, the more approachable and relaxed he became.

He let her pick the place where they stopped. It was too beautiful a day to try to win bits and pieces of victories that he didn't care about. It was nice to agree about something for a change.

"What, no camera?" he asked as they wandered, hand in hand, down an isolated, scenic path that seemed to highlight nature at its best. "I would have thought you'd be taking tons of pictures." It was the kind of thing she'd do. He'd seen the photo album on her coffee table, crammed full of photographs, of memories. He envied her that.

"I am." When he looked at her quizzically, she touched a finger to her temple. "Up here. It's all being stored up here."

He looked amused as he brushed a hair away from her temple. "How will you ever find it again?"

"Very funny." She tightened her fingers around his. "You know, you're coming along, Sullivan. You're really coming along."

"Please, don't depress me."

She lifted herself up on her toes to lightly brush a kiss on his lips. A butterfly landing on a flower was heavier. The impression it made on his soul couldn't begin to be measured. "Not a chance, Marc."

He was enjoying himself, enjoying her. He felt, as they wandered around the tall redwood giants that had been there before man had felt a need to communicate with others of his species, as if he were seeing all this for the first time.

The afternoon was a joyous celebration of life itself. She had taken his hand easily and never released it. He found that there was a certain warmth, a certain feeling of well-being because her hand was curled in his. It felt, he realized, as if this was the way it was meant to be.

For the day, just for today, he could pretend to believe that.

Maybe he was getting too caught up in the romance of his story. He knew the danger in that. On paper, he could control the situation, could fix anything that got out of hand. If something didn't turn out the way he wanted it to, there was a delete button on his computer to press. Life didn't quite work like that. The only way to avoid having something turn sour was not to have it happen in the first place.

That meant having choices, implementing them, sticking to them once they were made. He had made his when she walked into his life, but he hadn't stuck to it. And now, as he sat cross-legged beneath a tree, watching her unwrap lunch, he had a feeling that the condemned man was having a last hearty lunch before the trap beneath his feet was sprung.

There was no way out.

Like a man gripping the sides of a toboggan that was poised on the very top of a snow-covered peak, Marcus knew his fate. He was about to go plummeting down. And all he could do was hang on.

Unless, of course, he thought as he sipped the wine, watching her every movement, he somehow managed to get up off the toboggan before it took that first plunge.

Fat chance.

She had been talking all this while, steadily and without more than a few seconds' pause between observations and thoughts. It didn't seem to disturb her, he noted, that he made little response.

"Do you realize that you talk while you chew? I didn't think a person could do that without choking." She didn't look the slightest bit chagrined when he pointed that fact out to her. "You talk incessantly."

She wiped her fingers slowly on a linen napkin. He couldn't help wondering what those fingers would feel like, moving that slowly along his flesh. "That's because you don't talk at all. Natures balances things out."

"Nature has nothing in its bag of tricks to balance you out." He paused, studying her. "Are you afraid of being alone with your thoughts?"

The slight wince told him that he had hit the mark, even

though he hadn't really meant to. He hadn't meant to hurt her. He was just being philosophical.

"Sometimes."

His thoughts about being a condemned man faded as he stepped further into the trap. "Why?"

She shrugged, looking off into the distance. "Long story."

"And you're not up to it?" An incredulous note came into his voice. "This from a woman who just talked over a hundred and fifty miles? I find that rather hard to believe."

She smiled, but it was a smile tinged in sadness. A squirrel darted between two trees, then stopped, frozen, to stare. Annie pretended to be engrossed with it. "Some thoughts are private." She tossed the animal a bit of her bread.

The tables were turned. He found that incredible. "Mine aren't to you."

Nervously she tore off another bit of bread and threw it. "That's because I want to get to know you, the real you. The man I met in your books." The squirrel darted away, frightened, but scrub jays flew down to make off with what he had left behind.

Marcus placed his hand over hers, covering it. "Suppose I want to get to know you?"

She felt her heart beat harder. "Do you? Do you really?"

Yes, he thought, he did. He waited, but the sinking sensation did not come. "I don't say things I don't mean. There's not enough time in life for lies."

She liked that, liked that honesty in him. Whatever else he might be, he was a good man. An honest man.

For a moment, she said nothing. The fabric of the napkin seemed to hold her mesmerized. Just as he was about to say something, he heard her voice, low and still, as if she were afraid to let go of the emotion bound up within her. "I was in love once."

He felt a spasmodic tightening in his midsection and

wondered hotly why that fact should bother him so much. But it did. Selfishly he hadn't wanted her to have loved someone else.

Nonsense, all nonsense, he told himself.

She had no idea what was running through his mind. "I thought that Charlie was my happily-ever-after person, like in the stories. I guess I was a product of my environment." A bittersweet smile creased her lips. "Movies."

"He left you?" Though he had voiced sentiments to the contrary, he couldn't picture anyone walking out on her. Not permanently. Except, of course, for him, but that was another matter. It didn't have anything to do with her. Just with him. And survival.

She closed her eyes, remembering. "Not of his own free will," she said softly.

"Then why?"

He wasn't prepared for the hurt in her eyes when she opened them again.

"He died. A little over a year ago. Very suddenly." Her words were short and rushed, pushed out in small staccato bursts as if she couldn't manage to say them any other way. "One of those stupid boat races. He hadn't even wanted to go, but his buddies talked him into it. One of them needed a first mate, or whatever those people are called who help steer." She looked up at him, tears shining in her eyes. Tears for the horrible waste it had all been. "It doesn't matter what they're called, I guess." She gestured helplessly. "I just like being accurate around you."

The smile she had on her face was brave and sad and wounded him. He grieved for her hurt even as he was jealous of the man who had created it.

"This time, you don't have to be. I don't know what they're called, either."

Because there was nothing else he could do, Marcus gathered her into his arms and kissed her. To wipe away her pain and to share it with her.

Chapter Fourteen

It was a soft, gentle kiss, with only the barest hint of what existed hidden beyond the barrier he was struggling to keep in place. It was all he could allow himself to do against the fear of exposing his emotions without having the certainty of being accepted. If he let the kiss deepen even the slightest bit, this time she would see the force of the emotions that he held in check. Emotions that even surprised him.

Her mouth was sweet, pliant. He had only to let himself go. Only to—

There were no happily-ever-afters. Believing in them was for fools.

He felt she wanted him, but did she? She was so different, so unpredictable. Maybe what he interpreted as interest in him was just her way of maintaining a friendly business relationship and nothing more. He created complex people on the page, but there he could control them. In real life, he found complexity overwhelming. He gravitated to order, predictability.

There was a faint rumble in the distance and the sun retreated, leaving only shadows in its wake, across the land, across his soul.

There was a storm approaching.

He pressed a kiss to her temple. "I think perhaps we'd better be getting back."

She sighed as he released her, trying to hide the deep frustration and the annoyance that was building up within her. For a moment, he had been kind, tender, and she had hoped that he might cross the imaginary line that separated them. It couldn't all be up to her. Not if it was to matter.

Each time that they were like this, each time he held her, kissed her, he'd bring her that much closer to the brink. This last time, she knew she was about to tumble over. But it had to be with him, not alone. And at the last moment, he had pulled away, leaving her emotionally stranded, as he sought refuge in that haven only he occupied.

For the first time, desperation clawed at her. She wanted to beat on him with both fists. To yell at him. To demand to know what it was that had rendered him an emotional cripple.

But what good would it do? He'd just look at her with those intense eyes of his, making her feel as if there was something the matter with her instead of the other way around.

What was she doing to herself, anyway, hitching a ride on this emotional yo-yo?

There was no way around it. She had to be crazy. And yet…

And yet, he *wanted* her, she knew it. She could taste it in his kiss, feel it in his touch, see it in his eyes. He was too straightforward a person to be pretending to care. Damn him, anyway.

Antsy, uncertain, Annie started placing the dishes into

the hamper, although she would have rather thrown them at him. Maybe that would have gotten a rise out of the man. "I guess we've absorbed enough atmosphere for one day."

She leaned forward to pack what was left of the picnic into the basket. Her blouse fell forward, exposing the swell of her breast above her bra. She could see his reflection in the bottle. Without moving she glanced up at him and could see the desire on his face. Was it just a physical reaction? Or more? God, he had her so confused.

Marcus watched her as she cleared the blanket, saw the tension in her shoulders and knew it was because of him. He shoved his hands deep into his pockets and stared into the distance. "More than enough."

Now what was that supposed to mean? It was about time he did some explaining. She stopped packing and rocked back on her heels. "You seem interested, yet you back off as soon as things get started. Are you just playing some sort of a game with me? Is this your idea of fun?"

The hurt, angry tone in her voice surprised him. He wanted to protect himself, not wound her. "No, it's not any kind of a game." He swung around to look at her. "Look, I won't deny that I'm attracted to you, that I don't feel some—some kind of pull every time I kiss you."

She wasn't satisfied with that. She wanted more. She wanted reasons. "But?"

He blew out a sigh. "But I'm just not in the market for a relationship."

Annie jerked the blanket and pounded it into quarters as she folded it. She wished that it was him instead. "I didn't know you could find those kinds of things in a market, although laundromats seem to be up-and-coming among single people." With a thrust, she shoved the blanket on top of the hamper. "They say they might even take the place of a singles' bar."

He was trying to explain his feelings, a difficult thing for him at best, and she was talking about socks bringing people together. "Is everything a joke to you?" Grabbing the blanket, he held it in one hand and took the hamper in the other.

"Consider yourself lucky. If I wasn't making a joke, I'd be hitting you in the teeth. Take your choice. Lose them or use them."

He had never cared for her flippant remarks less. "You're right. We've absorbed enough atmosphere for today." The convertible was parked on the road a short distance away. He made for it. "Look, I've got enough in my life right now."

Annie walked behind him, mentally counting to ten. "It's just brimming to the top."

He had had just about enough of her high-handed opinions. The world did not operate according to her rules no matter what she thought. In addition, he was getting frustrated with his inability to express himself around her. "I've got my work."

She stared at the back of his head. It didn't look thicker than anyone else's. But it was. "Dandy substitute for living life firsthand."

Marcus tossed the hamper and blanket into the back seat of the convertible. The hamper tilted as it fell and the contents threatened to spill out. He left it where it was. "And a boy I'm not too sure what to do with yet." Wasn't that enough for her? How could he take on more now, no matter what his emotions said to the contrary?

"Do with?" she repeated, incredulously. Tired of looking at the back of his head, she placed a hand on his shoulder and made him turn around. "You make him sound like an erector set. You don't *do* anything with a boy like Nathan. You love him."

He was trying, but it wasn't that easy for him. "I have trouble relating to people." He had no idea why he was even bothering to explain himself.

Annie leaned against the car. "Why doesn't that surprise me?"

He raised his hands in exasperation. What did she want, blood? "I've already decided not to send him to military school—"

Her eyes wide. "Military school?" Was he out of his mind? Nathan would shrivel up and die in a military school. "You were actually considering sending him to military school?"

"Yes." Although he had rejected the idea, he grew defensive in the face of her attack. After all, he had only considered it because he thought it would help Nathan. "What's so wrong with that?"

If he didn't know, she didn't know how to tell him. Maybe she had been wrong about him after all. "You have no heart, Marc."

That was exactly his problem. He did. And it could feel pain. "Yes I do."

Then why are you always backing away from me? "Who says?"

"My doctor. It showed up in the X ray." My God, he was beginning to talk like her. His condition was getting serious.

She stared at him. How could he have even contemplated flushing the boy from his life like that? Easy, wasn't he trying to do the same with her? "Well, that's probably the only place it showed up."

Marcus clenched his hands at his sides. She was pushing him. "For two cents I'd—I'd—"

Annie raised her chin. "Yes?"

It was a tempting target. A very tempting target. He clenched his hands harder. "Nothing."

There were oaths she had heard her brother use once when he had lost a championship tennis match that would fit this occasion, but she kept them to herself. She was crazy, absolutely crazy to have thought that she was falling in love with this man. She was just fascinated by insanity, that was all, nothing more. Tall, dark and handsome only went so far. And in this case, not nearly far enough.

Annie surrendered. Maybe she had been wrong all along. It had been known to happen once or twice.

Feeling dejected, Annie climbed into the car on the passenger side. ''Okay, let's go home.'' There was a note of resignation in her voice.

It was better this way, he told himself. They'd keep their relationship strictly professional. He'd been a fool to even entertain the idea that anything else was possible. Marcus got in and shoved the key into the ignition. When he turned it, nothing happened. He swore as he tried again.

The silence was ominous. ''What's the matter?''

He didn't even look her way. ''It won't start.''

It's not the only thing, she thought. ''Jiggle the key.'' Annie leaned over, her hand raised, ready to do it herself.

One dark look from Marcus had her withdrawing her hand. ''I could jiggle the damn key until my hand fell off,'' he told her, ''the car still won't start.''

A fat drop fell on her face, followed immediately by another of equal size. Within a minute, a steady rhythm had begun. *Perfect, just perfect.* She glanced up, then down again quickly, as the rain increased. ''Doesn't it know that it's not supposed to rain in July?''

Rain was beginning to plaster her hair to her face. She looked exactly the same way she had the first day she had burst into his life. Wet. Why was that so damn appealing? How could he feel drawn to her at the same time he wanted to strangle her?

''Maybe it's never read the California handbook.'' He really *was* beginning to talk like her.

But there was no time to contemplate the fatal consequences of that. Rain began falling with alarming force. Marcus looked at the top of his convertible neatly folded at the rear. He and Annie were already soaked, as was the interior of the car. He remembered seeing a house not too far back. "There was a house back on the road. Want to make a run for it?"

"What about your car?"

The interior would get soaked, but that could be remedied. Right now, he wanted to get her safe, out of the storm. "We'll worry about that later." The storm was getting worse. "Let's go!"

Annie was already out of the car. "Sounds good to me. I never cared too much for drowning."

Without thinking, he grabbed her hand and they made a dash for shelter.

The house, a modest one-story, wood-frame building, was further away than he remembered. By the time they got to it, they were both soaked to the skin. Marcus knocked on the door several times, but there was no answer.

They couldn't just stand out here all night. There were lights coming from within, but those could have been set on timers. "We give them one more chance," Annie decided, "and then we break in."

Marcus stared at her, trying to make sense out of what she was saying. She probably thought of this as an enactment of "Goldilocks and the Three Bears". He knew how her mind worked. "We can't just break in."

She rubbed her nose. It tickled, which meant there was a cold in the making. "Breaking in sounds a whole lot better than pneumonia."

She was definitely one of a kind. "But not better than jail," he pointed out.

The door swung open, ending the debate. The elderly woman inside the house took one look at them and then immediately stepped back. "Come in, come in," she urged, taking hold of Annie and ushering her inside. She was totally unfazed by the fact that a good deal of rain came in with them. "Henry," she called, "we have guests."

"More like drowned rats," Annie laughed, pushing wet bangs out of her eyes. "Hello." She extended her hand to the woman. "I'm Annie de Witt and this is Marc—"

The woman enveloped Annie's hand in both of hers. Her hands felt warm, inviting, as did her smile. "Your husband?" the woman supplied, beaming at Marcus. She looked down at Annie's hand, which was still cradled in hers. Annie's ring gleamed in the lamp light.

"Yes." If he was interrogated for the rest of his life, Marcus would never be able to explain what had possessed him to voice that lie. It had just come out, perhaps because it was a lot simpler than explaining. He put his hand out and shook hers.

"I'm Polly Flynn and this is Henry." She beckoned to the man who was just stepping into the living room.

The man was tall and loose-limbed and looked as if his bones jiggled with each step he took. His wife was short and round, with a wide face that seemed to naturally fill out with a smile. They made Annie think of the nursery rhyme about Jack Spratt and his wife. Annie liked them both instantly.

"Hello." Annie nodded toward the man. "We're awfully sorry to barge in on you like this."

Marcus hooked an arm around her waist as if the action could somehow keep her anchored. He had an uneasy feeling that she'd be off and running any second. "I'm afraid our car broke down about half a mile from here," he explained to the older man.

Marcus looked into the living room and tried to see if there was a telephone. There was none visible from his vantage point. "If we could use your phone to call a garage, we'll be out of your hair as soon as possible."

The man scratched the few remaining hairs that stubbornly clung to his head. "Only garage in the area closes at five." Henry's brows raised up high on his wide forehead as he looked at his watch. "It's half past that now. 'Fraid you're out of luck."

"You're welcome to spend the night here." The invitation was genuine, one look at Polly's eyes told them that. "We have a spare bedroom."

"We couldn't possibly put you out, Mrs. Flynn," Annie began.

"Polly," the woman corrected her, a finely wrinkled hand patting Annie's shoulder. "If you're going to spend the night under my roof, you'll have to call me Polly."

"All right, Polly." Annie grinned. "Thank you both. We appreciate your generosity."

Annie seemed to take this all in stride, but for Marcus this was all much harder to comprehend. "You'd take us in? Just like that?" He looked from the man to his wife. "But you don't know us."

"Of course we do," Polly smiled at his confusion and spoke slowly, the way one did to a dim-witted child. "You just introduced yourselves." Polly turned on her heel and beckoned for them to follow. "Now come with me and I'll get you each something dry to put on."

"Could we use your phone first?" Annie asked before Polly could lead them to the laundry room. Annie saw the confused look Marcus gave her over the request. "We have to call Nathan," she told him.

He didn't understand her reasoning. The boy was safe with the housekeeper. "Why?"

Impatience highlighted her face. How could he be so thick-headed? "So he won't worry."

"Is Nathan your son?" Polly asked. "Children do get frightened," she went on, assuming the answer to her question was yes, "if their parents don't come home when they're supposed to."

Marcus thought of the way Nathan must have felt when he waited for his parents to return and they never did. Annoyed, he upbraided himself for his own stupidity. He saw the look on Annie's face. Trust her to think of it. This time he was grateful that she had.

"We'd like to call him as soon as possible," Marcus put in. "I'll reverse the charges."

"Never gave it a thought," Polly clucked, pointing out the phone in the corner of the living room.

"I didn't think people like that existed outside of fantasies," Marcus said to Annie after Polly had brought them to their room for the night. Gingerly he closed the door behind them. She seemed to be making herself right at home, he thought, watching Annie.

He hiked up one drooping suspender. He was wearing a pair of baggy, faded, cuffed, gray trousers that were a size too large. The trousers and his plaid shirt were a loan from Henry until his own clothes had dried. They had spent a far more pleasant evening than he would have anticipated learning about the woman's family and Henry's career as a carpenter over dinner. They had been born, met and married in a small town in Kansas. After forty years, they had moved to California and settled in Santa Barbara.

Annie tightened the huge pink robe that Polly had pressed on her. It gave new meaning to the word roomy. "People aren't as dark and horrid as you'd like to believe."

He watched her as she crossed to the only bed in the room. Her body was hidden in the folds of the robe, her outline was not. He looked away. That sort of thing wasn't going to help get him through the night. "It's not something I'd like to believe, Annie, it just is."

Annie sat down on the bed. The robe parted and one long limb was exposed before she pulled the robe over it. Marcus paced the room restlessly.

The man was utterly hopeless. "Right. Then how do you explain those people we spent the evening with?"

"Easy," he said dryly. "They're a figment of your imagination.'' He tried to block out the sound of her laugh and the effect it had on him.

He looked around the room. It was small and cozy, just like the rest of the house. The furniture was worn, but looked comfortable. Rather than illuminate it, the light from the single lamp by the bed made the room appear that much more intimate. The double bed dominated the room. There was a bureau and a stuffed armchair that didn't seem to match anything but somehow just belonged.

He moved toward the chair. This, he supposed, would be his bed for the night. The idea of successfully sharing a bed with Annie didn't even remotely present itself as having a snowball's chance in hell. ''You don't have to worry.''

Outside, the wind howled. The rain was still falling in sheets. She was grateful to be on this side of the window. ''About what?''

He lowered himself into the armchair. ''I intend to be a perfect gentleman about the situation.''

Their definition of gentleman differed. A gentleman wasn't supposed to cut up your heart. ''I never had any doubts.''

Why did her voice sound so distant when she said that, so frosty? Didn't she realize what a struggle it was for him not to take what he wanted so desperately? What a struggle it was for him not to give in to the storm that raged within him, more violent than the one outside the house?

''Just as long as we understand each other.''

''I don't think that'll happen in a million years,'' Annie murmured. She looked down at the huge robe she was wearing. ''Actually I was going to ask you if you wanted to share my robe. There's room enough here for two, possibly three.'' She laughed softly, disparagingly. ''Never mind, I've probably shocked you again.''

He didn't care for her sarcasm. He didn't care for the situation, not any of it. Least of all, he didn't care for the fact that he couldn't let go like any other man and take advantage of the opportunity. But he didn't believe in taking advantage. There was too much at stake.

"Look, I—" He glanced over toward Annie. She had gotten into bed. The robe lay on the flowered circular rug, a soft pool of pink. Marcus felt every inch of his body tighten. He licked his lips, trying to raise a little moisture for a mouth that had suddenly gone very dry. "What are you doing?"

She turned toward him. "I thought it was obvious."

He tried not to think about the fact that she was several feet away from him, dressed in a smile and percale sheets. "The robe—"

"Would probably smother me in my sleep during the night. Besides, it's hot tonight." The rain had only succeeded in making the air sticky.

And it was getting hotter all the time, Marcus thought. He tried not to think about what she was like underneath the sheets.

He couldn't think of anything else.

"I'll take the chair," he mumbled needlessly.

"Fine."

It wasn't fine. It was torture. If ever a piece of furniture had been deceptively presented, it was the armchair. There wasn't a comfortable position to be found on it.

Annie listened to him move restlessly around for ten minutes. Finally she raised herself up on her elbows, tucking the sheet around her breasts. He was an idiot, but she felt sorry for him.

"There's room enough for two in this bed, Marc." With a nod of her head, she indicated the other side. "And we can still stay very adult about it. People share beds all the time without anything happening." A smile twisted her lips as she thought of their screenplay. "If it makes you feel any better, you can pretend it's a foxhole during the war."

It felt like war, all right, he thought as he rose. A war that he was losing no matter what the outcome.

Annie turned away and faced the window. She had extended the offer because if she didn't neither one of them would get any sleep. He was thrashing around in that chair like a fish out of water. If he thought there was something more to the invitation, he was mistaken. She had decided to let him retreat behind his barriers. She wasn't going to let her feelings run away with her any longer. She had been rebuffed by him enough times to qualify her as a volleyball. Any moves whatsoever were all going to be his from here on in. If he was made of stone, that was his problem, not hers.

The hell it was. Annie gathered the sheet to her and prayed for sleep.

He knew he had made a mistake as soon as his body touched the mattress. He stripped off his shirt and let it drop on the floor, then laid down on top of the bed, purposely keeping the sheet between them as a barrier.

It didn't help. Even at a distance of a good nine inches and with a sheet between them, he could swear he felt the heat of her body searing up toward his. There was only so much a man could humanly withstand.

Marcus raised himself up on his elbow and turned in her direction. The light from the lamp was playing on her hair, creating scattered shafts of blazing gold through it. Hesitating for a moment, he touched it, letting it shimmer through his fingers like golden rain. The desire only grew. "This isn't going to work, you know."

Her breath caught in her throat, Annie turned toward him slowly. His fingers skimmed along the hollow of her cheek. She fought to keep her eyes from fluttering shut as anticipation vibrated through her.

"That depends." Her voice was husky as she felt her heart beating wildly in her throat. So much for promises about not letting her feelings surface.

"On what?"

Her eyes never left his face. She was searching for signs of a retreat. There were none. "On what you mean by working."

"I haven't the vaguest idea what I mean. I can't seem to think straight around you."

"Why is that?" she heard herself ask. He traced his fingers along one smooth, bare shoulder, dipping down to the planes of her breasts. Slowly he tugged the sheet loose. She shuddered. And so did he.

"Because I want you." There was no use in denying it any longer. No point in denying it. Softly he kissed her temple. "I want to hold you, to kiss you until I can't make my lips form a whistle."

Her laughter warmed him. "A fate worse than death," she agreed.

She was impossible. Totally and utterly impossible. And he had never wanted a woman more. "I want to make love to you until you can't make wisecracks anymore."

The suspender sagged again and Annie slipped it all the way from his shoulder, her fingertips splaying across his chest. She felt the muscle there tighten beneath her palm. "That might take some time."

He gathered her close to him. The outline of her body thrilled him, aroused him until he knew he couldn't bear any more. "That's what I'm counting on."

Annie framed his face with her hands. "Countdown," she whispered, pressing her lips to his throat, "begins now." She felt his pulse there jump.

She was brazen and she knew it, but she had never wanted like this, never felt like this, not even with Charlie. It was as if everything within her had caught on fire and she was going to die if he didn't make love with her. With hands that felt oddly steady, even as everything else within her shook, she undid his trousers.

Marcus shucked them off with a sure, swift motion, kicking them to the foot of the bed. Every inch of his body was as taut, as ready, as a finely tuned instrument about to be played.

But it still didn't change anything. He ran his hand slowly along her body until his outstretched fingers touched her breast. He watched her lids lower as he cupped his hand around it. "This is all wrong, you know."

She focused on his face. For now, despite his words, there were no doubts in his eyes, only desire. "We'll argue about this later."

"Fine with me." His hands slid down her body, tangling in the sheets and then tossing them aside. They fell on the floor, covering the robe.

It was a night of passion that matched nothing in his memory. Her body, so small, so sleek, had been created for loving. Senses swimming, he explored it with the awe of man discovering a place where no one had ever been before. It delighted him to make her arch toward him, to moan when he pressed a kiss to the back of her knee, to the inside of her elbow, to the hollow of her throat.

With his heart beating in his ears, he took more, reveled in taking more. Each kiss built, flowered, exploded into a wondrous stepping-stone that took them both higher and higher, past a point of no return.

Annie loved the feel of his nude body against hers. She couldn't get enough of touching him, of feeling it grow harder in its desire for her. The heat was almost overpowering.

"I knew it," she whispered hoarsely.

His tongue poised over the swell of her breast, Marcus looked up. "Knew what?"

She tangled her fingers in his hair. It felt silky. "That it'd be like this with you."

He ran his tongue slowly along her nipple, watching it tighten. "How did you know?"

She smiled, her breath growing shorter. "Read your books."

"Later. I'm a little busy right now." He closed over the other nipple and Annie arched, muffling a cry.

It was a series of volleys fired and returned. He wasn't in control but it no longer mattered. What mattered was this sensation that traveled through his veins like trapped lightning. He wanted it to go on forever.

He wanted to take her now.

Somehow, he managed to hold back a little longer, long enough to let his hands memorize every line, every curve, to know the feel of her smooth skin. Long enough to only begin to satiate his longing for the taste of her. But when she touched him, when her long delicate fingers began to stroke, to possess, his control thinned out to barely a thread. Groaning her name, he raised himself over her and entered. He felt her body tense, then her legs wrap around him possessively. Slowly he began to move, his hands on her hips. There was no need to guide her. She anticipated his every rhythm, his every movement, hurrying with him to the summit. Once and then again. And again.

And somewhere in the heat of the long, endless night, Marcus found what he so desperately sought.

Pleasure took on a whole new meaning for him, an entire new scope. Life, he thought as he lost himself in her flavor, in the very scent of her, had picked him up and thrown him into the eye of a hurricane.

And he was going willingly.

Chapter Fifteen

Marcus lay in bed with his arm tucked under his head, staring at fading shadows stretching across the bedroom wall in the early dawn light. He recognized the sweet sensation blossoming in the center of his soul. Recognized it, cherished it. And feared it.

Happiness. Such a wonderful, frightening thing. So fleeting.

Annie stirred next to him, her body curving into his. It seemed so natural, having her sleep next to him. She snuggled against him. Trying to move into his space, he thought, smiling as he looked at her. Just like she did when she was awake.

He needed to get a grip on himself, on his feelings that threatened to burst free.

Threatened to? He laughed silently. They already had. There was no point in closing the barn door anymore. The horses had escaped. The only option he had now was to round them up before they were lost or hurt. That was the bottom line. First happiness, then sorrow. An even, eternal balance. He couldn't logically expect more. He had never had more.

Yet at this moment, even when he was trying to summon the melancholy numbness, he couldn't shake this feeling of happiness. Not with her beside him like this.

But it wouldn't last. He knew that. It was a given. Happiness was always transitory. And the greater the feeling of well-being, the greater the sense of loss at the end. He had learned to approach life like that, had learned at an early age that only sadness was dependable. Emptiness always won out in the end. If there was nothing to compare the emptiness to, then it wasn't so bad. He had accepted living in a gray world.

But Marcus couldn't force himself to retreat, not just yet.

Oh God, he wanted to savor this, wanted to believe with his whole heart and soul that what he felt at this very moment, what had spread through him in the night like silvery threads of tenacious nylon cord, would last. Would go on until there was no more life and breath left within him.

She was having too profound an influence on him. He was beginning to think like her. The lady held only disappointment for him in the end, nothing but pure disappointment, even if she didn't know it.

So why did disappointment have to come packaged so sensuously?

He sifted her hair through his fingers, watching the first rays of the morning sun nudge away the shadows in the room. That's what he had felt like inside when he had finally made love with her. Like the shadows in his soul were being nudged away by a force stronger than they were. Light always seemed stronger than dark. At least at dawn, he thought as a small smile quirked his lips. Midnight was another story.

And they were heading for midnight. It was only a matter of time.

He almost wished he had managed to retain that paralysis of the soul he had been living with for so long. At least then he had an excuse not to feel. There had been a certain amount of security in his gray, non-feeling world. This kaleidoscope world Annie had opened for him was fraught with uncertainty. No, he thought, the end result was certain, only the trip there would be a maze.

She stirred and reached out to him even in her sleep. Her hand fell over his chest. He felt his heartbeat quicken. Slowly he ran the back of his fingers along her cheek and watched as her eyes fluttered open. There was no dazed look, no single moment where orientation escaped her. She knew exactly where she was and why. Her smile was warm and just for him.

Annie touched her lips to his; just the slightest of kisses passed between them. It was enough to start him again. "'Morning."

He sighed, but for now it was a sigh of contentment. "Yes, it is."

Annie shifted closer and rested her head on his chest. She liked the sound of his heart beating beneath her cheek. It was a warm, comforting sound. A special excitement wafted through her as she felt his fingers glide along her shoulder. "So, that really was you last night. I thought I had dreamed it."

He could feel her lips form a smile along his skin. "It was me."

Annie laughed. "Talkative as always."

He tried not to react as her fingertips feathered along his waist slowly. He would have had more success bench-pressing a five-hundred-pound weight. "I'm not sure I know what to say."

She wondered if that meant that there hadn't been that many women in his life. She would have liked to think so. She wanted this to be special to him. "'You were magnificent' would be nice."

He laughed. "You were magnificent."

Annie raised her head. He was just parroting the words. "With feeling."

"With feeling," he echoed.

Laughing, she shook her head, her hair falling about her shoulders in golden, tangled waves. "You are impossible." She pulled herself up on her elbow until her lips were a whisper away from his. She searched his face, but there was none of that wariness that she had come to expect. Instead, there was an innocent confusion. She could work with that, she thought, relieved. "You're going to have to go the rest of the distance on your own, Sullivan."

"I think," he murmured as he cupped the back of her head and tilted her face so that his mouth came down on hers, "I already have."

Not yet, Marc, not yet. But soon, she thought, hoped, prayed. *Soon.*

She was impossible to resist. One kiss was like one bit of chocolate, one potato chip. There was no such thing as just one and he knew it. But knowing that didn't stop him. He couldn't deny himself another taste of her mouth in this strange, cozy little room, one more sampling of a paradise that couldn't be allowed to exist beyond this place, these walls.

It all seemed unreal. The place, the woman, the time. An adventure out of spun sugar. Something she might have conjured up. And since it was unreal, he could indulge and let his wildest fantasies come to fruition.

He could have her, love her.

Fantasizing hadn't been something he had done on any sort of a regular basis. Until Annie. It seemed that until she had burst into his life, everything had stayed on more or less an even keel. There had been Jason and his wife, but they had never disturbed his life the way she had. They had enhanced his life. Annie set it on its ear. Now he was in turbulent waters, holding on for dear life and loving every breathtaking second of it.

He had never felt so alive.

His mouth slid over hers, down to her throat. The moan that vibrated beneath his lips aroused and excited him, but this time, he forced himself to hold back, really hold himself back.

There was no need to grasp things with both hands quickly, or to be stunned by the intensity, the passion. This time, he knew, or thought he knew, the pleasures that were ahead for both of them. Pleasures he had never fully sampled before there was Annie. She had brought this wonder to him. Making love was an adventure, not a simple, pleasing event that left no imprint on his soul and didn't linger on the mind.

Every detail of last night lingered now, every movement burned into his brain with the hot branding iron of passion. As it came rushing back to him, he suddenly wanted the exhilaration he had experienced last night. He wanted to thrust himself into her, to feel her legs wrap around him again and ride, hell-bent for leather, to the top.

No, he wanted to hold back. Anticipation enriched the end reward.

It wasn't easy holding back. Not when she touched him like that, skimming her fingertips lightly over his skin, making it blaze. It wasn't easy holding back when he knew that she gave so much more than he thought he was taking, than he was giving. He was in awe of her, totally and utterly in awe. In awe of her body, in awe of the gift she gave him. She made love with him as if he were the only man she had ever done this with.

But he had seen the tears shining in her eyes when she had mentioned her other lover. This had happened before. Had the other man been her first? Was Marcus now her second? He didn't want to be the second. He wanted to be the first. He wanted to blot out the memory of every other man from her mind, the imprint of every other man from her body. He wanted to make love with her until there was nothing and no one but him.

It was important to Marcus. He didn't want to explore why. Not yet. The implications were far too earthshaking and numbing.

He stroked her until both their bodies hummed, found all her secret places again, first with his hands, then with his lips and tongue. Annie twisted and moaned, away from him when the pleasure was too great to bear, toward him as soon as the lack of it penetrated her consciousness and left her bereft.

The ground beneath her feet opened up, and suddenly she had nothing to grab on to except him. Her lips parted, inviting him to sample, to take, to possess. Because he did. He possessed her without ever wanting to enslave her. She was his for as long as he wanted her. Longer. She was his forever.

Annie's mind spun madly, yet she saw everything clearly, felt everything as if it were trapped beneath crystal for her to see and hear and touch. She reveled in the fact that he shuddered when she touched him. Just as she did with him. It magnified her own arousal.

There were no techniques, no him, no her, just an intense whirlwind of passion that engulfed them both. Each wanting to give the other pleasure.

Annie withered and arched as his mouth claimed all of her, marking a slow, maddening path to the core of her being, reminding her how much she needed to be loved, held, cherished, reduced to this pulsating mass of wants and desires. She grabbed fistfuls of the sheet beneath her as he explored the most secret part of her, bringing her up to thunderous peaks. Each time she fell to earth, spent, only to be lifted up again.

The lovemaking made her feel one with him. To her, it was special, private, a wondrous gift she had only given one other man, shared with only one other human being. And now she was sharing it with Marcus. She had a feeling that it was the same with him. He hadn't talked about women, but she sensed that they had drifted nameless, faceless, through his life, touching his body but not his soul. She had it just within her reach. Whether he knew it or not, he was offering it to her. And she wanted it.

It made her want to cry. It made her want to laugh. Above all, it made her want to hold on to this feeling with the last breath that was in her.

His body slick with sweat that belonged to both of them, Marcus raised himself on his elbows, his body hovering over hers. He loved the look in her eyes when they made love. Dark, smoky, only for him. This much he could believe, here and now. Only for him. For now, it was enough.

As they joined together, his hands tangling in her hair, framing her face with powerful fingers, his body arched over hers, she stifled the cry that rose to her lips. Euphoria and warmth laid claim to her in a fast, climaxing, fever pitch. She tightened her arms around him as the spiral twirled her faster and faster, the rhythm they achieved already in harmony. A blending. It was a blending of thoughts, of styles, of beings. Whether he believed it or not, Annie thought, whether he admitted it or not, he was her soulmate for all eternity. Annie opened her heart and let him in.

He held her against his heart, knowing it was dangerous, knowing he couldn't help himself.

Let me hang on to this feeling a little longer, he prayed, loving her, *just a little longer.*

"What," he whispered softly into her hair, hardly knowing he was saying the words aloud, "am I going to do about you?"

She raised her head slightly, her cheek brushing against the dark stubble on his chin. Slowly she ran her fingertip along his lips. "For the time being, I'd say you've done it."

She saw the desire still shining in his eyes. And the perimeter of fear bordering it. Why? What was there to be afraid of? This was the most natural thing in the world. The very best part.

Marcus pressed her fingers to his lips and kissed them one by one. Who would have ever thought that someone so overbearingly pushy would have held such appeal for him? "No, I meant—"

Annie sighed. Reality was already intruding. There were times she hated reality. "I know what you meant." She pulled the sheet back up around them, making a show of tucking it about her breasts primly. "You're going to look into that thesaurus you carry around in your brain and find another word for all this. Maybe 'coupling' will suit you," she suggested, wondering how long her patience would hold. "Or mindless melding, or something else, but whatever words you use, Marcus Sullivan—" she jabbed a finger into his chest "—I know the right ones."

For once, temper made her look adorable. He tried not to grin. "Which are?"

"We made love here."

He raised a brow. "And there's a difference?"

"Yes, there's a difference." Exasperation tinged her words. Why was he pretending to be so obtuse? He *knew* there was a difference. "I don't think either one of us take things like this lightly. I know I don't." She raised her eyes to his face. "I don't think you do, either."

She didn't take it lightly. It was something he wanted to know, wanted to hear, and yet hearing it had such grave implications, such huge consequences. Did she know? Could she possibly know what it would do to him when the time came and she left?

She had told him that she had loved once. She had to know what doing without it meant.

"And that's the word you're running from," she concluded, her voice dropping. "Love."

He was all set to argue with her. After all, that was what they were best at, arguing. But then she smiled at him with that damn inviting smile and he felt his flesh rebelling against his thoughts, against all thoughts. He felt himself wanting her, needing her again. It amazed him almost as much as she did.

Gathering her into his arms again, he shrugged in answer to the question in her eyes. "What the hell, I might as well have more of a reason to run."

The smile within her flowered to fill all the corners of her being. "By all means, let's have more of a reason."

With practiced ease, they both slipped back into ecstasy.

"I think," Annie said as she dragged a brush through her tangled hair, "that we should leave the Flynns some money."

Tucking his freshly laundered shirt into his jeans, Marcus looked at her curiously. That was a very practical statement for someone like Annie.

No, he amended, there *was* no one else like Annie.

"To buy new sheets," she explained. "These—" she held up a corner of one for his inspection "—are just about worn out." Her eyes full of mischief, she rubbed the section she was holding against her cheek and looked up at Marcus affectionately. "I wonder if they'd think I was strange if I asked to keep them as a souvenir."

He had been watching her get ready, fascinated by the intimacies of the act. He had made love to women before, enjoyed their company and then gone on his way. Try as he might, Marcus couldn't remember seeing a single one of those women getting dressed. He couldn't remember wanting to watch any of them comb their hair, or ache to undress them again once they *were* dressed.

He ran his hands though his own hair and tried his best

to look nonchalant. "No stranger than they probably already think you are."

Annie dropped her comb into her purse. "I'm glad to see that nothing has changed on the cerebral front." She brushed a quick kiss on his cheek. "I like matching words with you, Sullivan. It keeps me on my toes."

"No, nothing's changed," he echoed, but saying it didn't make it true. Things had changed, changed drastically, and would never be the same again. Not for him, not emotionally. And not ever again.

The overall picture, though, was still the same. Things ultimately would still be the way they were. He would grasp happiness only to have it slip through his fingers. And he was now trapped inside where he had sworn never to be.

Annie heard the sounds of a household starting a new day. "I think I hear the Flynns." She left the robe neatly folded on the bed and picked up her purse. "Want to go see about getting that mechanic to come up here and hopefully get your car going?"

He took her arm and she smiled to herself at the change, but said nothing. The old Marcus would have never taken that initiative. He would have instinctively backed away from contact.

You're coming along, Marc Sullivan. And you're taking me with you whether you like it or not.

Not only were Mr. and Mrs. Flynn up, but Henry Flynn had put in a call to his son Andy. Andy and Henry, Polly Flynn told them with pride she didn't bother hiding, were undoubtedly already working on the car even as they spoke, and more than likely, repairing it.

"There isn't a thing that man has made that my Andy can't fix," Polly told Annie and Marcus matter-of-factly as she served them breakfast in the tiny kitchen. There was just enough room for four at the table. "I expect he'll be done by the time you two finish breakfast."

Marcus discovered that he had an appetite. Breakfast was usually restricted by choice to black coffee. Now a hunger gnawed at his belly that made him look upon the pancakes, sausages and eggs that Polly pushed toward him as a blessing.

Must be all that lovemaking, he thought. It sapped a man's energy and built up his appetite—for more things than one, he added mentally, looking at Annie over the table.

Annie merely grinned, digging in as heartily as he was. But then, he remembered, she could always eat.

True to Polly's prediction, Annie heard the sound of a car pulling up just as Polly swept away the last of the dishes.

Shooing away Annie's offer of help, Polly deposited them into the old-fashioned sink she had told them she preferred to a dishwasher. "I'm too old to try new things," she had explained cheerfully. Annie had thought that she had never seen a woman look more youthful.

Henry and a younger, taller and rangier version of the old man walked in. "This is my boy, Andy," Henry said, nodding in the youth's direction as he cleaned his shoes on the worn mat just within the door. "Our youngest."

Annie judged the young man to be around twenty or so. A love child, she guessed, gauging the older couple's age.

Andy said nothing, just ducked his head in a quick, shy greeting. Annie put out her hand, and he was forced to take it, after first rubbing his own on the back of his jeans.

She was drawn to shyness like a magnet. Andy didn't stand a chance, Marcus thought with a touch of amusement.

"Were you able to figure out what was wrong with the car?" Annie asked the two men.

That was his line, Marcus thought, but for once it didn't

bother him that she had jumped in and beaten him to the punch. Maybe making love with her anesthetized certain parts of his brain, he mused.

"Yes," Andy mumbled in reply, not looking at either one of them.

"Your battery was dead," Henry explained. "Andy here recharged it for you. It'll get you to where you're going and then some. Andy helps out part-time at the garage. Kirby keeps him on as an apprentice." It was evident that Henry shared his wife's pride in his last born. "It seems to me, Kirby could stand to learn a few things from our boy."

"Dad." The single word, tinged in embarrassment, was deep and resonant as Andy flushed.

Marcus dug into his back pocket and took out his wallet. "What do we owe you?"

Speaking for both of them, Polly placed a wide, surprisingly soft hand over the wallet and pushed it back toward Marcus. "Keep your money, Marcus. It's the neighborly thing to do." The women winked at him.

She must have been a hell-raiser in her youth, Marcus thought. The wink gave her a flirtatious air.

"Maybe you can dedicate a book or movie to us someday." It was apparent that Polly Flynn was in awe of what he did for a living. Conversely Marcus was in awe over anyone who could fix machinery so easily.

"The very next one," Annie promised, taking Marcus's arm. "And now, we'd better hurry off. There's a screenplay waiting for us back home."

And once it's done, everything will be over, Marcus thought.

She tried to pretend she didn't see the frown that crossed Marcus's face before he hid it.

Now what had she said?

Chapter Sixteen

Dammit, why didn't she say something?

Marcus's hands tightened on the wheel. She had been sitting next to him, silent now, for the last hour, ever since they had gotten into the car. Was she having second thoughts? he wondered, trying to stave off nervousness. Was she sorry about what had happened last night? He hadn't forced himself on her. She had seemed willing, receptive. Had he misread her reaction? If not, why was she so quiet now?

Annie looked at his profile. Marcus was staring straight ahead, his eyes on the road. Over an hour had gone by and the only sound she had heard was the sound of the tires against the road.

Why didn't he say something to her? Anything. She didn't want to be the first to speak. She was always the first. She wanted him to take the lead, to make her feel that this situation between them was going to be all right. This wasn't just a game anymore.

Maybe it never had been.

But the closer they got to the city, the more distant he became. She hadn't expected reams of words from him or protestations of undying love. But after last night and this morning, she *had* expected something from him, a change, perhaps a small aura of romance, or at least some kindness. Instead, he was just the way he had been before. He was acting as if nothing had happened last night. Or worse, as if he was regretting what had happened between them.

She felt a horrible pang seize the center of her stomach.

The silence was driving him crazy. He had never thought he'd feel that way, but right now, he wanted her to say something, anything. He had made the first move last night. He would have thought that would have shown her how he felt, would have made her happy. But she obviously wasn't happy or else she'd be talking. He had made a mistake. He shouldn't have let last night happen.

Annie looked down at her hands. She was twisting the hem of her shirt. Dropping it, she sighed. Muhammad was going to have to pay another visit to the mountain before he twisted off his clothing. She wet her lips. "A dollar ninety-five, taking inflation into consideration, for your thoughts."

Vaguely her voice penetrated his thoughts. She sounded the way she always did. Nothing had changed for her. He had been right. Last night didn't mean to her what it had for him. When they returned to the city, they'd be writing partners again, nothing more. Last night had been a lovely aberration, brought on by circumstances, by rain and wind and redwoods. These things happen. There was no more to it than that.

Oh, but there was. And after last night, how could he just go on working with her side by side, and not touch her? Not make love with her again? He didn't see how that was possible. "Did you say something?"

Annie blew out an angry breath, telling herself *not* to get angry until he had had time to plead his case—as if he *had* a case. There was no excuse to treat her so shabbily. "Would it matter if I did?"

He tried to concentrate on what she was saying and make sense out of it. He never did have much luck at that, he thought wryly. "What?"

She turned on the radio, hoping that the lively music would break this mood she felt consuming her. "You seem to be off in your own little world. Is it a private planet, or can anyone journey there?"

"What are you talking about?"

"About being left out."

He glanced at her, then looked back at the road. Why the hell was he feeling guilty? There wasn't anything to feel guilty about. He slowed as the car took a curve. "Left out of what?"

Out of your life, you idiot, she answered silently. "You haven't said two words since we left the Flynns' house."

Neither have you, he thought. But maybe it was just as well. The time they had spent in Santa Barbara had been idyllic, wonderful. It had nothing to do, he tried to convince himself, with the people they were in their day-to-day lives. And they were returning to that world. They couldn't stay in that little house, enjoying each other, indefinitely. It would have been wonderful, but utterly impossible. That episode had been nothing more than a fantastic interlude. Now it was back to the real world. Back to reality. And reality meant that their project would end soon and their lives would go on. Separately. He couldn't believe in anything else, couldn't let newly flexed, raw emotions lead him into making mistaken assumptions.

Because they wouldn't be true.

But even if they weren't, he knew that he needed her. Already he could feel that terrible, overwhelming loneliness envelop him as he anticipated her leaving. There wasn't that much of the script left to work on. And then what? He could ask her to stay, to explore this relationship with him. But what if she said no? He couldn't risk that. It was better not to put his feelings into words than have his feelings thrown back at him. Her silence on the trip back was enough of an indication that she probably thought the whole thing had been a mistake. She *always* talked. The fact that she didn't was a dead giveaway. Right now, the relationship hadn't progressed very far, and though he felt hurt, it was just a wound. He was strong. He could regain his composure. It wasn't as bad as it could be. Like a recovering alcoholic who had slipped, he had managed to stop himself in time before the damage was too great.

He could see impatience on her face. Why? Was she annoyed with him? With herself? Maybe he was wrong. Maybe he had hurt her in some way. Maybe there was a chance for them—no, dammit, what was wrong with him? "I've been thinking," he said slowly, trying to find an excuse for his own silence.

"About what?" she prodded, desperately wanting him to go on talking. If they talked, the truth would come out and then maybe she'd know what was troubling him.

She kept hoping that if she said the right words, set up the right situation, she'd hear what she needed to hear. Make him say things she felt were in his heart. Or prayed that they were.

Words eluded him. He grasped at the thing that was closest at hand. "About the screenplay."

Annie leaned back against the seat, disappointed. *What else did you expect him to say?* They were collaborating, for heaven's sake.

She rested her arm on the open window. The wind played havoc with her hair, whipping it around. She didn't bother trying to tie it back. "I think the screenplay is going well."

She didn't want to talk about the damned screenplay. They almost always argued when they discussed it. She didn't want to argue. Not now. She wanted to talk about what had happened between them last night. She wanted to hold on to that sweetness.

The expression on his face told her that now was not the time to explore the significance of last night. She tried a different approach. "Sure you don't want me to drive?"

"No, I'm fine." Besides, if he didn't drive, he'd have more time to look at her. It wasn't a good idea.

Liar, Annie thought. *You are not fine, and I wish I could beat you about the head and shoulders and get you to admit it. Talk to me, damn you.* She blew out a frustrated breath. *Patience, Annie.* She wasn't so sure that she could follow her own advice.

He glanced at her and was captivated by the simple way the wind played with her hair, the way the sun seemed to be reflected in it. He found himself, despite all his well-thought-out arguments, wanting her again. Right here. Right now.

He drove past a sign announcing a motel just a couple of miles down the road. Impulsively he toyed with the idea of stopping. Why not turn off here? What was so important about reaching home within the next hour or so? He had time, time enough to make love with her until the stars blanketed the sky.

Marcus gripped the steering wheel. *Drive,* he told himself. *Just drive.*

Another lapse into silence. Dammit, he was going to drive her crazy. She was almost hungry for the sound of his voice, even if it was raised in argument.

"So," she said suddenly, "do you really think it's coming along well, Marc?" Not waiting for him to answer, she lowered her voice and pretended to be him. "Well, I think it'd be coming along a lot better if you stopped trying to change lines and passages that are perfectly acceptable." Out of the corner of her eye, Annie saw Marcus looking at her as if she had lost her mind. She kept going. "Marc, you have to learn how to bend. Things work in books that don't on screen.'' Again her voice dropped. ''I guess you're right, de Witt. Maybe it's time for a change. But don't let it go to your head.''

Signs proclaiming that L.A. was fifty miles away popped up on the road. Not soon enough for him, he decided. ''Are you feeling all right?'' he finally asked.

Annie wiggled her feet, trying to get comfortable. ''Sure,'' she said tersely, ''why?''

A crazy woman—he was emotionally hooked on a crazy woman. ''You're talking to yourself.''

''It's a dirty job, but someone has to do it.''

He started to laugh and shook his head. Life, he knew, was going to seem empty without her.

Life *was* empty, he reminded himself. There were only occasional disturbances to make it seem otherwise. ''You know, you really are crazy, absolutely crazy.''

Pleased to hear him laugh, she grinned. ''It's one of my better qualities.''

He thought of last night. The way she'd felt in his arms. The way her body seemed to meld with his. ''No, I wouldn't say that.''

Annie turned, tucking her feet under her, her expression eager. ''What would you say?'' Her hand was on his arm, coaxing. ''Anything, I'll settle for anything. I've had more spirited conversations with my shoes than I've had in this car in the last hour.''

''Annie.'' Marcus felt almost helpless with the situation, with himself. ''I don't know what to say.''

''That hasn't stopped you from criticizing me before.'' She stopped, then looked at him. ''Do you realize that that's the first time you've called me by my name of your own free will without my prodding you?''

That was impossible. They'd spent over a month together. He had to have used her name in all that time. Hadn't he? ''No, it's not.''

''Yes it is. Trust me, I've been listening.''

"With all your rhetoric?" he scoffed, turning the car down the serpentine road that twisted and curved. "When did you have time to hear?"

She winked. "I'm gifted."

There was no point in arguing with her. She'd win. She always seemed to.

A straight stretch of road gave Marcus the opportunity to look at her again. She was grinning. He wanted to kiss that impish expression until it changed into one of desire. He wanted her in his arms the way she had been last night by dim light, this morning by the first rays of dawn.

He wanted her forever.

Forever was a word in a dictionary. Nothing more.

"So you are," he agreed softly. She had gotten under his skin, hadn't she? Somehow gotten to him the way no other woman ever had. Gotten to him and dug in despite his best efforts to eradicate her. That made her unique. "Gifted" was stretching it, perhaps, but somehow it fitted.

"Say it again."

"Say what again?"

"My name." She propped her head up with her hand, leaning it against the headrest. Okay, so she was settling for crumbs. She'd work it up into a feast somehow later on. "I have a feeling I won't hear it once we're back at work. At least, not said that softly."

Feeling silly, he obliged. It wasn't that much to ask. "Annie." She had closed her eyes, he realized, and seemed to be savoring the sound.

Annie let the sound of his voice wash over her like a warm caress. No, she decided, she wasn't going to give up. Determination had always been her mainstay. When Charlie had died, it had been what she had clung to to dig herself out and live again. She wasn't about to let it slip through her fingers now. Marcus might have a problem, but it was no longer his alone. She was going to help.

She glanced at him now, her green eyes widening. *If*

you're going to try to retreat, Marcus Sullivan, you're going to have one hell of a fight on your hands, she promised herself. And him.

A motorcycle suddenly came up behind them and then whooshed off around them, disappearing down the road. Marcus realized that he was about ten miles under the speed limit and pressed down harder on the gas pedal. He saw her smile as he did so.

"Am I rubbing off on you?" He had told her before that she drove too fast.

Perhaps she was. But nothing was going to rub off the impression she had made on his life, he thought. It was now a matter of how much damage would be left in her wake once she was gone.

"No, I just wanted to get back. Why don't I drop you off at your place first?"

When he retreated, he did it quickly, she thought. "My car's at your place."

He had forgotten about that. "I can have someone drop that off later."

She wasn't about to be obliging. "No need," she said cheerfully. "It'll still be early. We can get some more work done. That should make you happy."

He didn't know what would make him happy anymore. Certainly not the future. He tried to concentrate on the present. For she was in it.

Marcus had scarcely managed to pull his convertible up into the driveway and park it before the front door flew open. Holly, her hands on her ample hips, stood in the doorway glaring at him the way his mother had never been moved to do. His mother hadn't cared enough about his activities to take notice of his comings and goings. Holly, it seemed, did.

"So, you're back."

"Yes," Marcus answered, wondering what had gotten

into his placid housekeeper, "we are. What's the matter with you, Holly?"

Annie was out of the car in a heartbeat and at the woman's side. "Has something happened to Nathan?"

The possibility hadn't even occurred to him. "Has it?" he demanded.

Seeing Marcus's concern, Holly relented a bit. "I'm not sure he can walk anymore," she sniffed.

"What?" Had he been in some sort of an accident? Annie looked toward the house, then grabbed Holly by the shoulders. "What happened? Where is he?"

In reply, Holly turned on her heel and stalked back into the house.

"Holly," Marcus demanded, hurrying after her, his hand on Annie's arm, "what the hell are all these dramatics? Has the boy been hurt?"

Holly didn't answer. Instead, she pointed toward the front room like an avenging angel. "He's over there on the window seat, where he's been since early this morning. Probably," she amended, her expression accusing, "since last night after I went to bed."

Marcus walked into the living room quickly, but Annie was faster. Her heart almost broke when she saw the boy, his back to them, his slight shoulders moving as if trying to silence a sob. The puppy dozed at his feet.

She knelt by Nathan's side, but he kept his face averted. He didn't want them guessing that he had been crying.

"Nathan, honey." He wouldn't look at her. Annie put her hand on his arm and felt it stiffen slightly. "What's wrong?"

"My guess is that he's been waiting for you to come home." There was no mistaking the censure in Holly's voice, or whose side she was on. Marcus might pay her salary, but it was the motherless boy at the window seat who had won her heart.

Marcus didn't care for being on the defensive. Lately that

was all he seemed to be doing. ''We called you last night,'' he pointed out.

''Yes, about something being wrong with the car,'' Holly recalled. ''You were in a car, Mr. Sullivan.'' She emphasized the word car and neither one of them needed a diagram as to what went on in the boy's mind.

Marcus looked at Nathan, not knowing what to say. It was all well and good to talk about logic, but what place did logic have in the mind of a small boy who had already lived through one tragedy that had turned his entire life upside down?

Slowly Annie stroked the boy's hair. She felt the stiffness abating. ''Honey, I told you last night we'd be back today.''

Nathan sniffled hard, determined not to cry. He passed the back of his hand over his damp cheeks. Somehow, the gentleness in Annie's voice made it worse. He shifted around in his seat to look at her. The sleeping puppy at his feet yelped a little before settling back down. ''My mom and dad said the same thing before—'' His lower lip trembled. The words wouldn't come out. ''Before—''

She had enjoyed a night of passion while a small boy had gone through hell. Her feeling of contrition was almost insurmountable. ''Oh, darling, I'm so sorry.'' Annie's heart ached as she took Nathan in her arms and held him to her. ''I'm so very, very sorry if we made you worry.''

For a moment, there was only the sound of Nathan sobbing against her shoulder. Annie stroked his head, shedding silent tears while Marcus wrestled with guilt he felt was unreasonable.

But beneath the guilt was the realization that the boy had transferred his affections, his love, to him. It took Marcus's breath away. More than that, Nathan had encompassed Annie in this transfer. Marcus knew that for however long it took, he would be there for Nathan. But as far as Annie went, that was another matter. The boy shouldn't count on her. It wouldn't be fair to either of them.

Marcus regretted the day he had agreed to this damn screenplay.

But if he hadn't, a small voice whispered, he wouldn't have had last night. And last night had been worth all the agony that hell had to offer.

"I thought you were never coming back again," Nathan sobbed.

Annie kissed Nathan's forehead. "We'll always be here for you." It was a promise she intended keeping.

Nathan blinked back tears. The puppy, awake, wagged his tail and jumped into his lap. "Promise?" He looked at her hopefully. If she said yes, he knew he could believe her. She wouldn't break her word to him.

Annie raised her hand and said solemnly, "Promise." Elaborately she crossed her heart. "If you ever need me, all you ever have to do is call." She looked back at Marcus and saw that he was watching her. "Marc has my number."

Yes, Marcus thought, I have your number.

Her very answer reinforced his thoughts. If Nathan needed her, he would have to call her. At her house. Because after they finished the screenplay, that's where she would be. It was her way of saying that she would go on with her life and it would be a life separate from his.

It was what he expected. Yet he couldn't help the angry feeling that sprang up in its wake. He had known that all along, told himself that all along. But when the words were out of her mouth, they stung.

She saw Marcus stiffen and hadn't the vaguest notion why. Was he annoyed at the boy's attachment to her? Jealous of it? Threatened by it? What?

You are a damn hard man to love, and I should have my head examined for it. But, God help me, I do love you. And on my tombstone they shall write, she thought wryly, *that 'she loved not wisely, but all too well.'*

With a resigned sigh, Annie rose to her feet. It wasn't easy to put these feelings aside, but she gave it her best shot. "Why don't we go out for a soda and celebrate our homecoming? And after that, Marc and I are going to have to settle back down in front of our computers and make up for lost time." She looked at Marcus, daring him to say something different, daring him to send her home. "That all right with you, Sullivan?"

She was taking charge again, Marcus thought, but it didn't really matter, did it? She'd be gone soon. Too soon.

He looked at Nathan. An emotion that he could only identify as paternal and which fascinated him, tugged at his heart. "As long as the puppy stays here."

"Here," Holly gathered up the squirming mass. She was licked for her trouble and pretended to scowl. "I'll take him." She gave Annie a sharp look. "You might have at least housebroken him before you dropped him off."

Annie linked an arm through Marcus's elbow and placed a hand on Nathan's shoulder. "And have Sullivan here miss the fun? Not on your life, Holly."

"Fun?" he echoed, then found that he was smiling. "Is that what we call it?"

Annie lifted her chin. "That is precisely what we call it." Her eyes danced at she looked down at Nathan. "Right, Nathan?"

"Right." The boy beamed.

Who was he to argue? Marcus thought. At least for the time being.

Chapter Seventeen

The sun was shining and the world outside the den window looked bright and cheery. Annie shivered and ran her hands up and down her arms. The sunshine hadn't managed to penetrate the interior of the room. At least, not in the way that counted. Feeling oddly out of sorts, Annie watched a bluebird soar up in the sky until he faded into nothingness.

Was that all that there had been between them that night? Just a glimmer of a moment, a flash of feeling, and then fading away like a bird soaring out of sight?

Maybe it was her fault for wanting too much. She smiled sadly to herself. It seemed as if instead of her endless optimism rubbing off on him, his dark view of life had rubbed off on her.

How had he engineered it? she wondered. How had he managed to work beside her day after day and still reconstruct those damn walls of his? Except when Nathan was around, for all intents and purposes, Marcus had withdrawn into himself right after they had returned from their outing. That had been over a week ago. Eight days. Eight days of hell to endure, eight days of being shut out.

He hadn't changed. He was still the same removed, antiseptic man. Although not totally. Every now and then, he'd slip. But, like a well-trained tightrope walker, he always regained his balance. That night together, she had shaken his rope and yet he *still* regained his balance. What did it take to shake him up?

She didn't understand. It was as if that wonderful man who had brought her to the brink of ecstasy and beyond hadn't really existed, had been only a figment of her overactive imagination.

Annie pressed her fingers into her palms until her nails dug in. But he had been real, she thought as a fragment of a memory skimmed over the outskirts of her mind. Marcus, his dark, manly scent seeping into her, filling her senses as he kissed her. Involuntarily Annie's body tightened like the strings of a violin that needed playing, that ached to make music but couldn't on its own. *He* made the music within her, his hands had strummed the right chords, had found the right notes.

Annie leaned her forehead against the window. She needed him, the big idiot. And he needed her. Didn't he see that?

They were alone in the big house. She had brought Stevie and Erin with her, and Holly had taken the lot out to Knott's Berry Farm, bless her, after the "joyful noise" had proven to be too much to creatively compete with.

Alone. It should have been an ideal time to recapture what they had discovered a week ago. She had secretly hoped they might. But he had only grown more distant.

She looked at him. He was bent over the computer, pecking out words. It never ceased to amaze her that the man who produced such wonderful books was a three-fingered typist who couldn't seem to commit the keyboard to memory.

Annie dragged her hands through her hair and then let them fall again. They might as well have been on separate islands for all the good being left alone did. They were alone all right. Together, they were very much alone. She ached from the loneliness.

It made her angry.

She left the shelter of the window seat and crossed to his side of the desk. Looking over his shoulder for a minute, Annie contemplated her options. She could beat him on his thick skull. She rather liked that option. No court in the world, once it knew him, would convict her.

Or she could forget about her hurt self-respect and try again.

Once more with feeling. "Looks like another wonderful day in paradise."

"What?" He glanced at her, slightly bewildered. It always took him a moment to refocus when he left the dimensions of the world he was creating.

He sounded as if he was snapping at her, she thought. He had been snapping at her constantly this past week. Maybe she was turning into one of those masochists, she mused, who thrived on adversity.

"I said it's a beautiful day." She sat down on his desk and slid back, her hands braced on either side. His pages were neatly stacked to her left and she saw him eye them protectively, as if he were afraid she'd knock them over. "You haven't smiled lately, Marcus."

He wished she'd just concentrate on doing the job they were supposed to be doing. It was hard enough trying to refortify the boundaries of his life without her pushing at them every time he turned around. "I didn't know that smiling was in our contract." He pecked out another three words.

She deliberated shutting off his computer to get his full

attention, but since he was working, that was too drastic a measure. Not, she thought, that he didn't deserve it. "It's right after the paragraph that allows you to bite off my head only twice per session."

It was no use. He stopped typing. "Are you trying to tell me something?"

"Desperately." She leaned over, and he put a protective hand over the off switch on his computer. "I'm not going to shut anything off," she said tersely. "That's your department."

"You'll get to the point, I trust, before I apply for social security."

"Security?" she echoed angrily, her emotions finally erupting. "You have so much damned security in that high-walled life of yours, I sincerely doubt that you'll ever need any more."

A lot you know, he thought. Trust her to pick up on the one word that would send her verbally off and running. "Annie—"

But she was in no mood to listen to a formal tirade. "Where *are* you, Sullivan?" She jabbed an impatient finger at his chest, her eyes smoldering. "And I warn you, if you give me some pat answer with your address in it, I won't be held responsible for what I do to you."

He was having trouble curbing his own temper. "I don't know what you're talking about." So what else was new?

She felt like hurling things, hurling expletives, but what good would it do? She couldn't make him leave that world he had retreated to. Not if he didn't want to. But she'd be damned if she was going to take the insult lying down.

With more temper than she had ever displayed in her life, she shoved the pages they had been working on aside with the back of her hand, sending a shower of white onto the carpet.

"What the—?" He pushed back his chair, ready to scoop the pages up.

"Leave them there!" she ordered.

It was a side of her he hadn't seen before. He rose to his feet, concern warring with anger. "What's come over you?"

She lifted up her chin. "Maybe a belated attack of pride."

He saw the fire in her eyes. He saw the hurt as well. Had he caused that? He didn't want to hurt her, just to get out before there *was* no getting out. It was a mess all right. "Annie, I—"

She had had enough of excuses. "Damn you." Annie doubled her fists and punched him in the chest, frustrated beyond words.

He grabbed her wrists. She was *not* as fragile as she looked. He had to exert effort to hold on to her. "Stop it!"

But she went on struggling, trying to get free. She wanted to land just one more blow to make up for all the blows that he had given her. "I'm not just some one-night stand," she cried.

My God, was that what she thought? That he saw her as someone on whom to exercise his rutting libido? "Annie, I know that."

Annie yanked at her wrists, but he wouldn't let go of them. "Then why do you treat me like one?" She could see he didn't understand. He was so enmeshed in his own problems that he didn't know what she was talking about. "Why don't you just let things evolve? Why won't you let them go on the way they started?"

She wasn't going to cry. She wasn't going to give him the satisfaction of crying in front of him. She'd deck him and then cry her eyes out in the privacy of her own home, if he'd only let go of her hands.

He didn't know when her struggling burned away his anger and formed a new crack in his armor, he only knew it did. He wanted to hold her, to make love with her until he was too exhausted to breathe. At night, she haunted his dreams. By day, she haunted his mind, not to mention his house. But the consequences of giving in were so great, so painful. "Because one day, you'll walk away."

That was it? He didn't want it to start because he didn't want it to end? She stared at him, dazed. How could he think that way? What had happened to him to make him this wary, this skeptical?

"Only if you tell me to." She relaxed her hands and he released them. Annie reached out to touch his cheek. She saw him watch her hand warily. "Trust me, Marc. I don't know what happened in your life to make you like this, but trust me," she whispered the words, a plea in them. "Let me in."

"Let you in?" he repeated incredulously. "Let you in?" Didn't she see? Didn't she know that she was going to be his undoing? He surrendered to the battle that raged within him and took hold of her. "Damn you, you already *are* in." Marcus covered her mouth with his own, his lips hot, demanding, extracting her soul from the depths of her very being.

Annie twisted against him, wanting to savor every moment, every sensation he created within her.

Oh God, if she died now, Annie thought, threading her fingers in his hair, it would be all right. She wanted to go on a rising crest of happiness, and she didn't want to hear any words that would rob her of this later. She stood high on her toes, bending her body into his like a flower trying to absorb all the sunlight it could before darkness enveloped it.

Breathless, Marcus drew away from her. Her eyes had a dazed, unfocused look, her pupils wide, disoriented. But her mind, he knew, was clear. It was always clear. The woman would never feel desire to the extent he did. He doubted that anyone ever could. She had had love in her life. There had been her family, her fiancé. For Marcus, there had been no family, only three people beneath a roof, united by a common last name. It had sapped his ability to love, beating it back. But no one could have hungered for love the way he had.

"Tell me," she said in a whisper that was barely audible. "Tell me everything."

He didn't know what she wanted from him or if it was in his power to give it. "What?"

"I have to know about you, Marc. You're a good, decent man who's trying so hard to hide the sensitivity inside him with harsh words and barbed-wire retorts." Her eyes held him, asking him for the truth. "Why?"

"Annie, don't—" He turned away, unable to face the look in her eyes.

He was always turning away from her. And this time, it hurt more than she could bear. She was far too vulnerable to rally. "Don't what? Love you? Too late for that, I'm afraid." The words were tinged with sarcasm. He had no way of knowing it was aimed at herself. "I won't tax you with it. It's my burden, not yours."

She wouldn't have believed that she was susceptible to pride, but something stung now. Pride? Hurt feelings? She didn't know the right term, she didn't care. She just wanted the pain to go away.

Pressing her lips together, she forced the tears back and bent down to pick up the pages she had scattered. "Look." Her breath hitched. She tried again more slowly. "This is our last scene. Maybe—" *Don't cry, darn you, don't cry.* "Maybe I can just take it home and work on it and then send it to you."

Running. By God, she was running for the first time in her life. She hated him for doing this to her.

He saw the pain, the vulnerability as she was stripped bare before him. "Annie." Taking her free hand in his, he brought her up to her feet. "I never meant to hurt you."

"Funny thing for a man holding a bloodied spear in his hands to be saying." She was clinging to quips when everything inside of her was suddenly going dead. He didn't trust her. She couldn't force him to. A tear she couldn't stop seeped out of the corner of her eye.

Fascinated, Marcus touched the teardrop and let it melt onto his fingertip. She was crying because of him. And last week, Nathan had done the same. He had never meant enough to anyone before to cause tears.

Gently he took the pages from her hand. Annie stared at him, numb, striving to rally, striving to keep in mind who and what she was. She'd been a person before she had fallen in love with him. She had to recover that person. "I need those pages, Sullivan, if I'm to fix them."

He let them drop on his desk without looking to see if he had hit the mark. He hadn't. They fell to the floor and he made no effort to retrieve them. "Later."

Hope snapped up its head. Annie smiled. Just a little. "Want to wrestle me for them?"

"No." His hands skimmed along her arms. He felt her shiver and felt her fight to keep her crumbling composure. "I don't want to wrestle at all."

"What do you want to do?"

He surrendered. If there had been a white flag handy, he would have waved it. Later he would gather his protective shield back around him, do what he knew was right, what he had to do. But for now, fighting off this feeling that had him in a death grip didn't even make sense. Nothing made sense except holding her, kissing her, making love with her.

What she had said was true. This was the last scene left for them to work out in the screenplay. After this, there would be no more work sessions, no more reasons to have her here. He knew what she had said about not walking away, but he wouldn't hold her to that. She would move on to another project, taking her sunshine with her and he would move about in the darkness that was his lot. He accepted that.

But right now, he wanted the light. Her light. He wanted to bask in her sunshine just one more time.

What did he want to do? he repeated her question in his mind. "Guess."

His eyes held her captive. He was unbuttoning her blouse, and Annie thought she had never felt anything so sensuous in her life. The man blew hot and cold and drove her mad, but she didn't care how he blew, as long as he was here, with her. As long as he wanted her half as fiercely as she wanted him.

"I dunno." She kept her expression innocent as he pulled her blouse from her waistband. His fingers slipped beneath it, to the small thing she wore that served as a bra. "Give me another clue." She felt the clasp release at her back and the bra slip forward. His hands cupped her breasts. "I haven't got it yet," she murmured as her pulses scrambled. She braced her hands on his forearms. "But I know I'm getting warmer. Definitely warmer." Her head dropped back as he lowered his mouth across her cheek, down to her neck. Her breath quickened, becoming rapid and shallow as he found an erotic point on her throat. Annie moaned.

"Do you ever stop talking?"

"Multiple questions. I don't think—" she tugged at the bottom of his shirt, pulling it free "—that I'm up to functioning on two levels."

"You," he murmured, feeling his excitement pulsate through his loins, his belly, his very being, "can function on *all* levels."

She had to concentrate to look at him and not give in to the flood of emotions threatening to drown her. "That's the nicest thing you ever said to me. So far."

With hands that were suddenly clumsy, she worked the buttons on his shirt loose, wanting to feel his chest against hers. She caught her breath as his arms enveloped her, stroking her back. The soft, dark hairs on his chest tickled her. She arched her back as his kisses lowered to her breasts. He moved his face against them, rubbing his cheek along the sensitive skin as his hands cupped her hips.

Slowly he sank to his knees in front of her.

Annie braced her hands on his shoulders, gripping hard in anticipation. "You don't have to beg for forgiveness. I accept your apology."

He chuckled softly to himself as he undid her shorts and let them sink unnoticed to the floor. She was truly something else.

Annie's stomach quivered as Marcus languidly trailed his tongue lower and lower. She felt his moist tongue through the delicate fabric of her panties as he reached journey's end. She wanted to rip away the barrier, but her hands couldn't move. Her arms were limp, too heavy to lift.

"I think I'm beginning to figure it out," she rasped, her throat dry as words were getting harder to say. His hands were stroking the sensitive part inside her thigh until a fever pitch raged all through her.

Holding her, he lowered Annie to the floor, then loomed over her, his body so close that shafts of heat passed between them. "Annie."

She struggled to think within the thick cloud forming in her brain. "Yes?"

"Shut up."

"Gladly." She pulled his head down to her and kissed him as if her very life depended on it. Because, at this moment in time, it did.

Hours passed. Holly had called to say that she and the children were staying a little longer at Knott's Berry Farm than anticipated. Perhaps until seven. There was no threat of being interrupted. They had time to enjoy each other in peace and in excitement. And they did. But during it all, Annie had the feeling that there was something final happening. It was as if he were saying goodbye.

She wasn't about to let him.

"You know," Annie said teasingly as she shut the door behind the courier who was hand-carrying their finished product to Addison, "for a stuffed shirt, you've come a long way." Not far enough to share what troubled his soul, but that would come. She hoped.

He told himself that it would do him no good to try to memorize her every movement. It would only make matters worse in the long run. "This is just an interlude."

If he had taken a knife and plunged it into her, it wouldn't have hurt any more.

She took a deep breath, telling herself to calm down and not say anything that she would be sorry for. They had made love, then, inspired, had rewritten the last scene. The script was finished. Addison would be reading it before the evening was out. Everything should have been perfect.

Should have been.

Was she going to have to go through this with him each and every time? Make love with him, then watch him rebuild his barriers? Were they on some kind of tumblers that he could pull them up so quickly? Or didn't she matter to him? Didn't what was happening here count?

Holly was due back at any time now. Annie busied herself with getting her things together. The children would be tired and there was no reason to hang around tonight. Not if he was going to be like this. She was suddenly much too tired to fight.

"I don't know what I'm going to do, Marc," she said tersely, "not having you around to properly label things for me."

Not having him around. It was her way of saying that things were over, with no more meaning than he should have attached to them. He had given her an opportunity to deny it, but she hadn't. He had known all along.

Knowing didn't help. "I suspect you'll manage," he said quietly.

"I always have." The words were cheerfully said. Her throat felt hollow. He was pushing her out of his life, sweeping her away neatly. She wanted to say something to him, but couldn't summon the words. She wasn't going to beg, and she had come as far as she could on her own.

The noise in the hallway and the slam of the front door told her that Holly had returned with Nathan and her niece and nephew. "Right on cue," she said brightly. "I'd better collect what's mine and leave."

Before I do something that's everlastingly stupid, she thought, willing her tears to stay in place until she had driven off.

The tears nearly came when she said goodbye to Nathan, who seemed to sense that this was more than just the usual leave-taking, despite the smile on her face.

"You won't be back?" he asked.

She heard the fear in his voice. "Sure." She tousled his hair. "But you have to invite me. I can't just barge in." She looked over his head toward Marcus. "I don't do things like that."

"Ha." The single sound escaped his lips.

She rose and took a step back toward the sleepy boy and girl waiting for her. "Well, kids, I'd better get you back to your mother before she thinks I sold you off to the gypsies." She looked at Marcus, but didn't trust herself to say anything to him. Instead, she looked back to Nathan. "Take care of him, Nathan. He has trouble telling his left foot from his right—unless he's chewing on them."

He wanted to stop her. He didn't know how. Pride wouldn't let him. Marcus leaned against the wall, his arms crossed before him. "Charming, as always."

"I try not to disappoint," Annie tossed off. "Goodbye, Holly," she said in a voice that was oddly hoarse. "And thank you."

Holly waited until after the door was closed to glare at Marcus. She took Nathan's hand and walked out of the room to the kitchen. "I doubt, Nathan," she said in a voice that carried quite well, "if you'll ever see two stupider, more stubborn people in your life than you just saw now."

Chapter Eighteen

The mug warmed her hands even as the early morning breeze from the sea drifted over her in waves, making Annie shiver beneath the heavy sweatshirt she wore.

Warm hands, cold heart.

The singsong refrain kept echoing through her head. She watched two sea gulls disappear into the haze that hung over the ocean. She doubted that anything would ever warm her heart again.

Two weeks. Two whole, long, endless weeks that restlessly fed into each other, forming a chain that was about to drive her mad. Two weeks had passed. Not a word. Not a damn word. No messages, no notes, no pretexts. Nothing. He had totally and effectively evaporated from her life like a pool of water beneath the desert sun.

She took a sip of coffee, trying to find it in her heart to hate him. There was anger and hurt in overwhelming proportions, but hatred wouldn't come.

He had physically disappeared out of her life, but he still

lived and breathed and haunted her every move. In her mind. She kept finding excuses not to leave the house for fear she'd miss him if he showed up. She was just now beginning to realize that he wasn't going to show up.

It was a bitter pill for a die-hard optimist to swallow. She stared down into the mug, feeling the steam rise and curl around her face. Cold. She felt so cold, so alone. This time, she wasn't sure if she could regroup. She didn't know if she had the strength.

And for what? To go on alone? Whoever it was who had said that it was better to have loved and lost than never to have loved at all was a raving maniac and should have been put away.

The sharp cry of two more sea gulls pierced the air. For a moment, she watched them as they swooped down, intent on some prey that they saw from their lofty positions. They came away empty.

She lifted her mug in a toast. "Welcome to the club, fellas."

"Always talk to sea gulls?"

Her hand tightened on the mug as she told her heart it had no business leaping up that high in her body. People didn't function with hearts lodged in their throats.

She wanted to laugh; she wanted to cry. She wanted to beat on him until he gave her answers. "What kept you?" she murmured, not trusting herself to look his way.

She hadn't skipped a beat, he marveled. It was as if she had been expecting him. But then, she had always known him better than he knew himself.

All the way here, he had rehearsed what he was going to say. He was going to explain things to her, make her understand that, difficult as it was to admit, he was terrified of getting close to a person. Close enough to be locked out. But he *had* gotten close to a person despite his resolutions. He had gotten close to her.

Now his mind was blank. As blank as his soul had been

these last two weeks without her. He had tried to hold out. Lord knew he had tried, until it had finally hit him. Hold out against what? Against grabbing on to a little bit of happiness? Was he crazy?

Probably.

There were no guarantees in life, but that didn't mean he had to accept living in a void. Some people went their entire lives without having anything to show for it but mundane routines. There was no overwhelming love in their lives, no bombs bursting in the air. No hurricanes with blond manes blowing through their day-to-day existences. He found he had a weakness for hurricanes that started with the letter *A*. He suddenly realized that if he was backing away from a relationship because he was afraid of losing her, well, then, he was just going to have to learn how to fight to keep her *in* his life. It was as simple and as complex as that.

The plague he had once thought was descending upon his life was nothing short of a blessing in disguise.

Why was he just standing there, looking at her like that? Why wasn't he saying anything? she wondered. Suddenly she felt awkward and shy. A first.

"Talkative as ever, I see." She nodded at the chair next to her. "Sit down. I still don't bite."

I don't know about that, he thought, sitting down. "That is a matter of opinion."

She allowed herself a tentative smile. At least they were back on some sort of a footing.

Stop dreaming, she thought. Dreaming was what had started the problem in the first place.

He's here, isn't he? an argumentative voice rose within her, fiercely holding on to this newest scrap of hope. With extreme control, she looked out at the sea. The sea gulls were gone. "How's Nathan?"

"He's fine. Still adjusting." Marcus thought of the talk he and the boy had had last night, the words that had clinched what Marcus was going to do with his future. With both their futures. Strange how sometimes a seven-year-old could see things more clearly than an adult. "He misses you."

She smiled and then sighed. "I miss him." And she did. Missed him terribly. It was funny how quickly some people became a part of her life. A part of her.

The ocean breeze whipped her hair about her face. She didn't bother pushing it aside. It would only fly around again. One didn't win against the wind. Annie glanced at him. Or against set natures.

God, she was beautiful, he thought, looking at her profile. He *had* been crazy to run from her, from himself. Everything in life had a price. If there was a price for this, he'd pay it later. Whatever it was, he knew now that it would be worth it. He found that he couldn't live in his empty world any longer. Not another moment.

He only hoped it wasn't too late.

But how to tell her, how to make her see that he had changed? Maybe he should have brought Nathan with him. The boy somehow always managed to break the ice. Marcus looked down at his clasped hands. Perhaps he should have written her instead. He was eloquent on paper. Thoughts, feelings, always flowed on paper. It was in his mouth that the words seemed to die.

"So." She moved the mug back and forth between her hands. It was cooling rapidly. She tried not to shiver. "Everything's all right with Nathan?"

"Yes."

Any second now, she was going to start pounding on him with her fists. *Talk to me, darn you.* "Is this a social call?"

"Not exactly."

"Then what, exactly?" She tried, unsuccessfully, to keep the growing edginess out of her voice.

"I've, um, come about a rewrite." He felt positively

tongue-tied again and was annoyed with himself for it, but it didn't ease the situation.

She looked at him, her eyes narrowing. Business? This was about business? Of course, why should she have thought differently? *Because you're an idiot, that's why.*

"A rewrite?" Annie shook her head and banged down the mug against the small patio table in front of her with such force that it had her wondering if she had cracked the glass. "That's absolutely impossible."

He wanted to kiss her, to hold her. He sat where he was, watching fury build in her eyes and thinking that she looked utterly magnificent. He had been running from *this?* No wonder she kept losing patience with him. "Why?"

She threw up her hands. "Addison can't possibly want a rewrite. The movie is into production. They're shooting next week. Besides, he would have called me about it. He would have—"

She didn't finish. Instead, she got up, ready to go call Addison at his house.

Marcus caught her by the wrist. She was getting a full head of steam and that always seemed to help spur him on. The survival instinct kicking in, he realized. "Actually," he began, his voice softening, "Addison doesn't want the rewrite—"

Annie swung around. "Then who?" she asked suspiciously.

He spread his hands wide. "Me."

"You?" Annie slid back into her chair, staring at him. "That's doesn't make sense."

"Oh yes it does." He leaned forward and took her hands in his. "It makes perfect sense."

She blew out an exasperated breath, catching her bangs in the gust. "Sullivan, I know you're a perfectionist, but once the movie is filming and the producer is happy, it's time to back off, sharpen your pencils and work on something else." She wished he'd let go of her hands. She was having trouble keeping control of her emotions when he touched her. Shoe on the other foot, she thought.

"I'm not talking about the script."

Now he had lost her. The only path open was one she refused to entertain. She'd been hurt enough by him, and she'd think twice before leaping forward to impale herself again.

"Then what are you talking about?"

"I want a rewrite of my life."

"Oh?" There was her heart, back in her throat again. She had to squeeze the words out. "What sort of a rewrite do you have in mind?"

He didn't answer right away. He wanted to touch her, to feel her face in his hands, to trace the slope of those delicate cheekbones, to reassure himself that this, unlike what he had conjured up these past two weeks, was not an apparition.

He watched in fascination as a faint trace of pink rose to her cheeks. "Something along the lines of a permanent collaboration." She parted her lips. He placed his finger across them. "You don't have to give me an answer right away."

But she wanted to. She knew if she didn't strike now, an opportunity would be lost. "In order to do a rewrite, Marc, I have to know what was there before." She looked into his eyes, searching. He was offering her himself and she knew that she should snatch this moment, snatch this emotion and run, but what if it faded? What if there was trouble down the line? She couldn't fight, she couldn't hold her own against something she didn't understand. She'd learned that once. "Tell me."

She didn't have to say any more than that. He knew what she wanted. He knew he owed it to her. Yet he didn't know if he could bare his soul. "There was nothing before."

No, no, there was no longer time for evasions. A hand

to his shoulder, she tried to coax it from him, for both their sakes. "Marcus," she whispered.

"Now you get formal on me." A cryptic smile lifted his lips for a fleeting second. "I mean it, Annie. There was *nothing*. I wish there was. It would have given me a foundation for what was happening here between us. I never saw any love between my parents, never felt any from them. I was just an extension of what they were, like their cars and their clothes." He paused, trying to thrust aside the memories that suddenly came flooding back, drenching him. "I think it hurt...a lot...to feel what I did for them and not to feel anything in return." Marcus ran his hands through his hair, struggling with his ghosts. "I'm not making any sense."

Now she understood everything, his distance, his fatalistic philosophy. It was all to hide the hurt he kept locked up inside. She ached for the boy he must have been, like Nathan, yet not like him. Nathan had had parents who cared. She wanted desperately to make it up to Marcus. To spend her life making it up to him. "You're making perfect sense."

He looked at her, surprised. She understood. He had rambled and she had understood.

"Only you could say that." He stood up and went to the railing. Now that he had opened up, he had trouble looking at her, afraid of what he would see in her eyes. Would she pity him? Back away? More than anything, he was afraid that she would turn him down. It would serve him right. He had waited too long. But he had needed time to sort things through, time to see that for him, there could no longer be another way. Not if he wanted to be more than just half alive. "Did I tell you that I'm adopting Nathan?"

"No," she said, joining him at the railing. She noticed that the haze was lifting from the ocean. It was going to be another beautiful day. A very beautiful day. "When did you decide?"

"Last night. We discussed it." He turned to look at her. There was nothing but love in her eyes. "He has no objections."

She fell in love all over again, her heart full. "No, I don't see how he could."

He framed her face with his hands. "No barbs?"

She shook her head slowly from side to side, savoring the feel of his hands. "None come to mind."

It gave him hope. "We did a lot of talking last night, about his parents, about how it was all right to miss them and still find things to be happy about. I think he's going to be just fine. Nathan's promised to teach me football."

She laughed. "Brave of him."

"And we need a wide receiver."

Her eyes widened as she pretended offense. "Is that a crack about my bottom?"

"No," he said softly, "that's an observation about your heart."

"Poetry, Marc? That's not like you."

Slowly he let his hand slide down to her shoulders, his anticipation, hopes, heightening as he did so. "I'm not like me when I'm around you. You've changed me."

But she knew better. Annie placed her hands on his chest, absorbing the heat. She'd been wrong about her heart never feeling warm again. "No one changes a person. I just brought things out in you that you've kept hidden."

"You bring out a lot of things." Softly he kissed her forehead. "There's been no sunshine since you left, Annie. And no inspiration. I can't write. Not a word. It's hopeless." The desolation had been utterly overwhelming for him. He had gained nothing by trying to keep her at arm's length and had lost everything. "Marry me, Annie. I love you. You've got to come back."

She entwined her arms around his neck, her heart brimming over. "Twist my arm."

"I'd rather kiss you."

Annie pressed her lips together, pretending to consider that. "You drive a hard bargain, but I'm a magnanimous woman." She grinned broadly. "The answer's yes. It's always been yes."

Marcus kissed her then, stopping any further words. It made her head swim, made the entire world slip away, sea gulls, mist, ocean and all. She shut her eyes tight to keep the tears of joy from falling.

When she opened them again, they were shining, but with a radiance that gave Marcus his final answer.

"I'd like to get to work on the inspiration part as soon as possible, Sullivan."

He swept her up into his arms and nudged the terrace door aside with his shoulder before lightly brushing his lips against hers. "It's about time we started blending our styles again. Let's get to work, partner."

For once, Annie couldn't think of a single argument against that.

* * * * *

Dear Reader,

When I married my college sweetheart, we were barely more than babies ourselves. Wisely we agreed to put off having a family until we were out of college. We knew how much time children could take. After college we decided to wait until we had established our careers. We knew how expensive children could be. After the careers took off we decided to buy and remodel our first home. We knew how much room children needed. After we remodeled the first house we were exhausted. Let's travel, we said, before the children come. We knew how hard it would be to travel with children.

Throughout the years, friends and family would urge us to get started on that baby. We would look at each other and smile knowingly. We knew misery loved company. Finally we ran out of excuses, and on the day of our sixteenth wedding anniversary we welcomed Madeline to our family. Four years later Olivia joined her big sister. And, with their awesome, miraculous births, we learned something that only these precious gifts from God could teach us. No college degree or career, no house or vacation, nothing material this world has to offer could ever equal the magic these beautiful little girls have brought to our lives.

I wish you the happiness and love with your families that we have found with ours.

My best,

Carolyn Zane

THE BABY FACTOR

Carolyn Zane

Dedication:

To the Lord,
with many unending thanks for blessing us
with Madeline Alexa, our own little Bundle of Joy.
Thanks to: My mother, Mary Patricia, for everything....
And to the doctors, nurses and birth class
at Newberg Hospital, who—thankfully—
in no way resemble the characters in this book.

Acknowledgment:
Last but not least, Doug and Bob,
for the brainstorming sessions.

Prologue

"You're pregnant."

Dr. Hanson nodded over his bifocals as he tossed Elaine Lewis's file onto his ink blotter. "Congratulations." He smiled reassuringly at her and, groaning, settled his aging frame into the seat behind his desk.

Elaine blinked and attempted to focus her eyes away from the many framed diplomas and certificates on the wall. She was certain her heart had stopped beating as she digested her obstetrician's staggering announcement.

"Oh." Somehow she'd managed to overlook the obvious symptoms.

However, considering the severe emotional trauma she'd been through this past month, it was no small wonder. Her hands moved stiffly to the expensive silk scarf she wore knotted at her throat.

What in heaven's name am I going to do now? she wondered, numb with shock. She tugged at the colorful knot in an effort to fight back the wave of hysteria that threatened to finally send her over the edge.

This was too much. Her eyes darted wildly around the room as her brain tried to compute and file this latest bit of devastating data.

She was pregnant. With child. She, Elaine Lewis. Single, powerful, network television executive. Pregnant at thirty-three.

This wasn't how it was supposed to happen. This is not what she had planned at all. Although, nothing in her usually well-disciplined life had gone according to plan since the first of the year.

Her voice shook as she leveled her gaze at the older man. "You're sure?"

Dr. Hanson chuckled and folded his hands comfortably over his generous abdomen. "I'm sure. In fact, I want to see you back here in four weeks for your first prenatal visit, okay? Until then," he scribbled quickly on his prescription pad, tore off a sheet and handed it to her, "I want you to take one of these vitamins every day, watch what you eat, no alcohol or tobacco, and keep the heart rate below 120 beats a minute when you exercise. Any questions?"

No. Yes. Was it too late to back out? she wondered frantically, running the palm of her hand over the suit jacket that lay so snugly over her flat stomach. *What have I done?*

"I guess not," she answered dully, as the stark reality of what she now faced began to dawn on her.

"Okay. I'll see you next month then." Dr. Hanson rose from his seat with a broad smile and extended his hand. "Congratulations, Elaine. You've all worked so hard for this moment. I know how happy you must be."

Happy? Unfortunately, Dr. Hanson didn't know the tragic truth yet. She fought the irrational urge to laugh. No, happy didn't begin to describe the barrage of emotions that she felt. She was going to have a baby. Unfortunately she had no desire to be a mother.

Too shell-shocked to even try to explain the mess she now found herself in, she nodded weakly, shook the doctor's hand and headed in a depressed fog toward the door.

Once outside in the parking lot of Chicago Central Hospital, she leaned unsteadily against her Jaguar and inhaled great gulps of fresh, morning air. A stiff spring breeze whipped across the lake, tugging tendrils of hair loose from her smooth chignon and blowing them into her eyes. She fumbled for a moment with her keys and finally succeeded in opening her door.

Rigidly she held her tears in check. She couldn't lose it now. Over the past month she'd managed to hang on to her precious control through the most horrifying weeks of her life.

Her orderly, regimented routine was the only thing that had kept her from a complete and total nervous breakdown. And it would keep her from falling apart now, she thought, angrily swiping at an errant tear that had managed to squeeze past her tightly shut eyes.

Sliding into the leather-upholstered interior of her car, she shoved her key into the ignition and took yet another deep, steadying breath. She would just have to deal with all of this later, she decided, stoutly refusing to give in to the desperation that clawed at her throat. Thinking and feeling were luxuries she couldn't afford. Right now she had to get back to the station and begin producing Chicago's premiere five-o'clock news show.

The show that would still go on, even though she, the producer, was pregnant.

Chapter One

"Elaine?"

Taking a deep breath, Elaine stopped in her tracks and then exhaled in irritation. The last thing she wanted to do was stand in the hallway and make idle chitchat with one of her reporters. Why they called it morning sickness was beyond her, she thought, feeling her cheeks and forehead with the back of her hand. It was late Friday afternoon, and she still felt positively green.

"Yes?" She hoped her tone conveyed her reluctance to dally.

Brent Clark's dark head popped out of the editing bay into the hallway, and he squinted at her through his horn-rimmed reading glasses. "When you have a minute, I need to talk to you." He grinned cordially.

It looked like he had cut his hair with a weed whacker or some other equally blunt-bladed farm equipment. She was going to have to have a talk with him. Maybe out there in corn county—or wherever it was that Clark hailed from—a reporter could get away with that windblown haystack look, but not here.

"Can it wait for a few minutes?" She doubted it would take very long to throw up the crackers she'd managed to eat for lunch. She felt as if they were trying to swim upstream now.

Brent shrugged with the easy-going, laid-back charm that—for reasons that continued to boggle her mind—delighted the Chicago population at large. "Sure." He nodded affably and leaned back to allow his production assistant into the room with a cup of coffee.

The smell of the java was her undoing. "Good," she managed to say, before turning and tearing down the hallway toward the ladies' room.

Brent shook his head slightly and pushed his hair away from his face. If Elaine didn't slow down one of these days, she was going to end up suffering from some kind of stress-related health problem.

"Here, you look like you could use this."

"Thanks, Debbie." Brent took the steaming cup of coffee from the perky, young production assistant's hand and shifted his attention back to the video monitor.

Debbie peered over Brent's shoulder in the cramped editing bay of the newsroom at WCH. "What are you working on?"

"I'm putting the finishing touches on a fire safety series that will air late next month during May sweeps."

"Wow. Some fire," she breathed and scooted in closer for a better look. "This should win the spring ratings battle."

He could feel Debbie's warm breath tickle the hair at the back of his neck. The young girl made no secret of her crush on him, but, as cute as she was, he wasn't interested. She was just a little too fresh off the cheer squad for his blood. "Mmm." Taking a swig of his coffee, Brent shook his head and ran a weary hand over his jaw. "We shot this five or six weeks ago, when that high-rise condo on the shore of Lake Michigan burned down.''

Debbie's wide blue eyes narrowed thoughtfully. ''Oh, yeah. Now I remember.''

''Tragic. Never should have happened. These exclusive high rises,'' he said, pointing to the flaming apartment complex on the screen, ''aren't supposed to burn like that. The local building codes require sprinklers these days. This must have been an older building. Slipped through the cracks, I guess.'' He shrugged.

At times like these, Brent almost wished he'd gone into another profession. Sometimes it seemed like there just wasn't any good news left to report, and the rash of fires he'd covered lately didn't do much to improve his outlook. Today he felt far older than his thirty-four years.

Sighing sadly, Debbie shook her head. ''Didn't a bunch of people die in that fire?''

''Yeah. About a dozen. There were at least six people living on the top floor that didn't make it out.'' Brent searched forward on the tape. ''You can see why.''

The sound of his lanky cameraman flopping down into the seat next to him drew Brent's eyes.

''Man, I'm bushed.'' Ray Freed yawned noisily at the ceiling. ''I'm gettin' too old for these all-nighters. How does the stuff we shot in the wee hours look?''

''Terrific.'' Brent referred to the footage of yet another fire that they had shot late last night. ''You do good work, my man.''

''Too bad The Barracuda will find some reason to rag on it.'' Ray snorted and mimicked Elaine. ''Why didn't you get closer? Why didn't you get some interior shots? Videotape doesn't melt *that* easy.''

''Geez, Ray, why don't you talk a little louder? I don't think they can hear you down in the studio.'' Brent cast Ray a sardonic look and the cameraman grinned sheepishly.

It was true, Brent thought, Elaine was a demanding producer. But she wasn't as bad as Ray made her out to be. She was the reason their show was number one, and everyone knew it. She certainly didn't deserve the title they hung on her behind her back, he mused. Okay, so she was tough as nails, but he suspected that—somewhere beneath her rather unapproachable demeanor—she had a softer side she didn't bring to the station. And, Brent grinned to himself, for a barracuda she had great legs.

Ray glanced around nervously. "Where is Elaine, anyway? I haven't seen her all day."

"She said something about having another one of her mysterious doctor's appointments this morning." Debbie grinned. "Maybe she's having the barnacles scraped off her rusty little heart."

"Or maybe we'll be really lucky and she has a terminal case of lockjaw." Ray twisted in his seat and winked back at Debbie.

Brent's mustache quirked in aggravation. "For your information, she's back. In fact, she should be here in a few minutes. Why don't you guys go find something constructive to do, instead of sitting around griping about the boss?" he muttered, scowling at them.

Throwing her hands up in exasperation, Debbie said, "I don't get you. Why do you always defend her? You know she thinks you're nothing but a country bumpkin. You're her star reporter and she treats you like something she stepped in out in the barnyard."

Brent grinned at Debbie's righteous indignation. It was true. Elaine, when she bothered to notice him at all, tended to peer down her delicate nose at his Iowa broadcast experience. He knew, being the new kid on the block, that he had to pay his dues.

Though sometimes it really rankled him that she saw him in a less savvy and sophisticated light than his hip, happening, designer-clad co-workers. Nobody else held his small-town background over his head the way she did.

However, it was not in his nature to bad-mouth the boss behind her back, no matter how superior her attitude.

"Come on, Deb." Brent remonstrated. "If you can't say something nice..." Although, he had to admit, when it came to Elaine, he could understand how the young woman would be hard-pressed to come up with something. Especially lately.

"Ha," she retorted huffily. "I think you have a thing for Ms. Barracuda. Too bad." She ruffled his overlong hair and looked at him appreciatively. "I bet when you take off these ridiculous glasses, style this mop of yours, trim your mustache and put on an outfit from this decade you're adorable." She turned and grinned at Ray. "The gals in the secretarial pool say his rugged good looks make all the other reporters look like sissies."

"Macho man!" Ray thumped Brent good-naturedly on his large bicep.

Brent squirmed under their scrutiny.

"Yeah. A real heartthrob." She wriggled her eyebrows suggestively. "Anyway," she said, incredulous, "I just don't understand why you always stick up for the one woman who thinks you're a complete corn dog. What is it with you men?" Her sigh was heartfelt. "You need to get your priorities straight, doll face."

"Thanks for the free analysis, but if you don't mind, I have work to do." Just because he didn't want to hop on the gossip bandwagon and play shred the producer, didn't mean he was in love with the woman, for crying out loud. Brent pulled his reading glasses off and tossed them on the table. Stretching, he rolled his head tiredly from side to side and trained a bleary eye on Ray and Debbie. "So," he waved his hands at them, "get outta here, will you?"

Ray clumsily levered himself out of his chair and grabbed Debbie's hand. "I can tell when we're not wanted. See you at The Pub for a couple cold ones tonight, Brent?" The cameraman referred to the small Chicago microbrewery around the corner where the WCH news gang—with the exception of Elaine—gathered every Friday night after work.

"Yeah, sure," Brent mumbled distractedly. "Whatever." Shrugging them off, he went back to his project. It was nearly perfect. Hopefully Elaine would agree.

As he transcribed some of the comments the fire marshall had to say, he wondered why Elaine had gone to the doctor. "Barnacles scraped off her heart." He chuckled to himself and shook his head. Well, even though Elaine could be a complete and total pain in the neck at times, he hoped with all his heart that she was okay.

"You didn't wear *that* in the piece you shot last night, I hope," Elaine snapped, taking in Brent's rumpled appearance. Squeezing into the editing bay, she stood beside him and stared in frank disapproval at his clothing. It had been a long day for her. Nausea, meetings, nausea, doctor's appointment, nausea...she was in no mood to deal with the slovenly work habits of her staff.

Brent shuffled through his notes and nodded absently. "It was dark when I got dressed in the middle of the night, and I was in a hurry. Besides, my clothes are barely noticeable."

Elaine, annoyed at his lack of concern, said, "You could take a minute to turn on the light. You're representing WCH for crying out loud. We have an image to maintain."

Brent's chair squeaked as he dropped his head back and sighed up at her in exasperation. "Elaine, the place was burning down. I didn't have time to worry about making a fashion statement."

Glancing at the image on the screen, she blanched and felt the blood drain from her cheeks. Good Lord. Not another fire. She gripped the edge of the counter and, swallowing the urge to scream, waited for the sudden wave of nausea to pass. It was okay. She was a big girl. She could handle this.

"Well—" she blinked away the last of the black dots that danced before her eyes "—at least get a haircut." Her eyes drifted to the thick, dark locks that fell in an unruly mess across his forehead. "And when you get home, toss the corduroys, okay? It looks like you wore them in high school."

"I did."

Shaking her head she ran a fluttery hand over her abdomen.

She had yet to adjust to this pregnancy thing. And what on earth would her staff think when she announced that she was with child? Farm boy here, would probably drop dead from corn-fed horror.

Maybe she would keep it a secret and let everyone think she was getting fat. What the heck? Just another reason for them to make snide remarks about her behind her back.

"I was just putting the finishing touches on part one of the fire safety series." He punched the Rewind button. "And I wanted to get your feedback. Want to take a peek?"

No! she wanted to shriek. But she couldn't. Instead she glanced at the clock and wished she had an excuse to avoid sitting through a program that—for personal reasons—would be hell for her to watch.

"I guess so." Pulling a chair up beside him she sank tiredly into its seat. "Okay," she said, feeling like a wilted flower, "let's get this show on the road."

Brent shot her a curious look as she fidgeted.

Casting him her haughtiest I'm-your-superior-so-mind-your-own-darn-business expression, she stared pointedly at the screen. "I haven't got all day."

Searching back to the beginning of his piece, Brent leaned forward and nodded at the footage that flickered across the screen. "We got a few really fantastic shots out of some stuff we had on file. And the shots Ray got last night will fill in nicely. Some of these sound bites are real tearjerkers."

Elaine nodded uneasily, and her heart began to pump faster than the images that sped backward across the glowing monitor. She was incredibly uncomfortable with the subject matter of his series.

Even so, she had to give Brent his due. He may have earned his stripes reporting out in the boondocks, but his stuff was always on the cutting edge. Feeling sicker with each passing moment, she tried to feign a serene interest in fire safety.

"I bought a brand new shirt and tie, just for this series." He smiled genially at her as he cued his tape to the opening segment. "No corduroys on camera."

She bobbed her head curtly as the story began. "Good."

Brent's thoughtful, engaging copy drew her into the story as it unfolded, and again she was forced to admit that he was good at his job. They were extremely lucky he'd joined the news team at WCH last year. And, even though his small-town charm and easy-going manner made him a hit with the Chicago audience, she couldn't seem to resist giving him a hard time about being from Iowa. Sometimes he was just such a hick. Glancing over at his frown of concentration, she wanted to smile. Until the images on the screen pulled her back to reality.

As the camera zoomed out to reveal the facade of a flaming building, Elaine stiffened and felt her pulse begin to roar in her ears.

No. It couldn't be.

"Uh, Clark." Calling him by his last name, her voice cracked as she stared in morbid fascination at the screen. "Back up. I want to take another look at that last shot." The sudden wave of sickness that had washed over her had nothing to do with her condition.

Brent backed the tape up and sent Elaine a questioning look.

She felt faint. ‘‘When did you shoot this?’’

‘‘Waverly Towers? About a month and a half ago. You were out of the office for a couple of days, so I never got a chance to show it to you....’’

‘‘I don’t want you to use this,’’ she said suddenly. Trembling so violently she could hardly speak she whispered, ‘‘Take it out, okay?’’

Brent’s brow furrowed in confusion. ‘‘Oh, uh...why?’’

Her head spinning dizzily, she had to force the words past the fingers of doom that squeezed her throat. ‘‘Because I don’t like it.’’

Brent drew his lower lip into his mouth in consternation. ‘‘Hey now, wait just a minute here, Elaine. This scene is integral to the—’’

‘‘I don’t care. Just do it,’’ she barked. Abruptly standing on shaky legs, she walked from the room, leaving him to stare after her with raised eyebrows.

‘‘Another round for my friends.’’ Stuart Aldridge, another of WCH’s evening news reporters, tossed his credit card grandly onto the table and lifted his glass to the group in celebration. ‘‘Here’s to a stellar series on fire safety. May it save many lives, and kill the competition during spring sweeps.’’

Stu saluted Brent and the rest of the WCH crew who had gathered at The Pub after that evening’s show. The crowded establishment was filled to bursting with the Friday night, after-work set.

‘‘I’ll drink to that,’’ Ray shouted above the din and clinked his glass noisily into Debbie’s. ‘‘That series ought to make The Barracuda sit up and take notice. What happened to her, anyway?’’ he asked curiously, and handed his empty glass to the harried cocktail waitress. ‘‘I saw her tear out of the editing bay this afternoon like she was running from a fire. Looked a little freaked,'' he mused, tossing a peanut into the air and attempting—unsuccessfully—to catch it with his mouth.

Brent rubbed his darkened jaw and frowned. ''I don't know. She told me to eighty-six a shot in part one of the fire safety series, and then she never came back.'' Another opportunity to impress her down the tubes, he lamented, and reached for a handful of peanuts.

''That figures.'' Debbie looked disgustedly around the table. ''We bust our butts working late into the night to put together a darn good story to win her all kinds of acclaim for May sweeps, and we don't get any credit.''

''What's this 'we' stuff?'' Ray said crabbily. ''I didn't see you there last night serving up a pot of that sludge you call coffee.''

Debbie pursed her rosy lips in annoyance. ''Hey, I make great coffee. Besides, you know what I mean. Brent knocks himself out putting in overtime, and she doesn't notice. Typical.'' She leaned chummily against Brent's shoulder. ''But I noticed, honey. You were great, as usual.''

''Thanks.'' Brent smiled at Debbie. ''I just hope she's okay.'' He'd never seen his unflappable boss so shaken up.

''She has been going to a lot of 'doctor appointments' lately,'' Debbie confided smugly, tossing her juicy tidbit out to her inquiring-minded audience.

''I'd lay odds on an ulcer. You just can't live at the station the way she does. Any takers?'' Ray tossed some bills into their traditional Friday-night betting pool.

Brent shook his head. ''I think there's a lot more to it than that. She never gets that upset over a simple piece of video.''

Stu snorted. ''What rock have you been living under?'' Opening his wallet, he dug out a bill. ''I've got five that says it's a hangnail. That would explain the thorn in her paw lately.''

''Oh, sure. That would explain everything.'' Brent's

mouth curved in wry humor as he set his glass down and pushed back his chair. The noise, smoke and insipid gossip were beginning to get to him. It was time to call it a day. "I'm beat. See you clowns Monday morning."

"You're not going dancing with us?" Debbie whined, her lower lip protruding petulantly.

"No." Brent stood. "But thanks for the invite. I have some stuff to wrap up back at the station before I turn in for the night. You guys have fun, though."

"You're going back to the *office?* Aww, buddy. Get a clue," Stu advised. "Come with us and let us perk up that corpse you call a social life. We'll show you how it's done in the big city." He high-fived Ray across the table. They bayed and barked at the ceiling, causing the eyes of amused patrons to turn to their table.

"No, thanks." Brent smiled affably and slung his jacket over his shoulder. Big-city night life held no appeal. It was at times like these that he wished he had a loving wife and a passle of kids to head home to, instead of after hours at the station and then his lonely, cheerless apartment. "Some other time." Waving at his rowdy co-workers, he threaded his way through the hazy room and set off for the station.

Brent paused outside Elaine's office and noticed a dim light glowing from under her door. Glancing at his watch, he was surprised at the late hour. What was she still doing here? She worked far too hard. Ray was probably right. If she kept up this pace, an ulcer would be the least of her worries.

He hesitated, wondering if he should poke his head in and say hello. If he mentioned the time, she may take the hint and head home for the weekend. Wherever home was. He didn't know much about Elaine's personal life. No one at the station did. She was an extremely private person.

It was rumored, however, that she didn't have much family. He had that in common with her. And from what he could tell by the schedule she kept at the station, she didn't have much of a social life, either.

Oh, hell, he decided, as he buttoned his down ski jacket. She probably wouldn't appreciate any interference from a lowly employee. Especially from this lowly employee. He could tell Elaine wasn't the type who took kindly to well-meaning advice. "Her loss," he said under his breath.

Reaching into his pocket, he pulled out his wool scarf. The spring evenings still had a bit of a bite, and it had smelled like rain outside.

Better let stubborn bosses lie, he decided, and turned in the dim hallway to leave. The eleven-o'clock news crew was still here. Someone from security would undoubtedly make sure she made it to her fancy sports car in one piece.

As he moved away from her door, he thought he heard the sound of a muffled cry. Cocking his head, he tried to figure out where it had come from. Another sorrow-filled sob reached his ears, and he backed up several paces. Who would be here crying at this time of night? he wondered and waited for the sound to continue.

Again, the haunting, anguished cries reached his ears, leading him directly back to Elaine's door. Someone was crying in Elaine's office. Someone obviously in a great deal of pain. Was it Elaine?

He vacillated.

Should he knock? Or should he just go in? It was a tough call. Knowing Elaine—if it was Elaine—she would probably want to be left alone. Too bad he couldn't summon the wherewithal to force his feet to move. It was a character flaw he couldn't seem to overcome. When someone was in trouble, Brent felt the uncontrollable urge to go to the rescue. No matter how irritating the damsel in distress.

Standing helplessly outside her door, he listened to the pitiful, heart-wrenching sobs. Aww, geez. He hated it when women cried. Oh well, might as well get this over with, because there was no way he could leave now and still have his conscience intact.

At his tentative knock, the crying stopped.

"Yes?" came the feeble query.

It was Elaine.

"Uh, Elaine? It's me, Brent." He could feel his heart pick up speed.

"Oh." She sniffed. "What can I do for you?" she called, her voice breathy with emotion.

He pushed the door open. "I was...uh...just passing by and thought I'd say good-night. Are you all right?"

She eyed him through bleary, swollen, red-rimmed eyes. "I'm fine," she whispered, not convincing either of them.

"No," he said gently. "You're not." She looked like hell, which was amazing to him considering she usually looked like she'd just stepped off the cover of *Cosmo.*

Closing the door quietly behind him, he crossed the room and sat down in one of the plush leather chairs situated directly in front of her large, executive desk. Her office was opulently decorated, the walls adorned with numerous awards and photos of her with various celebrities and local officials. Unfortunately the tragic figure seated behind the desk looked anything but a powerful executive.

"Tell me about it," he coaxed and at the same time wondered what the heck he was setting himself up for.

She didn't seem to notice his breach in office protocol. "No, I'll be all right."

The reporter in him surged to the surface. Brent studied her tear-stained cheeks and knew she was lying to save face for some reason. She was far from all right. In fact, she'd seemed far from all right for weeks now. Call him a masochist, but he made up his mind he wasn't leaving until he found out what the problem was.

Taking a deep calming breath, he decided to take a chance on Debbie's comment about her many trips to the doctor of late. He knew she would probably consider this an extreme infringement on her personal life, but at this point he didn't care.

"Did you get some bad news from the doctor?" His fingers tightened imperceptibly on the arms of his chair, and he hoped that this wasn't the case. Good grief, what would he say if she announced that she was dying?

She shook her head and mopped the tears that welled in her eyes with the sleeve of her silk blouse. "No, really, thanks for your concern, but I'm—" she tried to smile "—healthy."

That was a relief. But whatever it was that bothered her was obviously serious business, and he could see that she needed to talk about it with someone. She seemed so alone.

"Elaine." He spoke the single word with a heart full of compassion. He knew what it was like to be alone, even in the middle of a crowd. "What then?"

Leaning forward in his chair, he braced his elbows on his knees and let his hands dangle between his legs.

As though figuring she had nothing to lose by confessing to him, she slumped pathetically across her desk top and plucked at her damp sleeves. Her breathing was jerky, wracking her slender body as she fought for control.

She stared blankly at Brent and began to speak.

"You know that…um, fire you covered about a month and a half ago?" she asked, her voice barely audible in the intimate hush of her office after hours. "The one I told you to cut today?"

"Yes." He answered softly, not wanting to interrupt.

She opened her mouth to speak, but swallowed a sob instead.

Brent waited as patiently as he could for her to continue, an unknown fear gripping his belly.

Drawing on her waning inner strength, she continued. "I, uh…knew two of the people who died. In fact," she whispered, "I was related to them."

He closed his eyes, feeling her pain. He could understand now, why she'd been so upset recently.

A small, self-deprecating laugh hiccuped past her lips before she choked on another sob. ''And to make matters worse—'' she trained her large, tearful, brown eyes on him ''—I'm pregnant with their child.''

Chapter Two

Elaine twisted the soggy tissue in her hands and surreptitiously studied Brent for his reaction. Thankfully, he didn't look appalled or disgusted at her predicament. That was something she didn't think she could take.

Instead he sat in silence and allowed her to cry. Handing her tissues from the box on her desk from time to time, he waited quietly for her to continue. It was evident that he wanted to help somehow, and curiously, she was grateful.

Up till now, Elaine had never felt the need to confide in anyone. She'd always considered that a sign of weakness. However, as of a month and a half ago, she was left completely alone in this world. No family. No friends to speak of. And, because there was no one else to share her grief with—and because he was there—Brent was elected.

"She was my cousin." Elaine sighed raggedly. Her eyes darted to her hands and then back up to Brent's gentle face. "Sara, and her husband Bobby Johnson, were the only family I had left. My parents passed away several years back."

Nodding sympathetically, Brent drew his ankle up over his knee and settled in to listen.

"I guess there was so much...smoke." Her throat constricted, and she shut her eyes, temporarily unable to continue.

"I know," Brent murmured. He'd been there. He remembered.

"And," she breathed, when she was able to speak, "I never even got to say goodbye. I never even got a chance to tell them—" her voice dropped to a whisper "—about their baby. Oh, dear God." Elaine buried her face in her arms and let the despair overtake her for a moment.

Brent felt his own heart grow heavy with her sorrow.

She looked up to find him watching her, compassion filling his face. Never in a million years would she be able to explain why she suddenly wanted to spill her guts to him. Must be part of the reason he was such a good reporter.

She brushed her hair back from her face and blew her nose, attempting to pull herself together. "They were so young," she continued, and felt her eyes glaze over as the memories flooded back.

"Sara wanted a baby more than anything. Bobby, too." Elaine's smile was tremulous. "Personally, I can't imagine that." She shook her head.

"But Sara was different. The only problem was, she couldn't get pregnant. They tried everything science had to offer. Then Sara got the idea to ask me to act as a surrogate. Bobby agreed since he had no family to speak of, either, with the exception of his mother, and from what I gather she wasn't exactly surrogate material."

Leaning forward Brent nodded and, intent on her words, encouraged her to continue.

"At first I wanted nothing to do with their crazy plan." Her chin tilted stubbornly. "After all, I'm busy with my career. Far too busy to become involved in their problems.

"So they continued to explore other avenues—adoption,

other surrogate options—but nothing seemed destined to work out. All the while, Sara kept badgering me. 'C'mon, Lainey' she'd say. 'Please just consider it. Who better to carry our baby than someone we love?'"

The tiny lines at the corners of Brent's eyes crinkled softly. He leaned his elbow on the armrest of the chair, cupping his jaw in his hand, fully engrossed in her compelling story.

Tears trembled on her eyelids, blinding her as she shook her head. "Anyway—" she sighed and allowed her head to drop against the back of her chair "—when my thirty-third birthday rolled around, I realized I wasn't getting any younger. I knew I probably wasn't the type to ever marry and have children of my own, and something inside of me just seemed to snap. The old biological clock, I guess," she reflected, lost in the past. "Curiosity must have gotten the better of me, because I decided that with this plan, I could have the experience of pregnancy and childbirth, and none of the responsibility."

"Why?" Brent asked, unable to stave off the reporter's need to know. "Why didn't you want to get married and have a family someday?" Shoot, if he could find the right person, he'd love nothing more than to do just that. He'd never be able to understand why anyone in their right mind would actually choose career over family.

She smiled a tiny smile. "That's a loaded question with about a dozen different answers. Suffice it to say that my own mother gave up a brilliant career as a concert pianist to marry my father and raise me. And she never let either one of us forget it." Her laughter echoed hollowly around the room. "She made sure that I learned from her mistakes and did something with my talents. Besides," her smile was defensive, "like my mother, I don't exactly think the wife and mother routine is my forte. And I love my job. I'm good at it."

Brent nodded in agreement. It was true. She was good at her job.

"Anyway," she said haltingly, and steered herself back to the original subject, "it seemed perfect. Her egg, his sperm, my body. I would be able to satisfy my biological urges, go back to my orderly, executive life, and Sara and Bobby would become parents. So we saw a lawyer and drew up an agreement. I wanted to make sure that my responsibilities ended with the birth."

Elaine took the tissue that Brent offered and wiped her eyes. She felt disoriented, lost in the surroundings of her own familiar office. Distant sounds of the city, an occasional siren and car horn, filtered up from the busy city below, where life went on, oblivious to the devastating situation within which she now found herself.

How could it be, she wondered, that the earth continued to rotate and people carried on normally, when her whole world had shattered? It all seemed so surreal. Slowly she lifted her heavy lids and stared at the man who sat patiently waiting for her to finish her story. He didn't seem to be in any particular hurry, she mused distractedly. That was nice. She'd never needed to talk to anyone so badly before.

"I never knew anyone like Sara. So sweet...so gentle. Her mother died when we were kids, and she came to live with me and my folks. She was the younger sister I never had. I think she knew I'd do anything for her. And she was right."

Pushing back her chair, Elaine stood, walked to the window, and stared into the city lights below. Her shoulders slumped pathetically as she leaned against the window casing.

"What am I going to do?" she asked the darkness.

Her torment was more than Brent could bear. Standing, he came up behind her and rested a light hand on her shoulder. "You don't have to do anything tonight."

Elaine closed her eyes for a moment against the soothing

tone of his low voice. She felt a fortifying strength radiate from his warm touch and turned to face him. He was standing so close, she could see the gold flecks in the deep green of his eyes. With the exception of the street noises that sifted up to them from the dusky city, they were alone in the silent world of her office.

She found his steady breathing comforting in its rhythm. Ever so slowly, he ran his hand down her arm and twined their fingers together. A thousand unshed tears pricked the backs of her eyes as she tried to swallow the hot lump in her throat. Why was her heart still beating? Surely a heart that was so badly broken could never sustain life.

"I feel like a part of me...died with them," she moaned, her voice low and broken with misery. "I'm so scared. I don't think I'm strong enough to go on living."

Brent's throat tightened painfully, and unable to fight his instincts, he pulled her into his embrace. Her situation struck a particular responsive chord in him. His own mother had gone through a similar ordeal, and he supposed he could understand better than most how she felt.

Bringing her head against his chest, he rocked back and forth and whispered words of comfort. He couldn't be sure how long they'd stood there, locked together by this tidal wave of emotion, when she finally pushed herself out of his embrace.

Smoothing her sleek, shiny, jaw-length hair, and scrubbing at her face with her shredded wad of tissue, she took a deep breath and tried to mask her pain with a watery smile.

"Thanks," she said attempting to effect an airiness she obviously didn't feel. "I...uh...don't usually fall apart like that."

Shades of Elaine the corporate dragon lady were beginning to reappear. Brent recognized this protective wall for what it was and took a respectful step back. Nodding pleasantly, he decided to let her handle what had just happened between them her own way.

"I'm sorry I...uh, took it out on you, there, uh, Clark." Running her fingers through her dark hair, she took a cleansing breath and strode back to her desk on unsteady legs.

He didn't think he'd ever heard her refer to him by his first name.

"No problem," he said, rounding her desk and pulling his satchel out of the chair he'd occupied earlier.

She turned to face him. "Look, I don't usually bare my soul to a mere acquaintance this way." Pink blotches stained her cheeks; her expression was pinched and drawn.

Brent tried to ignore the sting of her verbal slap. This was just her way of keeping him at arm's length...of coping.

"Um," he nodded blandly.

"And so I'd appreciate it if you kept everything I told you to yourself. I haven't figured out exactly what I'm going to do about...my job and the baby, and whatnot, so until then, please don't say anything to anyone about any of this. Okay?" Her voice carried the clipped tone of an order not to be ignored.

"Sure."

"Good." The word was spoken with breathy relief. Her burst of defiance flagged a little. "Thanks." Removing her coat from the closet, she slipped it over her shoulders.

Brent came up behind her. "If you're ready to go, I'll walk you to your car," he offered, unable to shake the surge of protectiveness he felt, in spite of her prickly attitude.

She seemed to consider his words, then nodded. "All right," she whispered, before she turned out the light and followed him into the night.

"Pssst! Brent! C'mere!" Debbie looked up and down the hallway, before motioning Brent into the employee coffee lounge. Stu and Ray were sitting around a table drinking coffee and shooting the breeze during their Monday morning break.

"What's up?" Brent grinned at Debbie's cloak-and-dagger routine.

Pulling him over to the table, she pushed him into a metal chair and asked, "We just wanted to know... What's the deal with The Barracuda?"

Brent glanced tentatively around the table at the interested eyes of his co-workers. "What are you talking about?"

"Cut the act, Brent." Debbie slugged him in the arm as she took a seat next to him. "One of the guys saw you walk Elaine to her car in the station parking lot late Friday night. And—" she narrowed her eyes "—I could hardly believe this, but he says he saw you *hug* her!" She appeared revolted by the very idea.

"That's right, buddy," Stu said, nodding smugly. "You should know better than to try to pull one over on us news hounds," he crowed. "Hey, if you can get the ice maiden to thaw, more power to you, right guys?"

Enthusiastic fist waving and woofing came from the admiring group at the table.

"Yeah, go for it, Brent," Ray advised, giving him the thumbs-up. "Put a smile on her face. For all of our sakes."

Stu drew himself up manfully. "I'd have done it myself, a long time ago, but—" he grinned at his friends "—she scares the hell out of me."

Ribald laughter rocked the break room, and more bawdy comments were made about Brent's apparent virility in the face of danger. It seemed that although everyone found Elaine physically desirable, her managerial style sent fear into the hearts of mere mortal men.

Last week, he'd have found this conversation as amusing as the next guy, but now, knowing what he did about

Elaine's situation, it just ticked him off. As much as he wanted to wipe the knowing, self-satisfied looks off the faces of the cozy group at the table with the truth, he couldn't. He'd promised Elaine that he would keep her secret. And, as much as it pained him to let them think the worst about her, a promise was a promise. Brent never went back on his word.

He had a feeling they would sing another tune if they were aware of the selfless act of love their so-called Barracuda had agreed to give to a childless couple. A childless couple that had tragically died only a little over a month ago and left her holding the bag.

"Careful, Brent." Stu assumed the role of relationship mentor. "You being an Iowa farm boy and all, she could chew you up and spit you out. Don't want to lose your job, buddy-boy." He leaned forward and spoke confidentially. "But, hey. If you manage to get up close and personal with her, try to get us a raise."

The raucous group laughed and beat the table top.

Brent's brow wrinkled in annoyance. He didn't need their unsolicited advice. He was perfectly capable of holding his own with any woman. Even Elaine.

"So, what's the deal? Are you two an item, or what?" Debbie demanded.

Slowly Brent shook his head and took in the wolfish, interested stares of his peers, and was suddenly turned off. Criminy, why hadn't he noticed how obnoxious these characters could be? Thank heavens he was leaving on vacation next week to visit his hometown. He could use a dose of civilization.

"I don't believe you guys." Letting out a weary breath, Brent pushed back his chair and headed, without a backward glance, toward the break room door.

Birds twittered in the perfumed air of the blossoming trees. Spring was literally exploding in a riot of noisy, colorful life around the cemetery. Two gravestones—a stark reminder that she was well and truly alone—marked the final resting place of Robert Johnson, Jr. and his beloved wife Sara. How incongruous it all seemed, Elaine thought morosely, adjusting her sunglasses to better conceal her grief-ravaged eyes.

It was at times like this that Elaine almost wished she had someone to lean on. Someone to share her sorrow with. Someone who understood her pain. Someone like Brent Clark.

She would never forget his kindness the other night. It was his understanding, sympathetic face that had saved her from dying of a broken heart, she was sure.

A gentle breeze teased the unruly wisps of hair around her face and cavorted in a carefree dance through the treetops. It was so unfair. April marched in, burgeoning with life, seeming to mock the solemn block of granite that bore her cousin's name.

What am I going to do? she wondered, virtually filled with despair. She'd always considered herself to be a strong person, but she knew she wasn't strong enough to deal with this incomprehensible situation all by herself. Her two best friends in the world were gone, and she was pregnant—out of wedlock—with their child. A child she'd neither wanted nor planned for. Dear God in heaven, how had this happened to her?

As she stared, bereft and desolate, at her cousin's final resting place, a feeling of Sara's presence—so strong that it caused her to look around—washed over her.

Words, carried to her on the lively spring breezes and whispered in Sara's voice, filled her head.

Be strong, Elaine. Be strong.

Brent poured a cup of Debbie's thick, murky-looking coffee and found himself experiencing a rare moment of blessed solitude in the otherwise chaotic break room. He had missed the station more than he cared to admit these past two weeks. Even though he'd enjoyed visiting with his mother, Margaret, and his friends back in Iowa, Brent was glad to return to the station. After working for WCH for a year, he'd finally earned a vacation, and at his mother's insistence, spent it unwinding on her front porch, eating her home-cooked meals. But, as much as he preferred her mouth-watering pot roast to his usual fast-food fare, there was nothing like sleeping in his own bed in his own apartment.

For some reason, he hadn't gotten a decent night's sleep the entire time he was in Iowa. It could have been the squishy, man-eating mattress on his mother's Hide-A-Bed.... Then again, it could have been the fact that he hadn't been able to get Elaine out of his head. Every evening, just as he'd been about to catch the train to dreamland, her large, haunted, tear-filled eyes had pulled him back to consciousness. He'd spent a good deal of each day, as well, wondering how she was faring.

He'd been tempted to confide in his mother about Elaine's problem, to get a woman's perspective. For who better than Margaret to understand what she must be going through? But he'd thought better of the idea and had respected her privacy even over the miles.

"You're back."

Elaine's cultured voice pulled him out of his reflections and back to the present. He hadn't laid eyes on her since that night in her office, two weeks ago, and he was surprised at how exhausted she looked. Her usually perfect complexion was marred by dark shadows under her eyes, and her cheeks looked sunken and hollow, as though she'd lost some weight.

This couldn't be good. Not for her. Definitely not for the baby. Once again he felt a magnetic wave of protectiveness toward her draw him under its spell.

"How was your vacation?" she asked, moving behind

him to the coffeemaker, where she fixed herself a cup of herbal tea.

"Fine, fine. Got a lot of rest," he lied. Yeah. About as much rest as she'd obviously been getting, he thought. If she didn't get some sleep pretty soon, she was going to fall over.

"Good," she said, sighing heavily. "I'm glad you're back. We need to talk about November sweeps. I know it's several months away, but I want to be better prepared than we were last fall. Lately, your pieces have done really well in the ratings, so I'd like you to work on something really special for this coming November."

"Sure." Brent sipped his coffee as he followed her to a table and joined her there. "What did you have in mind?" he asked and covertly watched her cross her legs. For a pregnant lady, she had great ankles. Hell, for a fashion model she had great ankles.

"I don't know. We need something big. Something sensational. We're slipping slightly in the ratings, and if we're going to stay on top, we have to pull a rabbit or two out of the hat." Turning, she pinned him with an uneasy look. "I was thinking about something like your, uh, fire safety series. Those are always popular." She swallowed, as though trying to deal with a bad taste in her mouth. "Only this time, maybe you could tackle accidents in the home. It could be interesting if you visited some emergency rooms and got the story from a 911-type perspective. I don't know...." She toyed absently with her tea bag, her mind obviously not on the conversation at hand. "Gang and homicide stories are always popular. Just be thinking about it, okay?"

"Okay." He nodded, although the fall sweeps were the last thing he wanted to think about. As much as he admired the way Elaine was handling her personal crisis so stoically, he wished she could just forget about work for a while and take some time off to heal.

He sat for a moment and watched her stare off into space, wondering what she was thinking about. Whatever it was, it filled her face with a sadness that he would give anything to be able to erase.

As the break room began to fill with the sack lunch crowd, Brent regretted that their time alone together had come to an end. He felt a certain...camaraderie of sorts with her now, since she'd trusted him with her secret, and he'd wanted to ask her how she was doing both physically and emotionally.

Unfortunately he couldn't do that now. No matter. He'd catch her alone at the next available opportunity.

Later that week, after having abandoned the gang at The Pub, Brent returned to the station and tapped lightly on Elaine's office door. He'd seen the dim light of her solitary lamp glowing forlornly from within and decided there was no time like the present to talk with her. Having no idea how she'd receive another late-night visit, he steeled himself emotionally against her wrath. He'd trumped up a weak reason to be there—that he needed her opinion on a story he was working on.

"Elaine," he called softly and opened her door an inch, "It's me, Brent."

"What is it?" she asked, lifting a wary eye from her paperwork and training it on him.

Waving his copy sheets like a white flag, he entered her private sanctuary and crossed the floor to her desk.

He cleared his throat. "I...uh, just thought I'd get your take on this story I've been working on for November sweeps."

"Oh?" She raised a skeptical eyebrow.

"Yeah," he said offhandedly and tossed the papers on her desk. "I need your approval before I go any further."

"You've got it," she said, pushing the copy back toward

him as he settled into one of the chairs in front of her highly polished desk.

"Just like that?" He was surprised. Usually she scrutinized every move he made.

"Just like that." She sighed tiredly.

Too bad she picked now to trust his judgment, he thought, looking at the proposal in dismay. The story he'd proposed was really weak, scratched on a cocktail napkin at The Pub, then pounded out on his computer only moments ago. He was sure that under any other circumstances, she would hate it. It was merely an excuse to see her.

The dark circles still marred the alabaster skin under her beautiful brown eyes. As he took in the subtle signs of her emotional struggle, he wondered how she managed to keep up the high standards of her professional appearance. Although, he guessed, it probably wasn't that hard. She was a natural beauty. She had the kind of gossamer, straight hair that he just knew would be softer than angels' wings to the touch. Not that she would ever let him touch it. No, every inch of her perfect, shapely body screamed "off limits." It was a pity. She reminded him of a priceless art piece kept crated and stored in a collector's closet. What a waste.

Pulling himself back to the business at hand, he said, "Oh...uh, great. Thanks." He picked up his sheets of pathetic copy and, rolling them distractedly, tapped his leg. "So, how are you doing?"

So what if she seemed uncommunicative. What the hell? He was feeling a little reckless. Why not push the envelope?

"I'm fine," she answered primly, in an attempt to stave off any further probing and send him on his way. She was tired, and the curious looks of her staff over the last month had drained her precious reserves.

Brent shook his head, obviously disbelieving. "Really?"

Pulling her lower lip into her mouth, Elaine shook her

head. What was it about his down-home, countrified goodness that made her want to throw herself on her office couch and bare her soul? No wonder people found it nearly impossible not to open up to him and tell all. She felt herself melting under his sympathetic gaze, her carefully built facade crumbling.

Had to be her hormones, she reasoned. She was never this easily persuaded to talk.

Setting her pencil down, she slanted her gaze at him, absently taking in his rumpled clothing and disheveled curls. "No. Not really."

"Been rough?"

"Hell." She suddenly found herself basking in the comfort of his nearness.

"I can imagine."

For some reason, she almost believed he could. For some reason, he seemed to understand.

He twisted into a more comfortable position and plowed his fingers through his untamed mop. "Have you given any more thought to what you're going to do about—" he paused, his eyes locking with hers "—the baby?"

She drew an unconscious hand over her still-flat belly. "No. I'm not sure I can keep it."

Leaning forward he asked, "Why not?"

She shrugged. "Because at this point in time, it's overwhelming. And I didn't sign up for this, that's why." She picked up her pencil and rolled it between her fingers as the silence in the room became almost deafening. "Can you imagine me as somebody's mother?"

"Yes."

"Well, I can't," she snapped and tossed the pencil into her desk drawer. "I'm—" hesitating, she cast her eyes guiltily around the room "—considering my options."

"Which are?" Brent tightened his grip on the armrests, and his breathing became shallow. What the hell was wrong with him? he wondered, amazed at his unusual behavior. It was none of his damn business.

"Adoption." Her eyes darted to his.

Agitated, he leapt to his feet and began to pace the room. "Elaine, this baby is all the family you've got left in the world, doesn't that mean anything to you?"

He knew he had no right to talk to her this way, but he couldn't seem to stop himself. It was the strangest thing, but he felt exceedingly protective of the little life she carried. Again, he thought back to his own mother's similar circumstance, and could feel the slender, delicate thread of common experience that had begun to form between them.

"Of course it does," she whispered, nearly as horrified by the option as he was. "What do you think I am? Heartless? But what choice have I got?"

"Certainly not giving it up."

She flushed guiltily at his earnest expression.

"I think you'd be a great mom." His voice lowered to a nearly inaudible level, and he was amazed to find that he actually believed what he was saying to her. "After all, you're a great boss..."

She snorted skeptically and stared at him. "Why do you care what I do?"

Taking a deep breath, Brent rotated his head from side to side and tried to rub the tenseness from between his shoulders. "I don't know." He ambled back to his seat and sank tiredly into its depths. "I guess..." His voice trailed off and his eyes strayed to the window.

"What?" she pressed.

He continued to stare at the bright city lights, as though mesmerized, and began to reminisce.

"My parents were never married, and I was raised by my mother."

Elaine closed her eyes, shook her head slightly and tried to stifle a groan. She could see where he was going with this already.

Seeming not to notice her impatience, Brent continued. "My mother won't talk much about what happened, but from what little I've been able to gather, she fell in love with a wealthy playboy. But, unfortunately for her, she was from the wrong side of the tracks. By the time she found out she was pregnant with me, it was too late. My father had bowed to family pressure and left my mother for a woman from his social circle, whose name my mother still cannot bring herself to utter." Brent grinned ruefully as his gaze wandered back to her. "It's true what they say about a woman scorned."

Elaine arched a delicate eyebrow.

"Mom won't tell me anything about him or his wife, so I have a pretty limited picture of them. I only know he married someone worse than Satan himself just to keep up his family's image." A deep dimple appeared in Brent's cheek. "Mom's a little bitter."

A ghost of a smile tugged at Elaine's lips.

"Anyway, my mother considered putting me up for adoption. But at the last minute, changed her mind. Instead, she packed our bags and moved us from Chicago back to Iowa, where she was born. She raised me in the same small town where she grew up."

A look of longing filled his eyes. "As much as I regret not growing up in a two-parent household, I guess I really can't complain. Mom was always there when I needed her. I'll always be grateful that she had the courage to raise me. We're still pretty close."

Her troubles momentarily forgotten, Elaine's eyes clung to him as he shared the situation that was so like her own. "She sounds like an extraordinary woman."

"She is."

"Whatever happened to your father?"

Brent shook his head. "I don't have a clue, but I'm guessing he and his wife made a life for themselves somewhere here, in Chicago. Mom won't talk about him."

He could tell he had her interest and leaned forward to drive home his point.

"The way I see it, our situations are somewhat similar. I was raised by a single woman, who contemplated not keeping me, and hey, I think I turned out okay." His mouth quirked in a rueful grin.

The pensive lines around Elaine's eyes relaxed. "Yes," she murmured, "you did."

They smiled at each other for a moment.

"Elaine," Brent's voice was gentle. "Not all children are lucky enough to be born into the perfect situation. I'm living proof of that."

She abruptly averted her eyes. "But they should be." A defensive veil clouded her face.

"It doesn't always work out that way, though. And a loving environment can make up for a lot."

She stiffened. "What are you trying to say?"

He thought back to his mother's brave choice to have him. "Only that I think you should consider keeping the baby."

She squirmed uncomfortably. "I'm not sure it's such a good idea."

"Why not?"

"Clark, I'm not like your mother."

His eyes swept appreciatively over her chic hairstyle and expensive tailored suit. "No, you're not."

"I made up my mind a long time ago. I have no desire to be a mother. I doubt that I ever will."

"Elaine," he looked her straight in the eye, "why don't you sleep on it some more?"

Sighing in exasperation, she began to tidy the mess on her desk, to show Brent she considered the subject closed.

"Clark, I think I know myself better than you do. And—" he stood and nodded curtly at the door "—I'd like to keep it that way. Good night."

Disappointed, Brent walked slowly to the door. "Good night," he murmured with a smile, before disappearing into the hall.

Chapter Three

"You know, I thought she looked like she was putting on a little weight, but I never dreamed she was *pregnant.*" Debbie leaned forward on the break room table, her eyes wide with wonder.

The regular WCH news staff had gathered for their morning break to discuss Elaine's announcement that she was over four months along. Nearly two months had passed since she had confided in Brent, and it had finally become impossible for her to hide the burgeoning truth from her curious staff any longer.

"It was a shock all right," Ray agreed as he refilled his coffee cup before dropping into the vacant chair next to Brent. "Elaine's one of those people you never quite believe is human." He blew thoughtfully into his cup. "The fact that she has a personal life blows my mind."

Brent pretended to stare at the blaring break room TV that was tuned to their station, in a vain attempt to ignore the trite conversation that went on around him. The group at the table reminded him of a pack of vultures circling a fresh kill.

"Man," Stu mumbled around a mouthful of Danish. "Pregnant. Wow."

Yes, Brent decided as he watched everyone buzzing, agog with the deliciousness of Elaine's news, these unfeeling clods needed something else to talk about. In an effort to divert their attention to someone who deserved it, he slipped his foot behind the rear legs of Ray's chair and gave it a quick tug.

Eyes bulging, Ray's arms flailed frantically for balance. He reached for Brent like a drowning man after a life raft, but a final, innocent nudge sent the gangly cameraman backward into a vending machine.

Howls of laughter filled the crowded room as Ray rolled around on the floor and tried to disentangle his long legs from those of the chair.

Debbie rolled her eyes in disgust. "I told you that would happen." She reached for the phone that rang on the wall by her head. "Break room," she shouted into the instrument in an attempt to be heard above the hilarity. "Brent," she called and caught his eye. "It's for you." With narrowed eyes, she mouthed the word *barracuda*.

Brent stepped over the still-prostrate Ray and took the phone. "This is Brent."

The professional, clipped tones of Elaine's voice filled his ear. "My office," she barked. "Now."

"Have a seat." Elaine motioned Brent into one of the chairs situated directly in front of her desk. Her expression was pained as she let her eyes slowly cruise over his attire.

Wiping his hands self-consciously on his blue jeans, Brent crossed the room and took the seat she indicated. He pushed his glasses higher on his nose and wished he'd bothered to tuck in his shirttails before he'd entered the pristine, orderly inner sanctum of Elaine's office.

Something about her cool, tailored appearance always made him feel like such a disheveled hayseed, and that was really beginning to get on his nerves. Dammit anyway, covering the street beat didn't always require pinstripes and wing tips. He'd like to see *her* chase down a story—by showtime, for crying out loud—wearing those impossibly pointy little shoes of hers. She'd be jumping into a pair of sneakers before he could say "fallen arches."

As he sank into his seat, he could tell she was cranking up to nag him about image. Well, he was sick and tired of it. While he was in here, he might as well set her straight on the clothes issue, he thought, noticing her expensive-looking maternity getup. She looked fantastic. But that was her job. He, on the other hand, liked his old corduroys. They were comfortable, and he almost never wore them on the air.

So what if he didn't go for the slick, prissy look of some of his co-workers. So what if he wasn't in touch with his feminine side. In fact, he doubted that he even had one. Big deal. If she thought she could call him in here and rag on him about his appearance again, she could just...

Brent felt his ill humor dissolve as he watched her battle to maintain the tenuous hold she had on her control. She looked kind of strange. Nervous. Worried. Human.

"I heard the commotion in the break room." The mangled paper clip she twisted between her fingertips betrayed the calm tone of her voice. She sighed, and her shoulders slumped in resignation. "They were talking about my announcement at the staff meeting this morning, weren't they?"

Brent shifted uncomfortably. It wasn't in his nature to lie. However, in light of the circumstances, he decided to hedge away from the entire truth.

"Ray was leaning back in his chair, and the hind legs gave way." He grinned good-naturedly, avoiding her question, thankful that for once it wasn't his apparel that was on the line.

"Oh."

"He's always doing something...like...that..." He could tell she wasn't buying his evasive tactics.

"How did they react?"

"They laughed, but then he deserved it."

Her eyes snapped in exasperation. "To my announcement."

"Surprised." Brent's gaze collided with hers. "They were surprised."

"Surprised," she repeated flatly. "I'm sure they were." She dropped the paper clip and rubbed her throbbing temples, "Clark, I'm well aware of the fact that I'm not very popular around here. You can tell me the truth." She regarded him with hooded eyes.

Maybe, he thought. But she looked so vulnerable sitting there, trying to pretend that she was above caring what anyone thought. Brent could, at that moment, imagine what she must have looked like as a young girl. The plaintive expression on her face moved him.

Once again he was struck by the similarity of her experience, and that of his own mother. Both women struggled with a great deal of grief, both found themselves unprepared for motherhood, both were completely alone in the world.

It was just the kind of predicament that—much to his annoyance—brought out the rescuing tendencies in him.

He knew how hard the loneliness had been on his mother. No one should ever have to go through something like that alone. Not even the cranky, obstinate Elaine. He had a feeling that she still didn't fully realize what lay ahead for her. The physical pain of childbirth, the emotional pain of parting with the baby...

"So, have you decided if you're going to keep the baby?" He winced at his brazen question. What the devil was he trying to do? Knowing he was way out of line, he wondered why was he trying so hard to get himself fired these days.

She sent him a beleaguered look. "Not yet."

"Oh." Brent was crestfallen.

"I'm just taking one day at a time."

Brent nodded. That made sense for now, although eventually she would have to make a decision. In his mind, however, there was no question. Babies were a blessing. Especially this baby. It was probably still too soon for her to see that.

Maybe it was because he'd been raised as an only child, but Brent had always longed for lots of babies of his own. And, as soon as he met a woman who had the right combination of maternal instinct and independence, he'd get himself hitched and get started on that family. Why it should matter so much to him whether or not Elaine wanted to keep her baby escaped him, but it did. Not keeping the baby seemed like a big mistake in light of the fact that she had no other living relatives. For crying in the night, didn't she realize how much a person needed a family?

"Have you got a labor coach?" he heard himself unexpectedly blurting out. Even if she gave the baby up for adoption, she'd still need someone to give her a hand at the hospital. She probably hadn't thought about that yet, he mused, and tried to stifle a grin at the look of shock that stole across her regal features.

She picked up her twisted paper clip and regarded him warily. "A what?"

"A labor coach? Someone to help you breathe?"

She was looking at him as though he'd just stepped off a spaceship.

Feeling the need to breathe a little more deeply himself, Brent fumbled awkwardly with the buttons at his collar. "You know, like they do on TV. Hoo, hoo, hee...hoo, hoo..." He felt stupid.

Elaine blew at her wispy bangs, annoyed. "Clark, I've been breathing without any help for the past thirty-three years. Childbirth can't be that hard, people have been doing it for centuries. Why would I need someone to help me breathe, for heaven's sake?"

He waved his hands in an impatient dismissal of her obvious ignorance on the subject. "Because you will, that's why."

Straightening in her chair, she tossed her silky, dark hair away from her face. "I don't know anyone that I would feel comfortable asking. Besides, I'll be fine by myself."

He couldn't believe that, and felt compelled to set her straight. He hoped his candor wouldn't land him in the unemployment line.

"Yeah, right. Come on, Elaine, surely there must be someone you could ask," he pushed. He hadn't just stumbled out of the cabbage patch. He'd learned a lot about the labor experience the time he'd produced that documentary on childbirth for the independent station back in Iowa. "The Miracle of Life." He'd won a couple of awards for that one.

Labor was hard enough with someone in your court. He couldn't imagine the frightened woman behind the desk—who was trying so hard to be brave—going through such an intense experience without someone there to hold her hand. She obviously hadn't thought this through. She needed his expert advice.

Elaine exhaled noisily. "Clark, as you may or may not have noticed, I spend a great deal of time here at the station. I don't have time for a social life, or...close friends. Since—" pausing, she swallowed "—Sara passed away, I don't have anybody. I'd have to hire someone to coach me, and that's just too humiliating."

"Well, it would be a hell of a lot better than going it alone. I don't think you have any idea what you're in for."

Agitated, she picked up her appointment calendar and snapped it shut. "And you do?"

"I have a little background on the subject. This will probably be the hardest thing you've ever done, and I think you're going to need some help."

Quirking a delicate eyebrow, she stared down her nose at him. "So, why is it, Clark," she asked, settling back into her plush, leather desk chair, "that you happen to know so much about childbirth?"

Brent feigned offense. "You mean you didn't see my award-winning documentary on childbirth? It was a big hit back in Iowa."

She smiled ruefully. "Sorry, I don't get the hayseed channel where I live," she scoffed.

"Too bad. You missed out," he said dismissively, eager to get back to the topic of her own situation. "Elaine..."

"Brent, why don't you just quit while you're ahead, okay?"

The woman could be so hard-headed, he thought, exasperated.

Changing the subject, she picked a file up off her desk and opened it. "Why don't you tell me about that project you're doing for fall sweeps?" she suggested, and looked expectantly at him. "If we're going to win the ratings game we need to get moving on it."

Uh-oh. She was referring to that bogus proposal he'd said he was working on that night in her office. He'd forgotten all about it. In fact, he couldn't even remember the idea. Something about the importance of flossing? Whatever it was, it certainly wouldn't win the ratings game. No. He needed to come up with an award-winning plan. And judging by the increasingly impatient look on Elaine's face, it would seem that he needed to do it now.

Too bad he didn't have another "The Miracle of Life" up his sleeve. His gaze wandered to Elaine's softly rounded midsection. Or did he?

Clearing his throat, he said, "Oh, sure. I thought we could do a series about childbirth. Like "The Miracle of Life" documentary I did in Iowa? It got a lot of critical acclaim. Of course," he cast her a sideways glance, "you'd have to have the hayseed channel to know that."

She frowned. "Miracle of Life?"

"Yes." He leaned forward, suddenly enthusiastic. A wild idea was beginning to form in his head. "It won a bunch of awards, and it's perfect for November sweeps." He feigned innocence. "I thought that's why you approved it."

"I did?"

"Sure did." He reminded her about the night he'd asked for her approval. "You didn't exactly study the copy, but you seemed to think it was a good idea," he said, bluffing.

Elaine squinted skeptically. "Refresh my memory."

"Well..." Brent's mind was racing. It was perfect. He knew that this time around, he could do an even better job on this series than he had in Iowa. He'd learned a lot the first time, and had countless ideas for the new and improved version for the Chicago audience. Talk about ratings. Elaine would have him knighted when he was finished with this piece. And, the best part of all, it would force Elaine to start preparing for the birth of her own baby. However, this would take some pretty tricky footwork to get her to agree.

"Basically we follow a woman and her labor coach through the pregnancy and labor. It's really emotion-packed stuff. The audience eats it up. Nobody can resist a baby. That's why they use them in advertising all the time," he said, improvising. "Babies, puppies and uh...sex are all surefire sales tools."

"Do tell," Elaine said dryly. "And just who were you planning on having play the part of the pregnant woman?"

"I thought we agreed that you would do that."

"What?" she gasped. "No way."

"Oh. Well, in that case I don't see how we can get the

thing done in time for November sweeps.'' He shook his head sadly. ''We need to get started right away. It would be so convenient to use you as the talent.'' Pinching the bridge of his nose, Brent racked his brain for plausible reasons to convince her to play the part. He knew it was the only way she would ever take any help in the form of a birth partner.

''I don't remember agreeing to any such thing,'' she said suspiciously.

Ignoring her skepticism, Brent decided it was time to pull out the big guns. ''Elaine, think of the ratings. Come on. This is a sure thing.''

She looked torn, he was pleased to note. He should have known that the way to her heart was through the numbers.

''Okay.'' She sighed. ''I'll buy that.'' Pulling a pencil from behind her ear, she pointed it at him. ''But there's no way I'm going to give birth in front of the Chicago general public.''

''I promise, the way I'll do it, no one will ever know it's you.''

Tenting her fingers in front of her lips, she attempted to hide the smile she felt threatening. ''Just how do you propose to work that little problem out? Have me wear a wig?'' As much as she hated herself for giving in to his enthusiasm, she knew he was right. It was a great idea. Having someone to help her over the rough spots when the time came was just an added bonus.

He laughed. He could tell that she liked the idea from an audience standpoint. ''No,'' Shaking his head, he explained his idea. ''We'll do it from the mother's perspective. She is the camera, so to speak.''

''Brent, I don't want a camera crew in the labor room with me.'' The thought of the ill-mannered pack down in the break room capturing her *en deshabille* for posterity was just too mortifying to contemplate.

"No problem. We'll set the camera up on a tripod, lock it down and let it roll."

"We?"

"Elaine, somebody has to set up the camera. And—" he went in for the kill "—the way I have it scripted, somebody has to be your labor coach. That's why," he lied, "I was wondering if you picked someone out for that job." Taking advantage of her nonplussed expression, he continued. "But, since you don't have anyone, and since I'll be there with the gear anyway, I should probably just act as coach." He frowned thoughtfully, hoping she would go for it.

Brent held his breath. It was important to him that she have a labor coach, and someday, if he was lucky, he just may figure out why. But for now, he'd just go with his reporter's instinct and rely on the fact that it was good for Elaine and the baby to have a coach. And since nobody seemed to be rushing forward to volunteer, he would just take on the responsibility himself.

All of the women in his documentary had sworn that they never would have gotten through labor without the support of a good coach. After seeing an actual labor, he could see why. It was a painful experience. Elaine had no idea.

Hadn't she been through enough lately without adding a solo labor experience to her list of hardships? Yes, he decided, looking into her large brown eyes. Those eyes that had haunted him day and night since he'd learned of her pregnancy. She'd gotten under his skin. Maybe he could work through it by helping her, he reasoned.

Elaine stared at Brent. "The Miracle of Life" idea had definite appeal. Especially at this stage in her life. Everything he was saying made perfect sense, and she supposed that's what scared her. Good heavens, he wanted to be her labor coach. She hadn't even realized she would need one. Then again, she supposed it would be possible to fill the

Library of Congress with all she didn't know about having babies.

She guessed she should be grateful that anyone was interested in coaching her at all. Even if it was only in order to get a story. She tried to quell the wave of loneliness that suddenly settled over her.

In some respects she imagined he had a point. She was definitely not looking forward to labor. Sara had wanted to be with her in the delivery room in the original plan. Her heart twisted painfully at the memory of her young cousin's excitement over the prospect.

It was a moot point now, she thought grimly, looking at Brent's boyish face. His youthful appearance belied the mid-thirties she knew him to be. Something in his gentle expression reminded her of Sara's husband, Bobby. He'd been a cockeyed optimist, too.

What did she have to lose? Nothing it seemed. And she had everything to gain, if Brent knew what he was talking about.

Her response was solemn. "Okay."

"Okay?" Like the sun peeking out from behind a cloud, Brent shot her a disarming grin and beamed at her. "Great. When do we get started?"

Elaine's lips twitched in exasperation. Dammit, how the heck should she know? He was Mr. Miracle of Life. Not her.

"What do you mean, 'get started'? The baby isn't due until October. This is only the end of May. We can get started on the details of this whole thing sometime at the end of summer. Until then, you work on your part of the program, and," she patted her stomach, "I'll work on mine. Sometime around Halloween, I'll call you and we'll go to the hospital and breathe. Okay?" There. That seemed simple enough. Perhaps this wouldn't be so bad after all. She strode around her desk, sank into her seat and considered the matter settled.

It wasn't.

"Ohhh-nooo."

She watched Brent remove and begin to thoughtfully polish his reading glasses. Why on earth did he wear those hideous things? she wondered. Someone should tell him he'd look much better in contacts. Without those nerdy horn-rims, he wasn't that bad looking. Although, she decided, as her eyes dropped to his upper lip, she wasn't much on mustaches.

"What, ohhh-nooo?" she asked, mimicking him.

He grinned. "You can't just march into the labor room and start breathing."

"Why not?"

"Because that's not the way it works. You have to take classes to learn how to breathe. I'll get you a copy of the proposed idea," he told her, knowing that he would be up all night typing. "That will really help you understand why you have to go to birth class."

"Class? You're kidding." Elaine blew impatiently at a wisp of hair that tickled her cheek.

"No. And listen, you'll be glad you took them when the time comes. You'll learn everything you need to know about delivering this baby. Anyway—" he leaned forward enthusiastically, warming to his subject "—you'll need to take a series of classes for about seven or eight weeks and—"

Elaine cut him off. "Seven or eight *weeks?*"

"Sure. Don't worry, I'll be there, too," he said, oblivious to her horror, "gathering information for the series. And I should probably take you to a few of your doctor's appointments as well. You know, so that I can get to know him and anticipate any problems we might have."

Noting her dazed expression, he laughed. "Don't worry, Elaine. We'll only shoot footage of the labor. Tasteful footage," he promised. "The rest of the classes and doctor's appointments are just for background information. We'll leave the camera out of it. It will all come together and be just great, trust me.''

Looking into his clear green eyes, she was surprised to realize she did trust him. More than she cared to admit. As he continued with his enthusiastic plans, Elaine, for the first time in weeks, began to feel her spirits rise.

She—of all people—was having a baby. With a country boy cowpuncher as her labor coach, no less. Maybe it would all work out after all.

It certainly couldn't get any worse.

''Mom? It's me.'' That night Brent went home to his apartment and rooted the phone out from under a pile of laundry. He hadn't talked to his mother in over a week, and after his planning session with Elaine that afternoon, he suddenly had the urge to hear her voice.

''Hi, honey. How's it going?'' Margaret Clark's youthful tones carried across the miles, bringing him home to Iowa.

''Fine.'' He sighed and lifted his feet up onto the stack of newspapers that flowed over his coffee table. ''Just wanted to hear your voice.''

''That's nice, honey,'' Margaret sounded skeptical, ''but you don't sound fine. What's the matter?''

He never could pull anything over on her maternal radar. ''Nothing, really. It's just...''

''Just what?'' she pressed.

''Mom, what was it like when you found out you were pregnant with me?''

''Oh, Brent.''

He could tell that, as usual, she had no desire to discuss the past. ''Humor me, Mom.''

''It was such a long time ago. What could it possibly matter to you now?''

''I have a friend in a similar situation, and I need to know.''

Margaret was silent so long Brent was beginning to wonder if she'd hung up. "Brent? This friend of yours... You're not the father, are you?"

Brent chuckled at her obvious mortification. "No, Mom. You can relax. I just work with her. Right now she's all alone in the world, and I was wondering how I could help. Thought maybe you could shed some light on the subject."

"It does sound familiar," Margaret mused. "Poor thing. What's the story here? Did the father leave her for another woman?" Her voice was filled with a bitterness that was years old.

Apparently Margaret still hadn't forgiven the evil socialite that had married his father. He knew better than to quiz her about either of them. Nothing would bring their conversation to a screeching halt faster than to ask her anything about his father or his scheming wife.

"No. Nothing like that. It's a long story, but suffice it to say that she has no one but me right now, and maybe it's because of you...I don't know, but I want to help."

"You're a sweet man, Brent," Margaret said with obvious pride. "I must have done something right when you were growing up. I would have loved to have had a friend like you when I was in her shoes."

"You would have?"

"Most certainly." Her voice took on the melancholy quality it always did, whenever she allowed herself to travel briefly down the path to the past. "It was probably the loneliest time of my life. I was frightened and ashamed. But," she said, sounding almost amused at the irony of her words, "I had my anger to keep me going. And then, of course, there was you. The sweetest, most adorable little boy in the whole state of Iowa."

Brent's nose wrinkled tolerantly as he pulled his reading glasses off and tossed them on the table. "Mom, please."

"Sorry. Anyway, how is it that you're going to be helping this poor girl?"

He'd never heard Elaine described as a poor girl before.

That would most certainly get her undies in a bunch, he thought, grinning to himself.

"I'm going to be her labor coach. You know, support her in the labor room when she delivers the baby. Help her breathe, hold her hand, that kind of thing." He wasn't sure why, but he didn't feel like telling his mom about the series of reports on childbirth they were planning.

"My, my. The times they are a-changin'." Margaret laughed. "Well, good for you. That sounds just fine."

"It does?"

"Sure. It will probably do you some good, too. Get you into the swing of things. You spend far too much time by yourself, since you moved to Chicago." She paused. "Or do you? Have you met anyone and started dating yet?"

Brent hated to disappoint his mother. She was always nagging at him to find some nice girl and settle down and give her a bunch of grandchildren. And, he would like nothing better himself. The trouble was finding someone who fit the bill. There weren't very many single, sharp, independent thinkers who shared his interest in his career—kind of like Elaine, he mused—who also shared his desire to have a big family. Unfortunately, that was where he and Elaine parted viewpoints.

"No, Mom. Not dating anyone. But you'll be the first to know," he teased.

"Oh, sure."

They both knew he'd cut the apron strings when he was still in short pants. Brent never had been a mama's boy, much to Margaret's mutual pride and regret. They chatted for a while longer, catching each other up on their separate lives. Then, after bidding his mother a fond good-night, Brent lay, sprawled out on his couch and drifted off to sleep, dreaming of chubby babies with Elaine's big brown eyes.

* * *

"Hi. Come on in." Elaine motioned Brent into her stark, designer-perfect house.

Brent glanced around the sterile interior, wondering where on earth she would ever fit a child among the expensive art pieces and gleaming white carpet.

"Can I get you something to drink? Juice? Mineral water?" Her eyes wandered to his Cubs baseball jersey and faded jeans. "Beer?"

"No, thanks." Brent glanced pointedly at his watch. "We should probably get going. We don't want to keep the doctor waiting...unless you want something?"

"No." Her lips curved ruefully. "My teeth are floating as it is."

They'd taken the warm spring afternoon off to attend Elaine's first ultrasound appointment at twenty weeks, and Dr. Hanson had advised a full bladder for the best possible view of the baby.

Her hands fluttered nervously to her linen blazer, and she tried unsuccessfully to button it. "You don't have to do this," she said, giving him an out. "I can go by myself. I won't mind. Really." She searched his face for signs that he'd changed his mind about doing the story. Part of her almost hoped he would. And part of her was terrified that he would.

Brent smiled warmly. "Of course I do. I'm really looking forward to it." Truth be told, he was more excited about this appointment than he'd been about anything in a long time. A little baby seemed so...refreshing. Especially in light of the depressing news stories he reported day in and day out.

Relief seemed to sweep over her as her button finally found its proper hole. He could see that she was glad he was coming along, although he knew she would never admit it. It went against her grain to depend on anyone for anything. Letting him in on this private experience would take some getting used to for someone like Elaine.

"Okay, then." She took a deep, cleansing breath. "I'm uh—" placing a hand lightly on her swelling abdomen, she stole a glance at him "—a little nervous."

He nodded in understanding and took a step toward her. "You don't have anything to be afraid of. I remember when we shot the documentary, that ultrasound is a piece of cake."

"Oh, I know."

"What is it, then?"

"It's probably silly," she explained, averting her eyes to inspect her spotless carpet, "but I'm worried that he might find something wrong with the baby. I—" she pressed the back of her hand against her pale cheeks in a gesture that spoke of her fear "—don't think I could handle that."

Tiny jolts of joy chased each other down Brent's spine and into his stomach. She was beginning to care about the baby. Would she consider keeping it as well? Maybe there was some hope after all.

"Well, there is always that chance. But it's a small one." He reached out and tugged on her sleeve. "Try not to worry, okay?"

"Okay."

"Other than that, how are you feeling?" He didn't like the look of the dark circles that still shadowed her eyes.

"Fat," she retorted, eyeing her thickening middle.

Brent laughed and threw a companionable arm around her shoulders. "You don't look fat."

She looked tentatively up into his face. "Really?"

"Really. In fact, you look quite—" He wanted to say *sexy*. In his mind there was nothing sexier than a woman blooming with the life of an unborn child. Especially when that woman was the already-sexy-as-hell Elaine Lewis. "—businesslike."

"Thanks." She sighed and turned to inspect his attire. "I just wish I could say the same for you. Well then, come on," she ordered, taking charge in her usual style, "we don't want to be... Oh!'' Eyes wide, her hands flew to her stomach.

Brent's heart leapt to his throat. ''What?'' he barked, fear filling his gut. ''What's wrong?''

''I'm not sure, but I think—'' a tiny smile began to tug at the corners of her mouth ''—I just felt the baby move.''

A sudden grin split Brent's face. ''Are you sure?''

Taking his hand, she guided it to her abdomen and pressed against it with her own. ''You tell me,'' she murmured, wonder filling her eyes as she gazed up at him. They both stood silently, barely daring to breathe for fear they'd miss the tiny signs of life.

And then, like the first, tentative green shoots poking up from the ashes of a forest fire, they felt it.

''Well,'' Brent whispered in awe, ''I'll be darned.''

Chapter Four

"Hey," Brent admonished, as he took in the white-knuckled death grip Elaine had on her handbag, "try to relax, will you? You're about ready to tear the handle off your poor purse."

Smiling apprehensively over at Brent, Elaine made a concerted effort to compose her runaway fears and set her handbag on the floor next to her chair in Dr. Hanson's waiting room.

"You're right," she breathed, willing her pulse to slow. "It's just that I've never done this before, and I'm nervous. I mean, what if he finds some kind of problem? I'm not exactly a kid anymore." Filled with anxiety, her eyes locked with his, seeking reassurance.

Laughing, Brent reached over, took her cold, fragile hand in his large, warm one and gave it a squeeze. "Elaine, no amount of worrying is going to change anything. Lighten up. You're not exactly over the hill—yet," he teased, attempting to distract her.

"Yes, well, I am still your boss, Clark. Remarks like that could get you into trouble." A tiny smile played at her lips.

"Listen," he murmured. "You're going to be just fine."

"Provided my bladder can hold out." She sent him a baleful look. "What's taking so darn long, anyway?"

Glancing over at Dr. Hanson's grumpy receptionist, she smiled insincerely and, lowering her voice, confided in Brent. "I think she does this on purpose. It's a power trip," she griped, thoroughly annoyed at being made to wait.

Brent nodded conspiratorially. "Her eyes do seem a little beady."

Swinging her head toward Brent, Elaine caught him smiling at her in that lazy cowpoke way of his and bristled. He was making fun of her. Although, as much as she hated to admit it, it was good to have him along. Her hand, still clasped tightly in his, drew her eyes, and she could feel his calming presence travel up her arm and begin to work on her frayed nerves.

"I guess that where you come from, out on the farm, having a baby is probably no big deal." As gracefully as she could, she extracted her hand from his.

An easy grin tipped the corners of Brent's mouth.

"But," she said, "to me, it's..." Pausing, she groped for the words to explain how she felt. "It's just that it's a mystery to me. I know that to most women this is a natural, beautiful experience. But I'm not most women." She searched his face for understanding and, thankfully, found it.

"Why don't you just try to think of this appointment as part of the research we're doing for our November sweeps project, instead of a doctor's appointment," he suggested.

"Okay," she sighed, liking that suggestion. Work was something she knew about. "Have you got your notepad?"

He nodded and tapped his pocket.

"Ms. Lewis? The doctor will see you now." The grandmotherly nurse smiled broadly at them and held open the door that led to the dreaded hallway beyond.

"It's about time," Elaine muttered under her breath, and grabbing her purse, allowed Brent to help her to her feet.

His hand rested comfortingly on her lower back as he guided her to the examining room that the nurse indicated.

"Here we are," she chirped cheerfully and ushered them inside. Picking up Elaine's chart, she waved them into the chairs that were situated against the wall. "Dr. Hanson will be here in a moment, but first I want to find out how we're doing."

"We're bloated and ugly," Elaine sighed, as the nurse slipped the blood pressure cuff over her arm.

Chuckling good-naturedly, the older woman winked at Brent. "They all say that," she said. "But I think pregnancy enhances a woman's beauty."

"Me, too," Brent put in boyishly, leaning forward for a better look at the proceedings.

Eyes twinkling, the nurse noted the reading on Elaine's chart. "Well now, isn't she lucky to have you?" She patted Brent fondly on the shoulder as she motioned for Elaine to hop up on the scale.

Elaine grimaced. It was obvious that Nurse Grandma here was under the misguided impression that they were a couple. And Brent, grinning like an idiot, played the role of proud papa to a tee.

"Good girl," he said to Elaine, when the nurse made positive comments regarding her moderate weight gain and low blood pressure.

She felt her cheeks grow suddenly warm. Never before had one of her staff called her a "good girl." It was clear that she was going to have yet another talk with him. He was carrying this reporter/labor coach thing a bit too far. Although, she decided, as the nurse continued to put her through her medical paces, in some respects it was rather nice.

Still, she didn't want him becoming too emotionally involved. For heaven's sake—*she* didn't want to become too emotionally involved. That's what had landed her in this predicament in the first place. No, getting overly wrapped up in this whole thing would only make it that much harder when it came time to give the baby up. She sighed as a feeling of melancholy overtook her. Why did life have to be so complicated?

"Here you go, honey." The nurse handed her a paper gown. "Take off your clothes and put this on. Dr. Hanson will be here in a moment."

Unfolding the ridiculously small square of tissue, Elaine stared after the retreating woman's back.

"I'm supposed to wear this?" she asked incredulously, holding the crinkly garment up for Brent's amused inspection. "It looks like something I'd use to blot my lips. She must be kidding."

"Better put it on. The doctor will be here any minute," Brent advised, and sitting back in his chair, prepared to enjoy the show.

Clutching the paper to her chest, Elaine vigorously shook her head. "Oh, no. I'm not putting this thing on in front of you." She pointed at the door. "You can wait out there."

Brent snorted, not budging. "For the love of Mike, Elaine. Don't you think your modesty is a bit misplaced, considering what we're going to be doing together in a few months?"

Her fiery cheeks paled. She hadn't thought about the more delicate aspects of this coaching business. How could she gracefully back out of their agreement now? The sudden mental image of giving birth with Brent in the room was extremely disturbing. However, even more disturbing was the fact that she was beginning to rely on his involvement in this experience.

Giving birth in front of one of her employees may not

be high on her list of things to do, but then again, neither was going it alone. At least not anymore.

No, she huffed, kicking off her shoes, Brent had gone and made himself indispensable. He had a way of doing that, she noted churlishly, reflecting on his outstanding talents as a reporter.

"Besides," he continued affably, "I'm a farmboy, remember? I've seen it all."

The glint in his eyes told her that he wasn't overly impressed with her silly prudishness.

"Hurry up. Don't want the doc to catch you in the altogether, now, do you?" He pinched the corners of his mouth between his fingers as though trying not to laugh.

Once again, she had the feeling he was poking fun at her. Gritting her teeth, Elaine impatiently shook out the paper gown, unfurling it in his direction. "The least you could do is cover your eyes," she snapped.

"Yes, ma'am," he drawled and tipped the brim of an imaginary cowboy hat at her.

Elaine had no sooner stripped and scuttled into her less than proper attire, when there came a knock at the door.

"Are you decent?" Dr. Hanson called.

Brent snickered.

"Shut up," she groused at Brent, and in a louder voice invited the obstetrician to join them.

Dr. Hanson came into the examination room and grasped Brent's hand in a firm handshake. "I'm so glad that you'll be here for Elaine. This has been a very stressful time for her. Your support means a lot."

Brent nodded. "Just let me know how I can help."

The kindly physician had been extremely sorry to learn of the Johnsons' death and had taken a special interest in Elaine's case.

After the introductions had been made, Dr. Hanson set to work preparing the ultrasound equipment, and then dimmed the overhead lights. Turning the video monitor to give Brent a better view, he instructed Elaine to make herself comfortable on the examination table.

Clutching the sides of the table—as though it might decide to run away with her—Elaine lay back so stiffly that anyone who didn't know better might assume that rigor mortis had set in.

"Try to relax," Dr. Hanson urged, frowning as he began to scan her belly for signs of the baby.

Elaine let go of the breath she'd been holding and glanced uncertainly at Brent. As she tried valiantly not to panic, Brent reached out and pulled a stray wisp of hair away from her lower lip, and then traced its fullness with the pad of his thumb.

"Come on now, honey," he coaxed, scooting his chair up next to her and whispering soothingly in her ear, "take a deep breath."

"I didn't know I'd need you to help me breathe at the ultrasound," she quipped, her voice sounded shaky and feeble even to her own ears.

Squeezing her arm, he chuckled. "See? I told you it would come in handy."

After what seemed like a lifetime, Dr. Hanson finally smiled. "Ah, here were are."

Unable to contain his excitement, Brent leaned forward over Elaine and peered at the video screen. Together they watched in amazement as the outline of what looked like a perfectly formed little spine came into view.

"That's your baby's back," Dr. Hanson informed them, before moving around to show them a set of miniature feet.

Fumbling around in the darkened room, Elaine found Brent's hand and twined her fingers with his. It was well and truly the most miraculous sight she'd ever seen. Her throat constricted tightly with some nameless emotion. Slowly, Dr. Hanson took them on a guided tour of the tiny life, pointing out each incredible new body part as he went.

Brent pointed in fascination at the baby's image. ''What are those flashing dots?''

Dr. Hanson paused and pushing a button, magnified the view. ''That's the baby's heartbeat. I'll turn on the audio so you can hear it...''

Crackling noises filled the room as he adjusted his sound equipment. ''There's a lot of static,'' he commented, searching for the elusive pulse of life. ''Probably because you're so nervous.''

Elaine tightened her grip on Brent's hand.

''Relax,'' Brent murmured, squeezing back.

''I'm trying.'' Her voice was breathy with emotion, as her eyes clung to his. ''Really. I'm trying to be calm so I can hear it. But,'' she whispered, ''it's so hard.''

Gently Brent smoothed her hair away from her face. ''You're doing great,'' he encouraged.

Elaine closed her eyes and concentrated.

Listen hard, Elaine.

Once more Sara's voice echoed whisper soft in her mind, filling her with an overwhelming sense of peace.

The static on the audio monitor suddenly became rhythmic. Whoosh, whoosh, whoosh, came the delicate cadence.

Slowly opening her eyes, Elaine found Brent watching the image on the screen, his face mirroring her own sense of wonder at the magic of life. Whoosh, whoosh, whoosh. Together, they listened, awestruck. There were no words in the English language that could ever explain the intense poignancy of the moment.

Misty-eyed, Brent smiled at her with incredible tenderness, before leaning down to kiss her gently on the forehead.

Whoosh, whoosh, whoosh. The little heartbeat was strong.

Hear your miracle, Elaine.

Elaine took a ragged breath, as one by one the tears ran down her face.

* * *

"Well, will you look at that?" Stu pointed toward the front entryway of The Pub. All heads at the usual Friday-night table swiveled, following the direction of his finger through the smoggy throng.

There, clutching her small handbag to her chest and looking like a lost child, stood Elaine. Brent felt a tingle of excitement run down his spine at the sight of her. Somehow, in the darkened examination room of Dr. Hanson's office that afternoon, he'd bonded with her—and her baby. It didn't matter to him that the bond was one-sided. Big deal. So she wasn't the bonding type. He glanced around at the tight little clique at the table and decided he liked that about Elaine.

He was delighted to see her.

"What the hell is she doing here?" Ray wanted to know, bringing the front legs of his chair to the floor with a thud.

"Slumming." Dismay tarnished Debbie's gamin features. Huffing noisily, she plucked the paper umbrella from her drink and stuck it in her hair at a saucy angle.

The muscles in Brent's jaw worked in agitation as he listened to their catty comments. Elaine had just as much right to be here as they did. Although why she'd want to subject herself to the inane nightlife of The Pub puzzled him. The smoke, not to mention the lukewarm reception of the WCH staff, should be enough to drive her back to the safety of her office. Especially in her condition.

Catching her eye, he smiled warmly and, much to the chagrin of the folks at his table, beckoned her to join them. Relief seemed to flood through her body as she tentatively returned his smile and began to thread her way through the crowd toward their table.

"Brent," Debbie hissed, under her breath. "What are you doing? We come here to get away from the office, you big goober."

"The party's over," Stu warbled and grinned as Ray began to hum along.

Brent's eyes narrowed threateningly. "Can it," he ordered and, looking back up at Elaine, pulled an extra chair over to the table.

Wound as tightly as a toy soldier, Elaine woodenly approached the gaping group and wondered what in heaven's name she'd been thinking. She didn't belong here. She didn't fit in with these people. Dollars to doughnuts they thought she was out of her mind, and she didn't blame them.

It had seemed like such a good idea back at the office. Friday night had loomed so depressingly ahead of her, and with nothing better to do than go back to her sterile home and feel sorry for herself, she'd decided to take a chance on finding Brent.

Still high from the emotional experience she'd shared with him that afternoon, she got the silly idea that he might want to talk about it. Now she wasn't so sure. Obviously he had his own life—she glanced uneasily at the perky young Debbie's pouty expression—and his own friends.

Brent moved around behind her and offered to help her with her coat.

"Oh, no," she said, suddenly changing her mind about socializing with Brent. "Really, I can't stay." She knew her smile was probably tighter than a pair of control-top panty hose, but she couldn't help it. Her mind reeled, searching for a plausible excuse for showing up uninvited like this. An annoying blush stole from her neck to her cheeks, sending heat all the way to the top of her head.

"Oh, that's too bad," Debbie murmured and nudged Ray with her knee.

Pretending not to notice, Elaine swallowed against her wounded feelings and turned to smile brightly at Brent. "Actually," she said, bluffing, "I wanted to check briefly with you about some questions I had about your November sweeps piece.'' Her voice trailed off as she ran out of steam. ''So, if you have a minute?''

''Sure.'' Brent sent a departing scowl over his shoulder at Debbie, and followed Elaine toward the door. ''You have a question about—?'' he started to ask as they reached the street.

''That's okay,'' she said, interrupting. She didn't have any questions. She just wanted the sidewalk to open up and swallow her whole. ''It's nothing that can't wait till Monday. Really.'' She studied her shoes.

''Oh.'' He smiled winsomely at her.

''Well... I should probably be...going.'' If she hurried, she could probably make it home in time to wash and dry her hair. ''I also just wanted to let you know that I'm considering taking your advice.''

His brow furrowed in confusion. ''Oh?''

''Yes. About, you know, keeping the baby...''

Brent's face glowed with surprised pleasure. ''You are?'' he breathed, quite obviously thrilled at the prospect.

''Thinking about it, yes.'' She smiled.

''Hey, this calls for a celebration,'' he crowed, oblivious to the interested stares of passersby. ''Let me take you out to dinner.''

Elaine's heart hammered against her ribs. ''Now?''

''Sure! Why not?'' His laughter was giddy.

''What about your friends?'' She nodded at the front door of The Pub.

''They're not invited,'' he said with a grin, and not waiting for her to refuse, hailed a cab.

''You what?''

''I signed us up for a breast-feeding class.'' Pulling his napkin across his lap, Brent smiled sheepishly at Elaine across the candle-lit table of the small Italian restaurant.

Realizing her jaw was hanging open, Elaine clamped her lips shut and scowled at Brent. ''When?''

"Yesterday," he admitted. "It might come in handy for the story. And, I had a feeling you might change your mind about keeping the baby." His smile could light up a ballpark.

"Oh, you did, did you?" Her expression softened. Why not lose herself in his enthusiasm for a moment? she reasoned. Life had been dismal enough lately. Feeling a tiny bubble of joy rise into her throat, she decided to go with the flow tonight. After all, life seemed to go on, whether she wanted it to or not. Might as well try to enjoy it.

"Yeah," he mumbled around a mouthful of antipasto. "I'm really glad. You're going to make a great mom."

"What makes you so sure?"

He stopped chewing and regarded her with solemn eyes. "You remind me of my mother. She's beautiful, bright and tough as nails. Kind of like you."

"I'll take that as a compliment."

"Oh, it is." He winked lazily at her.

Elaine wriggled in her chair. *He thinks I'm beautiful?* The guy really was a cornball. Nobody in their right mind would ever classify her as beautiful. Not with this case of midriff bulge. Why then, under his unfathomable gaze did she suddenly feel so attractive?

Get a grip, she sternly told herself. He probably looked at a new tractor with the same admiration. Still, it was nice to hear a personal compliment. With her social life, they were few and far between.

"So," she said airily, attempting to steer the conversation to safer ground, "you signed us up for a breast-feeding class." Okay, maybe not safer ground. Different ground.

"Umm-hmm." He popped a green olive into his mouth and chewed thoughtfully. "I've been doing some reading about the subject."

Good heavens. She stared at Brent, mystified. He never ceased to amaze her. Why hadn't some nice girl snagged him and given him a batch of children. "You have?"

"Yep. Did you know that on the average, breast-fed babies are eight IQ points higher than bottle-fed babies?" His face was animated as he dug a pamphlet out of his jacket pocket and handed it to her across the table.

"No. I...can't say that I did." She stared at the pink paper she held in her hand. "Breast-feeding Made Easy," it read. Elaine rolled her eyes. How hard could it be?

"Well, they are. Plus, it's really healthy, for you and the baby. Don't worry about having to go alone. Birth partners are encouraged to attend. See—" he pointed at the back page "—it's a two-day deal. Pretty neat, huh? We'll learn everything we need to know about feeding little peanut."

"Peanut?" she asked, still stunned that he had taken this on himself. Whatever happened to her resolve to keep him from getting too involved? she wondered absently. Maybe she should tell him no on this thing. Then again, maybe the birth coach was supposed to get somewhat involved. Hell, she didn't know. This was all new to her. At any rate, it probably wouldn't hurt to explore the breast-feeding issue. But a two-day class?

"Two days?" Frowning, Elaine looked up from the etching of the serene Madonna figure happily pressing her babe to her breast. "What on earth could take two days to learn about?"

Brent shrugged. "Lots of stuff. Breast pumps, how to hold the baby, colic, you know, lots of stuff. Come on, it'll be fun."

Elaine sighed. "For you, sure. A class about breasts is bound to be interesting."

Chapter Five

Scrambling like a contestant on a game show, Brent dashed through his apartment, attempting to put it into some semblance of order before Elaine's arrival. Unfortunately, he lamented, as he stopped his whirlwind of activity and stood listening to the incessant ring of his phone, he couldn't remember where he'd stored that particular item. He finally managed to home in on the sound and rescued the poor instrument from under a pile of mail that littered his desk.

"Oh, hi, Mom." Tucking the cordless phone between his shoulder and ear, he opened a desk drawer and shoved great piles of debris inside before squeezing it closed. "What's up?"

"Nothing," Margaret Clark's smiling voice filled his ear. "I just called to say hi. You sound a little out of breath."

"Yeah." Opening the hall closet, Brent kicked his jacket inside and slammed the door before an avalanche of sports paraphernalia could escape. "I'm—" he huffed, picking his coffee table up and tilting it into a waiting wastebasket "—cleaning house. I've got…company coming."

"Oh?" Margaret's interest was piqued. "Company."

Brent sighed. He didn't have time to go into it now. "Yeah. Remember? I told you about Elaine Lewis. The producer of the five-o'clock news."

"Ah, yes. The pregnant one."

"The one." Grinning, Brent strode to his kitchen, opened the cabinet under his sink and began loading it with a mountain of dirty dishes.

"Brent, try washing your dishes once in a while, will you?"

He glanced around in amazement. How did she know? She was in Iowa, wasn't she? "Yes, ma'am."

"So, you're having company." Margaret was never easily dissuaded from discussing the possibility of a relationship for her bachelor son. "I take it this friendship is blossoming?"

"Mom, I hate to disappoint you, but I'm just her labor coach." This was true enough, although lately, he'd caught himself daydreaming about Elaine in a most uncoachlike way. Not that he'd ever confide his fantasy life to his mother. "She's going to meet me here any minute now. We are going to our first birthing class."

"Already? How far along is she, anyway?"

Pausing, Brent counted on his fingers. "Let's see. This is August, and she's due the end of October, so…I guess about seven months, more or less."

Margaret hummed thoughtfully. "How is she doing? Last time we spoke, you told me she was finally beginning to recover from the death of her cousin."

"She has her days, but she's working through it." The doorbell rang. "Listen, Mom, she's here. I gotta go."

"Okay, honey. Have fun at birthing class." Margaret chuckled and rang off.

He jammed the antenna back into his phone and raced

to the door. Pausing for a quick glance in the hall mirror to check his appearance, he threaded quaking fingers through his unruly curls and tried to get a handle on his emotions.

But it was hard. Ever since the day of the ultrasound, he ceased to be simply a reporter researching a story. Over these past weeks, he'd done his best to remain detached. This was no time to develop a thing for his pregnant boss. Elaine had made it perfectly clear that she had no room in her life for a serious relationship. The fact that she'd decided to keep the baby was a major concession to her usual free-wheeling, workaholic life-style. He knew that for her to make room for a man, as well, would be too much of a stretch. At least at this point.

However, try as he might not to let it bother him, it did. She was going to need some help with this baby. Unfortunately she was just too hard-headed to realize it yet.

Besides, when—and if—the time came for Elaine to go man hunting, it wouldn't be for a guy like him. When she did find time to date, she probably went for those slick-haired yuppie types.

With a momentous effort, Brent managed to swallow the sudden feelings of jealousy that squeezed his heart at the thought of another guy taking his place with Elaine and her baby.

Inhaling deeply, he decided he could wallow in self-pity another day. Right now, he had a birthing class to attend.

"Hi," he breathed, feeling like a teenager in the throes of his first crush as he pulled open his door and invited her into his home. He hoped it looked presentable. He'd never been much of a housekeeper.

"Hi," she answered, entering his apartment and glancing curiously around at his lived-in living room.

Suddenly flustered, Brent closed the front door behind her and, bounding over to his couch, grabbed a newspaper off the cushions. "Here, you should probably sit down."

"Thanks." Following him, Elaine perched awkwardly at the edge of the couch. She smiled nervously up at him. "So. Birth class."

"Yeah. Birth class." He adjusted his reading glasses and glanced at his watch. Claiming the seat next to her, he said, "We're a little early, still. Can I get you something to drink?"

"Sure."

Brent sprang to his feet and headed to the kitchen.

"Actually," her voice startled him, as she peered over his shoulder into his refrigerator, "I'd prefer some ice cream, if you have it."

The corners of his eyes crinkled in amusement as he glanced back at her. "Ice cream?"

Nodding, Elaine pulled open his freezer. "I can't seem to get enough of the stuff. I never cared about it before, but suddenly it's so...*good.* Any flavor will be— Clark—" she turned and shot him a funny look "—what are your tennis shoes doing in the freezer?"

Damn. How was he supposed to know that she'd go snooping around in his kitchen? Next time, he'd just leave the place a mess. "I like to keep them there. They stay fresher..." he explained hurriedly as he pulled a carton of fudge ripple out of the freezer and slammed it shut before she could discover his sweat socks.

Elaine looked at him skeptically and took a seat at his kitchen table. After he'd loaded up a bowl for each of them, he joined her.

"This should be fun." He winced. Where was the clever repartee he'd rehearsed in front of the mirror all week? Why was he suddenly feeling so shy? Shoot, he'd never worried this much about making an impression on her at work. Maybe he should try remembering that the truth of the matter was, he *was* at work. Elaine viewed his part in this whole thing as nothing more than research, and that was probably how he should view it, too. But it was so hard, he thought, watching her tongue rim the lucky spoon she held in her hand. It sure didn't feel like work. He tightened his grip on his own spoon and began shoveling his ice cream into his mouth.

"Umm." She nodded noncommittally.

They ate in silence for what seemed to Brent like an eternity. Unable to stand it any longer, he racked his brain for something interesting to say. This uncomfortable silence was not what he'd planned as he'd prepared for her visit that afternoon. No, he'd envisioned a far different scenario in which he would amuse her with his snappy, quick-witted humor. And she, for the first time, would begin to see him through different eyes.

"You have the pillows?" Oh well, so much for the witty repartee she probably indulged in with her high-falutin social circle. But heck, anything was better than the silence that threatened to deafen him.

"In the car. Clark—" amusement dimpled her cheeks as she pointed at him with her spoon "—you're not going to ask a bunch of silly questions tonight, are you?"

Silly questions? He stopped eating and looked at her. "What are you talking about?"

"Like you did at the breast-feeding class." She laughed. "I thought I'd die when you asked how I'd feed the baby if I broke both my arms."

"That wasn't such a dumb question," he retorted defensively.

"Okay, then how about when you whipped out your calculator and estimated the per day cost of each breast pump?" She giggled over another large spoonful of fudge ripple.

"You want to be sure you get the most bang for your buck on equipment, Elaine." He glared at her.

Elaine nearly lost her mouthful of ice cream. Eyes dancing with mirth, she leaned forward, teasing him. "Well, when it came to nursing the baby doll with the plastic breast, I have to admit, you had us all beat.'' She hooted with glee. ''Are you going to include that scene in your November sweeps series? The ratings will definitely go through the roof.''

''Oh, for crying out loud. Are you done with that?'' He pointed at her empty bowl.

''Yep.'' Still giggling, she pushed her dish over to him and watched in amazement as he bent down and stuffed it under his sink with the rest of his dirty dishes. ''Don't tell me,'' she said dryly, ''they stay fresher down there.''

Grinning, he crossed the room and pulled her to her feet. ''Something like that.''

So much for getting her to see him in a new—and improved—light, he thought resignedly. Dropping a companionable arm over her shoulders, he led her to his front door.

Elaine's gaze cruised apprehensively around the eclectic array of parents-to-be that filled the classroom at Chicago Central Hospital. To say that it was an interesting group was to put it mildly. She glanced over at Brent as they took their seats and was suddenly—and exceeding—grateful for his strong, solid presence. She knew Brent was right, that taking these classes was the proper thing to do. She was also aware that it took all kinds to make a world. But, good gracious…just what had they gotten themselves into?

Clutching the pillows that the literature had advised they bring, she settled in next to Brent, and wished once again that Sara and Bobby could be here to share in what was, by all accounts, supposed to be an awesome learning experience.

Then again, she decided, scrutinizing the diminutive, aging nurse who strode purposefully to the head of the class, perhaps this experience was more the fearsome variety.

''Hello, everyone, I am Ruby Shocktaag,'' she barked, ''no nonsense'' deeply etched into lines on her time-weathered face.

A half a dozen or so expecting couples, including Brent and Elaine, sat in a semicircle facing the chalkboard that hung on the wall up front. After scratching her name in huge letters on the board, the tiny dynamo turned to face the class and smiled rigidly.

"When I call the names," she ordered in her heavy, Latvian accent, "you will tell me you are here, no? Then tell little something about yourself. We must get to know each other, because perhaps I will be with you when you give birth." Snatching a pencil from her tightly coiled bun, Ruby tapped it against her pointed nose and stared with razor-sharp eyes at her clipboard.

Elaine swallowed and blinked at Brent. For heaven's sake, wasn't giving birth scary enough without Nurse Shocktaag and her militant bedside manner? She nervously nibbled her lower lip.

As if reading her mind, Brent smiled reassuringly and took her hand.

Ruby touched the tip of her pencil to her tongue. "Mary and Dick Olsen?"

"Yo," Dick shouted. The balding man grinned Cheshire cat style at the group. Not a large man to begin with, Dick's tan polyester leisure suit appeared to be at least two sizes too big. "I'm Dick, and this is Mary," he bellowed and threw a casual arm around his equally tiny, and terminally shy, wife. "I'm in sales. Cars. This—" he pointed proudly at Mary's middle "—is our first."

Dragging her eyes from the fascinating Mr. Olsen, Elaine darted a quick peek at Brent and unconsciously tightened her grip on his hand. The slight lift at the corner of his mouth was her only indication that he found Dick as unusual as she did.

Ruby's nod was curt. "Vicky and Jason DuShane?"

"Here." Jason DuShane said, his voice cracking, and he promptly turned a brilliant shade of crimson.

Why, he's just a baby himself, Elaine thought sadly, staring at the gangly teen. Maybe her situation wasn't a dream scenario when it came to giving birth, but at least she was old enough to vote.

Shielding her face with her hand, she grimaced covertly at Brent and knew he received and understood her private message. And as much as she wanted to deny it, she was beginning to like his ability to read her innermost thoughts. It was kind of fun to have somebody to gossip with. Somehow it kept her from feeling quite so alone. Although it was almost eerie the way he could tune in to her thought processes.

But then again, any reporter worth his salt should be able to do that, she reasoned, attempting to shrug off the warning bells that sounded in her head. Bells that cautioned her against letting anyone get too close.

"And this is my wife, Vicky," Jason gestured awkwardly toward the homecoming queen at his side, "and this is our first." Giggling, she snapped her gum and thumped Jason's arm in girlish embarrassment. "We're still in school...." He stared at his shoes.

Bobbing her head imperceptibly, Ruby scratched a check mark on her roll sheet. "Liz and Danny Martin?"

Liz smiled placidly at her rotund husband, whose wild hair and beard flowed unfettered over his leather jacket. She tossed her own waist-length hair over her shoulder and raised her hand.

"Here. I'm Liz and this is Danny. We own a motorcycle shop. And this is our first baby, too." Danny's affable grunt could have signaled anything from a casual greeting to a bad case of heartburn.

Elaine nudged Brent with her elbow. Suddenly her unusual predicament seemed almost normal, in light of the interesting cast of characters that made up their birthing class. His answering nudge was playful.

"Brent and Elaine Clark?" Ruby's hawklike eyes scanned the group.

Elaine opened her mouth to speak, but before she could set the authoritative Ruby straight on their marital status, Brent spoke up.

"Here." He smiled genially at the group. "I'm Brent Clark, and this is Elaine. We work for the news department at WCH here in Chicago."

Marking them present, Ruby went on to the next couple.

"Clark," Elaine whispered warningly and pulled his ear down to her mouth, "what are you doing?"

"What's wrong?" he whispered back.

For someone so in tune with her every thought, he could certainly be obtuse. "They think I'm having your baby," she snapped, scandalized.

"Big deal." His brow knit in annoyance.

Grabbing a handful of his midnight curls, she tugged his ear back to her lips. "It *is* a big deal. You're a local celebrity…kind of. What happens when word gets out that I'm having your baby?" Good heavens. He hadn't even kissed her yet.

Yet? Where had that come from?

"Fine." He sighed in exasperation. "As soon as she's done, I'll explain that you're a surrogate mother, and I'm a reporter here to gather information for a show we're doing."

Okay, she thought, loosening her hold on his earlobe and looking around the room. So he had a point. No use going into detail about their particular circumstances. Pursing her lips she squinted at him through narrowed eyes.

He grinned and much to her dismay—and pleasure—kissed the tip of her nose with all the indulgence of a typical father-to-be.

Elaine squirmed uncomfortably. She really shouldn't enjoy his company so darn much. It's just that his neophyte charm had a way of getting under her skin.

He really was a good guy, she mused, comparing him to the other male members of the group. Compared to Brent they were all pretty lame. Personally she couldn't envision herself married to any of these oddballs, let alone giving the world an oddball junior. No, she decided as she counted the gold chains that ornamented Dick's furry chest, she was definitely the luckiest woman in the room.

Suddenly realizing that she'd been woolgathering for quite a while, Elaine hoped that Brent had been paying attention and tried to catch up with the lessons that had gone on without her.

"...and breathing is of utmost importance," Ruby announced. "With pillows you bring to class, take seats on floor."

Brent shot Elaine an I-told-you-breathing-was-important look, as he helped her out of her chair and onto the pillows she'd brought along.

Following their tiny dictator's instruction, Elaine leaned back against Brent and tucked the pillows under her legs. She could only hope, as he rested his hands comfortably around her blossoming waist, that he couldn't feel the resounding thunder of her heartbeat. What came so naturally to every other couple in the room seemed exceedingly intimate to Elaine. She could feel his breath tickling the back of her neck. He was so warm, she noted, settling gingerly into position. And so soft. No, hard really. Hard and soft. And warm. She hated herself for noticing how wonderful, and how right, it felt to recline into his embrace. It had been so long since she'd been held.

Nurse Shocktaag marched to the middle of the floor and crouched into a ball.

"I am the contraction," she thundered and slowly returned to an upright position. "Come now. Breathe with me." Jerking her body back into a ball, she puckered her thin lips and began to exhale. "Contraction is beginning now! Hoo, hoo, hee!"

"See?" Brent arched a superior brow.

"Yeah, yeah, yeah." Elaine rolled her eyes.

Ruby looked at them sternly. ‘‘Mr. and Mrs. Clark! No time for talking. Hoo, hoo, hee.’’ She made the words sound like firing bullets.

After what seemed to Elaine like an inordinate amount of practice, the class finally mastered the art of hoo-hoo-heeing and moved on to hee-ha-hoo and an assortment of other varied and uninteresting breathing patterns.

Then, as part of that evening’s grand finale, Ruby ordered everyone back into their seats and turned to face her class.

‘‘Now we will get to know each other a little bit. We will go around to see what each man thinks of becoming Daddy, and why he is taking class with Mama,’’ she announced. ‘‘Jason, you will begin,’’ Nurse Shocktaag informed the red-faced teen.

Elaine’s head snapped up. Oh dear, she thought wildly, what were they going to do? Brent wasn’t becoming Daddy. He was just along for the ride. Maybe they should leave. She scanned the room for the nearest and most unobtrusive, exit.

All eyes in the room focused on the visibly shaken Jason.

‘‘I’m…uh,’’ he squeaked, ‘‘mostly scared. But then, I don’t have much to go by.’’ His youthful voice carried the weight of the world. ‘‘My old man split when I was just a kid.’’ He paused and glanced at his young bride. ‘‘I’m here to learn how to help Vicky. I guess I’ll just try to do my best.’’

‘‘Good.’’ Nurse Ruby nodded. ‘‘Dick?’’

The bantamweight car salesman sat up straight in his chair, his chain-link chest expanding pridefully. ‘‘I’m attending because Mary here twisted my arm.’’ Dick chortled gleefully, enjoying his own peculiar brand of humor.

‘‘All kidding aside—’’ his thoughtful frown was practiced ‘‘—I think having a kid will be a giant kick in the head. Can’t wait to meet the little beggar. But to tell the truth, I’d rather sit in the waiting room when the time comes and let Mary here do her thing. But, hey, if she needs me, I'm there. Know what I mean?'' His brash laughter filled the silent room.

Ruby scowled. ''Okay. Danny?''

Danny grunted and adjusted his leather jacket over the Grateful Dead insignia on his T-shirt.

''Uh, I'm here to try to convince Liz that we don't want to try this at home. She has it in her head that a hospital would give the kid bad karma or something. Also, I think she should go for the drugs.'' His bushy beard twitched in amusement. ''Hell, I would.''

''Thank you, Danny.'' The muscles in Ruby's jaw jumped spastically as she swung to face Brent. ''Brent?''

Closing her eyes tightly, Elaine braced herself for whatever her pseudohusband might get it in his head to say.

Brent let his gaze wander slowly around the room, a soft smile adorning his gentle face. Leaning forward he braced his elbows on his knees and pulled Elaine's hand into his lap.

''I think that being there to welcome a tiny new life into the world,'' he began, ''will probably be the most powerful, humbling experience I'll ever have. It's such a mystery...I seriously doubt that there is anything on this earth that will compare to the feeling of holding a newborn child in my arms for the first time.'' He spoke in a tone filled with awe and respect.

''To me, being a father figure means being there. To help mend broken hearts and to help make dreams come true. To hold and comfort them when they're scared of the dark.'' His expression was sympathetic as he looked over at Jason. ''Never leaving.''

Tears brimmed into Elaine's eyes, and she felt her throat suddenly fill with a hot lump. Sara would have loved him.

Brent sighed, his honest expression filled with the hope of his small-town upbringing. ''In my line of work, I see so much sorrow and despair. But the way I look at it, babies, so pure and innocent, are a gift from heaven. It's like…everything is shiny and new. I don't know," he shook his head and smiled at Elaine, "they give me hope. I wouldn't miss this for anything. I'm here to support Elaine. And when the time comes, to be there for the baby."

Ruby Shocktaag's face relaxed into a soft smile for the first time in probably fifty years.

"Thank you, Daddy," she whispered, before moving on.

"Stop it!" Elaine squealed, wiping the tears of mirth that streamed down her cheeks. "I mean it, if you don't quit, I'm going to have this baby right here in your car."

Brent pulled his car to a stop near the spot where Elaine's Jaguar was parked in front of his apartment. Jumping out, he rounded his vehicle and, pulling open his passenger door, helped Elaine—still laughing helplessly—to her feet.

"Hey, Shecky, get the jet. I'm outta here!" he yodeled, continuing his impression of the flamboyant Dick Olsen as he took her by the elbow and walked with her to her car. It was a mild summer evening, and the scent of newly mown lawns and flower blossoms followed them through the twilight to her waiting Jaguar. He stood patiently while she tried to pull herself together enough to locate her keys.

"Yes, no, yes, yes, no," he muttered under his breath, as she dissolved into laughter, abandoning the search through her purse. He was feeling buoyant, not just from the birth class experience they'd just shared, but from the easy camaraderie they'd fallen into on the way home. The atypical mothers- and fathers-to-be, provided an endless source of fodder for making Elaine laugh. He loved her deep, throaty laugh. It was sexy as hell.

Giggling, Elaine hiccuped. "Would you just *stop?*"

"Yes, no, yes, yes, no." Brent grinned and grabbed her purse out of her hands. At the rate she was going, they'd be out here in the parking lot all night. "Don't mind me, I'm just..."

"Matching you to a car!" they both crowed in unison, then fell against each other in paroxysms of laughter.

"What on earth was that man talking about?" Elaine referred once again to the tiny car salesman with the big voice, her eyes dancing up into Brent's.

He looked down into her relaxed expression and was once again struck by how beautiful she could be. It had been a long time since he'd seen her smile like this. "I don't know, but half the time I got the feeling he was communicating with another world." Brent fished the keys out of her purse and handed them to her.

Taking her purse from him, she looped its handle over her shoulder and leaned back against her car. "Can you believe he's going to be that poor kid's dad?" She ran her ignition key over her full lower lip.

Unable to stop, Brent found himself staring, mesmerized, at the thoughtful gesture. "Almost makes me grateful for my fatherless childhood," he murmured teasingly.

"You know, the sad thing is, he wasn't the nuttiest guy in the bunch, either." Elaine caressed her tummy with a protective hand.

"True, but at least he seems to care."

"Yes," she admitted, "he does seem to care."

Not wanting the evening to end, but at the same time unsure about inviting her in for coffee, Brent racked his brain for ways to keep her from going home. "How about that couple, what was their name? The ones that dressed exactly alike?"

Her merriment rippled through the fresh summer air. "The Harlows? I thought they looked cute."

"Oh, sure. Come on, they looked like pigs in a blanket and you know it."

"Brent!" Elaine gasped with surprise.

His face flushed with pleasure. He wondered if she realized she'd called him by his first name. "Well, really, Elaine. When you wear matching brown sweatsuits at this stage of the game, you're asking for trouble. Can you imagine us dressing exactly alike?" His observant gaze roamed over her lush figure.

"Well, no, not exactly, but you haven't got Mr. Harlow's beer belly, either." She returned his bold inspection, letting her eyes flick over his trim waist and narrow hips. "Actually," she teased, "I think you'd look good in something like Dick wore tonight."

"Ha. I may have terrible taste in clothes, but even I'm not that bad."

"No," she agreed. "You're not." Her eyes drifted up to his. "Not bad at all."

"You're not so bad yourself, little Mama."

"You think?" she asked, and he could feel her need for his reassurance. The kind of reassurance that only a man can give a woman.

"Mmm. Not bad at all."

He reached up, as she leaned back against her car, and traced her jaw with his fingertips. He loved this vulnerable side of her personality. It was a side that she so seldom let steal to the surface of her corporate persona.

"Thanks," she whispered up at him. Twining her fingers with his, she captured them in a gentle squeeze between her cheek and shoulder. "And, thanks for going with me tonight."

"I wouldn't have missed it for the world," he said and knew that it was true. Wild horses couldn't have kept him away. And unfortunately it was beginning to feel as though those same wild horses couldn't keep him from making a colossal fool of himself right now. Because it was at that moment he knew he had to kiss Elaine or die trying.

To hell with the fact that she was his boss. His pregnant boss, at that. And to hell with the fact that she fancied him to be nothing more than a hick from the sticks. There had been far too much happening between them. He needed a physical outlet for the connection he felt with her. Hoping against hope that she would understand, or at the very least let him keep his job, he rested a palm on the roof of her car and lowered his mouth to hers.

Chapter Six

Elaine could scarcely believe that she was allowing one of her reporters to kiss her good-night, let alone the fact that she was enjoying it so...immensely. She was seven months pregnant, for heaven's sake. She had no business enjoying herself this way.

And with Brent Clark, of all people. What on earth was the world coming to, she thought fuzzily, loving the feel of his mustache as it tickled her upper lip. Closing her eyes against the hazy fog that swirled around her dizzily spinning head, she clutched his well-muscled upper arms and leaned into him for support.

"Lordy, Lordy," she whispered against his warm, supple mouth. The man sure could kiss. Merciful heavens, he must have put in a few very heavy practice sessions with some neighbor girl or another out behind the barn.

"Pardon?" Brent breathed raggedly, as he briefly tore his lips from hers only long enough to rain kisses down her jawline and across her chin.

"Nothing," she managed to answer, just before he claimed her mouth again.

What was happening here? She tried to analyze the situation, but it was hopeless. She was hopeless. Hopelessly caught up in the moment. Sliding her hands over his tightly corded shoulders, she twisted her fingers together and locked them behind his strong neck. Funny, she'd never noticed how…large, he was before. Even in her present condition, he made her feel almost petite. She'd always thought of him as being much smaller. An underling.

So much for that theory, she mused, nearly drunk with her need for his touch. It had been so long since she'd been touched, she supposed it could be possible that her tastes in men had changed—but really—*Brent Clark?* New kid on the WCH block, she thought, angling her head to give Brent better access to her mouth.

She would definitely have to give this some thought. Later. When she could think straight. Not now. The mind-numbing desire that had somehow become a roaring backdraft between them, made any kind of rational thought completely impossible.

She clung to Brent as her legs turned to Jell-O beneath her, and savored the warm, sweet taste of his kiss. It was so exquisite. How could this be? Her head was reeling. Obviously she needed professional help. Yes. Counseling to discover why, in less than one short year, she'd managed to sabotage her upwardly mobile, fast-track-to-success life with a baby and this…this…labor coach. However, when she factored in the thrill she was getting from kissing him, it almost didn't seem like such a raw deal. Maybe the upwardly mobile, fast track wasn't all it was cracked up to be.

"Elaine?"

The husky word was sharp and hot in her ear.

Who was Elaine? Ahhh, yes. She was. Of course.

"Yes?" Letting her head fall back, she breathed her

question and gazed up at Brent through the half-open slits of her eyelids.

Brent pulled her hands from around his neck and clasped them firmly in front of his body. ''You should probably be on your way. It's getting late...''

He had a very strange look on his face.

Groaning inwardly, Elaine felt the heat of a thousand white-hot suns burn her cheeks. How mortifying. She, Elaine Lewis—much-sought-after, hotshot Chicago news producer—was being sent home.

And why not? What man in his right mind, even a gentleman like Clark, would want a disagreeable unwed mother, complete with water-retention problems, throwing herself at him? She was supposed to be helping him research a story, not jumping his bones in the parking lot of an apartment complex. She could just die. What on earth had possessed her to allow this to happen? *Ohhhh.* Why didn't someone just shoot her and put her out of her misery?

She tried to swallow past the sudden dryness in her mouth.

''Of course. You're right.'' Smiling weakly, she fumbled with her car keys in the uncomfortably confining space between Brent and her car. Why did he have to stand so damn close? Especially since he was in such a hurry to get rid of her. After several unsuccessful attempts, she was finally able to unlock her door and slip into the cool, leather interior of the Jaguar.

Gunning the engine, she rolled her window down, and avoiding Brent's eyes said, ''Thanks, Clark. It was a great class.''

Too humiliated to wait for his response, she backed out of her parking spot and roared off into the sunset.

Later that night Brent lay in his bed, filled with angst, tossing and turning and waiting for that elusive train to dreamland. But it was a fool's errand. No way in hell was he going to get a lick of sleep. Not after the stunt he'd pulled earlier with Elaine.

What an idiot! What in heaven's name had convinced him that kissing his boss would be a good idea? Especially since it had taken him so long to gain her trust both as a reporter and a labor coach. Thank God he'd at least come to his senses long enough to send her on her way, before he did something really stupid that she'd never be able to forgive him for.

All he could do now, he decided as he quite literally punched the stuffing out of his pillow, was pray that his error in judgment hadn't killed their fragile bond of trust.

Exhaling in misery, he flopped over onto his back and stared, unseeing, through the darkness at the shadows on his ceiling. He'd always prided himself on his ability to stay objective in any situation. It was part of what made him so good at his job. Why then, had he thrown caution to the wind and come on to Elaine the way he had?

And, why did it have to be so damn good?

Of course, once he'd finally come to his senses—before he took her right then and there out in the parking lot—she'd taken off like a bat out of hell. Couldn't wait to get away from his clumsy, unsophisticated advances. Probably went home to call her lawyer and see about slapping him with a sexual harassment suit.

"Ohhh man," he groaned and pulled his pillow up over his face.

Gosh darn it anyway, it had been such a nice evening, too. Before he'd gone and messed it up. All through birthing class he could almost imagine that he and Elaine were married. He felt the most mysterious connection with her. Almost as if it were his baby she was carrying. The mere thought made the blood run hot through his body.

No. He'd never get to sleep tonight. Wouldn't the guys at the station have a field day over this? He groaned again and pounded his forehead with his fist until his ears began to ring. And ring.

He stopped hitting his head and listened. Fumbling in the dark, he reached for, and finally found, his phone.

"Hello?" His heart pounded the way it did every time his phone rang this late at night. It was usually always the station. It was usually always bad news.

"Clark?"

It was Elaine. Her voice sounded shaky. This was it. She was calling him to chew him out.

"Yes..."

"I hate to bother you this late at night, but something's wrong."

Brent cringed as he sucked his lower lip into his mouth. Yep. She was going to tell him that they could no longer work together after he'd mauled her the way he had down in the parking lot earlier.

"And," she continued in the same quavering voice, "I didn't know who else to call."

What was she talking about? Surely if she was going to read him the riot act, she'd dialed the right number.

She moaned slightly, breathing heavily into the phone. "Clark, I think I'm in labor."

Brent suddenly found himself standing next to his bed, as though some giant puppeteer had yanked him to his feet. Labor? It couldn't be. It was too early. "Are you sure?" Using his best reporter's voice, he tried to keep his panic from showing. It was far too early. She was only seven months along.

"Clark," she cried in exasperation. "How should I know? I've never done this before. I'm having regular contractions, and—" her voice dropped to a frightened whisper "—I'm scared."

Pulling his jeans on over his pajama bottoms, Brent hopped around his bed and searched for his shirt and shoes.

"Stay where you are," he barked, feeling his pants pockets for his car keys. "I'll be right there."

"But I don't want to stay in bed. This is ridiculous. I feel just fine." Elaine sighed as she flopped back on her pillows and watched Brent fold her large, fluffy, white comforter. He tossed it onto the pine chest that stood at the foot of her four-poster bed and, turning to her, yawned broadly.

"Good. I'm glad you feel fine. But you heard Dr. Hanson. He wants you to stay in bed for the rest of your pregnancy, or you could lose the baby." Lifting his arms up loosely above his shoulders, he stretched and rotated his head. "You're lucky he didn't make you stay at the hospital tonight. High blood pressure is nothing to fool around with, Elaine. You don't want to have the baby now," he said as he pinched the muscles in his neck.

He looked tired, she noted. It was no small wonder, considering it must be after three in the morning. Glancing at her bedside clock, she saw she was right.

"But I have work to do," she moaned petulantly. "Tons of work. I simply can't stay in bed. And what about our story for November sweeps?"

Brent snorted. "Elaine, to hell with the sweeps story. As far as I'm concerned, we can do something else. The life of your unborn child is far more important than any stupid news story. Give it a rest, okay?" His expression was haggard. "I'm sure the station will get along just fine without you for a while."

Twisting her freshly laundered sheets into a mangled ball, Elaine tried to stem the tears she felt welling to the surface. Damn her hormones. Would she never be free of these impossible mood swings?

Seeming to read her distress, Brent's face softened. "Okay, maybe we won't get along just fine, exactly, but we'll muddle through. Hey, give us some credit. We've probably learned a thing or two from watching you."

"You're just saying that." She could feel one lone tear blaze a trail down her cheek.

Brent settled next to her on the edge of her bed and reached out to tuck an errant strand of hair behind her ear. Then, extracting the crumpled ball of her sheet from her hand, he gently touched it to her damp cheek. "Oh, honey. Listen. We'll find a way to win the ratings game," he reassured her, misunderstanding the reason for her depression. "Until then, you just need to take it easy."

She didn't give a damn about the ratings anymore. She only wanted to make sure that he would still be her birth partner. Her doctor's appointment partner. Her birth class partner. Her partner. "Brent?"

"Hmm?"

"I know that you—" feeling silly and emotional, she sniffed and reached over to her nightstand for a tissue "—probably have better things to do with your time, now that we won't be working on our project together, so I understand if you—" she swallowed, the tears beginning to flow in earnest now "—you know, don't want to…uh, coach me, now…."

Brent reached over and gathered her into his arms. "Sweetheart, if you're trying to get rid of me, you can forget it. I'm coaching you and that's final, got it?"

Sighing raggedly, she whispered, "Got it."

He had far too much time invested in this project to call it quits now.

That was a lie.

He had far too much emotion invested in Elaine to call it quits now.

But he couldn't tell her that. Swaying slightly, he rocked her to and fro as she slumped tiredly against him. She must weigh no more than a feather, baby and all, he mused, enjoying her body warmth as it seeped through his shirt.

He planted a few kisses into the fragrant tresses at the top of her head. She smelled of lilacs. He loved the smell of lilacs. It reminded him of springtime back home.

Elaine closed her eyes and enjoyed the hypnotic rhythm of his relaxing movement. She could feel Brent's cheek lift slightly as he smiled against the top of her head.

It seemed so right, having him there at three in the morning. How strange. Never before had she allowed anyone to see her this way—tired, frightened, bloated. She must look a perfect wreck.

Then again, when had what she looked like in front of Brent become so important? That was one question she didn't want to face. Because the answer—since he'd kissed her earlier—was mind-boggling. Especially at this hour. She was still reeling from the potency of that kiss. And from the humiliation.

It had been sheer, unadulterated terror that had prompted her to dial his number and ask for his help. Because just as she'd vowed that she was never going to let him get that close to her again, the pains had started. He, unfortunately, was the only person in the entire world she could think of to call. Sweet, dependable, salt-of-the-earth Brent.

How pathetic that he was the only person that had come to mind. Really, she thought tiredly, as soon as she was able, she was going to have to do something to remedy this situation. Cultivate some new relationships. Go out on a date or two.

Elaine stifled a yawn against Brent's steadily beating heart. Oh, um humm, right. She was going to start dating with an infant on her hands. Life. She smothered another yawn. Sometimes it was just so unfair.

Brent's voice rumbled comfortingly in her ear as he spoke.

"You know," he said, the stubble from the day's growth on his jaw made an interesting sound as it rubbed against her hair, "I was really scared when you called and said you were in labor."

"You were?" Elaine lifted her cheek off his chest and looked up into his eyes. They were such nice eyes, really, when he wasn't wearing those dopey glasses. "Why?"

The tiny hairs at the side of her face stirred as he huffed. "Because I'm concerned about you. And the baby."

"You are?" She eyed him speculatively. Why should he care? Good heavens, even on her best day at work, she was nothing but a pain in his side. Her expectations were always higher of him than of the rest of the crew. She rode him, because she knew he could take it. Because he was better than they were. No, her constant harping certainly couldn't have endeared her to him, could it?

"Yes." There was a quiet emphasis on the word.

His gaze lowered, as did his voice, and Elaine felt the same fire that had flashed between them that afternoon begin to spark. Oh no. She'd promised herself that she wouldn't let this happen again. Why then, did she feel herself once more beginning to melt under those unfathomable, sea green eyes of his? He shifted his position slightly, and suddenly, she found herself half lying across his lap.

"Why?" she breathed, hoping against hope that she was more than just a story to him.

He shook his head and inhaled deeply. "I'm really not exactly sure. Lots of reasons, I guess. And no reason at all. It's a mystery."

She nodded, trying to understand.

"Elaine?" His lips hovered a hair's breadth above hers.

"Hmm?" She felt so delightfully warm and wonderful.

"I really think—" he sighed heavily and, moaning, shifted her off his lap "—that I should be going home. Because the way I'm feeling, if I don't leave right now, I'll be here all night."

Her stomach tightened. Of course. He had to leave. He must be exhausted. How thoughtless of her. Flames of humiliation licked her cheeks. She was really batting a thousand with him today.

"Sure. Go. Go." Smiling brightly, she shooed him toward the door. "I'll be fine."

"Good. But, if anything, and I mean *anything,* should happen, I want you to call me immediately. Okay?"

"Okay."

"Well, then." He paused at her bedroom door and smiled down at her. "Don't get up," he teased, "I can find my way out."

Surely her face would crack from the effort it took to smile so cheerfully. "Okay," she chirped again.

"I'll call you in the morning," he promised.

Elaine listened as he locked and closed her front door. "Okay," she whispered and, burying her face in her pillow, suddenly felt lonelier than she'd ever felt in her life.

"What have you got?"

"Chinese."

"No," Elaine huffed, cranky, frustrated and bored out of her gourd. "Not the food." She pointed to the pile of folders Brent balanced under his arm, along with the bag that was emitting the most enticing smells of ginger and sweet-and-sour sauce. "Those."

Brent dropped his load on what had become "his side" of her bed. During the two months since Elaine had been confined to bed, he'd taken to bringing her dinner, magazines and assorted toys to amuse her, and bits and pieces of work that the higher-ups at the station felt she could handle from her home. He would spread the food, picnic-style over her covers, and they would spend a companionable hour or two together before he headed home to his place.

"Debbie sent these." He pushed the files in her direction. "Says they need your signature. Also, Stu wanted you to take a look at a story proposal he's hot to do on some women's wrestling team. Thought it might be a good one for November sweeps.'' He dug through the bag of food and tossed her a pair of chopsticks.

Elaine sent him a baleful look. ''Sounds like his kind of story,'' she sighed. ''Not exactly what I had in mind to win the ratings war, though.''

''Brent laughed. ''Oh well. He also said something about wanting to go undercover to expose them, or something like that. It's all in there.'' He gestured to the pile of work with his own chopsticks. ''Hope you feel like Szechwan.''

''I feel like a beached whale,'' she said crabbily. ''But, Szechwan will be fine.''

Brent smiled indulgently and handed her a carton of rice and a paper plate. ''You're in a good mood. Maybe we should talk to Stu about getting you on that wrestling team.''

That made Elaine grin. ''Well, for crying out loud, I want to get out of bed. I feel fine. I really don't see what difference it would make, considering I'm due next week, anyway.''

Brent stopped eating and stared at her. ''Already?'' Was it the end of October? How could that be? He wasn't ready. Even though Dr. Hanson had okayed their weekly attendance at birthing class, he still wasn't sure he'd learned everything he needed to know to help Elaine get through labor.

''Yes,'' she mumbled around a mouthful of sesame beef, and then, suddenly remembering her news, her eyes lit up. ''Oh! Guess who called!''

Shrugging, Brent scraped the rest of the cashew chicken out of the carton and onto his plate. He'd gained at least ten pounds since Elaine had gotten pregnant. He almost couldn't fit into those old high school corduroys of his. ''I give.''

''Liz Martin. She says Dick and Mary Olsen had their baby yesterday.''

"Really?" Leaning forward, he grinned, eager for her news.

"Yes," Elaine crowed, bouncing up and down on the mattress. "And you'll never guess what! He fainted!" She screamed with glee.

"He did?" Brent breathed, his eyes wide with wonder. "Man. I sure as hell hope I don't do that."

Shaking her head with a confidence he was nowhere near feeling, Elaine said, "Oh, you won't."

"What makes you so sure?" He looked at her, curious.

"Because you're not a little wimp like Dick."

He wasn't? Of course, *he* knew that, but Elaine? Well, he couldn't ever really be sure exactly what she thought of him as a man. She was always so busy bossing him around as an employee. And as her assistant in this pregnancy.

"I'm not?" he asked dryly.

"No," she regarded him thoughtfully for a moment. "You're made of much sturdier stuff."

Not entirely dying to know what "sturdier stuff" was composed of, Brent asked, "What'd they have?"

"A boy. Richard Olsen, Jr. Five pounds even and eighteen inches long. Must take after his folks," she mused.

Brent shook his head and smiled broadly at Elaine. It was happening. The babies were beginning to come. "In the immortal words of Dick Olsen—Shecky, get the jet," he roared, in a tribute of sorts to the new father, and they laughed together, sharing their private joke.

"Do you want me to call 911 now, or would you rather I wait until you keel over?" Brent asked churlishly, eyeing with disgust the jelly doughnut Ray was dipping into his coffee cup.

"What's the bee in your boxers?" Ray's eyes narrowed defensively before he stuffed the soggy confection into his mouth. "You've been a bear all week," he mumbled, and looked across the break room table at Stu and Debbie who were nodding in agreement.

Brent shrugged impatiently and checked the battery in his pager for the umpteenth time. Ray was right. He'd been jumpier than a cat in a roomful of rocking chairs. Elaine was five days past due now, and he was beginning to wonder if everything was all right. If she didn't have this baby pretty soon, he was going to lose what was left of his mind.

It didn't help matters that he couldn't explain his antsy behavior to his co-workers. Elaine still preferred to keep their relationship private. And, looking at the powdered sugar that adorned Ray's nose and chin as he polished off the rest of Debbie's Danish, he couldn't say that he blamed her. He rolled his eyes. These clowns would certainly be no help.

Even his mother's assurance that he'd been two weeks late when she'd gone into labor with him hadn't enabled him sleep any better last night.

Debbie studied him thoughtfully. "You haven't joined us for Friday night at The Pub in ages. Why don't you come with us tonight? Get out and have a little fun." She grinned. "They've got a new karaoke machine. You have to hear Stu sing 'Feelings.' It's really horrible."

"Hey." Stu looked wounded.

As the conversation turned to the Friday night hit parade at The Pub, Brent's thoughts wandered back to Elaine. She was even more anxious than he was. So far everyone from birth class had had their babies without a hitch, but that didn't stop Elaine from worrying about her own imminent labor. And he had to admit that he himself would be much happier once the whole thing was over. Well, maybe not happier, exactly, but at least he and Elaine could get back to their respective lives.

Shifting uncomfortably in his chair, the thought of relinquishing his role in her personal life saddened him. The dismal prospect of a future spent listening to Stu sing "Feelings" every Friday night loomed depressingly ahead.

Unfortunately he'd allowed himself to become a little more attached to Elaine than he'd planned on. He dreaded going back to eating his dinner alone. And he dreaded missing the way her eyes lit up when he came into her bedroom every night, missing the curve of her lips when she smiled at him, the smell of her fragrant hair, the lilt of her throaty laughter as they shared a joke...but mostly, he supposed, he dreaded not being needed anymore.

A little more attached than he'd planned. Ha. Talk about denial. He was in this thing way over his head and he knew it.

Balancing his elbows on the break room table, Brent cradled his head in his hands and gingerly massaged his throbbing temples. No, he was beginning to realize, simply working with her here at the station in the future wouldn't be the same at all. She was completely different here at work than she was at home. At home she was free to be herself with him. Here she was the boss, and they would have to go back to their respective roles.

He exhaled mightily, wishing he could blow away the hollow feeling in his gut. The room had grown strangely quiet, and as Brent surfaced from his reverie, he noticed all eyes were trained curiously on the break room door. Turning in his chair, he followed their gaze. Elaine, her cheeks unusually flushed, was leaning unsteadily against the doorjamb. His heart began to thud erratically in his chest.

For crying out loud, she was supposed to be at home in bed. What could be so important that she couldn't wait for him to bring it home tonight? Pushing his chair back from the table, his eyes glittered dangerously at her.

"What the hell are you doing here?"

"Is that any way to address your boss?" she snapped. Shuffling over to the couch behind him, she lowered herself awkwardly into its depth. "Besides, if memory serves, I work here. At least I used to,'' she muttered, aware of the furtive glances exchanged by her subordinates.

The muscles in Brent's jaw jumped angrily as he stood, nearly knocking his chair over in the process. ''You should be in bed.''

The collective group of eyes swung from Brent back to Elaine, soaking up with fascination this unusual byplay between their producer and the newest member of the news team.

''My water broke this morning while I was fixing my breakfast. I thought I'd swing by here and pick you up on my way to the hospital.'' Leaning back on the couch, Elaine swung her feet up onto the cushions and, for once, enjoyed the slack-jawed and bug-eyed reaction of the gossipmongers at the table, as they shifted their eager focus back to Brent.

The blood drained from Brent's face as he sank back down into his chair in shock.

''You...what?'' he stammered.

''Her water broke,'' Stu supplied helpfully.

''Oh. Right.'' Brent tried to swallow as he struggled to recall what Nurse Shocktaag had instructed, once the bag of waters ruptured. ''Okay, okay...'' He raked his hands through his hair. ''Everyone, stay calm,'' he ordered, wishing to hell he could follow his own advice.

''Wow,'' Debbie murmured, looking in admiration at Elaine. ''You're doing great. Not like that woman I saw last night on 'Rescue Cops.' ''

Ray leaned forward, his eyes animated. ''I saw that,'' he cried exuberantly. ''Man, that was something.''

''Yeah.'' Debbie's nod was emphatic as she turned back to Elaine. ''This woman's water broke while she was on the Ferris wheel. And she started having these horrible contractions immediately. So she starts screaming, but the guy operating the Ferris wheel was off smoking or something, anyway—''

"Smoking, right!" Ray interrupted, swept up in the story.

"Right, right—" Debbie waved him aside "—anyway the baby was coming. I mean, then and there! Can you believe it? I didn't know they let pregnant women even ride those things...."

"I think it's okay, if it's not the kind of ride that throws you all around," Stu interjected.

Brent's head swam as he watched Elaine smiling benignly at the news crew as they regaled her with the horrors of childbirth. Shouldn't he be timing her contractions? Or boiling water? Or, according to Debbie, preparing to deliver this baby right here in the break room? And why didn't Elaine seem the least bit worried?

Taking a deep breath, he willed himself to get a grip on his runaway pulse. This was no time to panic. No. There was no time for that. Panicking was not good. So he wouldn't. Panic, that is.

Thank heavens they'd canned "The Miracle of Life" idea. Because there was no way in hell he'd ever be able to document his own name, let alone the birth of Elaine's baby.

Standing, he crossed over to Elaine and squeezed between her and her sudden admiration society. "Come on now," he barked, his frayed nerves jangling. "You guys give her some air, will you?" He reached down and pulled her to her feet. "Stay calm and whatever you do, don't panic," he advised, more to himself than anyone.

Elaine felt as though she were standing in the eye of a hurricane. "I'm calm," she assured him, smiling as her usually calm, cool and collected star reporter struggled to shove his head through the sleeve of his jacket. Good heavens, she thought, watching him battle his way into his poor, tangled garment, if they made it through this day, it would be a miracle.

She could hardly believe it. It was finally happening. A

shiver of excitement ran down her spine. They were having a baby. Lost in thought, she watched Brent spin in circles, chasing his sleeve, until the first contraction hit.

Panting, she grabbed Brent's arm and forced him to stop for a moment. She leaned against him, her face ashen as the pain gripped her belly.

"Shecky," she whispered, "get the jet. I'm—" grimacing, she clutched his arm "—outta here."

Chapter Seven

"Three centimeters?" Elaine caught Brent's shirttail and tugged him over to the hospital bed where she'd been laboring for the past several hours. "That can't be right," she groaned, and pushed the damp strands of hair away from her face with a free hand. "I was dilated to three centimeters an hour ago." Apparently she could forget having this baby anytime soon. Ten centimeters seemed a grueling lifetime away.

"You're making progress, Elaine," Brent reassured her. "You're effacing, and that's what's important here. Remember?"

"Umm." She smiled weakly up at him, then tried to focus her attention on the formidable Nurse Shocktaag as she bustled in and out of the room. The efficient woman was preparing the equipment Dr. Hanson would require when the time came. And it couldn't come soon enough to suit her, Elaine thought, wincing as she grasped Brent's bicep in a death grip. The pain was unbearable. Couldn't the old biddy see that? What was taking so blasted long? She wanted drugs, and she wanted them now.

"I demand a recount," she whimpered up at Brent as he leaned over her and lightly stroked her cheek with the backs of his fingers.

The birthing suite at Chicago Central was cheerfully decorated in lovely shades of pastel, with a window seat that made into a bed for the labor coach, a television and stereo for the patient's entertainment pleasure and a tasteful seating area for guests. Elaine would most likely have found herself enjoying her stay if it weren't for the excruciating cramps that seized her midsection every two minutes.

Brent reached over to the small table situated next to the hospital bed, retrieved a cool, damp cloth and arranged it over Elaine's forehead.

"Hang in there, honey," he encouraged. "Ruby says that the anesthesiologist should be here in about an hour or so. Once you get the epidural you'll feel a lot better."

Elaine shot him a withering look. "Oh, sure. Easy for you to say. I can't wait that long," she gasped and then moaned. "At this point I'd settle for a quick blow to the head with a hammer."

Chuckling sympathetically, Brent lifted the cloth from her forehead and replaced it with his lips, bestowing a tender kiss. "There," he murmured, "does that help?"

"Umm," Elaine nodded and sighed. "Some."

He really was very sweet. Why hadn't she ever noticed what a rock he was before? How could she have mistaken his quiet strength for the country bumpkin she'd pigeonholed him to be when he'd joined the WCH news team last year? Just never took the time to look beneath the outdated clothes and ugly horn-rims, she guessed. At any rate she was incredibly grateful for his steady, fortifying presence.

"Thanks," she whispered as he dropped an ice chip into her mouth. She'd never been so thirsty in her life.

Leaning back against the cool, crisp linen case that covered her pillow, she wondered why anyone in her right mind would ever have more than one baby. Why, some people actually went through labor a half a dozen times or more. Good heavens, were they masochists? At this point she couldn't imagine ever wanting to have another child.

She inhaled deeply and glanced over at Brent. Thank God he was here for her. He was the only thing that kept her going. Her salvation, really. Elaine had to admit, as she watched him thoughtfully studying the baby monitor that was attached to her abdomen, he was right about how much she would need him.

It was amazing how comfortable she was, having him here. He was the only person she could envision sharing this moment with. The only person she felt sure would understand her vast array of emotions. Both the pain and the joy. Because between contractions, she could almost relax long enough to become excited about meeting Sara and Bobby's baby.

Whoosh, whoosh, whoosh. The sweet life song penetrated her reverie.

She closed her eyes and listened to the reassuring sound of the baby's strong heartbeat coming from the machine that Brent hovered so protectively over, when he wasn't busy being her bastion of strength. The steady rhythm reminded her that it was all worth it. Every last pain. Ruby had explained earlier that the monitor that churned out endless yards of white graph paper kept track of both the fetal heartbeat and her contractions. Fascinated by the buttons and dials, Brent had taken to the machine like a cowboy to his horse. She smiled as he pushed his glasses up higher on the bridge of his nose.

"Clark," she whispered, catching his attention. "I don't suppose you could talk that old killjoy, Shocktaag into some pain medication before the anesthesiologist gets here?"

Turning his attention from the hypnotic thrumming of

the baby's heartbeat, Brent removed his glasses and smiled sympathetically. "I'll ask her just as soon as she comes back," he assured her.

Elaine regarded him through her half-closed eyelids. "That would be great."

It was odd how she'd never really noticed how nice looking he was before, either. Without those glasses, he was really quite handsome, she mused, trying to busy her mind with something other than the impending contraction that lurked just ahead. He even managed to look quite fetching in that faded gray sweatshirt and those impossibly tight jeans he'd retrieved from the trunk of his car once they'd arrived at the hospital. Come to think of it, that outfit suited him. In the future, she would also spend more time appreciating the advantages of casual wear, she thought, eyeing his narrow hips and well-muscled thighs.

But not now. No. Now she was going to have a contraction.

Noticing the look of pain that flashed across her face, Brent glanced at the monitor and nodded. "It looks like you're going into another contraction," he told her and took her hand. "Come on now, sweetheart, breathe." His eyes locked with hers as he began the breathing pattern they'd learned in class.

He whispered encouragement, and she nodded, transfixed on his face. Cast adrift on a sea of pain, Elaine clung to the lifeline that was Brent's strong hand. Focusing on his unwavering gaze, she weathered yet another contraction and allowed her mind to take flight. And it was then, as a barrage of muddled, incoherent thoughts flitted through her subconscious, that she began to realize just how much she'd come to depend on Brent.

There was no way she'd ever have been able to go through this by herself, she knew, as he led her to the crest of the pain and down the other side. He was not only her partner and coach, he was her friend. Somehow he'd managed to sneak past her arsenal of defensive weapons and worm his way into her heart. Great. Just what she needed. To fall in love with a co-worker.

Fall in love? That couldn't be right. She was probably just confused from the pain. Or was she? If being in love meant needing and wanting someone as badly as she'd come to need and want to be near him, then she had it for him, and she had it bad.

''Ohhh,'' she moaned, wrestling with a pain in her heart that had absolutely no connection to bearing this child. This couldn't be happening. She was setting herself up for a terrible fall. What man in reasonable control of his faculties would want someone as unlovable as herself? And then again, there was the matter of the ready-made family she was preparing to bring into this world.... *''Ohhh.''* She writhed and moaned again.

''I'm so sorry, honey. I know it hurts. Hang on, though. Ruby just came back, and I'll see about getting you something for the pain.''

His gentle expression was so sympathetic, Elaine wanted to weep. How would she ever be able to get through another day without him? He left her side, and she watched while Brent briefly conferred with Nurse Shocktaag. A moment later he returned, smiling triumphantly, Ruby at his side.

''So, you are ready for some relief?'' The older woman peered down her pointed nose at Elaine and nodded curtly.

''Yes,'' Elaine breathed, wishing there were an immunization for broken hearts in the competent nurse's bag of tricks.

Brent laced his fingers with hers as Ruby administered a dose of pain medication into the IV. The drug began to take effect almost immediately.

''Is that a little better?'' he asked, squinting at the printout of the baby's heartbeat as it rolled out of the monitor.

Feeling suddenly intoxicated, Elaine smiled giddily.

"Yessssir," she slurred and pulled his hand up to her cheek. "Lotss better. Hey," her head lolled onto his hand as she gazed up at him. "Thankss. You're so nice. I know," she continued, feeling suddenly quite glib, "that I haven't told you how much all your help meanss to me. But, it doess. Really." She could feel her eyes drifting shut, and she continued woozily, "I love it. You. I mean... I...love...you...."

Nurse Shocktaag smiled at Brent as the anesthesiologist arrived in the room along with a younger nurse. "Allow her to rest for a moment. And you take a break. I will stay with her while she gets the epidural. I will come for you when we are done." She pointed at the door and shooed him toward it. "Go. Go. Eat some lunch."

Dazed, Brent nodded and, following her instructions, moved across the room, through the blurry haze of Elaine's announcement and into the hallway. His stomach crowded into his throat as he wandered down the hall through the OB wing and stopped before a large plate glass window. He felt his eyes glaze over as he stared out the window and over the endless expanse of Lake Michigan. Oblivious to the colorful sailboats that skimmed bravely over the water's choppy surface beneath the cloudy fall sky, he tried to assimilate the meaning of Elaine's words.

She had said she loved him! Never mind that she was under the influence of heaven only knew what. On some level he was sure that the truth had surfaced.

Then again, there were many different kinds of love, and he doubted that Elaine could ever feel for him as deeply as he'd come to feel for her. The fragile bubble of excitement burst as reality dawned. It was just the drug talking. He'd do well to keep that in mind. Feeling as though the wind in his own sail had abruptly died, he turned away from the window and slogged down to the hospital cafeteria in search of something edible.

If ever he needed his strength, it was now.

* * *

She looked like an angel. Too bad the gang at the station couldn't see their Barracuda now. Brent stood next to Elaine's bed and watched her sleep. The epidural had evidently worked its magic, and she was sound asleep, exhausted after a morning of some pretty heavy suffering. Her face, so girlish in repose, drew him like a magnet, and he was unable to resist touching his lips to the smooth porcelain of her cheeks. He'd never be able to understand how, even in the throes of labor, and without a speck of makeup, she managed to look so beautiful.

Full lips, almond-shaped eyes fringed with thick, dark lashes, high cheekbones... If this baby managed to inherit even one of these attributes from her side of the family, it would be an amazingly handsome child.

If he could, he would gladly suffer the pain in her place. He hated the feeling of helplessness that overcame him as she endured each increasingly painful contraction. Picking up one of her delicate hands in his, he rubbed it absently with the pad of his thumb. Now, more than ever before, he admired her strength. Elaine Lewis was an amazing woman.

She stirred in her sleep, and he backed away from the bed and settled onto the window seat where he could keep an eye on her. He was tired, but knew that he was far too keyed up to drift off. Soon the baby would make its appearance, and he didn't want to miss a second of the impending miracle.

No, he would just put his feet up and rest for a moment. He'd stay awake. Elaine might...need...him....

Elaine was groggy. Her eyelids felt as though they weighed a ton, and her mouth was so parched she was sure that if she didn't drink at least a gallon of water within the next minute or two, she'd die of thirst. Rolling her head to a more comfortable position on the pillow, Ruby's tight, gray bun came into view as the older woman bent over the fetal monitor.

She touched her tongue to her dry lips in an effort to moisten them, but it was almost as if someone had packed her mouth with cotton. "Where is Brent?" she whispered hoarsely, tapping the bed rail to gain the nurse's attention.

"Shh," Ruby rightened to her usual ramrod posture and touched a bony finger to her tightly pursed lips. "He sleeps by the window. He is very tired from helping all day. I tell him to take more breaks, but he is protective, no?" A begrudging smile tipped the corners of her mouth.

Elaine shifted her gaze to the window seat, where she found Brent sprawled out, one arm flung over his eyes, the other, dangling off the edge of his bed. Her heart constricted at the touching sight, and she felt her eyes grow misty. The shadows of his lashes rested lightly across his cheeks, and his strongly chiseled lips puffed softly as his chest rose and fell with the breath of deep slumber.

"You know," Ruby whispered in a rare moment of chummy candor, "I never see a father so excited as this one. He is a lovely man."

"Yes." Elaine's gaze swung back to the prunish woman. "Yes, he is."

As the shifts changed, Ruby efficiently introduced the nurses who would be assisting in the birth once she left, then she squeezed Elaine's knee with her knobby hand. "You will be fine with these girls," she told her, indicating the cheery-faced Sandy and Clarejoy. "I wish you both luck," she said, her hawklike eyes darting from her to Brent as he slept. "I have a feeling you will be just right as parents, no? Love each other and love the little one."

Suddenly Elaine desperately wanted the curmudgeonly woman to stay. She felt the childish urge to burst into tears and beg her to work yet another shift. But even the militant nurse must have a family that she had to get home to, Elaine knew. Everyone had families, it seemed. Everyone but herself. Family had never been important to her before. But now, as she watched Ruby fuss with her covers, she desperately longed for her mother's soothing presence and a husband to call her own. Someone to walk out of the hospital with her and into the rest of her life. Resisting the tears that threatened at Ruby's imminent departure, she set her chin bravely.

"Thank you," she murmured. "I'll see you at the birth class reunion."

"Ahh, yes." Ruby's sudden smile was radiant. "You will meet the babies. That Olsen baby...he is a cutie. Life has some pleasant surprises, no?" On that note she turned without a backward glance and marched out the door.

Feeling bereft, Elaine smiled tentatively as the nurse Ruby had introduced as Sandy snapped on a pair of latex gloves.

"Hi, there," Sandy said, smiling, and looked down into Elaine's face. "I'm going to be taking care of you during transition, and once the baby is here, I'll assist Dr. Hanson, while Clarejoy takes care of your newborn. But first, I want to see how far we've come."

"Okay," Elaine sighed and submitted to yet another check to discover how far she'd managed to dilate while she slept.

Sandy finished her task and nodded approvingly at Elaine. "Good job." She pulled off her gloves. "I'll call Dr. Hanson now. And we'll get the anesthesiologist back here to turn down your epidural so you'll be able to feel the contractions. You, my dear, are ready to start pushing."

"I am?" Elaine's eyes grew wide with wonder. Dilating from zero to three had been much worse than three to ten. Thank heavens for modern science.

"Yes indeedy," she chirped, motioning for Clarejoy to give her a hand preparing Elaine's bed for birth.

The bed came apart in the middle and the lower section was whisked away, and two footrests were attached in its place. Equipment was rearranged around the bed, and Sandy briefed Elaine on the use of the handlebars at the side of the bed.

"Just hold these like so," she instructed, "and when the time comes, use them to help yourself bear down." Pressing a button at the side of the bed, she elevated the back to an angle more conducive to childbirth.

"And," Elaine quipped, "if it gets too rough, I can just peddle on out of here, right?"

Sandy laughed. "You might want to wait until after the baby comes. And judging from the look of things, that will be pretty soon now."

Elaine felt a pleasant flush steal into her cheeks. Sara's baby was coming. Ruby was right, she decided, glancing over at the still-deeply sleeping Brent. Life did have a few pleasant surprises.

Brent had no idea how long he'd been asleep, when the sound of Dr. Hanson's voice roused him. Jumping to a standing position, he stumbled to Elaine's side on wobbly legs, rubbing his eyes and feeling guilty at having fallen asleep. The room had mysteriously transformed from the comfy suite at the Ritz, to a sterile labor room. Ruby had disappeared and been replaced by two younger nurses, and Elaine was chatting calmly with Dr. Hanson.

He felt strangely left out of the proceedings. They all seemed to be getting along just fine without him. Fighting the temptation to feel sorry for himself, he tucked his shirttails into his jeans, straightened the sweatshirt he wore over that, and waited patiently for someone to notice him. Much to his relief, it was worth the wait.

The smile Elaine bestowed upon him could have thawed an iceberg with its warmth.

"It's about time you woke up, sleepyhead," she teased, sounding drained. Her smile faded. "I'm glad you're here." She clasped his hand in a firm grip and winced.

"They turned off my epidural. I'm starting to feel the pain again." She moaned.

"This is it, then," Brent said and glanced at the monitor. She was having a contraction, and it looked like a big one if the squiggly lines on the graph paper were any indication. Squeezing her hand to get her attention, he lowered his face to hers and began coaching, as Dr. Hanson adjusted his stool and studied his tray of tools down at the other end of the bed.

"Yesss." The word came out as a painful hiss from between Elaine's lips. "This is it," she said, panting.

Seconds ticked past, turning into minutes, which in turn became an hour. Contractions came and went, gaining in momentum and intensity, until Brent was sure Elaine would never make it to the end. Actually, he was almost more worried about making it to the end himself. He didn't want to alarm Elaine with his worries, but as the sands sifted through the hourglass, he was beginning to wonder if this baby would ever be born. Did it always take this long? he wondered. He had a sudden new and profound respect for his mother.

Dr. Hanson seemed to feel that everything was progressing nicely, so Brent decided he would just have to take his word for it. Still, if he felt this drained, he could only begin to imagine what Elaine must be going through.

Elaine moaned audibly with each breath. "Ohhh..."

"Shh, honey. Save your energy. Try to breathe slower." Brent pushed several damp strands of hair out of her eyes as she writhed in pain. He reached for the cup of ice and held a chip to her lips.

"*You* breathe slower," she ordered, her eyes wild. "Get that away from me." She pushed at the cup in his hand. "I...think...I'm...hyper...ventilating," she managed to whisper, her shadowed eyes were filled with fear. "Brent...I can't...stop.... Ohhh..."

"Elaine. Listen to me." He grasped her face between his

hands and looked into her eyes. ''Breathe with me. Elaine. Breathe with me, honey.'' He fell into one of the patterns they'd learned in class, breathing slowly, his eyes locked with hers, and as though hypnotized, Elaine followed his lead. ''That's better. Good girl,'' he praised.

''Where is the ice?''

''Here.'' He picked up the cup she'd pushed away earlier and ran a cube over her lips.

''Thanks,'' she whispered gratefully, and gazed up at him, adoration filling her eyes. ''Sorry I'm such a grouch. I think I've been invaded by aliens.''

''Hey. You're doing just great. I'm proud of you.''

''You are?'' She looked up at him for his approval, her girlish vulnerability obliterating any trace of Elaine Lewis, corporate broadcaster.

Here their roles had reversed. Here he was in command, and she was subject to his leadership. He had to admit it was refreshing for a change. ''Yes. I am.''

''Oh, Brent,'' she clutched his hand in what felt to him like an attempt to amputate his thumb with her fingernails. Lifting her head off the pillow, she hunched forward. ''Here we go again.'' She cried out in agony as she assisted Sara's little life into the world.

This next contraction finally brought the baby's head to a bulging crown.

''Good job,'' Dr. Hanson said. ''Just a couple more pushes and I can introduce you to your baby.''

Electric jolts of excitement shot down Brent's spine. He felt like a kid at Christmas. Only this was a million times better. This was quite possibly the most exciting, most beautiful thing he'd ever experienced.

''I feel another one,'' Elaine moaned, weak with exhaustion. ''But I'm too tired to push anymore.'' She suddenly burst into tears and looked up at Brent with panic-stricken eyes. ''I can't do this, Brent. Really. I want to stop. Let's just call it a day, okay? Please. Tell them I want to go home now," she pleaded, growing increasingly hysterical with fright. "Brent…oh, Brent. It hurts so bad."

He let go of his heart forever in that moment, as it went out to her in her pain. It amazed him how a heart so swollen with love for another human being could continue to beat. Once again Brent pulled her eyes into his steady, unwavering gaze. "Elaine. Listen to me now, honey. The baby is almost here. If you can summon enough energy for just one or two more pushes, the pain will stop and it will all be over. Then," he promised, coaxing her to relax, "we can go home. Okay?"

"Okay." She managed to grit this out through her tightly clenched jaw.

The raw trust in her expression was unmistakable. It was heady stuff, and Brent vowed then and there that he would always—if she would allow it—be there for her in some capacity or another.

"Brent."

"I know." He could see that she had to bear down. Her lithe body quaked with her effort, and beads of sweat broke out anew on her forehead. His eyes penetrated hers, and together they rode the crest of the pain.

"Terrific!" Dr. Hanson pulled his rolling tray of tools closer to his side. "Once more, Elaine."

"Is it born yet?" she asked, delirious from the tidal waves of torment that washed over her.

"The head!" Brent crowed, jubilantly, leaving her side briefly to inspect the baby. "The head is here! And, Elaine, it looks great. Beautiful. Awesome."

Time seemed to suspend for Brent, as Elaine, with one final grunt, expelled the tiny life from the safe haven of her body. The baby emerged, red-faced and squalling, its arms waving jerkily in the sudden freedom of the surrounding space. A giant lump thickly crowded Brent's throat as he moved toward Dr. Hanson to get a better look at the newborn.

It was a girl. A healthy, gorgeous baby girl.

"Elaine. We have a girl," he managed to say, past the growing emotional obstruction in his air passage. And, for the first time since he was a small boy living in his mother's home back in Iowa, he felt tears spring unbidden to his eyes. "She's beautiful, Elaine."

Sandy peered indulgently at the baby and then up at Brent. "She sure looks like her daddy."

Knowing that this was impossible, Brent, nevertheless, felt his chest swell with pride.

"Thanks." He beamed at the nurse.

Elaine's smile was tremulous.

He moved back to her side and smoothed her hair away from her face, feeling the dampness from the tears that flowed down her cheeks. Perching next to her on the bed, he gathered her into his embrace, their tears of awe and happiness mingling as he kissed her and held her tight.

Elaine relaxed against the strong wall of Brent's chest as Dr. Hanson placed the baby on her tummy for a moment while he clamped and severed the umbilical cord. The baby's tiny, mewling cry reminded her of the bleat of a spring lamb, and she looked up at Brent, her eyes glistening.

"She is beautiful, isn't she?"

"Like her mother."

Elaine leaned forward and touched her lips to the incredibly soft skin of the baby's cheek. And as the tiny eyes blinked up at her, seeming to contain the wisdom of the ages, she again heard the echo of Sara's sweet voice.

Love her, Elaine, it seemed to say. *Love her.*

Chapter Eight

"You know, we're going to have to think of something to call her other than 'Peanut.'"

Brent smiled over at Elaine from the rocking chair he occupied next to her bed in the birthing suite. Looking fondly down into the sleeping face of the cherub he held in his arms, he said, "It kind of suits her now, but I can't imagine her going through life with that handle."

Elaine laughed. Nearly twenty-four hours had passed since the baby had been born, and after some sporadic sleep during the night, she was beginning to feel a little bit like her old self. Long shadows from the setting sun slanted in through the window, and a single lamp in the corner of the room glowed cheerily. They would spend one more night in the hospital before they were discharged in the morning.

"You're right." She sighed, turning onto her side so that she could watch Brent rock the tiny bundle in his arms. "Peanut Lewis, CEO, just doesn't make it."

"Neither does Grandma Peanut. Not very adult." He

laughed as the baby yawned and stretched in her sleep. The beginnings of a light beard shadowed his square jaw, and once again Elaine found herself marveling at how she'd never noticed his good looks before. Clearly she spent far too much time glued to a video monitor. Her eyes wandered to his well-shaped hands as he stroked the soft fuzz that adorned the top of the baby's head.

"She sure does sleep a lot," he commented. Leaning back he rolled the baby onto her stomach across his chest.

Already he handled the baby like a pro. Unlike herself. "Hmm. Not really. She woke up at least three times last night, looking for food." Elaine sighed ruefully.

Brent lifted his chin off his chest and looked over at her. "I must have slept through it. How'd it go?"

She felt herself grow warm beneath his unfathomable gaze. "Painful. They never mentioned that particular tidbit in breast-feeding class. I had a whole slew of different nurses in here last night, trying to explain the mechanics. I'm not kidding, Brent, it may look easy, but I swear, you need at least six arms."

His eyes twinkled as he watched her over the top of the baby's head. "Aren't you glad we took that class?"

"I guess. We muddled through while you were in the cafeteria for breakfast and lunch today, but it was mostly a fiasco. They say practice makes perfect, but I'm beginning to wonder." Elaine sent Brent a doubtful look. "I wish we could just give her a sandwich."

Brent chuckled and peered down at the baby. "Would you like a sandwich?" He pretended to listen as she nuzzled his neck. "Nope. She says she'll wait till she has some teeth."

Smiling, Elaine pulled the blanket up over her shoulders and gazed on in contentment as Brent closed his eyes and slowly rocked the baby.

It had been a wonderful day. The station had sent a giant bouquet of flowers along with a card expressing best wishes, and some of the news crew had stopped by with gifts for the baby. She smiled at the image of Stu and Ray awkwardly holding the infant, blushing delightedly when she'd gripped their fingers with her tiny hands. Debbie had accompanied them, complaining loudly that they were hogging the baby. Not to mention the fact that the silly men were holding her all wrong. The young woman had rolled her eyes in feminine camaraderie at Elaine, and for the first time, Elaine had begun to feel like one of the gang.

Although, she had a sneaking suspicion that they were more interested in her relationship with Brent than they were in the baby...but it was nice to have visitors. She'd been beginning to wonder if anyone would remember her at all. But even Brent's mother had wired a lovely plant. She'd have to send her a thank-you card, she thought making a mental note. Margaret Clark must be a wonderful woman—her eyes strayed from the leafy foliage back to Brent—because she certainly had a wonderful son.

And then there were the roses. Their delicate scent filled the room. One dozen of the most beautiful red roses she'd ever laid eyes on. From Brent. She couldn't remember the last time anyone had given her roses, and his thoughtful gesture meant more to her than she could ever say.

"So," Brent murmured, his eyes still closed, "what'll it be?"

"What?"

"Her name?"

"Oh." Elaine's brow puckered as a wave of melancholy washed over her. "I don't know. What do you think about Sara?" It seemed only fitting, she mused, wishing she knew what her cousin and her husband had planned to name their child.

Brent opened his eyes and slowly smiled at her. "I love it."

"Me, too."

They smiled indulgently at the baby for a moment before he asked, "What about her middle name?"

Elaine's eyes found his. "I'd love to name her after you." She frowned. "But Sara Brent is a little strange. Why don't you pick?"

He beamed. "I've always been partial to Margaret. For my mother."

"Margaret." Elaine rolled the word across her tongue, as though sampling an expensive wine. "We could call her Meg."

"How about that, Meg?" Brent looked proudly down at the baby, who chose that moment to open her eyes. "She likes it," he decided. "You know," he confided uneasily, glancing up at Elaine, "the nurse brought in a packet of paperwork for us to fill out this morning."

"Oh?"

He nodded and continued to gently rock the baby. "Now that we've chosen her name, I can fill out the birth announcement for the newspaper. But that still leaves the question of the birth certificate."

Elaine was puzzled. "What's the problem?"

The rocker squeaked pleasantly as his eyes darted from the baby to her and back to the baby again. "I need to know who to write down as mother."

Her brow furrowed. That was a good question. Sara was, after all, the biological mother. But she was the birth mother. The baby squirmed and clutched a handful of Brent's shirt in her tiny fist, and Elaine's heart constricted painfully. By all rights, it should be Bobby and Sara rocking their newborn. It should be Bobby and Sara filling out the paperwork, receiving congratulations, celebrating life.

Life. Sometimes it was so unbelievably fragile. As she contemplated the little orphan who rested—unaware of the tragic circumstances of her birth—in Brent's strong arms, she made a decision. A decision of which she felt sure both Sara and Bobby would approve. Maybe she was just caught up in the post-partum emotional aftermath. Or maybe it was raging hormones. She would probably never know for sure. But, if she had any choice in the matter, this child would have a live mother and father to call her own.

"Put me down for the mother." Her eyes caught his and held. "And," she suggested shyly, "put yourself down for the father." Elaine braced herself for his refusal. She wouldn't blame him for declining the nomination. That would certainly go far above and beyond the call of duty as a caring labor coach. Still, even though it meant setting herself up for possible humiliation, she wanted to give him the chance. He was the closest thing to a father little Meg would probably ever have.

Brent stopped rocking, his eyes wide. "Me?"

"No, no," she hastily reassured him, backpedaling some. "Not if you don't want to, of course. I doubt that it would be legally binding or anything, and you wouldn't be obligated to care for her in the future, I was just thinking that, you know, since you were here for the birth and, you know—" she continued, babbling, embarrassed "—she doesn't have any family at all, no one to teach her how to play ball, or whatever it is that a father does...."

"Elaine—" Brent interrupted in exasperation "—shut up."

Mortified, her eyes flew to her hands as she nervously plucked the balls of fluff from her blanket. He was right. It was a foolish idea. She didn't know what had possessed her.

"I would be honored." His voice was hushed, filled with emotion and his eyes were suddenly bright.

"You would?" she whispered, afraid that if she spoke out loud, she could break the magic spell that seemed to bind the three of them together.

He pressed his lips to Meg's downy curls. "I wouldn't have it any other way," he whispered back, grinning foolishly.

* * *

Elaine hobbled painfully across the room and eyed her suitcase. It was checkout time. Time to leave the relative safety of the hospital and rejoin the real world. Time to begin her new life as mother to little Sara Margaret. The prospect seemed overwhelming, considering she needed help just getting in and out of bed. How would she ever manage?

"We're all squared away at the front desk," Brent informed her, coming briskly back into the room. "So, if you're ready, I'll take you home."

"I guess so," she responded warily. "I still have some packing to do...."

"It's okay. Take your time. We still have several hours before we have to be out of here." His eyes searched the suite. "What did you do with the car seat?"

Elaine stopped in her tracks and slowly turned to face him. "What car seat?"

Dragging his fingers through his hair, Brent sighed. "We don't have a car seat?"

"Uh...no. I didn't know we'd need one."

He nodded. "It's the law. What about some clothes and diapers and things for the baby? The stuff she's wearing now belongs to the hospital. Except for the disposable diaper she's got on," he amended.

She shrugged and gripped the handrails of the bed for support. Man. She felt as though she'd been run over by a truck. Everything ached. Even her hair. "I didn't think about that," she breathed, wanting desperately to sit down, but fearing the consequences.

Brent snorted. "Well, we can't exactly take her home naked, now can we? It's cold out there."

Tears threatened the already tenuous hold she had on her composure. She was a terrible mother. So far she was miserable at feeding the innocent creature that was her daughter and a complete failure at clothing her. Not to mention the fact that she had no way to get the poor kid home. This was much harder than she'd expected.

Seeming to read her considerable distress, Brent strode to her side and helped her over to the window seat. "Oh, honey, don't cry. I'm sorry. I know you didn't have much chance to get out and shop. I should have thought of that."

"It's just that...huh," she blubbered, "Dr. Hanson told me I couldn't...huh g-g-get out of bed...."

He sank down beside her and pulled her into his arms. "Shh. Hey. Why don't I go get us a car seat and a few clothes and meet you back here in a couple hours. You pack and get the baby fed." He peered into her face, then kissed her eyelids.

She nestled into his comforting embrace, never wanting to leave the security she found there. He smelled pleasantly of a masculine mixture of spicy soap and after-shave, and his heartbeat thudded reassuringly beneath her cheek. Locking her arms around his trim waist, she exhaled contentedly and asked, "How will you know what to get?"

His lips twitched in amusement. "I'll ask. That's my job, remember? Asking questions?"

Pushing her hair away from her face, she smiled, feeling suddenly buoyant. "Thanks." Everything would be all right. Brent was there.

He brushed his lips quickly across hers before he stood. "Get dressed. I'll take care of everything."

Yes, she thought, watching him leave the room, *he would.*

Brent pulled the station's remote van to a stop in front of Elaine's house and hopped out. Coming around to the passenger side, he opened the door and helped her untangle the car seat from the safety belt that held the peacefully sleeping Meg securely in place.

"Really, Brent," she said with a resigned sigh. "I don't

know why you had to abscond with the company van. Are you trying to get us both fired?''

Grinning, he assisted her to her feet and lifted the car seat into his arms. ''Stop bossing me around,'' he commanded her good-naturedly. ''We're not at work.''

Elaine shook her head. ''You're getting a little too big for your britches, buddy,'' she teased, and taking his arm, walked with him to her front door. Feeling suddenly awkward, she searched for the words to thank him for everything he'd done as he opened her front door and let them inside. It was then that reality dawned. He was leaving. How was she going to do this without her partner? Her heart thudded dismally.

She looked around at the familiar walls, trying to orient herself and quell the panic she felt rising at the prospect of single motherhood. Strange, how her home looked exactly the same, when everything else in her life had turned on its ear she mused, slinging her purse onto her coffee table and turning to make her goodbyes.

''Brent,'' she began, and then discovered she was talking to herself. Meg blinked up at her from where Brent had planted her on the sofa, her miniature toes peeking out from beneath her new blanket. ''You is not Brent,'' she said in affectionate, motherly gibberish. ''You is Meg.'' Her heart swelled with love as the baby sneezed, then looked at her with owlish surprise.

Where had he disappeared to? she wondered. Moving to the window, she watched in mute amazement as he opened the back of the van and began unloading what appeared to be a mountain of baby paraphernalia. Realizing her mouth was hanging open, she snapped it shut and smiled. From the look of things, he'd purchased the entire infant section from some lucky store.

''Where do you want this stuff?'' He grunted, wrestling a huge box that obviously contained a crib through her front door.

"Uh," she said, limping over to the hallway that led to the spare bedroom and pointing at the door. "In there, I guess. What on earth have you done?"

"Don't give me a hard time about this, Elaine," he insisted, depositing the crib in the room. "You're going to need this stuff, and I didn't have time to consult you about decor and the like." Brushing past her, he headed out to the van for another load. And another. And...another....

Brent nearly wore a path in her snow-white carpet as he delivered his booty. A changing table, several boxes of disposable diapers, a battery-operated swing, a deluxe stroller, a bassinet, an infant bathing tub—complete with rubber ducky, a half dozen bags of odds and ends for baby maintenance and enough clothing to see Meg well into the first grade.

"I don't suppose you have a partridge in a pear tree in there?" Elaine murmured, sure now more than ever that she was head over heels in love with this crazy cowboy.

Staggering under the weight of a highchair and a host of stuffed animals, Brent shook his head. "No...the lady at Baby World didn't mention that," he responded, taking her seriously. "But I've got several bears, bunnies and a lamb that bleats somewhere in here." He dumped his load in the middle of her living room.

"Hey, Lainey," he enthused, unconsciously calling her by Sara's nickname for her, "take a look at this." Rummaging around in the pile, he found and withdrew a Mother Goose mobile and wound it up. The tune to "Rock-a-bye Baby" tinkled as the little chicks slowly rotated. "When the bough breaks," he sang softly along, "the cradle will fall, and down will come baby—" he looked over at Meg, his eyes loving "—cradle and all."

How had she gotten so lucky? she wondered, sending a silent prayer of thanksgiving heavenward. She didn't deserve him. She would certainly never be able to thank him.

"Brent," she began helplessly, "I..."

"Hold that thought," he ordered, and rushed back out to the van. Returning moments later with a suitcase and sleeping bag, he closed and locked her front door.

She glanced at him in confusion. "What's that?"

Shrugging, he tossed his bag into a chair and arched his back, stretching his shirt tightly over his fascinating physique. "I stopped by my place and picked up a few things."

"You did?" What was he talking about?

"Yes. You're going to need a hand with the baby. And because you don't have a mother, and knowing that you probably hadn't arranged for a nurse, since you weren't even aware you needed a car seat—" he grinned "—I figured I'd volunteer for the job. That is," he said, pausing uncertainly, "if you'll have me...."

The weakness in her knees was not related to the fact that she had just had a baby. Knowing it was probably a horrendous mistake to grow any more dependent on him than she already was, she heard herself whisper, "I'll have you."

She must be nuts. Everyone she'd ever loved had eventually, one way or another, left her. Would he? It was too depressing to contemplate.

"Great," he breathed, relief spreading over his handsome features. "Great!" Crowing happily, he swept her into his arms and crushed her enthusiastically to his chest until she begged for mercy. They stood, holding each other for a supercharged moment, awareness crackling between them, before Brent lowered his head and touched his lips to hers for a brief moment.

Then, sighing, he squeezed her arms and fought for self-control. She looked far better than any new mother had a right to look, he thought, as she gazed up at him. Battling the urge to kiss her senseless, he released her and forced his eyes to the pile of Meg's new furnishings.

"I guess I'd better get started putting some of this stuff together," he said ruefully. He'd have to keep himself busy. Living with Elaine would definitely test his willpower. Feeling a restless arousal grip his belly, he exhaled deeply and rotated his head from side to side. Perhaps he should have bought the kid a car. One that needed a complete engine overhaul. That would keep him occupied. Because if Elaine kept smiling at him in that unguarded, sexy way, he was going to lose it.

''Elaine, what's wrong?''

''Nothing. Go away,'' she snapped testily, her frustration obvious even through the nursery door. It sounded to him as though she'd been crying. He took a deep breath. Dealing with this newer, more emotional version of his usually self-confident boss would take some adjustment. And understanding.

''Don't be ridiculous,'' he cajoled, cracking the door open and poking his head inside. There he found Elaine, sitting in a rocker, staring in dismay at the squalling Meg. He could tell by her fussy cry that the kid was hungry. Why wasn't Elaine feeding her? ''What's the problem, Elaine?'' he asked, coming over and kneeling down next to her.

She turned her large eyes balefully to him and, hesitating, seemed to search for the words to explain her predicament. She looked almost embarrassed. ''Brent, do you remember in class when they taught us how the baby is supposed to latch on to the breast?''

Nodding thoughtfully he responded, ''Yes.''

A small flicker of hope flared in her eyes. ''Oh, good.'' Her sigh contained quiet desperation. ''And do you remember what they said to do if the mother becomes engorged?'' She raised her voice to be heard over the baby.

He frowned. ''Sort of.''

''Sort of? Brent, that's not good enough,'' she cried. ''Think! You have to remember. If you don't I'm afraid this kid is going to starve to death.''

Meg's pitiful cry was growing steadily angrier, and Elaine's panic seemed to run parallel to the baby's outrage.

His eyes dropped to her considerable bustline, which was prominent beneath her nightgown, and he immediately averted his eyes. Though breast-feeding was the most natural thing in the world, and it had even been his idea in the first place, there was something incredibly intimate about discussing Elaine's breasts with her. In class it had seemed so clinical. Here it seemed so...personal. "She's not latching on?"

"Obviously not," she complained, bouncing the baby stiffly on her knee. "I don't know how she could, seeing that I have two bowling balls on my chest at the moment. There is nothing to latch on to! Arnold Schwarzenegger couldn't latch on to these babies. I could star in a Madonna video. Without the metal bra," she nearly shouted, her hysteria rising.

He bit the inside of his cheek to keep from laughing. It was true. She could. As far as he was concerned, she looked great. But telling her that now probably wouldn't win him any points in the tact department.

"Look," he said, rising to his feet and lifting the baby to his arms. "I seem to remember them saying something about wet heat for this kind of problem. Why don't you go take a hot shower and relax? I'll take care of Meg. She won't starve to death, trust me. She's as healthy as a horse."

Elaine looked doubtful.

"Go on. We'll be fine, won't we, sweetheart?" He looked down at Meg who'd grown quiet in his arms.

"Oh, sure," Elaine huffed, as she took his advice and headed slowly toward the door. "She's quiet for you. I think the men should have to feed the baby," she continued grumpily and her voice grew dimmer as she headed—griping all the way—down the hall to the bathroom.

Brent smiled down at the baby. "Be patient, sweetie. She's learning."

A half hour later, Elaine returned, considerably refreshed and ready to try again. Settling herself back into the rocker, she looked up at Brent and held her arms out for the baby. "Umm," she began, feeling quite awkward, "I don't suppose you could give me a hand here. After all, you were pretty good at this in class, as I recall."

"Uh, sure." Brent couldn't quite seem to meet her eyes as he lowered the baby to her lap. "I would try the football hold."

"Right," she said with a grin. "Like I know how to hold a football. Men."

Grinning, but still not able to look at her, Brent positioned the baby in her lap. "Here," he said, his breath tickling her neck as he placed her arms around Meg's tiny body. "Just tuck her feet under your arm and her head should go right about, uh...here." His eyes shot to hers and then to the wall behind her head as he held the baby to her breast. "I think you'll be just fine now, so I'll leave you to it," he said nervously. Slipping his hand from under the baby's head, it brushed against her breast and even though she was still modestly covered by her gown, he froze. "Sorry."

"Brent," she admonished, smiling. "It's okay."

"Okay," he breathed, smiling back. "I'll be in the living room, if you need anything. So, uh...good luck."

"Thanks." She looked gratefully up at him.

"Anytime." He winked, and she watched as he strode across the room and gently clicked the door shut behind him.

Much to her amazement, Brent's reporterlike attention to detail in class proved invaluable, and Meg proceeded to fill her tummy with gusto. "He's pretty cool, huh?" Elaine asked the busily feeding baby. "He says it's okay if you want to call him Daddy someday. Isn't that neat? You'll learn to love him," she whispered confidentially. "I did."

The fire Brent had laid earlier that evening crackled merrily in the fireplace, casting a warm glow across the living room. Elaine stretched contentedly and snuggled into the corner of her sofa, enjoying the peaceful moments of solitude while Brent put Meg down for the night. The weeks since the baby's birth had passed in a foggy haze of night feedings and diaper changes for Elaine, as she adjusted to her new life. And, much to her disbelief, she was loving every minute of motherhood. Thanks to Brent.

He'd been so wonderful. Each night after work he'd come home and taken care of the baby, handling her with the skill of a seasoned father. Watching him in action never ceased to bring a lump of joy to her throat. And after Meg had gone to bed each evening, he would regale her with tales from the office, keeping her in touch with the goings on. It still surprised her how little she thought about, or missed, the station. She was quite content to stay home and nurture her daughter and enjoy Brent's company. Soon enough she would have to return to the daily grind.

They never seemed to run out of things to talk about, though the conversation—thankfully—revolved mostly around Meg's brilliant achievements. Elaine carefully avoided discussing their relationship for fear she might blurt out her innermost feelings toward him and drive him screaming out the door.

Her eyes glazed over as she stared at the dancing flames. Her contentment was marred only by the niggling doubts she had, concerning the feelings she was forming for Brent. And, on the rare occasion that she could bring herself to face the facts, she worried about the unbreakable bond that had formed between him and the baby, as well. Both mother and child were beginning to need and depend on him so much, Elaine dreaded the day when he would pack up his sleeping bag and head back to his cluttered apartment.

How could she ever return to her old life? She couldn't imagine. Not after having sampled the heaven of family. Her eyes shifted from the fire to the Christmas tree Brent had brought home after Thanksgiving last week. He was so thoughtful. Someday he would make some lucky woman a wonderful husband. The thought was completely and utterly depressing.

How on earth had this happened? Just last year at this time, she was telling Sara that she couldn't even begin to understand her intense desire for a family, and now, well, now she could understand perfectly.

Suddenly she wished she could discuss her predicament with her sweet, sympathetic cousin. Elaine missed her desperately. The yawning chasm Sara had left in her heart was slowly being filled by her daughter and Brent, but the scar would be with her always.

"She's sound asleep."

Pulling her focus from the fire, she turned to smile at Brent as he flopped down on the couch beside her. "I'm glad," she murmured sleepily. "We had a long day today. I'm tired."

Brent lifted his feet to her coffee table and, shoving a stack of magazines to the floor, made himself comfortable. It continued to confound her that his slovenly housekeeping habits didn't matter to her. She'd certainly changed. For some reason she found his messy little quirks endearing. Her priorities were so different now, sometimes she barely recognized herself.

"You look sleepy," he commented, thoughtfully studying her face. "How are you feeling these days, anyway?"

"Terrific. Back to normal, pretty much. I won't be doing any gymnastics in the near future," she teased, "but cartwheels never really were my forte."

"You certainly have bounced back quickly," he noted

approvingly. "No one would ever be able to guess you gave birth just over a month ago."

She was inordinately pleased that he'd noticed. Smiling modestly, she said, "I'm doing okay, for an old broad."

He shook his head and laughed. "You're not old."

"Maybe, but if I don't get to bed soon, I'll fall asleep right here on the couch. Ten years ago, I could easily stay up all night long, but these days..." She sighed. "Well, anyway, you have to get up early, and I'm sitting on your bed," she paused awkwardly, suddenly aware that she was indeed sitting on his bed. Saying it out loud seemed incredibly intimate, and with his uncanny ability to read her thoughts, she decided she'd better get out of there. "So, uh, good night."

Their eyes collided and locked. She could tell he hadn't missed the reference to his bed, or her apparent uneasiness about being there with him at this late hour. The look she encountered in the deep recesses of his dark green gaze sent a rush of new and unexpected feelings coursing through her. Feelings of desire and longing. For the first time in her life, Elaine was beginning to understand what it meant to be completely in love, and her heart pounded wildly with exhilaration. He was able to make her feel so feminine. Not at all the barracuda she knew the rest of the news crew saw her to be.

Standing on unsteady legs, she tried to appear nonchalant. "Good night," she said airily, and before she could say anything further that would undoubtedly humiliate her, she headed for the safety of her room.

The tiny mewling of Meg's nighttime cry finally penetrated the pleasant dreams that flitted through Elaine's subconscious. Dreams of Brent and white picket fences and loving all the time. And more babies that looked like Meg and Brent. Struggling back to wakefulness from the elusive

Shangri-la of her dreams, she sat up, pulled on her robe and, standing slowly, proceeded to stagger to the nursery.

But the nursery was empty. Confused, Elaine left the baby's room and made her way to the living room, where she paused at the doorway and took in the poignant scene before her.

Brent, clad only in a pair of loose-fitting pajama bottoms, held little Meg against the powerful wall of his bare chest and walked slowly around the room, babbling to her in tender baby talk. She stood, drinking in the sight for a moment, amazed at how his imposing physique contrasted with the fragile babe in his arms. It was so unbelievably sweet.

She cleared her throat slightly, to make her presence known, and he looked up at her and smiled a smile that sent shock waves through her heart. How could she have been so blind where he was concerned? She'd actually managed to convince herself that this hunk of a man was nothing but a hick from the sticks.

He was anything but that. Brent Clark was a man among men. No wonder everyone in the secretarial pool was enamored of him. He was not only the nicest man she'd ever met, but he was also stunningly gorgeous. She shivered, reacting to the raw, animal magnetism that was palpable from clear across the room.

"She just needed a change, I think," he whispered, moving toward her through the flickering shadows that emanated from the fireplace. "I didn't want to wake you, considering how tired you've been." Tucking his chin to his chest, he smiled at the baby's cherubic face. "I was just going to put her down."

Elaine could only nod, too overcome by the need that had sprung to life deep in the well-guarded recesses of her soul, and followed him numbly to the nursery. Standing next to him as he lowered the baby into her crib and tucked her in, she knew that she should go back to her room. He had everything under control here. But try as she might, she couldn't seem to make her heart obey the dictates of her mind. She stood helplessly as he finished his task and turned to look at her.

And, convincing her once and for all that he could truly read her mind, he slowly reached out and pulled her into his arms.

Chapter Nine

Brent gathered her body up against his, and Elaine was filled with a breathless wonderment at the raw power of his embrace. Running her fingertips over the heated curves of his well-muscled, delightfully bare chest, she suddenly knew that she hadn't even begun to realize how much she'd craved his touch. Elaine caught her breath as he eased them down into the rocker and cradled her in his lap. The slow, rocking sensation, coupled with the breathtaking kisses he rained across her cheeks before returning to her mouth, was the most erotic experience she'd ever had.

The day that Brent had moved in with her, she'd persuaded herself that there would be no problem keeping their relationship strictly platonic. After all, he was far too level-headed to become involved with a hormonal basket case like herself. Not to mention the fact that she was also his boss. The kisses they had shared before he'd moved in had merely been a reaction to the nightmares she'd endured at the loss of Sara and Bobby. His embrace had been a healing balm to her battered soul, and she had known instinctively that she could trust him.

But could she trust herself?

It was becoming increasingly clear that the answer to that question was no.

His kiss was gentle, but it was evident by his tortured touch, that he was exercising restraint. And when she didn't resist his advances, but instead, responded to him with abandon, he yielded to temptation and gave in to the lure of their passion. His kiss deepened with an urgency that sent shock waves of need down her spine and into her stomach.

Elaine's pulse was a raging timpani against her breast. Never before had she seen such a special look in a man's eyes. A look that told her how infinitely desirable she was to him. A look that told her without words just how badly he wanted her. And his increasing fervor ignited a matching blaze in her.

After all they'd been through together, bringing Meg into the world and learning to love her, being here with Brent this way seemed the most natural thing in the world. She didn't stop to analyze. She wanted him, and nothing had ever felt so right.

Their kiss was ardent, feverish in its intensity, driving Elaine half out of her mind from need. His mouth fitted hers oh, so exquisitely. She loved the sensation of his mustache as it tickled her upper lip, her neck and that special spot behind her ear.

His mustache suited his face, too, she decided woozily, running her hands through the ebony curls at the nape of his neck. It gave him a rugged, masculine look. And as his hands traveled up over her hips to her waist and then higher still, she felt goose bumps of pleasure rise over her entire body. She grasped his steel biceps for support and shivered.

He whispered words of need and encouragement along her lips, into her ears, against her neck. Arching back in his arms to give him access to the place where her throat blended into her collarbone, she sighed as she attempted to satisfy her voracious craving for the man who held the key to her heart.

He paused for a moment, looking down at her, his eyes filled with such eloquence, it threatened to undo the last shred of her composure. In that moment Elaine became lost in the rapture of the virile man who held the power to steal her heart. And it was thrilling. Intoxicating. Exhilarating. Like nothing she'd ever experienced before.

Dragging his lips from hers, his voice was ragged and husky as he spoke. "Elaine, I think we should…"

He stopped abruptly at Meg's cry, and Elaine felt as if someone had tossed a bucket of cold water over them.

He groaned and kissed her hard one last time. "She sounds hungry," he said. Releasing Elaine from his grasp, he nudged her—dazed—to her feet. "I'm sorry," he said, and standing up beside her, raked an unsteady hand across his jaw. "I never meant for it to go that far."

Meg's cry escalated.

"Of course," she said, suddenly confused, unable to meet his penetrating gaze. *He never meant for it to go that far.* She wrestled for an instant with the meaning of those words. Words that seared so painfully through her heart she was unable to speak. Obviously she'd misinterpreted the look in his eyes. Assigned a deeper meaning. She could only conclude that he'd never really wanted her in that way, but instead had fallen victim once again to her neediness. For him it had been a mistake. Purely physical. She felt like a charity case. "Me, too," she agreed, because her pride prevented her from doing otherwise.

He stood uncertainly for a moment, as though trying to decide what he could do to put things back to rights.

Still reeling from the powerful effects of his passion, Elaine moved woodenly to the crib and bent to lift the baby into her arms. Meg was so warm and cuddly, but even the child's cherubic presence couldn't fill the aching void that suddenly threatened to tear her heart in two.

He'd never meant for it to go that far. Of course. She'd known that from the beginning. How had she managed to make him an accomplice in her pathetic vacuum of a life? Obviously she'd taken unfair advantage of the fact that he felt sorry for her.

Mortified at having coerced him into filling her endless list of needs, she clutched the innocent baby tightly in her arms and managed a weak smile.

"I'll...feed her...now," she told him haltingly, wondering how she'd ever be able to face him in the morning. But she knew she would have to find a way. She would rally. Go on as if nothing unusual had happened. She was after all, Elaine Lewis, tough-as-nails television producer. It was time to remember that. She sighed, knowing deep in her heart that it was no longer true. She wasn't the same woman anymore. Not the same at all.

Forcing herself to return his tentative smile, she watched in despair as he backed out of the room.

Brent sagged into the couch that had been his bed since the baby had been born and stared despondently into the fire. Never had a woman affected him the way Elaine did. He'd been around the relationship block a time or two in his life, but never with the intensity that he had with Elaine. And yet, he thought, closing his eyes in disgust, he'd nearly blown it just now. Nearly given in to the unbearable temptation to claim her as his own. To show her physically just what she'd come to mean to him.

What a clod. Wincing, he allowed his head to drop back against the back of the couch. What the hell had he been thinking? The woman had just given birth for crying out loud. The last thing he was sure she wanted at this point was to be pawed by a lust-crazed employee.

Except it wasn't lust. Groaning, he pulled one of her

afghans across his bare torso. It was love. He loved Elaine Lewis with every fiber of his being, and he was dying to show her. But he couldn't. Not now. She was still in mourning. Still healing mentally and physically from events she'd had no control over.

Oh, damn. He pummeled a needlepoint throw pillow and called himself every kind of fool. He'd really mucked it up back there, too. He'd wanted to make her understand how profoundly sorry he was that he'd taken advantage of the situation. To tell her that he understood how she felt, and what she was going through. To tell her that he loved her, but if she didn't return his feelings, that it was okay. He understood.

But no. Instead, he'd blurted out some gibberish about not wanting to go that far. What the hell did that mean? It was obvious that she'd been confused. Although, much to her credit, she'd been gracious and let him off the hook. He was probably lucky she didn't slap the living daylights out of him.

Balling the throw pillow up into a mangled wad, he made a vow, right there and then, that no matter how desperately he wanted her, he would wait until she was ready. No more physical contact. It would be torture, but then again, another incomplete encounter like the one in the nursery, just now, might possibly kill him.

In the meantime, he would become so indispensable to her that she couldn't envision life without him. And when he asked her to marry him, she wouldn't be able to refuse. Unless, of course, he'd blown it. If that was the case, he'd join a monastery, because life as he'd known it before Elaine was over.

Two weeks later the classroom at Chicago Central Hospital was decorated festively for Christmas. Everyone from the birth class was there to show off their new offspring, and Elaine and Brent were no exception.

Cornered at the punch bowl by the new mothers in the group, Elaine did her best to follow the conversation and at the same time keep an eye on her small family. Poor Brent stood at the other end of the room cradling Meg in his arms, held captive by Dick Olsen's incessant sales pitch. She felt sorry for him, and as soon as she got a chance, decided to rush over and rescue him.

Smiling, she caught his eye. He nodded imperceptibly in her direction, and without a word made it clear that the sooner she could come to his aid the better.

"Your husband sure is a proud papa," Dick's wife, Mary, said, nibbling on a Christmas cookie and following Elaine's gaze across the room. She shifted her son in her arms and inclined her head at Brent.

Liz Martin turned slightly to see what they were talking about. "He's really cute with her," she commented in agreement. "So protective. It's amazing how much Meg takes after him. You must hear that a lot."

Squinting, Elaine thoughtfully studied Brent and her baby. They were right. Meg's downy curls were the same dark shade, her eyes held the same sweet countenance, even her nose and chin were replicas in feminine form of Brent's. It was pretty uncanny. Funny how she'd never noticed that before.

"One of the nurses at the hospital mentioned that, just after she was born," Elaine said, remembering Sandy's remark. And though she knew it was impossible, it pleased her that everyone seemed to think that Brent really was Meg's father. In a way he was. Although she knew that no amount of wishing on her part could make it permanent. She would just have to enjoy these brief months of maternity leave together while she could. Then Brent would move on and leave her and the baby to face the world alone. Just like everyone else in her life.

This dismal train of thought didn't bear thinking about, she mentally chided herself. It was a party, for heaven's sake. She would just have to cross that bridge when she came to it. Too bad she couldn't blow the bridge up.

Mary's smile was shy. "I can see why the nurse would say that. They are two of a kind, aren't they?" She reached over and helped herself to several more cookies. "I don't think our boy looks like either of us. You're lucky, Elaine," she offered bashfully. "You and Brent are such a stunning couple, Meg is sure to be a beauty."

Taken aback, Elaine was at a total loss for words. *Stunning couple?* It was true that Brent looked quite handsome tonight in his faded jeans and cowboy boots. The casual shirt he wore was pressed for once, thanks to her. He wore it opened slightly at the collar, and the sleeves were rolled up revealing his strong forearms. His straight white teeth flashed beneath his dark mustache as an easy, tolerant grin stole across his face from time to time. He stood, his legs spread slightly for balance and rocked the baby back and forth as he patiently listened to Dick's endless diatribe. No wonder every woman he came in contact with fell in love with him.

Liz sighed. "I wish Danny would take half the interest in Harmony that Brent does in Meg." Pausing, she untangled Harmony's chubby fist from her long, ruler-straight hair. "Brent is so natural with her. Danny claims he's afraid of breaking Harmony. I think it's just an excuse to hide in the garage and work on his bike," she said confidentially.

Young Vicky jostled her squalling son in her arms, absorbing the conversation of the older mothers. "If you think that's bad, you should try living with a guy who works two jobs during the day and goes to school at night. I'm stuck with Trevor all by myself every day. None of my friends want to hang around us anymore, and I'm afraid that Jason is just going to take off someday, like his dad did to him."

The fear that flashed across her youthful face tore at Elaine's heart. In some ways she could identify with the girl.

Vicky looked over at Jason, who stood alone and visibly uncomfortable by the door. "I think you guys are lucky." She patted the fussy Trevor on his back. "Especially you." Vicky grinned up at Elaine. "He's cool," she pronounced, referring to Brent with all the wisdom of a teenage groupie.

"Yes." Elaine had to agree. He was very cool. Deciding that this was the perfect opportunity to make good her escape, Elaine excused herself from the gathering at the refreshment table and moved across the room toward Brent.

"I brought you some punch," she said, smiling as she extricated him from Dick's clutches and led him to a deserted section of the room where they could talk for a moment. Ever since the night of their fateful kiss in the nursery two weeks ago, they'd been somewhat formal with each other. Elaine hated that fact that their easy camaraderie was a thing of the past, and hoped that Brent's festive mood could help them get beyond that, for tonight at least. It seemed she was in luck.

"Thanks," he breathed, taking the cup of punch from her hand. "Dick had such a tight grip on my arm, I was afraid I was going to have to chew it off at the shoulder to get away."

Elaine laughed gleefully, drawing looks of envy from the other wives in the party. "He can be tenacious."

Brent snorted. "No lie. Did you know that we need a family car immediately? He wants us to come out to the lot tomorrow."

"What'd you say?"

"Shecky, get the jet."

They laughed, finally easy with each other again.

"Just kidding. I told him I had to talk to the little woman." He grinned at her. "It's not a bad idea, really. Your Jag isn't really made for family life, and I can't keep stealing the company van."

"True," Elaine agreed, "but do you think we should go to Dick?"

"Not without a bodyguard." His eyes twinkled pleasantly. "He's pretty upset that Mary hasn't lost any weight since the baby was born."

"What a creep," Elaine said, and smiled in greeting across the room at the Harlows in their matching red-and-green sweatsuits. Even Harlow, Jr., sported a tiny red-and-green sleeper. They looked festive. In a way she envied their corny little family.

"Yeah. Says she's still sleeping in the spare room." Brent wiggled his eyebrows, his expression loaded with meaning.

"Can you blame her?"

Brent shook his head. "No. He did want to know, however, if we were...uh, you know, back in the saddle, so to speak."

Elaine gasped and then giggled nervously. "What did you say?"

"I told him not for lack of trying."

"Brent!"

"What?" He feigned innocence. "I think he has a crush on you. He couldn't get over how fetching you look in this outfit." He tugged playfully on the sleeve of her red pantsuit. "He's right, you know. You are definitely the best looking woman in the room."

"Oh, for crying out loud..." Elaine huffed, knowing that he was teasing her, and loving it. Luckily, before their conversation could grow any more awkward, Nurse Shocktaag came over to make the obligatory party talk.

Ruby stared down her pointed nose at Meg, who stared back apprehensively at this new face. This was not Mommy or Daddy, her look seemed to say.

"Hello, little one." Ruby tickled her under the chin, and Meg smiled. "How are you liking your mother and father? Are they being good to you?"

"Brrbbtt." Meg drooled and blew bubbles.

"Ah, so you like them, no? This is good. I can tell they like you very much, too. You are daddy's princess?"

Meg waved her arms and squealed.

"Yes." The stern woman pursed her lips and winked knowingly at the baby. "I can see the bond. There is nothing like daddy to make us feel safe."

Brent smiled over the top of the baby's head at Elaine, and longing to linger in the delightful glow of this fairy tale, she smiled back.

"Hey. You're supposed to be asleep," Brent whispered to Meg, as he peered down into her crib at her. Lifting her up to his broad shoulder, he moved through the moonlight and settled with her in the rocker. Unable to drift off to sleep after the party, he'd decided to check on the baby. He was feeling decidedly restless. Elaine had looked so beautiful tonight. She stirred something in his gut that he was beginning to fear would never go away.

"So, what did you think of all those other babies tonight?" he asked the child who nestled securely against his chest. "They were kind of lame compared to you, huh? You were definitely the smartest kid in the bunch." He patted her back. "And," he murmured in quiet baby talk, loving the way she stared so contentedly up at him, "you is definitely the prettiest one, too. Just like mama."

He hummed a few bars of a lullaby from one of the tapes Elaine had bought, and her eyes began to drift shut as he rocked her back and forth. "You know," he whispered. "I wish you really were my little girl. I feel like your daddy already." Her eyes shut tight, and she gripped a lock of his hair in her tiny fist, melting his heart.

"I promise you, little one. I'm going to do everything in my power to convince your mama that she needs to marry me someday." He paused and stroked her soft curls with his finger. "I just have to figure out how I'm going to do it, that's all. I have to make her an offer she can't refuse."

He continued murmuring sweet nothings about a future together as the moon slowly rose in the winter sky. A future of Christmases and Birthdays, a future of bicycles and roller skates, a future of brothers and sisters who were as smart and beautiful as she and her mother were.

The next morning Elaine turned off the shower's rejuvenating spray and stood listening. It was quiet. Good. The baby hadn't awakened yet. She'd become quite adept at jumping in and out of the shower while the baby slept, all the while listening for her tiny cry.

As she stood toweling off, a sound reached her ears, but it wasn't the sound she'd been anticipating. It was the doorbell. Hurriedly, she reached to the back of the bathroom door for her robe and wondered who on earth it could be. Brent had left for work over an hour ago.

Wrapping the sash firmly around her waist, she twisted a fluffy bath towel around her head, and after a quick peek into the nursery at the still-sleeping Meg, went to see who would be calling at this hour of the morning.

She peered though the peephole and discovered an elegantly dressed, highly sophisticated-looking woman standing impatiently on her stoop. Elaine didn't recognize her, but deciding that she most likely wasn't here to rob the place, pulled open her front door and smiled a curious greeting.

"Hello." The regal woman's smile was polished. "I don't believe we've met. I'm looking for an Elaine Lewis?" She extended a perfectly manicured hand. "I'm Amanda Johnson. Bobby Johnson's mother."

Chapter Ten

"Oh." Flustered, Elaine grasped the proffered hand for a moment as a feeling of foreboding washed over her. Bobby's mother. Of course. She'd heard about her from Sara on occasion, but knew that there had been a certain amount of estrangement between the young couple and this intimidating woman. With the emotional upheaval of the past year, Elaine hadn't given much thought to Amanda Johnson, other than to wonder briefly why she hadn't attended her son's funeral.

"Won't you please come in?" she asked, self-consciously smoothing the towel that adorned her head.

Nodding confidently, Amanda brushed past Elaine, as a cloud of cloying, expensive perfume wafted after her into the foyer.

"Please, uh—come this way," Elaine invited awkwardly, leading Amanda to the living room and wishing she'd had a chance to straighten up. Brent's sleeping bag lay in a rumpled pile on the floor next to the couch, and his personal effects were strewn about in his typical happy-go-lucky style. The chaos hadn't bothered her until now.

Quickly shoving his bedding aside and tossing his dirty laundry into a pile in the corner, she turned and sent a flushed smile in her visitor's direction. "Please—" she gestured to the couch "—have a seat."

"Thank you," Amanda murmured, glancing disdainfully around the cluttered room.

It was obvious from the look on her face that she disapproved of Elaine's housekeeping abilities. Swallowing her embarrassment, Elaine tightened the sash to her robe and racked her brain to remember what Sara had told her about Bobby's mother.

Bits and pieces of previous conversations with her cousin flashed through her mind as she tried to organize what precious little she knew about the woman.

Amanda Johnson had never been much of a mother-in-law, as Elaine recalled. Always on the go, the socialite had made a career of seeing the world after her husband and Bobby's father—Robert Johnson, Sr.—had passed away several years ago.

Sara, bless her compassionate heart, had felt it was Amanda's way of dealing with the grief of losing her husband. To run away from it. She had defended Amanda's continued absence by saying that she was sure Bobby's mother would return to her home in Chicago as soon as she and Bobby presented her with a grandchild. Sara had loved the idea of a big family—complete with doting grandmother—no matter how spoiled its members were. And Sara had believed that if there was one thing in this world Amanda loved more than spending money and traveling, it was her only son. She would return soon, Sara had predicted, just wait and see.

Elaine had had a feeling her cousin had been suffering from a severe case of denial, considering Amanda had been conspicuously absent from their wedding, but Elaine had felt, if it made Sara happy to hope for the best, then so be it.

Unfortunately Elaine's feelings had not been unfounded. One day shortly after Robert passed away, Bobby had confided the truth to Elaine. And the truth of the matter had been that Amanda hadn't felt that Sara was in her son's league socially and had continually urged him to leave his young wife. Especially since the poor thing had been unable to bear him an heir. After a bitter argument, Amanda had stormed off to Europe, and as far as Elaine knew, never had the chance to make amends with her precious son. Beyond that, there was little else Elaine knew about Amanda.

Other than the fact that the woman was turning her into a nervous wreck at the moment. Fidgeting under her scrutiny, she wished that Amanda would stop staring at the towel she wore turban-style around her head and state her business.

"What can I do for you?" Elaine asked politely, trying to quell the disquieting feeling of doom that had followed Amanda into her home.

Amanda settled gingerly into her seat, crossed her long, shapely stocking-clad legs and smiled rigidly. "It is my understanding that you are Sara Johnson's first cousin."

Elaine nodded and wondered how appropriate it would be to offer condolences about the young couple to Amanda, considering the nature of her relationship with Bobby at the time of his death. She decided to wait and let his mother set the tone.

"Yes, that's true. Our mothers were sisters. When her parents passed on, she came to live with my folks until she married your son," she said. Adrenaline flowed through her veins, and she felt her body reacting instinctively to this perceived enemy. Although she couldn't quite put her finger on the problem, she could sense something was wrong. Very wrong.

Reaching into her small clutch bag, Amanda withdrew a packet of what appeared to be paperwork of some kind and then sat back in her chair and looked directly at Elaine.

"It is also my understanding that you were close to my son and his wife." It was more of a statement than a question. Elaine's radar clicked into overdrive as she wondered where the woman was leading with this.

"Yes. I loved them both very much."

What could have been a flash of pain briefly touched Amanda's eyes. "Yes." She nodded. "Then I'm sure you are aware that Bobby and I were very close until he decided to marry Sara."

"Uh," Elaine wet her dry lips with her tongue.

"It's all right." Amanda waved a dismissive hand in her direction. "He never did listen to me." Her face softened for a moment. "It's no secret that I felt he married beneath his social class. No offense," she hastened to loftily assure Elaine.

Insulted Elaine arched an eyebrow, tightening her grip on the arm of her chair.

"You are probably also aware," she continued, "that Bobby and I had a...falling out...before I left for France last year."

Noticing the visible anguish that tinged Amanda's cultured voice, Elaine nodded. Now that she was a mother herself, she could only imagine what it must be like to lose a child after a quarrel. She could almost feel sorry for the woman. Almost, but not quite.

"I did not learn of his death until after the funeral." Amanda's eyes glazed over. "His lawyer went to a considerable amount of trouble to find me, but by then it was too late. Bobby was gone." She sighed and shook her head as if to clear it from the demons that tormented her over the rift with her son. "I saw no point in coming home to a lot of unhappy memories, so I stayed in France with some old family friends and dealt with my grief." Her laugh was short and derisive. "There was no one left to come home to, anyway."

"I'm so sorry for your loss," Elaine murmured, uncomfortable with the personal nature of the conversation. For the life of her, Elaine couldn't figure out why Bobby's mother was here, telling her such confidences. And why now? She wriggled restlessly in her seat.

"I am, too." Amanda glanced down at the papers she held in her hands. "That brings me to why I'm here."

"Oh?" Finally. Dread filled her heart as she waited for the other shoe to drop.

"Yes. When I came home, I found some papers in my son's safe-deposit box. I contacted his lawyer and discussed them with him."

Elaine's eyes darted to Amanda's as the tiny hairs at the back of her neck stood at attention. *What papers?* she wondered anxiously.

Smiling and confident, Bobby's mother held the packet up for Elaine to see. "I was surprised to learn that you had entered into an agreement with my son and daughter-in-law to act as a surrogate mother for their child. I knew that they were exploring that option. At one point I think Sara even considered me." Her condescending smile was hard, and it was evident that she thought the very idea was ridiculous.

Elaine bristled. She probably didn't want to ruin her perfect figure, she thought uncharitably. Age certainly couldn't have been an issue. Platinum blond and wrinkle free, Amanda hardly looked old enough to be Bobby's mother.

It suddenly dawned on Elaine that some other woman could have given birth to Meg, and the thought was immensely disturbing. She couldn't envision Amanda as anybody's mother, let alone sweet, innocent little Meg. Never had she been more delighted than she was now, that she had agreed to give life to the baby. Besides Brent, it was the most wonderful, miraculous thing that had ever happened to her. No job or perfectly toned figure could ever give her the happiness she had now, thanks to her new little family. She doubted that someone like Amanda could ever understand that.

"Anyway, being that this child would be my granddaughter or grandson," Amanda continued, "I wanted to find out if anything had ever come of this agreement, and if so—" she eyed Elaine coolly "—I would like to file for adoption."

Adoption? Suddenly Elaine felt faint and her heart leapt into her throat. Dear Lord. This unfeeling, emotionless woman wanted to take her child from her? No! Every maternal instinct ever known to womankind sprang to life within Elaine as she felt herself tense for battle. Never. The only way this woman would ever get Meg was over her dead body.

Her mind reeled frantically. What would she do? Lie. Yes, that was it, she would tell the woman that there had never been a baby. Then, hopefully, Amanda would go away, back to some foreign country and leave them alone.

She opened her mouth to speak, but unfortunately Meg had other ideas and chose that moment to announce her existence to her grandmother.

Amanda's eyes widened with interest as she homed in on the cries that came from the nursery. "Is that the baby?" she asked, unable to contain her curiosity. "May I see him?"

No! Elaine wanted to scream. Grandmother or not, this woman couldn't just waltz in here and announce that she wanted to take her baby. Valiantly she struggled to understand the strain the woman must be under. To give her the benefit of the doubt. Perhaps she didn't really mean what she was saying. Perhaps it was just the grief talking. "Her," Elaine duly informed her. "It's a girl."

"A girl?" Shrugging off her disappointment, Amanda rose to her feet and followed the sound of Meg's voice.

Taken aback by her bold behavior, Elaine rushed after

and found the woman standing next to the crib. Amanda's perfectly manicured hand was covering her mouth and her eyes glistened with unshed tears.

"She's beautiful," she breathed, sorrow at all she had missed out on these past few years with her son filling her expression.

"Yes," Elaine agreed, apprehensively. "She is."

Amanda stood, staring at her granddaughter for a moment, then turned abruptly and left the room. Elaine picked up the fussy baby and held her tightly to her breast. She kissed Meg's sunny little face and whispered words of comfort and reassurance as she followed the baby's grandmother back to the living room on unsteady legs. Trying to rein in her runaway emotions, she patted the child's bottom and longed for Brent's comforting presence. He would know what to do with this...this...barracuda.

"I want her," Amanda announced without preamble. "I want to adopt her. She is all that I have left of my son."

She turned to confront Elaine. The cold, calculating look that crossed Amanda's face sent waves of terror rippling through her body. Gripping Meg so tightly that the child squeaked in protest, Elaine gallantly battled the hysterical urge to bolt.

"I imagine," Amanda continued, getting down to brass tacks, "since you are not the baby's biological mother, that you will be relieved to dispense of the burden of raising someone else's child. Since you are merely the surrogate, I feel that—as the child's grandmother—I have more of an emotional investment."

Elaine gasped, too shocked to respond to the woman's harsh words. "No," she whispered. When it came to emotional investment, she doubted that Amanda had a clue. Otherwise, she would leave the baby where she was.

"No?" Amanda's eyes narrowed. "Surely you can't mean that. It says right here," she waved the legal documents in her hand under Elaine's nose, "that you were planning to give the baby to Bobby. It say's right here in black and white that you wanted to make sure that your responsibility for the baby ended with the birth. Well—" her tight laughter tinkled sharply "—I'm here to take over."

Elaine longed to slap the smug look off the audacious woman's face. It had been a lifetime since she'd signed those papers. She was not the same woman who'd agreed to that arrangement a year ago. She was a mother now. And, like a she bear protecting her cub, she squared her shoulders in outrage.

"Mrs. Johnson, having just discovered the existence of the child, I don't believe you've had time to give this matter much thought," she said, her voice amazingly calm under the circumstances. "I'm sure once you have taken time to consider all that would be involved with raising this child, you'll agree that she is better off with me. I'm the only mother she has ever known. And," she continued, her voice vehement, "I want it to stay that way."

"Oh, but you're wrong," Bobby's mother bit out tersely. "I have given this a lot of thought. This is my chance to make amends to my son. By caring for his child. I can give the baby everything. I have money. I'm also going to be remarried this spring and can offer the child a father. My sources tell me that you are a single parent. What do you have to offer?" She glanced around at Elaine's messy house in disgust.

Shaking with rage, Elaine leveled her gaze at the regal woman. "Love," she said, her tone protective—deadly. "I can offer her love."

And that was something she felt quite sure that Amanda was in short supply of. Taking the baby because of some misplaced sense of guilt over a bad relationship with her first child certainly wouldn't do anybody any good.

Marching over to her front door, she yanked it open and

inclined her head toward her unwelcome visitor. "I'll thank you kindly to leave now."

"Certainly." Amanda seemed unfazed. "You'll be hearing from my lawyer in the next few days. You haven't heard the last of this," she promised, before stepping arrogantly to the porch.

Slamming the door behind her, Elaine sagged with the baby against its solid surface long enough to gather her wits, swallow the giant obstruction in her throat and blink away the tears that blinded her. *How dare she?* she raged, shifting Meg to a more comfortable position on her shoulder. *Never. Not in a million years.* Not even if she had to pack the baby up and move to outer Mongolia would she let that evil woman get her clutches on this child.

Striding back to the nursery, she laid the baby back down in her crib, then rushed to the phone to call Brent at work. Her fingers shook violently as she dialed the number. Taking several deep breaths to calm her shattered nerves, she knew that everything would be all right once she could hear Brent's voice. It always was.

"Oh, thank God!" Elaine breathed, and practically dragged the bewildered Brent into her house.

His eyes darted quickly around the foyer, worriedly looking for signs of trouble. "I got here as quickly as I could. What's going on? Is everything all right? Where is the baby?" he asked, fear unlike any he'd ever experienced before clawing at his throat. Elaine's frantic phone call had scared the hell out of him. He'd broken land speed records to get here, and now, seeing her tear-stained face, he felt his alarm begin to rise.

Grasping tight fistfuls of his jacket in her shaking hands, she looked miserably up at him and tried to speak. "She wants to take her away," she whispered, her anguished face pale. She was quivering like an aspen leaf.

"Who?" Brent framed her face between his hands and tilted it up to his. "Who wants to take who away?"

Elaine touched her tongue to her lower lip and closed her eyes. "Amanda Johnson. She wants to take Meg. Brent, she can't do this to us. It's Christmas next week," she added.

He cut her off. "What?" Brent stiffened. His stomach felt as though it had sunk clear to his shoes, and his heart stood still. Someone wanted to take Meg away? "Who's Amanda Johnson? Where is Meg?" The muscles worked convulsively in his jaw.

"She's asleep in the nursery." Elaine choked on a sob and lifted her tear-spiked lashes up to Brent. "She's taking her morning nap. Oh, Brent, she always takes her nap at this time every morning," she babbled, panic-stricken. "I know that. I'm her mother. No one else can ever care for her the way I can."

"Of course you're her mother," he said soothingly. Drawing her into his embrace he wondered what the devil she was getting at. He held her tightly for a moment then, taking her hands in his, he lead her to the living room and pulled her down next to him on the couch. "Why don't you tell me what's going on?" he instructed, trying to slow his own raging pulse. "Start at the beginning. Who is this Amanda Johnson?"

He sat on pins and needles, waiting for her to organize her muddled thoughts. She looked as if she'd seen a ghost, her anxiety was palpable.

"Amanda Johnson is Bobby's mother."

"Meg's father, Bobby?"

"Yes. She's Meg's biological grandmother. She wants to adopt Meg."

Brent sat stupefied as he tried to reconcile the meaning of Elaine's words. He couldn't believe it. He wouldn't believe it. No one would ever take Meg away as long as he had a breath of life left in his body. He would fight this battle for Elaine, and he would win. Of that he was confident. But first he had to size up his opponent.

"Why now? Why has she waited so long to come forward? Why haven't you mentioned her to me before?"

Elaine drew a deep shuddering breath and wrapped her arms protectively around her middle. She looked so frail and lost, Brent suddenly wanted to tear this rotten Amanda woman limb from limb.

"She was in Europe at the time of Bobby's death. She claims that she only just now discovered our agreement in his safe-deposit box."

"What agreement?" Brent was puzzled.

Elaine reached over to the coffee table and picked up a sheaf of papers. "The surrogacy agreement I signed with Bobby and Sara. I told you about it before, remember?" Brent nodded as she handed him the document. "This is my copy. I dug it out of my files after Amanda left."

Brent took the papers from her hand and removed his reading glasses from his jacket pocket. Frowning, he positioned the glasses on his nose and began to scan the document as Elaine poured out the details of Amanda's visit.

He nodded absently from time to time, listening with half an ear. Something about this whole thing just didn't add up. The reporter's blood in him surged through his veins. The more Elaine talked, the more Amanda was beginning to sound like a case. Bobby, on the other hand, sounded like a smart guy. Surely anyone with half a brain would know his mother might try to undermine this surrogacy project. Especially since it seemed that she disliked his young wife so much, he mused, scanning the document.

"Did you read this whole thing?" he asked Elaine, interrupting her tearful account of her unfortunate encounter with Bobby's mother.

"Um," she sniffed and her delicate brow furrowed together. "I think so. Most of it, anyway. I knew that Bobby and Sara would take care of me. I wasn't really that worried about the fine print."

"Mmm." Nodding, Brent ran his hand over his jaw.

"Why?"

"I don't know," he admitted, flipping through the pages. "I just have a feeling. I can't explain it, but from what you tell me about Amanda and Bobby, I just…get…the idea… that…" his voice trailed off as he squinted thoughtfully at the last page.

"What?" Elaine leaned over his body and tried to see what he was reading with such rapt attention.

He looked up at her and, for the first time since he'd walked through the door, grinned. Then, he kissed her on the nose.

"What?" She glanced up from the paperwork to him in confusion.

"I think that good old Bobby was a pretty smart guy. I like the way he thinks."

"Why?"

"Because it says right here, that in the event of his and Sara's death, you are to be named the baby's parent."

"What?" Elaine squealed, delighted. Relief flooded her beautiful features, and she smiled brilliantly, stealing Brent's breath for a moment. "That's fabulous!"

"Well, yes, but there is one provision." Pulling his reading glasses off, Brent chewed thoughtfully on the stem.

"What provision. Where?" Elaine snatched the document out of his hands and searched it to find what he was talking about.

"At the bottom there." Brent pointed to the specific clause. "It would seem that you need to be…married."

Chapter Eleven

"Oh, no," Elaine breathed, suddenly crestfallen. "That's terrible. I'm not married." Groaning, she pushed her hair away from her face and slumped dejectedly against Brent. "That must be why Amanda made a point of telling me that she was going to be remarried in the spring. Obviously Bobby wanted his child to have two parents."

Brent felt a surge of excitement rumble through his stomach. This could be just the opportunity he was looking for. If only he could convince Elaine.... He sat in silence for a moment, searching for a way to broach an idea that was beginning to form in his mind. He had to tread lightly. This was no time to scare her away. With a massive effort, he tried to swallow his zeal and appear nonchalant.

"I can see his point," he deadpanned, schooling his tone to reflect her agitation with this disappointing turn of events.

"But why?" she cried in frustration. "I'm a good mother."

"The best," he agreed. "But apparently, Bobby and Sara felt it was important that their baby have a father. They never discussed this with you?"

"No. I'm sure they never foresaw the need. How could they have known?"

"True," Brent mused, still trying to remain outwardly cool and at the same time keep from exploding with eagerness.

"What are we going to do?" Elaine was beginning to grow agitated again.

"I don't know," he said, frowning his thoughtful, reporter frown. "I suppose you could get married."

"Oh, sure," she sighed. "When they build a Tastee-Freez in hell. I haven't even been on a date in well over a year. Anyway, who would be crazy enough to marry someone who just had a baby?" She covered her face with her hands.

"It's not so crazy," Brent said offhandedly. "In fact, I can think of someone who'd be willing to help out."

"Oh, yeah? Who?" she asked through her fingers.

"Me."

Holding his breath, Brent watched her peel her hands away from the shocked expression on her face. *Please,* he prayed, *please don't say no.* Not yet.

Before she could object, he continued. "I've grown very fond of Meg. And her mother," he added, smiling, and reached out to pull her hands into his. "I'm probably as worried about Bobby's mother taking Meg away as you are. And considering it's my name listed as father on her birth certificate, who better to play the part?" He tightened his grip on her hands. "Elaine, marry me."

"Oh, Brent," Elaine whispered. "You don't have to do that. You've already done so much." Tears glistened in her eyes as she looked up into the face that had become so beautiful to her. This was the moment she'd come to dream about.

If she were honest with herself, she would have to admit that she wanted this more than she'd ever wanted anything else in her entire life. But how could she saddle him with even more responsibility? It didn't seem fair that he was constantly having to bail her out of every jam that came her way. Marriage was certainly above and beyond the call of duty for a reporter just doing his job. She doubted that Walter Cronkite would have gone this far just to get a story about childbirth.

The man was a saint. No wonder she loved him so much. But she would have to turn him down. It was only fair. When—and if—Brent ever proposed to her for real, she wanted it to be because he loved her and Meg as much as they'd come to love him. Then they could be the family of her dreams.

No. There had to be a better way.

"Elaine, if you won't do it for me, do it for Meg. We can't lose her. Not now. I don't think I could stand it." His steady gaze bore into her in silent challenge. "I want to be part of her life," he argued. "To teach her how to ride a bike. To interrogate her boyfriends when the time comes. To be there for her when she needs me."

She was beginning to melt. She must steel herself against her crazy impulse to give in to him. He didn't know what he was getting into.

Brent could tell she was waffling. He searched for a way to convince her that this was their only choice. "It could be a short-term agreement, if you like." Speaking quickly, he pulled out his trump card. He would give her an out. How could she resist such logic? "As soon as Amanda is taken care of, we could end the marriage…if you, you know…want to. We, uh, could figure that out later, of course." If it were up to him, the marriage wouldn't end until Willard Scott was wishing them happy record-breaking anniversary on national television.

Elaine felt an overwhelming wave of tenderness consume

her at the vulnerable expression on his face. Never had she known anyone as wonderful as Brent Clark. And it was then that she knew—as much as she wanted to set him free to find his own happiness in life, she needed him.

Meg needed him.

The thought of losing the angel that slept so peacefully in the next room was more than she could bear. She wasn't strong enough to sustain yet another loss of a loved one. And that included Brent.

If he was sincere, she would love nothing more than to become Mrs. Elaine Clark. Maybe, after they were married, she could find a way to make Brent love her. She knew he already loved Meg.

"Are you sure?" She gulped hard; hot tears slipping unnoticed down her cheeks.

"More sure than I've ever been about anything else in my life."

"Okay, then." She sighed, as a tentative smile played at her lips. "Yes. I'll marry you."

Brent exhaled mightily in relief. Closing his eyes, he sent a prayer of thanksgiving heavenward, and then leaning forward, pulled Elaine into his arms to seal their agreement. As he lost himself in the shy, feather softness of her kiss, he knew that once she was legally his, he would find a way to make her love him.

"You're going to *what?* Brent, it sounded like you said you're going to get married," Margaret's incredulous voice squealed across the line from her living room in Iowa.

Brent grinned, envisioning the look of shock that his mother must be wearing. "You heard right, Mom. So instead of me coming home for Christmas this year, why don't you come to Chicago for the wedding and spend the holidays with us?"

Margaret was rendered speechless.

"Mom?"

"Yes, honey. I'm here. Who's the lucky woman?"

"Elaine."

"The pregnant one?"

Brent laughed. "She's not pregnant anymore, Mom," he reminded her. "We want to get married as soon as possible, so that we can spend the holidays as a family." It was a tiny fib, really. He and Elaine had agreed it would be wise to keep the nature of their agreement a secret. At least until Amanda called off the dogs. Then, if Elaine wanted, they could begin divorce proceedings. But he sure as hell wasn't going to bring it up. He'd never been happier in his life. He was getting the most beautiful, intelligent, sexy woman on the face of this earth, and an adorable baby daughter to boot. How could he be so fortunate?

"Mom, I just know you're going to love her," he promised. "We thought we'd get married next week on the Saturday before Christmas. I'm sending you an airline ticket today. You'll get here Friday afternoon, and you can stay at my place..." His voice trailed off as the sound of some pretty heavy sniffing and squeaking reached his ears.

"Mom? What's wrong?"

"Nothing, honey. It's just that I'm so happy."

"Me, too, Mom." Brent smiled into the phone. "Me, too."

The break room went silent. All eyes stared in shock at Brent. Finally, after what seemed like an eternity to him, Ray broke into an ear-splitting grin and slapped him on the back in a gesture of hearty congratulation.

"You old son of a gun. We all wondered what the deal was between you and The Barr—" Ray went suddenly pink "—uh, Elaine, but we never dreamed you'd fallen in love with her."

Brent grinned at the amazed expressions that had greeted the announcement of his impending nuptials to the boss. He only wished Elaine could have been here to enjoy their slack-jawed wonder, but she was busy making last-minute arrangements for the ceremony. For once he had the dubious distinction of being the one with the juiciest piece of gossip. He was sure he could have knocked most of them over with a feather. This should give them fodder for endless discussions about the particulars of Meg's paternity. He didn't care. As far as he was concerned, he was the baby's father.

"You're getting married Saturday?" Debbie asked, her gamin face scrunched into a knot of wonder. "*This* Saturday?"

"Yep." Brent nodded pleasantly and glanced around the table. "You're all invited, of course. It's going to be a small affair, just a few friends and family. The Old Church on Front Street, downtown. I know it's awfully close to Christmas, but if you could attend, it would mean a lot to both of us. We didn't really have time to have invitations printed or anything, so I'll send out a memo on the particulars."

"Wow. Congratulations," Stu offered with a grin. "Some people will do anything for a raise."

"Yeah," Debbie murmured, unable to keep the disappointment from her voice.

"I guess that means we won't be able to complain about her in front of you anymore, huh?" Ray joked, leaning back on his chair's hind legs, as the room began to buzz with the amazing news.

"'Fraid not." Brent winked at Debbie who smiled slowly in return, apparently deciding that if you can't beat 'em, join 'em.

"She's okay," she admitted grudgingly. "We had a nice talk at the hospital, and the baby—" Debbie beamed "—is a little doll. Good for you, Brent. I hope she'll be good to you."

"She's the best thing that ever happened to me," he told them. He only wished that Elaine felt the same way about him.

* * *

Considering that it had been a hastily planned, last-minute affair, the wedding was beautiful. Elaine made a radiant bride, dressed in a winter white tailored suit that accentuated her newly trim waistline and the soft curves of motherhood. The only thing that would have completed her delirious happiness was the knowledge that Brent was in love with her. But since that wasn't the case, she made the best of the situation and threw herself into the moment. Knowing that this would be her first and last marriage, no matter what the outcome, only made it that much more poignant.

Brent was stunningly handsome in his expensively cut, form-fitting Italian suit. The double-breasted jacket drew attention to his square shoulders and broad chest, and the slacks fitted his long, well-muscled legs like a glove. And as she stood next to him, reciting the vows that would bind them together, if only temporarily, she felt her heart swell with pride. He was not only physically breathtaking, he was the missing piece of her oft-broken heart. She couldn't imagine ever finding anyone who suited her so perfectly.

A surprising number of people attended the wedding: the entire, rabidly curious WCH crew had turned out in droves; Dr. Hanson and his wife; most of the birthing class, who were astonished to find that the Clarks had never been married; a staid but beaming Nurse Shocktaag; several people from Brent's apartment building; little Meg and a tearfully joyous Margaret were all in attendance.

Though she'd only managed to spend a few hours with Brent's mother the evening before the wedding, Elaine had instantly loved her. It was no wonder Brent was such a marvelous man. And, call it woman's intuition, Elaine believed that the feeling was mutual. The fact that Margaret was wild about Meg only served to clinch the bond between the two women. Brent practically had to drag Margaret back to his place, where they'd spent the night. Teasingly, he'd told Elaine that it was bad luck to see the bride before the wedding, and after a lingering kiss that she was sure was mostly for his mother's benefit, he'd promised he'd see her at the altar.

And he'd kept his promise. They were man and wife. Elaine could scarcely believe her good fortune. After a small reception in The Old Church's basement, the newlyweds had climbed into the waiting limousine with Meg and Margaret and gone home to Elaine's.

"Surely, you can't be serious," Margaret said, her brows furrowing in consternation. "Why ever not? Even a day or two in the country would be better than nothing," she said, referring to Brent's announcement that they hadn't planned a honeymoon.

Glancing self-consciously at Elaine, Brent struggled for the words that would satisfy Margaret's obvious mortification. They hadn't planned a honeymoon because they weren't really married. At least not that way. At least not yet. But he couldn't tell that to Margaret.

Thank heavens she was staying at his place for the next few days. It would be impossible to explain the fact that he would be sleeping on the couch on his wedding night. Someday, hopefully sooner than later, he would rectify this painfully inconvenient situation, but not before Elaine was ready.

"Mom, since this is our first Christmas together as a family, Elaine and I thought it would be nice to stay home, you know, with the tree and the gifts and start some traditions of our own with Meg." Shooting a beseeching look in Elaine's direction, he nodded imperceptibly, encouraging her to back him up on this matter.

"Yes," she murmured, blushing furiously at him. "We, uh, wanted to spend the night, uh, together, uh, here, at my…our house here in, uh, the—our bed." She plucked nervously at the petals of her corsage.

Meg squirmed in Margaret's arms as the woman looked back and forth between her son and new daughter-in-law.

"That's just plain silly. Allow me to play the part of interfering in-law for a moment here and say that I think you are making a big mistake. But, it's your life." She sighed dramatically. "If I can't convince you to get away for a day or two, at least go out to dinner. I can take care of the baby. Please. I want to."

Cuddling the baby in her arms, Margaret tilted her head and planted a grandmotherly kiss on Meg's chubby cheek. Striding to the couch in Elaine's living room where she'd deposited her purse after the wedding, Margaret withdrew her billfold and tossed a credit card at Brent.

"Here. Take your beautiful new wife out to dinner," she ordered. "I mean it now. I won't take no for an answer. We'll be just fine, won't we, lovey dover?"

Meg blew a row of bubbles across her rosebud lips and stared happily up at Brent's mother.

Brent turned to Elaine and shrugged. "You heard her."

Elaine nodded and smiled. "Thank you," she murmured as Brent helped her on with her coat. "We'll be back soon."

After quickly deciding where they would go for dinner and finding the phone number in the yellow pages, Brent gave his mother the lowdown on the ins and outs of baby care.

"Her diapers are in here, and I always put this white rash prevention stuff on her bottom before I change her, and she likes to play with Mr. Bunny, and if you hold her facing out, she's happier. Also—" he dragged a pensive hand through his hair "—she only cries really hard if she has a bubble in her tummy. So what I usually do is—"

"Brent. Get out of here. I took care of you for years and you managed to live to tell the tale. Don't give us another thought," Margaret advised, shooing them out the door.

They hadn't been gone ten minutes when the doorbell rang. Looking down at the baby, Brent's mother pursed her lips in dismay. "I can see your mommy and daddy are worrywarts,'' she cooed in baby talk, as she made her way to the foyer with Meg in her arms. Pulling open the front door, she opened her mouth to chastise them, but instead gasped in shock.

''Amanda Johnson?''

Chapter Twelve

Brent watched Elaine take a sip of her coffee in the dim light of the romantic little bistro they'd chosen for dinner, and couldn't believe his good fortune. This heavenly creature was his wife. His blood ran hot at the thought. And this was their wedding day. Correction, wedding night.

Brent shifted uncomfortably in his chair. The annoyingly efficient waiter who had hovered over their table through most of their meal was back, consulting Elaine about dessert. The dessert he had in mind wasn't available on the waiter's little tray of goodies. Oh, no. But it would be the perfect capper to the meal.... Good grief. If he didn't stop this train of thought soon, he'd spontaneously combust.

It was just that he'd never envisioned actually being lucky enough to find someone who fit his requirements so perfectly. Elaine was independent, career oriented, a great conversationalist, wonderful mother, sexy as all get-out, and considering they came from such different backgrounds, they thought a lot alike. They were remarkably simpatico. He couldn't even begin to imagine how lost he would be to her, once they'd made love. Although, he thought morosely, that probably wouldn't happen right away. If ever. Oh, damn, how could he stand it?

Shaking her head politely at the waiter, she lifted her darkly lashed eyes shyly up to Brent's and smiled softly. His pulse roared so loudly in his ears he was afraid she could hear it, too. They'd been somewhat bashful around each other ever since the wedding. The parameters of this new relationship would take some getting used to on both their parts, Brent knew. If he had his way, they'd spend this night in bed...exploring the parameters. By morning they'd both know where they stood. They would be husband and wife in every sense of the word.

"She said Zimbabwe this morning." Elaine beamed up at Brent.

He stared at her, trying to make the quantum leap from their marriage bed, back to the restaurant. What the devil was she talking about?

"Actually, it wasn't Zimbabwe, exactly. It was more like, Zzahhmmwe. Then she said, 'Ahhhhh, ahhhh, ahhhh, zahhmmwe.' I think this bodes well for a career in news, don't you think?" Elaine twinkled mischievously at him.

Oh, she was talking about Meg. Brent gazed at her and smiled. Lordy, he loved the way she liked to chew on her luscious lower lip that way. It made the cutest dimples in the sides of her cheeks. Didn't she realize she was driving him nuts? Man, how he wished he could take his mother's advice about that honeymoon.

"I think she's brilliant and beautiful, like her mommy," Brent said, looking across the table at her through heavily hooded eyes.

Elaine colored girlishly. "Do you know that she is all we've talked about all evening?" Threading her fingers together, she rested her elbows on the table and supported her delicate chin with her hands, a smile playing at th corners of her mouth.

Only nodding because he wanted to remain agreeabl Brent suddenly realized that he didn't have much of a cl what they'd been talking about. Or what they'd eaten f that matter. All he could think about was taking his wi to bed.

"I was surprised at how many people turned out at th wedding today," she murmured, tilting her head at Bre and tossing her luxurious, shiny dark hair away from h delectable jaw. "The gang from the station really isn't s bad, once you get to know them."

"And once they get to know you. I think they' changed their tune about you since you had the baby. Brent wished he could push everything off the table on the floor and take her right there. It certainly wouldn't b as comfortable as a hotel suite, but he wouldn't have wait forever and a day to consummate this union, either.

For crying out loud. He was really beginning to lose i

"If I'd known having a baby would have made me s popular at work, I might have done it years ago," sh teased.

And, I'd have helped, Brent thought.

"You know, Brent, I really can't thank you enough fo well, you know…marrying me and Meg today." She stu ied her nails, embarrassed. "I know it was a real sacrifi for you, and I just don't know how I'm ever going to rep you."

Brent shifted self-consciously in his seat. She was ma ing him out to be some kind of saint. She would be shock if she knew how selfish his motivations had really bee Guilty at having deceived her this way, it seemed only fa to try to set the record straight. After all, she couldn't g around thinking he should be canonized. Especially consi ering the way he'd been mentally undressing her all throu the meal.

"Elaine, it wasn't a sacrifice. I wanted to help, and I have lots of reasons." He sat back in his chair and toyed with the napkin in his lap. "I care a lot about Meg. I love her, actually." His gaze met hers. "And, I care a lot about you...in fact, I—"

"Would you care for some more coffee?" a voice behind him inquired.

"I, uh, oh, sure." Brent leaned out of the way to allow their waiter to refill his cup, and he mentally beat the tar out of the insensitive server. Couldn't the clod see that he was trying to tell the woman that he cared about her? Loved her even?

He sighed and smiled a thanks for the refill. It was probably better this way. The way he was going, he'd have spilled his guts and told Elaine how madly in love with her he was and spoiled any chance he had of winning her heart. He had to remember: slow and steady wins the race.

"How about you ma'am?"

"Sure." Elaine wanted to tear this idiot's head off. Couldn't the waiter see that Brent had been going to say something that would clue her in to how he felt about her?

She sighed and smiled a thanks for the refill. It was surely better this way. He probably had no intention of declaring his undying love for her. No, with her luck, he'd most likely been on the verge of asking for a raise or something equally impersonal. He could never really love her the way she'd come to love him. Why ruin a perfectly lovely honeymoon dinner with the truth?

She wanted him to kiss her.

As she stood on her front porch, fumbling through her purse for her house keys, Elaine was incredibly aware of the man who hovered at her elbow. Jolts of electricity seemed to fairly crackle between them. Couldn't he feel it, too? Maybe if she fiddled around long enough out here, before they went inside to relieve Margaret of her baby-sitting duties, Brent would haul her into his arms and kis her into oblivion.

No, she decided—after rummaging for a ridiculousl long period of time while her handsome husband stood pa tiently waiting—she'd been wrong. If anyone was going t haul her anywhere, it should be away. To the loony bi She'd actually deluded herself into believing that this mar riage was real.

Sighing in resignation, she withdrew her elusive keys an held them out to him. Somewhere along the way he'd los his touch at reading her mind. Or, perhaps, she thoug morosely, watching him unlock the door, he just didn't fe like kissing her.

Brent pushed the door open and echoed her sigh. He wa beginning to think she'd never locate her blasted keys. had taken every bit of his dwindling willpower not to gra her and kiss her into oblivion. But he knew that if h started, he wouldn't be able to stop. With his luck, Elain would wallop him with her purse, and his mother woul call 911. Resting a light hand at her back, he led them int the house.

Once inside they both stopped dead in their tracks an stared in shock.

"Amanda," Elaine blurted out and tightly grippe Brent's arm. For there, sitting cozily in front of the livin room fireplace, bouncing a fussy Meg on her knee, wa Amanda Johnson. And Margaret was nowhere to be see Exchanging worried glances, they quickly stepped into th room.

"You're back!" Amanda smiled up at them in greetin "Good. I think she's hungry." Standing, she shrugged an held the whimpering Meg up to Elaine, as though it we the most natural thing on earth for her to be there, takin care of her granddaughter.

Elaine took the baby, who, back in familiar arm stopped fussing and smiled.

"She sure knows her mommy," Amanda mused, shaking her head. "I tried every trick in the book, walking, singing, rocking..." She peered into the baby's face. "But you wanted mama, isn't that right my little punkin doodle?" Noticing Brent for the first time, Amanda shifted her gaze to him, and her eyes widened as though in recognition. She regarded him with interest for a moment. "You must be Brent."

"Where's my mother?" Brent asked, his jaw set grimly as he took a protective step toward his wife and child.

Amanda waved an airy hand. "Oh, we had a nice long, very enlightening chat, and then, since it was getting so late, she went back to your place. She says to tell you that she'll call you tomorrow about getting together for Christmas." Then, as though she didn't have a care in the world, she began straightening up the toys that lay strewn about the room.

Still rendered speechless, Elaine could only watch as Bobby's mother put the room back to rights and then retrieved and donned her white wool cape. Who was this woman? she wondered in amazement. She certainly looked like Amanda Johnson. She arched an incredulous eyebrow at Brent whose answering look spoke of his own misgivings.

"Your mother is...a good woman, Brent," Amanda stated calmly, as she turned toward him and flung her expensive wrap around her slender shoulders. "She tells me that, among other things, congratulations are in order." Her smile was sincere as she held her hand out to him.

Shooting another quizzical look at Elaine, Brent took the proffered hand. "Thank you."

Suddenly Amanda's expression turned melancholy. "I only wish I'd been half as understanding and sweet about my own son's marriage." Her eyes misted slightly. "But, it's too late for that now, isn't it?" Obviously not expecting an answer to her rhetorical question, she sniffed daintily and swiped at her eyes with her diamond-encrusted fingers.

"I'll be on my way and leave you two newlyweds alone now. But before I go, I just wanted to let you know that as a wedding gift of sorts, I'm going to call off the adoption proceedings."

Feeling suddenly light-headed, Elaine leaned against Brent's solid body for support. "That's wonderful," she breathed. Brent circled her waist with his arm and squeezed.

Amanda smiled softly at the family that stood before her, united by love. "I know Bobby would have wanted it this way. He was a beautiful man." She shook her head slightly, as if to clear it of her emotional turmoil. "It's apparent to me that little Meg here will be better off with two parents who love her, and each other, so much. I'm only sorry to have upset you both with all this in the first place, but I didn't know that my granddaughter was in such fine hands. I thought she might make up for losing him. And—" She stopped speaking for a moment, as tears of genuine regret trailed down her flawless cheek. "I miss him so much," she whispered.

"I know," Elaine murmured sympathetically.

Amanda swallowed and blinked rapidly up at the ceiling. "I've made a lot of mistakes in my life. I've been known to run over a person or two in my time to get what I want." She shifted her gaze back to Elaine. "But it's never really made me happy. Take it from me, Elaine. The love of a good man and a healthy baby are far more important than any other of life's status symbols."

Leaning forward and kissing Meg tenderly on her chubby cheek, Bobby's mother squeezed Elaine's arm, and then moved out of the room toward the foyer. She paused at the front door.

"If neither of you have any objections, I'd love to see her from time to time." Amanda inclined her head at Meg

"I'm in the book. Well—" Pulling open the front door, she stepped out into the brisk night air. "Good luck to you all."

And with that, she was gone.

The fresh pine scent of the Christmas tree filled Elaine with a sense of nostalgia as she sat curled up on the couch, covered with an afghan. It was such a beautiful tree. She couldn't remember the last time she'd bothered to decorate her home for the holidays. It had seemed so pointless without someone to share it.

Brent was in the kitchen, fixing them a glass of eggnog, and the sounds of his clumsily masculine activity brought a smile to her lips. She'd fed and put Meg to bed after Amanda had left. Staring at the tree, she watched the colored lights blink cheerfully from its limbs, and was taken back to another place and time.

A place and time where she had lain awake with Sara, urging her young cousin to listen closely—did she hear the reindeer landing on the roof? Sara had loved the game, wriggling with excitement and trying to convince Elaine that they should run downstairs and trap Santa Claus in the closet. That way they could rush to the roof and take a quick spin in his sleigh.

Sara had been such a delight. Both as a child and a woman. Elaine could only hope that Meg had inherited her cousin's free spirit. Someday, it would be her daughter listening for the reindeer. There was a sad poignancy to the thought that Sara's life had finally come full circle.

A log fell suddenly in the fireplace, drawing her eyes and sending a cascade of sparks swirling up the chimney. She'd never understood why Amanda hadn't liked Sara. Until tonight. She supposed the drive to climb to the top socially could do strange things to people. If anyone could understand the drive to climb to the top, she could, Elaine thought, self-deprecatingly. Thank heaven Brent and Meg had changed her priorities. It was clear to her now, that nothing was more important than family.

But what had prompted the sudden change in Amanda? Had the Ghost of Christmas Past visited her? Shivering, Elaine tucked the afghan more firmly around her legs and snuggled into the couch.

Maybe Brent would be able to shed some light on the subject, she thought, as he continued to forage noisily around her kitchen. His reporter's instincts were generally on the money. When had she grown so dependent on his thoughts and opinions? she wondered. She respected his input on everything from diaper rash to the state of the union.

It was then that it suddenly dawned on her that she had better get his input on the state of their union. Now that Amanda had called off her bid for custody, what reason did they have to stay married? None that she knew of, other than the fact that she was terminally in love with the messy guy in the kitchen, who labored so endearingly over his batch of eggnog.

That was why she decided, her heart heavy, that if he wanted out, she would let him go. Because she loved him. A marriage where only one of the people involved was in love was no marriage at all. When it came to Brent, she wanted all or nothing. But even that would most likely prove impossible. After all, she still had to work with the man. And then there was his relationship with Meg....

Oh, how would she ever be able to let go? *Please God,* she whispered, sending a silent prayer heavenward, *don't let him go.*

Back in the kitchen, Brent took a sip of the eggnog and frowned. Aside from the stuff Debbie called coffee at work, he'd never tasted anything so vile. It was no small wonder, considering he couldn't concentrate on anything except the possibility of losing the woman in the next room. The woman he'd come to love more than life itself.

But, after carefully weighing the situation, he knew that Elaine would probably see no reason to continue their marriage. As a quiet desperation settled in his gut, he struggled to come to terms with the fact that if she wanted out, he would have to let go. Elaine was not the type of woman to be forced into any situation. It was one of the things he loved about her. However, a marriage where only one person was in love, was no marriage at all. He would make the offer of freedom, only because he loved her. If she accepted, he'd know that it was the way it was supposed to be.

Pouring the disgusting eggnog down the drain, Brent wondered absently what it was that had changed Amanda's mind about the adoption. Was it something his mother had said? Whatever it was, in some respects he was grateful, and in others he was out of his mind with worry. Taking a deep breath he pushed himself away from the counter and snapped off the kitchen light. It was now or never, he decided and moved through the darkness toward the cheerfully crackling fire where his wife sat waiting for him.

"Hi," she whispered, and pulled her knees up under her chin to make room for him. "Where's the eggnog?"

"Busily eroding your kitchen plumbing," he quipped dryly as he sank into the couch and pulled her legs across his lap.

"That bad?"

"Mmm," he murmured, training his eyes on the flames.

They sat in silence for a moment, neither wanting to address the question that lay so heavily on their hearts. Finally Brent could stand the suspense no longer.

"Elaine," he began dully, still staring unseeingly at the fire.

"Hmm?" Something in his tone had her heart leaping fearfully into her throat.

"Now that Amanda has decided against adopting Meg, was wondering...uh, just what you wanted to do about our marriage.'' *Please, God,* he prayed, *let her want it as much as I do.* Feeling duty bound by honor, he continued. ''Uh, I could look into beginning divorce proceedings. Or, um, there is always annulment, I guess, considering that we never, uh...actually consummated the vows, and you know...'' His voice trailed off miserably.

He sounded so miserable, Elaine wanted to curl up and die. The poor guy had really been through the ringer with her, she thought, studying his rugged profile in the firelight. As much as she wanted to throw a childish tantrum and rail against his words by kicking and screaming in agony, she knew it wouldn't be fair. Brent was the kind of guy who would stay with her out of a sense of duty. She couldn't allow it to go on any longer. It was time to let go.

Brokenhearted and not trusting herself to speak, she followed his eyes to the fire and nodded. Growing up, she had dreamed about and expected to be doing many things on her wedding night, with the man she loved, but discussing the dissolution of her marriage wasn't one of them.

''All right,'' she was finally able to whisper. ''Do whatever you see fit.''

His jaw grim in silhouette, he nodded quickly, not daring to look at her for fear he'd beg her to change her mind.

Elaine caught the movement out of the corner of her eye and bit her lip to keep from crying.

Chapter Thirteen

The holiday season had never seemed so bleak to Brent as he let himself into his apartment the next morning. He'd spent the night on Elaine's couch, unable to sleep and painfully aware that it would be one of his last nights under her roof. Preferring to avoid an awkward scene at breakfast that morning, he'd gotten up at the crack of dawn and headed home without seeing Elaine.

Soon he would need to pack his meager belongings and go back to his place to stay. It was hard enough contemplating not tucking Meg into bed each night, but when he thought about life without Elaine, well, it was decidedly more than he could bear. He'd made the fatal mistake of losing his heart to those two, and now he was going to have to pay the piper.

Shouldering his way through his front door, he kicked aside the pile of mail that had accumulated under his slot that morning and headed into the kitchen.

Margaret, who sat at his kitchen table browsing through

the morning paper, looked up from the cup of coffee she cradled in her hands in surprise.

"Hi, honey." Her smile was puzzled. "What on earth are you doing here? You're the last person I expected to see."

"Why's that?" Brent tried to effect a casualness he was far from feeling. After kissing his mother briefly on the cheek and pouring himself a cup of coffee, he joined her at the table.

"Need I remind you that last night was your wedding night? I thought for sure you would still be in bed recuperating from…your big night," she teased.

Brent shrugged and ran a weary hand across his jaw. He didn't find her attempt at humor particularly amusing this morning.

Sobering, Margaret reached out and squeezed her son's shoulder. "I get the feeling something's wrong."

Brent blew into his cup and took a sip of coffee. "Nah." He didn't feel like talking about it. He felt like punching something. But he couldn't. Margaret never had gone in for showy displays of temper.

"Would you like to talk about it?"

"No."

Margaret set her coffee cup down and, exhaling deeply, turned in her chair to face her son. "Brent." She swallowed and drew her cheek between her teeth, suddenly pensive. "I have a feeling I know what this is all about, and I think maybe I can help."

Brent's head snapped up sharply. "No, Mom. You can't, so just drop it, okay?" No amount of well-meaning, motherly advice could pull him out of this foul temper.

Sitting silently for a moment, Margaret appeared to make a decision. "Brent, I have something to tell you, and I want you to listen to me. I should have told you this a long time ago, but sometimes when things hurt too badly it's easier to just sweep them under the carpet and ignore them."

"Mom." Brent sighed. She never could take no for an answer. He knew she would tell him some cockamamie anecdote, designed to get him to spill his guts, and he wasn't in the mood. In an effort to spare them both, he decided there was no time like the present to come clean with her. She would eventually find out, anyway. "I'm not trying to sweep my troubles under the proverbial carpet. I'm just a little shell-shocked, that's all." He smiled wanly at her. "Elaine and I are going to get a divorce."

"What?" Margaret whispered in disbelief. *"Whatever for?"*

Beats the hell out of me, he wanted to say. "Because it never really was a marriage in the first place." At his mother's shocked expression, he hastily assured her. "Oh, it's legal, but the only reason we did it in the first place is because Amanda Johnson—you met her last night—"

Margaret nodded.

"She is Bobby's mother, and from what Elaine tells me, used to be a pretty rotten apple."

His mother's lips twitched.

"Anyway, she was threatening to file for custody of the baby. That scared the hell out of both of us. Luckily, her son Bobby had written a provision into the surrogate contract, stipulating that Elaine could keep the baby in the event that anything should happen to them—if she was married." He shrugged dejectedly. "So we got married. At the time it seemed like a good idea. And it must have worked, because last night, after we came home from dinner, she told us that she'd changed her mind about adopting Meg. So I guess something good did come of it after all."

Nodding, Margaret opened her mouth to speak, but Brent cut her off.

"Now there's no reason to continue the marriage." His eyes darted to his mother's. "Since Elaine doesn't love me, I decided to cut my losses and get out while my poor heart was still in one piece. Although," he mused morosely,

"I'm beginning to have my doubts." His laugh was sharp. "Anyway, someday I'm sure she'll find someone to share her life with. Someone who will love her and Meg as much as I do."

Her expression full of sympathy, Margaret reached out and drew her son's large hand into hers. "She already has," she murmured.

Eyes dull, Brent stared at his mother. What was she talking about now?

"Honey," Margaret leaned forward, and something in her tone caught his attention. "I want you to listen to me for a moment. I have something to tell you, and in light of the circumstances, I think you should know. I was going to wait till after Christmas to tell you, but now seems as good a time as any."

What choice did he have? he wondered impatiently and nodded for her to continue.

"Last night, almost immediately after you two had left for dinner, there was a knock at the door. I thought you had a typical case of the parental jitters and had returned to give me some more instructions." She smiled. "But when I got to the door, I discovered Amanda."

Pausing, she took a deep breath, and then, as though she were afraid she might lose her nerve, her words tumbled out in a rush.

"I hadn't seen her in thirty-five years. Even so, I recognized her immediately."

Brent frowned. She wasn't making any sense. "Mom, what are you getting at?"

"Honey, she was the woman who took your father away from me."

"Amanda?" His brows knotted in consternation. Amanda Johnson was the evil socialite who had schemed and plotted her way into his father's life? To say he was shocked was certainly an understatement. The fact that Bobby and Amanda carried his father's surname certainly never would have tipped him off. Johnson was a very common moniker. It had never been his family name. Margaret had given him her maiden name when he was born.

"Mmm." Margaret nodded, and her eyes became glassy as she began unfolding the past to her son. "Amanda." Her voice took on a reflective quality. "I never expected to see her again. But in a way it was good for me. I think it gave me a sense of closure, after all these years of bitterness and jealousy. It also helped me realize that much of what happened was partly my fault."

Brent shook his head in disbelief. This was his mother speaking? He hardly recognized her. For once, she was talking about the past without turning beet red.

"Yes." She smiled at Brent's incredulous expression. "I gave your father to her without much of a fight. You see, I was convinced that he would be better off without me. Kind of like you and Elaine," she noted. "I regret that he never knew about you."

She sat in silence for a moment, remembering, while Brent attempted to digest this startling revelation.

"Why didn't you tell me this before?" he whispered, prodding her out of her reflective pose.

She lifted and dropped her shoulders. "I couldn't face the fact that I'd made a terrible mistake. It was easier to blame Amanda for everything. Anyway, you can imagine my surprise at finding her there on Elaine's porch last night, claiming to be Bobby Johnson's mother. Meg's grandmother. Well, I just couldn't let her stand out there on the porch without explaining herself. Not to mention the fact that I had the most childish urge to tear every platinum blond hair out of her head."

Brent grinned.

"So, I invited her in. She recognized me, too, after a while. We had quite the conversation. It was very healing." At Brent's skeptical look, she smiled. "Really. She told me that she and Rob—that's your dad—only had one child together. Bobby. I could tell, Brent, that she loved him and missed him very much. As much as I hate to admit it, I was actually beginning to feel sorry for her. So, I let her keep her hair and continue with her incredible story. She's really not so bad…

"I was saddened to learn that she lost Rob several years ago. He was your father, after all, and at the time I loved him very much."

Margaret's eyes misted over as she regarded her son. "You look so much like him. Amanda must have seen it, too. He was a very handsome man. Anyway—" she brightened "—Bobby would have been your half brother, and best of all, little Meg is your niece."

His niece? Brent's pulse roared in his ears. "That explains why everyone keeps saying she looks just like me."

"Well, come to think of it, she does," Margaret agreed. "I've got baby pictures of you that could certainly pass for Meg."

Brent felt as if he were dreaming. He'd always known that it was a small world, but *this?* Out of all the people in the world, Elaine Lewis, the woman he loved, had given birth to his niece. As disappointing as it was to discover that he'd had an entire family that he would never have the pleasure of meeting, he couldn't get over the fact that he was an uncle to the sweetest little girl in the world. Surely Elaine wouldn't prevent him from visiting his own niece.

"I could tell that even though Amanda was crazy about Meg, she wasn't really ready for the diapering routine again. We had a long talk, and I think I persuaded her that touring the world with an infant might put a crimp in her style." Margaret grinned. "She ended up admitting that the baby would be better off with you and Elaine, because you both love the baby—and each other—so much. And, I couldn't agree more."

Brent only wished his mother's words were true. "Mom, you're right. I do love Elaine. With all my heart. But she doesn't love me. To her, I'm just a friend seeing her through a difficult period in her life.''

Margaret slapped the table with the palm of her hand so hard the coffee sloshed out of their cups.

''Are you crazy? That girl is head over heels in love with you, and if you can't see that, you are blind. Don't offer her a divorce, Brent. It's not what she wants. Please, learn from my mistakes. Don't give up the one you love because you are under the misguided impression that it's what they want.'' Her plea was impassioned. ''I did that with your father. I could have fought for him. Instead, I rolled over and let Amanda have him. I guess, looking back, there is a silver lining to my cloud because now we have darling little Meg, and you have Elaine. But if I had it to do all over again, I would fight for my man. I only regret that he passed away before I could tell him that.''

Completely stupefied by the incredible tale his mother had just told him, Brent could only sit and stare at her, numb with shock. Slowly his mind began to thaw, and he realized she was right.

He had to fight for Elaine.

Dammit, what did he have to lose? If he didn't take a chance and tell her how much he loved her, he'd lose her for sure. Besides, maybe she would consider staying married, once she realized that he, too, was related to the baby. Hell, considering the bizarre story his mother had just regaled him with, he could almost bring himself to believe anything.

Even the idea that—as his mother and Amanda seemed to believe—Elaine loved him.

Standing abruptly, Brent hauled his mother out of her chair and into his arms for a big bear hug. Setting her back down on her feet, he cupped her face in his hands and grinned.

''Thanks, Mom,'' he whispered. Before she could respond, he let go of her, spun on his heel and headed out to tell his wife how much he loved her.

He was gone.

Elaine stood in the middle of her living room and regarded the neatly stacked pile of Brent's belongings with apprehension. It appeared that he would be wasting no time moving out, now that they had agreed to dissolve their marriage. Her heart leaden, she turned toward the nursery, where Meg lay announcing to the world that she was hungry and, most likely, wet.

"Hi, little one," she cooed at the baby, who had looked at Elaine in surprise since her arrival and increased the pitch of her frantic wails. She wanted Daddy. Every morning, since the day she was born, Brent had made it his routine to get her out of bed and change her before he showered for work. Then he would stagger sleepily into Elaine's room and deposit Meg into Elaine's bed where she would nurse her back to sleep.

"I know, I know," she said, lifting the squalling baby into her arms and patting her gently on the back. "You want the guy with the mustache." She pressed her lips to the child's damp, wonderfully soft cheek. "I know how you feel."

Battling the tears that stung the backs of her eyelids, she settled into the rocker to feed Meg. "I want him, too," she whispered hoarsely.

Tomorrow was Christmas Eve. In the closet, hidden behind a pile of Meg's blankets, lay a pile of presents for Brent and the baby. Presents she'd wrapped with the tender care of a contented, deliriously happy woman in love. Over the past week, she had fantasized about their first Christmas together as a family, allowing herself this indulgence, even though she knew that it would never become a tradition. But she could dream. It had been years since she'd celebrated the day with family, and after years of lonely Christmases spent working at the station, she felt she deserved at least one holiday that she could reflect on in the forlorn years to come.

Now it seemed she could kiss even this slight consolation goodbye. At least she had Meg. But even though she loved this child with a mother's heart and soul, she would never get over losing Brent.

She'd never even had a chance to tell him how she felt. A bittersweet tear spilled over her lower lashes, down her cheek and onto Meg's. No, that wasn't exactly true, she amended to herself, as she stroked the dark fuzz at the nape of the baby's neck. She'd never had the courage to tell him how she felt.

What was wrong with her? She'd never have gotten anywhere in life, if she'd been this timid about everything. Top broadcast producers were generally never wilting lilies. Then why all the fear when it came to telling Brent how she felt about him? she wondered.

As she sat pondering this question, the answer began to make itself clear in her mind. Because she couldn't bear the thought of losing him. And secondly, because she was proud.

Well, she was losing him anyway, and her pride had already suffered a mortal blow, so what did she have to lose?

"Nothing," she stated so firmly that Meg started. "Sorry, honey," she said soothingly to the baby. "But Mommy just realized that she has to damn the torpedoes, so to speak and tell Daddy that she loves him."

"Zimbabwe," Meg babbled, then after a contented burp, went back to her meal.

"Elaine?" Brent let himself into her house with the key she had given him. Shrugging out of his jacket, he tossed it on the entry hall table and glanced into the empty living room. His heart sank as he noticed that she'd tidied up, removing all traces of his personal effects.

"In here," she called, and Brent followed the sound of her voice toward the nursery.

Rounding the corner to the baby's room, he found her there, slowly rocking their sleeping child. She smiled serenely up at him, and he felt his heart catch in his throat at the sight.

On the way over, he'd decided to skip the long, involved tale of Meg's family tree and cut to the chase. He'd wasted way too much time tiptoeing around the issue so far. She would either agree to remain his wife, or she wouldn't. It was a simple as that. And as complicated.

He stood in the doorway, opening and closing his fists, nervously wondering where he should start. It wasn't every day that he laid his heart on the line. All the words he'd so carefully rehearsed suddenly escaped him.

"Brent," she whispered, tensing slightly as she looked up at him. "I'm so glad you're back. I have something I need to say."

"Oh." She seemed so serious. Fear filled his gut. No. He couldn't let her speak before he declared his love. She might say something that would prevent him from accomplishing his mission. "That's great," he said, gripping either side of the doorjamb with his hands for support, "but first I have something to say to you...."

Interrupting, as though she hadn't heard him at all, she said, "And, I wish I had told you ages ago." She nervously touched the tip of her tongue to her lower lip.

That was fine with him. Right after he told her that he loved her. "That's great, honey. But first—"

"Although, I guess I was afraid to tell you that—"

Plowing a frustrated hand through his hair, Brent rested his forehead impatiently against the door. Couldn't the woman see that he was trying to tell her he loved her? Why did she have to choose this moment to drive him nuts with idle chitchat? He took a deep breath. He had to tell her that he loved her. Now. It was time. Whatever she had to say could wait. This couldn't.

"I love you," they both said in unison.

Exchanging shocked glances, they both asked, "What?"

"I love you," they answered together, then broke into matching radiant smiles, as they stared at each other in surprise.

"You do?" they whispered, then started to laugh. "Yes!" Their simultaneous declaration woke the sleeping Meg.

"Elaine!" Brent said, laughing as he crossed the room. "One at a time. Me first." Kneeling down beside the rocker, he cradled her cheeks in his hands and searched her face, the light of love and hope burning in his eyes. "Elaine Lewis, I love you. I've always loved you."

"You have?" she breathed, her eyes shining.

"Yes." He nodded solemnly. "And I want more than anything on this earth for us to stay married. Please say you will."

Her throat closed and Elaine was afraid she was going to cry. However, this time it wouldn't be from sorrow, but instead from spine-tingling, all-encompassing joy. She gazed up at the man who'd given so freely of himself and taught her the meaning of the word *love,* and then down at the tiny bundle in her arms. Nodding, she wondered how on earth she'd managed to get so lucky.

"Yes," she said when she was finally able to speak. "I can't think of anything I'd rather do than be wife and mother to you and Meg. I love you, too. Both of you." Lifting her tear-spiked lashes up to him, she promised, "With all my heart."

Groaning with relief, Brent pulled her close and covered her mouth with his.

And as he sealed their vows—to love, honor and cherish—Sara's voice echoed once more, deep in the secret shadows of Elaine's soul, granting her dearest Christmas wish and bringing her dreams to life.

Take care of them, Elaine... Came the whisper, soft and sweet. *They're yours now. Forever.*

Epilogue

"Good heavens, what is that horrible smell?" Amanda sighed in resignation as she glanced around at the happy mess that was the Clark household. Depositing several large bags of gifts on the floor, she removed her wrap and tossed it haphazardly over her booty. "When in Rome," she murmured and kicked off her pumps.

Kissing her on the cheek, Brent ushered her into the living room and placed the baby in her arms. "I sort of forgot about the turkey," he grinned. "I hope you like pizza."

"For Christmas?" She looked at the baby and tsked.

"That's what I say," Margaret said, emerging from the smoke-filled kitchen to join them in the living room. "Hello, Amanda." Smiling, she embraced Bobby's mother in welcome.

"Hi, Margaret. Where's Elaine?" Amanda asked, squinting through the haze.

"On the phone with Debbie and Ray. She's going to

have them pick up a couple of pizzas on their way over.'' Pursing her lips, she scowled at her son.

Brent shrugged good-naturedly. ''Hey, it was Elaine's idea to have me cook dinner. Being the liberated, working mother that she is, I've been trying to expand my culinary skills. I guess I have a thing or two to learn about preparing fowl....''

Amanda smiled. ''I think you've mastered the art of foul.''

A joyous squeal—coming from somewhere amidst the clouds that still belched from the oven—reached them only seconds before Meg did, her chubby legs pumping as she raced across the living room. ''Grandma!'' she shrieked in ecstasy as she hurled herself at Amanda's legs.

Amanda's face mirrored her granddaughter's delight. ''Darling!'' Handing little Bobby to Margaret, she bent down, scooped the excited Meg into her arms and planted loving kisses across her pink cheeks. ''Was Santa good to you this year?''

''Yes!'' she squealed. ''I was a good girl.''

''Most of the time, anyway,'' Elaine said with a smile, joining them and flapping a dish towel in an effort to clear the smog from the living room. ''Hi, Amanda.'' After a quick hug, she tugged her excited daughter out of her grandmother's arms and set her on the floor. ''Go wash up,'' she instructed her four-year-old bundle of energy. Turning to her guests she said, ''I'm sorry about the turkey.''

''Are you referring to your husband or our main course?'' Margaret asked dryly.

''Both.'' Elaine giggled and Brent grabbed her around the waist and growled in her ear. ''We've got pizza coming. And Dick and Mary are bringing a salad. If Liz and Danny bring dessert and Jason and Vicky bring something to drink we should have enough.'' She looked apologetically at the two grandmothers. ''I hope that will be okay.''

Amanda shrugged and nudged a pile of toys out of the middle of the floor with her foot. "It doesn't matter." She waved an airy hand. "To me, the important thing is family. As long as we're all here together, I'm happy." She smiled contentedly at the Clarks.

"Here, here," Brent murmured as he nuzzled his wife's neck. "I couldn't have said it better myself."

* * * * *

Silhouette®
SPECIAL EDITION™
Emotional, compelling stories that capture the intensity of living, loving and creating a family in today's world.
Silhouette®
Desire®
A highly passionate, emotionally powerful and always provocative read.
Silhouette®
Where love comes alive™
Silhouette®
INTIMATE MOMENTS™
A roller-coaster read that delivers romantic thrills in a world of suspense, adventure and more.
SILHOUETTE Romance®
From first love to forever, these love stories are for today's woman with traditional values.
Visit Silhouette at www.eHarlequin.com
SILGENINT

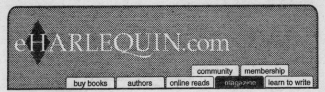